C000262006

"Funny, engaging, and pai

— Meg Gard

"In her debut novel, *Rapeseed*, Nancy Freund explores the phenomenon of synesthesia and manages to delight all of our senses with her vibrant prose. As Freund weaves and unravels the secrets of an American family living abroad in England, she takes care to consider the many ways a parent can not only harm but also save a child. *Rapeseed* is a novel of resilience and heart, of teenaged indiscretions and marital discontentment. With humor and reverence, Freund's characters strive to reconcile their childhood traumas with their adult longings. This moving portrayal of a family in crisis reveals Nancy Freund to be a writer of boundless compassion."

— Amber Dermont,
New York Times bestselling author of *The Starboard Sea*

"*Rapeseed* is a tender and evocative novel about the slippery nature of home and inheritance, an unflinching but ultimately hopeful examination of the sneaky distances that form between neighbors, between sisters, between husband and wife and child and parent. Nancy Freund writes with authority and charm."

— Nick Dybek, Hopwood Award-winning author of
When Captain Flint Was Still a Good Man

"Nancy Freund's luminous debut novel *Rapeseed* works to answer the age-old questions of what it means to be a family, and are we what we are born into? What she finds in her careful, and at times, heartbreaking, examination of American expatriates living in England is that true family are those who love us despite our flaws and that, ultimately, home is where the heart is."

— Myfanwy Collins, author of *Echolocation*

"Nancy Freund's *Rapeseed* is a rich portrait of an American family beset by displacement—by history, geography, and psychology, from relatives and nations and individual minds. Yet in their struggles to remain true to where they come from while making the most of where they are, her expatriate family, the Coopers, are in so many ways like all of us, and we are lucky to to have their example in the form of this smart, sharply observed debut."

— Steve Himmer, author of *The Bee-Loud Glade*

"*Rapeseed* spotlights the influence of a person's early life on the adult version of that self. Nancy Freund's style is clean, spotlessly competent in technique and logic, and always contains an irreverent note or a narrator with a mischievous glint in the eye. Her work contains echoes of American novelists Richard Russo, Jane Smiley, and Joyce Carol Oates as well as the English novelist Barbara Pym, a writer of "light women's fiction" but containing some of the darkest, hardest satire of her time."

— Michelle Bailat Jones, author of *Fog Island Mountains*

Praise for Nancy Freund's *Marcus*, winner of the 2013 Geneva Fiction Prize

"What I liked best about *Marcus* was the sort of disjointed, fragmented tone and texture of this stark and foreboding tale, A young man trying to figure things out, trying to figure how to tell his story, doing the best he can, and doing the wrong thing. A full and rich and startling story."

— Bret Lott, Oprah book club author of *Jewel*

NANCY FREUND

Rapeseed

a novel

To Val,
Enjoy !
Your Friend,
Nancy

Gaxwood
Sept. 21, 2022

Gobreau Press
Key Largo & Lausanne

Published by Gobreau Press LLC
First printing September, 2013

Cover design and interior formatting by www.jdsmith-design.com.
Author photo by Edward Fraser.

Freund, Nancy.
Rapeseed: a novel/by Nancy Freund.

Paperback ISBN 978-0-9887084-0-2
Ebook ISBN 978-0-9887084-1-9

Gobreau Press proudly supports global literacy.

For John

Chapter 1

Carolann tied a knot in the twine and tapped her birdfeeder. It was just the right place, stable and protected under the last of the season's pink roses. She checked her watch. It was an ideal time to have finished the job, and the perfect job for a free afternoon. If she hadn't spent the morning at the pub, of course, she would not have to focus on all her perfection. Though knowing the local pubs would fortify her marriage. Perfect.

The birdfeeder twisted in the breeze. Carolann had no idea what birds were native to southern England. For that matter, she'd never paid attention to birds in Kansas, other than the red cardinal with its pretty song. England definitely had no cardinals. Shame. A red bird would be lovely in a gray-green place.

There were more than 100,000 Americans in Greater London. They'd probably all agree London was gray-green, and the place would do well with a red bird's golden song. Perhaps not everyone would agree that cardinal song smelled like lavender. Carolann knew better than to discuss any of that.

"Yoo-hoo!" A woman's voice called in the distance. A breeze ruffled the leaves of the rose trellis. Carolann backed away from the tall hedge to peek through an arch to her front garden. Maybe her heavy-set neighbor was having an affair with the mailman. The *postman.*

No one was there. Such a quiet country. Cloud cover muted everything.

The postman must have been just out of sight, in his red van with its yellow crest of royal affiliation. He was probably parked in front of the neighbor's house. Gone was the American mail truck, the solid white Jeep with its familiar red, white and blue logo and its sleek eagle design cruising her stable Kansas neighborhood. The English post van looked like a life-sized toy or a theme-park ride. She was almost sorry not to see the neighbor-woman lumbering into the back of the little red truck. Carolann could run out with a wide roll of masking tape and Sharpie marker to make a bumper sticker: *When this van's a rockin', don't come knockin'*. Of course, if she got caught defacing government property, she'd be deported. She tapped the bird feeder, testing its weight on the twine. She wondered if their masking tape had come over with the early stuff in the air-shipment.

"Hello?"

Carolann froze and silence followed.

Gone was her reliable American once-a-day mail delivery. In England, sometimes the mail arrived twice in a day. It was impossible to plan a day by it. And gone was private mail pick up altogether, unless, she'd read in a guidebook, you were the Bishop of Canterbury or the Queen. And they claimed British society was no longer a class system.

"Yoo-hoo…" The hedge wobbled left and right, and the neighbor burst through it, branches cracking as she came.

Carolann jumped back. "Yes?"

The woman's home-knitted sweater vest snagged on a twig, and she yanked her shoulder from the bush. "Used to be a bigger gap there." She laughed. "Maybe I'm what's bigger." She seemed unfinished, like the knitter had run out of blue yarn for the sleeves. Surely, the unflattering style wasn't the intended plan. "Uh, hello?" Carolann said.

"I've been dragged through a hedge backward," the woman cackled and rubbed her fleshy pink arms. "Or forward! I'm Rowan."

Carolann wiped her hands on her apron. "Can I help you?"

"You're hard to reach. You've been in the house nearly a month, but every time I try, you're out."

"Yes." Carolann looked the woman up and down. "Three weeks."

"Lovely birdhouse." Rowan patted her bleached frizzy hair against her head. "Where did you come from?"

That same question again, the same phrasing. It had followed Carolann all the way across America and the Atlantic Ocean. *Where did you come from, little girl?* But of course this neighbor lady meant nothing by it. "The United States," she said. "Kansas."

"American! I heard your son's accent, and I thought… could be Canadian. But wonderful! You're American." Rowan reached forward as if to hug Carolann, but grabbed herself around her own fluffy turquoise torso instead, rocking her shoulders. "I lived in Austin, Texas for a while, which entitles me to membership in the American Women's Club. I'll bring you to a meeting."

"No, thank you." Carolann fingered the rubber handles of her garden shears in her pocket. If she wasn't careful, this neighbor-woman would swivel herself into the ground and grow roots in Carolann's yard. "Our relocation agent wants to register me, but I'm not interested in a women's club."

"It's not a bore. Nothing like Women's Institute or what do you have? Junior League? Rotary-Annes? Americans are lovely jubbly. If I could be re-incarnated, I'd come back a Texan. Although my ex-husband, bastard, still lives there, so perhaps not." She grimaced. "Shit head fuckface wankjerk bastard."

Carolann nodded slowly, her eyebrows raised.

"If you met him, you'd understand."

"I see." Despite herself, Carolann smiled.

"Burns me up he's taken Texas for himself. But I want to

know all about you." Rowan grabbed Carolann's shoulders.

"Not a lot to tell." Carolann pulled away. Rowan would plant herself there, awaiting Carolann's personal information pouring down on her like a watering can. "I'm afraid I am kind-of busy."

"But tell me about Kansas." The neighbor clapped her dimpled hands. "Like Dorothy in *The Wizard of Oz*. Tell me – do you and Dorothy and everyone in Kansas love a clambake?"

"No," she sighed. "We're rather known for wheat. Corn and a few alternative crops." She thought of the old lady still living next to her parents' house, and her dark basement science lab. "Biodiesels and cooking oils, I think."

"Poor Kansas." Rowan pouted. "No clams."

Carolann wiped the sweat from her palms inside her gardening apron pocket. Her maroon nail polish would look black in the darkness of the laminated fabric. Like witch's nails. If she snapped her fingers, maybe Rowan and her splotchy naked arms would vanish.

But Rowan smiled. A sparkling rarity among rainy gray people.

"We raise pigs and cattle," she said. "Kansas has excellent beef. No Mad Cow Disease, of course. But no clams."

"Well, Saturday next will be an adventure for both of us then, because it'll be my first clambake too. We'll find loads in common, I'm sure. It's all planned to welcome you to the neighborhood. Not this Saturday, but next. You Americans say next Saturday and it might be the soonest one. I learned that the hard way in Texas."

"We're not party people," Carolann said.

"Pardon?"

"We find party-style interaction stressful."

Rowan said, "Your son already told me you're free."

"Lyn tends ... We're from a tight-knit community. You talked to Chip?"

"But depending on the other neighbors, we'll postpone. I'll let you know." Rowan continued, "The last Americans in this house – great friends – came from Long Island, and they loved a clambake. 'Lawn guyland.'" Rowan laughed at her pronunciation. "So I sunk an old bathtub in my garden to try it, but then they moved to Brazil, wouldn't you know it? I've been praying for more Americans. Your house has been with renters for *yonks*. The family before you was German. Deutsche Bank. They stick with other Germans. Before them, Skandies. Fins or Danes – I don't know – but they weren't clambake people either. And now here you are – Americans!"

Carolann glanced at her watch again. She should have spent less time in the pub. Not so perfect, after all. When she worked full-time, it was easier to organize her days. "*Yonks?*" she repeated.

"Donkey's years. Years. Your English is no better than the Krauts." Rowan laughed. "I'm not xenophobic. Don't get me wrong. I love expats, exiles, immigrants of all kinds. But most of all Americans."

"I'm afraid I need to get to the garden center."

"Wonderful place. I love helping foreigners find their feet. I'll show you Hampton Court and Windsor Castle. We can road trip to Stoke-on-Trent's china factories, if you like. I prayed for Americans. You know you can buy china patterns that aren't even discontinued for the price of a paper plate. After you eat, you can throw it in the fire. Decadent! Not that I've ever done it myself."

"How wasteful." Not to mention the dangerous porcelain shards.

"Stonehenge! I am definitely taking you to Stonehenge. Do you believe in God?"

"Is Stonehenge for pagan worship?" Carolann asked.

Rowan slapped her own face, lightly. "You'll have to tell me when to shut up. Americans are so open, I get carried

away." She looked carefully at Carolann. "Maybe I'll take you
to Glastonbury." She nodded slowly. "To the Tor."

"Sounds like a lot of miles."

"Oh, I love driving," Rowan said. "Love the freedom. I
can fix my own car. Change a flat, replace headlamps. Wiper
blades. Not every woman knows what a sparkplug is or where
to pour their engine coolant. Glastonbury is… well… that's
a special one." She took a deep breath. "I go every year in the
spring."

Maybe Rowan would drive her to some of the obligatory
antiques stores her twin sister demanded that she visit. Or
the National Trust places. Maybe Rowan would take her to
the garden center.

Rowan exhaled. "You might like Glastonbury."

"Maybe." Carolann said.

"Six-thirty for seven alright for the clambake?"

"I don't think so. You mean Saturday? I'd have to check
with Lyn. My husband's very reserved."

"We can reschedule to suit you." Rowan reached into the
front of her sweater, extracting an oversized business card
from her cleavage. "My phone number. Anything you need,
just call. Anything. Boiler breaks down. Smell something
burning. Gypsies at the door trying to sell you kitchen
sponges, and you don't like the look of them. Anything. "

Carolann knew the card smelled like powder, and it would
be warm. She didn't want to touch it. Hoyt, Kansas had to
be the world's most old-fashioned town, and women there
stopped using their brassieres as handbags decades ago. She
opened her palm, and Rowan set the card in her hand, face-
up.

"Your vowels!" Carolann stared at the card, dizzy. The "a"
was red, which was right. But many of the others were wrong.
"Your letters are printed in colors."

"I paid extra." Rowan tapped her head. "Because that's
how I see them."

Carolann was stunned. "And you tell people?"

"Well, I'd hate for anyone to be jealous," Rowan said. "It's just luck. Maybe genetics. I rarely mention it, but you asked."

Had Rowan never been locked in a car while the family ate in a restaurant? Or spanked with a belt for hearing horns when no one else heard them? Had Rowan never been kept home from a swimming pool party because she saw numbers in blue? Did Rowan see conversations in color? Rowan was lucky?

"Synesthesia," Carolann said. She'd never said the word to another person, as many times as she'd rolled its familiar syllables through her head. The word played with her senses, her every event, every day, but it was not something she said out loud.

"You know it?" Rowan asked. "Are you...?"

Automatically, Carolann nodded. Her most personal detail, delivered.

"Letters and numbers? Do your colors match mine? What about shapes? Texture? Is it stronger when you're tired? Is it disruptive? Do you have it with food and music and days of the week and –"

"Experience," Carolann said. She took a deep breath. Even admitting it might bring it all back. "Memories."

Rowan nodded slowly. "My sister had that too. My twin."

Carolann froze. "You have a twin."

"I did." Rowan's face darkened. "Cancer."

In an instant, Carolann forgot her joyous new anonymity, the freedom she'd already found in being unknown and so far from Kansas. "I'm a twin too," she said, "Maryann has no synesthesia. We're not identical. In fact, we share very little." Carolann swallowed hard. There was also a lot they did share.

Quickly, she added, "What are the odds that we'd both be twins and both be synesthetes?" The word rolled out as if she'd always been comfortable with it. The mad knitter next door might truly become a friend. "Would you like to come in for a cup of tea?"

Rowan shook her head quickly. "No."

"Coffee?" Didn't English people invite one another in for tea?

"No, no, no. Another time." Rowan retreated back toward her house and disappeared.

Carolann stared at the hole in her hedge. Rowan was a synesthete, and even she seemed to react the same as everyone always had. The door slammed next door and the only sound remaining was the gentle creak of twine and the birdhouse.

Chapter 2

I'ma tell you something.
I maw?
I'm gonna.

Chip was a normal, healthy fourteen-year-old boy, and smart enough (self-aware enough) to know that when he felt alone or like a weirdo who wanted things no one else wanted, he was probably one of a gazillion fourteen-year-old boys thinking the same thing all over the world. However, Hoyt Kansas had a population of six people, and not one seemed like-minded to Chip Cooper. Now though, in England, maybe he'd find someone. Both of his parents had already made unexpected transitions. The family rules were unchanged, but both of them seemed more relaxed than ever – especially his mother.

It had to be England. If Carolann Cooper could relax, Chip could do anything. Be anything. Use any kind of language he wanted. The one thing Chip had wanted most, his whole life, he suddenly had, with this new venue. Possibility.

He held the fountain pen above the notebook and stared at his words. He looked back at the mirror, his lip curled, his chin thrust forward, his eyes cold. The tough and edgy expression fit together like a finished puzzle. On the surface, Chip liked what he saw, this image he'd created – but he also saw right through it to the agonizing truth.

He didn't know the word for what bothered him most.

Fraud? Failure? Anguish? Thanks to studying Milan Kundera, he had *litost*. Czech for torment of catching sight of one's own misery. Perfect word – though of course, it didn't make him feel any better.

Even with his hair slicked back with water, he'd never look like anything but a good kid from Kansas. One who'd just gotten out of the shower. So what if he could remember every vocab word from *The Unbearable Lightness of Being*, so what if he got A's in English Lit and every other class – he didn't see a rapper in the mirror, a tough guy from New York, LA, or Detroit. He saw a good boy, what everyone thought of as a perfect boy, and underneath it, where no one else could see it except himself, he saw suffering.

But he'd made a start. He liked the British ink flowing from his pen. The shared geography with Shakespeare and Byron and Chaucer. George Bernard Shaw. The Beatles. Like new vocabulary was suddenly available to him, even if it wasn't the street language of rappers. Back home, his identity was well established. Raines Charles Lynwood Cooper, Jr., only child of Carolann and Lyn Cooper Senior, very active members of the Heart of America Church of God. There, if Chip even thought about slicking his hair back, people talked.

Of course, England was not the birthplace of rap, but rap was nothing if not words, and England was the fountainhead of the English language. Chip already wrote like he was channeling the great dead writers. He was drinking the same water those important English guys did, if you followed the cycles through the clouds and the rain and the rivers enough times, Chip probably drank Shakespeare's water just this morning.

They spoke the same language in England, but all else was different. Right down to the red postbox down the street, and the double-decker busses in the city. So why not? Something Chip would send off in the red postbox might reach someone who'd like it. Chip could sell a song, make a friend, get a girlfriend or two.

He'd escaped Kansas, and that was *never* going to happen. People said his mother had no impulse control, not that Chip ever really knew why, but she was supposedly the reason they could never leave Hoyt – yet, here they were. Pharmaceutical Dad got a new job in a foreign country, and against all expectation, Chip's mother had packed their bags.

Chip nodded at his slicked-back hair in the mirror. Fuck the *litost*! He swallowed, his Adam's apple bobbing a little reprimand. The f-word was unnecessary, and it wasn't Chip Cooper. He could write his lines without that kind of language, and they'd be true to him. He turned away from the mirror, his hair drying now, his pen in hand.

My mom's wound so tight, she's surely gonna snap.
Wonder what would happen if she laid eyes on my rap.
But I've got one year here – shed the shackles, get clear
Of the shit life I come from. Done enough time acting deaf and dumb.
Done with other people's problems, past I can't define.
Why's everybody have to toe a nonexistent line?

Chapter 3

Carolann walked to Lloyds of London on the High Street to finally open a checking account. Letting Lyn's new secretary continue sorting out the details of their recent move was ridiculous, and using her American cash card to get English money must be costing a fortune. Her father was probably having heart palpitations back home every time she did it.

She couldn't pretend the Coopers were just visiting anymore. They needed a bank account. And she needed to figure out how to understand the English accent. It was the same language, for goodness sake.

The banker leaned in to the bullet-proof glass and said, "For a joint account, your husband will need to come in to open it, I'm afraid."

Carolann had a thousand pounds sterling in her bag. She really didn't want to walk around carrying that much cash. If her father knew what was in her purse that afternoon, he'd have more than palpitations – he'd have a coronary. Cyrus Field in the obituaries – free listing.

"Can I open an account in my name, and add Lyn's name later? We'll switch it to a joint account as soon as he takes a morning off work and I can get him in to the bank."

The banker looked Carolann up and down, but did not answer.

Perhaps she hadn't been heard through the glass. "That's how it works in the U.S.," she added.

"Not here." The banker woman said into her microphone,

"If you're married, you'll need your husband here to do it."

"So I can't even –"

"Sorry, no. I'm afraid not. Is that ok?"

Carolann was startled by the question. *No, it's not ok*, she wanted to answer. *Let me fill out the papers and do it now, since you're asking. Today is the day I decided to do it, so let me goddamn do it today.*

Carolann took a deep breath and looked at the banker through the bullet-proof glass. She saw an orange haze around the woman, tempered with purple. Normally conversations with blended color showed still gradations of color, not lava-lamp-style moving blobs of purple. This conversation, this color scheme, was something new.

In England, after a definitive answer was delivered, and Carolann's polite request was boldly denied, why would the follow-up be a meek-toned question? *Is that ok*? The echo of the woman's question went to lilac. Carolann might never learn to navigate the conversations in this country. She quietly left the bank, the offensive and worrying money still in her bag.

She walked as quickly as she dared toward the next bank. Too quick and she'd draw attention, or worse, she'd trip and fall, and the money might slide from her bag and out of her grasp. England was treacherous.

In gun-loving Kansas you could talk face-to-face to the bank tellers, but in this country, where even the police only had billy clubs and no guns, the bankers hid behind bullet-proof glass. Maybe it was just Lloyds. Carolann headed into Barclays Bank, her bag tight under her arm.

"Sorry, no," the next woman said into her microphone. Again, the orange haze, and then lilac.

At Abby National, Carolann recognized the pursed lips even before the teller spoke the now familiar words: "Sorry, no."

Back home, Carolann handled their family finances. Lyn

hadn't paid a bill or cashed a check or compared interest rates on their money market savings accounts since they'd been married. Growing up, Carolann's father's regular financial management discussions put her well in position to handle these things in adulthood. But in England, it seemed, she was expected to fix dinner for the family and keep out of the important stuff. Not that good nutrition wasn't important. Good nutrition probably mattered more than anything.

When Carolann neared the smallest bank on the High Street, HSBC, she saw her neighbor Rowan near the grocery store with her orange cart. Carolann waved, but Rowan didn't seem to see her. Still, maybe Rowan would soon head home and might finally come over for a chat. Carolann had called Rowan's house four times already. If she called again, she promised herself she'd leave a message.

Carolann was eager to ask about her synesthesia. Even in her head, the word was taboo. But Carolann wanted to know how old Rowan was when she first knew she was different, how gradual her discovery was, and how her family reacted. Were Rowan's parents afraid of it? Did they secretly take Rowan to the church? Did they tell everyone they spoke to not to tell anyone else? For the first time, Carolann actually wanted to talk about it. But before she could reach her neighbor on the street, the woman had disappeared, leaving Carolann with nothing but the thoughts in her head.

A waft of scented heat billowed out of the twins' mother's oven. They were seven years old. Invisible remains of past meals, warm and aromatic, escaped into the small kitchen. Barbara Ann scrubbed the oven clean each night, but there must have been tiny drips left behind, leaving their smells. She slid a glass casserole dish in and shut the oven, but Carolann still smelled it. Violins. Already, she knew no one understood what she meant.

Maryann came into the kitchen pulling at one of her

pigtails, straightening the dark spiral and letting it spring back into a loose coil. "Why do we have to go to the loony bird's house?"

"Don't call her that. She's had a hard time."

Maryann said, "What hard time? She's rich. Everyone knows the loony bird's rich."

"What everyone knows isn't always the truth." Barbara Ann watched the casserole through the oven door and slid her thumbs against one another. Barbara Ann only had one casserole dish – although she once had two, a big and a medium, unlike Buck's mother, who took the Sears catalog and had all three – big, medium, and small. Carolann often heard her mother mention those dishes – whenever Cyrus wasn't there to hear it. Every woman's kitchen should have all three.

Barbara Ann only had the one because one day she set her medium down too hard and broke it. Tuna noodle casserole with Saltine crackers. Barbara Ann wasn't paying attention to the family dinner, so it was her own damn fault.

Carolann doesn't believe in God. Maryann tattled on her sister.

I never said that, that's not what I said.

Yes, you did. That's what you said.

No, I didn't. Carolann could hardly see her family through the hazy blue veil that suddenly shrouded the scene. Age seven. She'd certainly begun to realize she was different by age seven. *I said what Daddy said, that human beings made Him up, because people are bad and God's like a big policeman.*

Cyrus? Barbara Ann had turned from the oven with the dinner, her ladybug oven mitts on her hands. Cyrus said nothing.

I said no one made Him up. He always was. *It's just people figured Him out – that He's there. That's what I said. He was real before people ever came to planet earth from outer space or wherever they came from.*

The ladybugs made tight fists on the glass dish. *Your father said what? Cyrus?*

Carolann said it. She doesn't –

I do believe in God! The blue shimmered, and the little girl tried not to cry. *...and Jesus and sin and I know people do bad things, but God forgives them. Not like the police. Policemen are people like you and Daddy and Buck's daddy and... just people.*

Maryann interrupted her sister. *God's stupid,* she said.

Barbara Ann slammed down the dinner, and the dish split right in half, and both little girls cried out and then became silent as small stones. Cyrus grabbed the serving spoon and served the noodles onto their plates.

Broken glass, Barbara Ann whispered. *Digestive tracts. They're just little girls.*

It's a clean cut. We'll eat it. Lord, bless this food. He made them sit still. *We implore you to bless this goddamn food.*

They ate till the noodles were gone. No one was sick in the digestive tract. God existed.

"I don't want to hear you call Mrs. Heaney a loony bird. Something happened to her in her past," Barbara Ann said. "And the bad feeling stays with her. She suffers already, and I don't want you girls being cruel to her."

Maryann said, "Joey-Scott Landsdowne says Mrs. Heaney has two heads, and one's empty, and every night, her brains pour out into the empty one so she can dry out the other side. Like eggshells and a yolk. She's a witch."

The word "witch" was sharp and dark green, even though the "w" was purple. The "itch" sound gave it its green. Carolann didn't say so. She had said it once before – just to Maryann – and learned not to mention it again.

"That's just silly," Barbara Ann said. "She's a perfectly nice lady. But you girls should understand, if you do something bad, it stays with you forever, even if you move away, even to another country, and even if you say you're sorry." She fixed her gaze on both daughters. "And it's the same if the bad thing happens to you. With girls, sometimes they make the bad things happen to them, so even the victim carries guilt."

"Even if she's not a witch, she might hurt us." Maryann dug her toe into the floor, and Carolann knew she thought it made her look adorable.

"She won't hurt you or anyone." Barbara Ann reached for the lipstick tube she kept on her spice rack between the black pepper and powdered mustard. The color was called Cotton Candy. She did her lips, hot pink, and Carolann smelled the yucky pink smell. She knew it wasn't real, that no one else could smell it. When had she found this out? If she didn't see the lipstick, if she closed her eyes, there was no smell. But as soon as she saw the color, she smelled burnt milk. The sight of that lipstick and her mother's pursed lips, and the sour pink smell of it made Carolann desperately lonely.

Over the years, as the colors and shapes and letters settled into place, Carolann grew to accept them, and her sense of desperation lifted, but the undercurrent of loneliness never did. She wanted to know if it was the same with Rowan. But Rowan was not on the street, and she hadn't come back to the Cooper's house since her first visit. Carolann would call her again.

When she got to the next bank – the last on the high street – she decided to skip it and go next door to spend some cash where it was welcome. It seemed that Lyn's presence would be required at any bank she'd try, and he wouldn't truly mind knowing she'd gone to the pub – even if he'd admonish her for it, in his way.

She knew she might be the only woman in that particular pub by the bank. It seemed to cater to men with jobs in construction. But it didn't matter. Even the roughest looking people in England all had a lovely, polite accent and wonderful manners. Not surprisingly, she hadn't had any trouble in a pub, and she'd already been in most of them at least once. It was the one thing she could count on, so far. In the pubs, regardless of what people were wearing or how they were speaking, or what they had to say to her and each other, everybody's colors were what Carolann knew to expect.

Chapter 4

Chip was first in the History classroom, and in the beautiful solitude, rhymes poured out of him. He scowled, tough guy, his new persona, and tapped his pen on the desk. Hard to write it right, think out all the nuances and fine-tune it so it could then flow out like genuine stuff. Maybe that's why all the famous writers were alcoholics. They had to drown the internal monitor to free themselves and write real.

Wherever I go, I end up here.
Farther from home, maybe, but still more near.
Chasing the thing I've been wanting so bad.
But what if what you want, you already had?
Try to get away to someplace new.
But wherever I go, damn if I'm there too.

He put down the pen. Chip's new life in England could start with the big Swedish guy from his bus. Henrik knew nothing of Chip's history. No one did. No one knew he taught Sunday School. No one knew of his grandfather's tobacco teeth and his scary briefcase full of numbers. No one knew of his crazy Uncle Buck's car dealership and tales of high school football glory. No one knew of his mother's twin sister, Chip's Aunt Maryann. No one knew the idiosyncrasies of Carolann Cooper.

Chip could have girls. A crowd. Screaming, fainting, tank

top girls. Step one, goal setting, like his dad taught his sales teams. Creative visualization. Chip knew all about self-talk. He grabbed the pen again.

I've got twelve months, and all twelve count
No past, no problems, no rumors to surmount.
Gonna meet some people who don't already know
Every goddamn thing about me, top of head to pinky toe,
Every move I'm gonna make, every place I'm gonna go.
I think I'm grown already, but now, maybe I'll grow.

The classroom door opened and a few students entered. Chip flipped his notebook closed. He'd written profanity in there. *Goddamn.* Chip had to make sure no one saw it.

The students sat down, uninterested in Chip and his writing. A tall Asian girl in tennis whites and two guys. Mr. Neame, the History teacher came in next, a stack of papers and notebooks balanced in his arms, and his curly brown hair trapped in a sloppy ponytail. He nodded at Chip and the others. "Greetings."

Chip mumbled hello and slid his notebook into his backpack. Fortunately, Carolann Cooper respected privacy. Chip didn't want to hold back in his writing. Sometimes that f-word seemed necessary. Back home, everyone was always f-this and f-that. Even smart kids said it. Probably, they even did it. Fornicate. The tennis girl adjusted the blinds to get the glare off her desk. Her bronze legs were skinny. She probably even did it. Once you did, Chip wondered, were you in some sort of club, where everyone could tell?

Two more girls came in, slid into chairs, and ignored Chip. Jeans and long hair. Mall girls who'd shop and drink sugared ice coffees and know the whole world thinks they're pretty. Thong underpants hiked up and visible, which either meant they did it, or did everything-but-it. Chip sighed.

He pulled the notebook out again and slouched low in his chair. He pushed his bulky basketball feet beyond the desk… stuck them into the classroom's central aisle just like Henrik did the whole first week, all big and Swedish in his skater t-shirts, his blond razor-cut hair and cheekbones. Chip wondered if Henrik was coming to class.

I'm gonna shed the shackles of this life I haul around,
Twelve months to find my feet, start running, hit the ground.

The bell rang and Mr. Neame sat on the edge of his desk to take roll. Henrik's name would be five after Chip's. He better hurry.

"Cooper." Check.

"D'Onghia." Check.

Chip's dad promised him a road trip to Liverpool for a Beatles Birthplace Tour. Chip knew rock-and-roll was born in black America of Big Mama Thornton, and Elvis shaped it later, but according to his dad, the Beatles defined it. So it started in America and came of age in England. Just like Chip would do now.

Chip's father promised, Chip's father delivered. Within a year, Chip would be a *goddamn* rapper.

"Kruidenier." Check.

And with a foreigner's accent in England, Chip was suddenly a minority. It didn't exactly qualify him as a rapper, but it was something. The darkest-skinned people Chip knew were brown, and he had only just met them. Indian, Cuban, and Pakistani.

"Olague." Check.

"Patel." Check.

And of course, having a parent once-accused of a crime didn't make Chip a gangster. Children punish themselves for the crimes of their parents, but it wasn't the same. Still, he had every right to put *goddamn* in a notebook. He wrote it again, thick, and he pressed hard, so the colorless impression could be read six or eight pages down. *Goddamn.*

She says she only wants what's best for me.
Let me be, Mama, let me be.
How do I make it clear? Set me free.

Neame called Henrik's name, and as if on cue, in he sauntered. The room smelled acrid and sharp, dry erase markers, Power Ade, and cologne, and Henrik swept through it, parting the waves as he ambled, broad-shouldered, down the central aisle. Everybody noticed him.

Henrik looked at Chip and nodded.

Chip pulled his big eager feet under his desk. Dialogue in his head threatened to tumble out uncontrolled, like the wafting chemical stink of energy drinks. *Hello, Henrik, how's it going,* pant-pant-human-puppy-dog, *how was rugby? Do they play rugby in Sweden?* Chip barely raised his eyelids.

Henrik dropped his backpack on the floor and slid into his desk chair.

Neame eyeballed the students and waved a stack of quiz papers. "Miss Olague? Do the honors?"

A black-haired girl in a purple tank top stood. Lots of braids, many of them sprouting little escaping bits of hair. Her jean jacket was tied around her waist. She took Neame's papers and shuffled them. Chip rubbed his fingertips on his notebook page and could read the impression like Braille. *Goddamn.*

Only one week of school, and Miss Olague seemed to know everyone's name. Chip watched her hand a quiz paper to Henrik, flipping her braids over her bare shoulder. "Impressive," she said.

Henrik rolled his eyes.

Chip saw the red ink, but he couldn't tell if Henrik got an A or an F. If Miss Olague was being sarcastic.

A or F. A or F.
How do you spell success?
I got an A, I wanted less.
At 14 years old, how to impress?

"Dude." Miss Olague jabbed a paper into Chip's chest. A perfect score.

Chip took the paper, staring at the badges pinned to the girl's jean jacket, pressing against his desk at hip-level. *I "heart" Macedonia.* And a smaller one. *Getting used to getting used.* "Cool button," he said.

She looked at her hip. "National Macedonia Day. Flag raising at noon."

"I meant the other one."

She stared at him. "It's ironic."

"I figured."

"Some don't." She raised an eyebrow.

Chip stared at her, the silence begging for another clever two-word response. Her eyes were blue, like Henrik's eyes, the color of swimming pool water, but hers were rimmed with black, like her hair. If he brought this girl home, Chip's mother would speak without thinking, and she'd owe all her loose change to the profanity jar.

Carolann wouldn't like Miss Olague one bit. She never liked anyone new, girl, boy, adult, child. Work colleague. No one.

Back home, everyone already knew everyone, and Chip suddenly realized he didn't know how to meet people. Not to mention the problem of his age. He stared at Miss Olague's braids, and his mouth dropped open, like a guppy, or the original village idiot.

"They think I'm advertising." She tapped the button. *Getting used to getting used.*

"People are dimwits," Chip said. His father's favorite explanation for anything.

She laughed, a sparkling, glittery, jingle-bell laugh. "How long you in for?" she asked. "Standard two to five?"

Chip stared at her.

"Your assignment. Your dad's overseas contract. Hit-and-run? Lifetime expat? You guys local? Is your mom the contract?"

"I, uhhh..." Chip stammered.

"Don't tell me you're a virgin."

Chip gasped. Of course, she didn't mean virgin-virgin, but what if she did? Was it obvious?

"Nothing wrong with it. I love virgins." The girl shook Chip's hand. "I'm Ticia Olague." She repeated it. "Tee-see-ya."

Her hand felt warm and small and strong. Her smile was pure sunshine.

She beamed and said, "Don't worry, virgin, I'll get you settled in."

Chapter 5

Carolann brought napkins to the dining room for Lyn and Chip. Dinner had come together relatively easily, once she'd realized the English called zucchini courgettes, and that eggplants went by their French translation, aubergines. Try as they might to distance themselves from France, the English couldn't help being a little Frenchy. Anyway, Carolann had nothing against the French. Even with all the butter in their recipes.

Lyn reached for the big bowl of pasta. "I feel like I can breathe in this country."

"The train in from Surrey isn't claustrophobic?" Carolann asked. "I'm sure I couldn't breathe at all."

"It's busy. But I don't know anyone. No one knows us. It's great. Right, Chip?"

He shrugged. "I wouldn't mind knowing a few people, maybe."

"But the congestion, the tall buildings. Everybody jostling and hustling, in such a hurry being important." Carolann sighed. "I'm not a city mouse, I guess."

"London's alive," Lyn said. "It's like it's buzzing. Samuel Johnson said, 'Why Sir, you find no man, at all intellectual, who is willing to leave London.'"

Chip added, "'When a man is tired of London, he is tired of life.' The headmaster's welcome assembly started with that quote."

Lyn looked at Chip and nodded. "Very good. Can you remember any other Johnson quotes?"

"Your old favorite: 'No people can be great who have ceased to be virtuous.'"

"That's the one." Lyn smiled.

"Well, in only one year, I'm not sure I'll get used to London before I can tire of it." Carolann laughed, but it wasn't an easy laugh.

Lyn poured his wife's wine glass full and winked at her. Nearly fifteen years of marriage, and he still winked. Carolann's friends at the hospital said their husbands and boyfriends never winked. Some didn't even bother in the beginning. But who were those women she had called her friends? Already, their names were starting to blend, the makes and colors of cars they drove had become indistinct. Two of them had husbands named Jim, one Jim might have had a mustache, one might have been bald. All Carolann remembered for sure was that neither of those men named Jim winked. What if at the end of a year, she couldn't recognize anyone she once knew? She'd worked with those people 40-hours-a-week, sometimes more, for years, and she didn't feel a single thread connecting back to them.

"This year is going to be great for you," Lyn said. "You might choose not to go back to nursing at all. You may discover a whole new Carolann Cooper over here, with new interests."

"I hope you're not tired of the old one." Carolann sipped her wine. It was from a German biodynamic vineyard. She'd never seen a biodynamic wine label at home, though she'd read about biodynamic farming. But the wine was expensive, so until raw data proved its benefits, she couldn't recommend it to her patients. Not to mention, it tasted like the stuff they bought in a box.

Lyn smiled. "I just mean it's nice not to have the family obligations – other than your sister's antiques store visits of course."

"I thought I'd miss church," Chip said. "But I don't. Is

that bad?"

"You just focus on school," Carolann said. "Regardless of the move, transition stress and all that, we expect nothing less than all A's." Carolann glanced at her wineglass. It had become empty. She frowned. If she wasn't careful, it might turn out she actually liked the stuff.

"You sure you don't want to join a church here?" Lyn refilled her glass and stared at the label. "I have it on good authority the Church of England is boilerplate American Protestantism."

"It's one year." Carolann interrupted him. "We'll go back to the Heart of America Church of God where we fit in, and where it serves our purpose. For one year, I'd like to think we can speak to God directly. Otherwise, what kind of Christians are we?"

"You don't have to convince me." Lyn salted his zucchini, and Carolann grimaced. Besides the blood pressure issues, and the water retention, salt just made people over-eat. The American way.

"Are you sure it's only one year?" Chip asked. "It seems like everybody at school has had plans change, countries change – this one kid had all his stuff on a boat to move back to Chicago from Singapore, and they had to redirect his shipment to here. His family's been expat for 13 years."

"We are 100% sure," Carolann stated. "We will be expat for one year. Now, do we talk about your school work first, or today's *Telegraph*?"

"We could talk about extending our contract here, if it all goes well," Lyn pressed.

Carolann glared at him.

"I read *The Mail* in the library," Chip said.

"Actually, I like the look of a job they've got going in Milan." Lyn laughed. "Health care consultancy could take me anywhere. You want me to put in for a move from here to Italy?"

"I most certainly do not. *The Daily Mail*?" Carolann shook her head at Chip.

Chip said, "We're not Catholic, we don't speak Italian. England's foreign enough. Let's find that Beemasters thing for Aunt Maryann and go home." He looked at his mother.

Carolann said. "Eleven daily papers in this town, and the boy finds one for illiterates. You need color pictures now, to understand a story? Sports? Celebrities? Naked ladies?"

"Mom, *The Mail's* not bad. But I read *The Times* too. You're the one who said to branch out."

"Right." Lyn nodded. "Carolann, we don't have a church, so let's at least explore the newspapers to find the right fit for our family."

Was he mocking her? Their impeccable church attendance was Lyn's commitment as much as hers. She glared at him. "You all want to find a church? Fine, we could find a church."

Lyn laughed. "Are you kidding? We have eleven daily papers to read. We won't have time for any church."

Chapter 6

Chip could see a small crowd in the distant flag courtyard. Ticia Olague led the singing of Mexico's National Anthem, loud enough that Chip could hear her voice distinct from the others.

Ticia was a faculty kid with Mexican ancestry, and she seemed to truly love the all-nations, enrichment by multiculturalism stuff. Chip, on the other hand, knew nothing about Mexico, and he was only just learning the distinction between multiculturalism and diversity. If he bumbled over to the Mexican flag for this ceremony, he'd look like a leach.

So he sat alone on the rock wall near the Peace for All People sculpture, his notebook open next to him. He ate a sandwich and listened to his headphones. Eminem. The king of self-deprecating lyrics, rhymes about vomit and fear and stuttering performance. How did Eminem get himself past the mumbling, upchucking idiocy?

Chip thought Ticia noticed him across the rugby pitch, and he lifted a hand to wave. She didn't wave back. He flipped his notebook closed, and back open.

Ticia had called his house two nights earlier to ask if his welcoming buddy had called yet, which he hadn't, and they stayed on the phone for 20 minutes. So of course, he should wave to her when he thought she was looking his way. He hoped she'd ditch the singers and come over solo.

Ticia hugged a girlfriend near the flagpole and walked toward Chip. He grabbed his notebook to look busy and wrote the only word repeating in his head as she approached.

He traced over it again and again. *Yes.*

"Hey, slim." Ticia kicked his tennis shoe. "Can I ask you something?"

Chip pulled his headphones down.

"Do you think I'm cute?" she asked.

Chip coughed. "That's kind-of a direct question."

"But do you? My boyfriend hasn't made contact in almost two weeks."

"You're shopping for a replacement?" He smiled.

"Are you proposing?" She flipped her hair. No longer in cornrows, now it was long and curly. "No. He moved to Austria, but we made plans, you know. Every day an email. Not all day contact. I'm talking one email. I don't think that's too much to ask."

"I don't know what you want me to say."

"The truth. Am I cute enough for a long-distance relationship? We went out all sophomore year."

"Well, examine your question." Chip cleared his throat. "If all he cares about is your looks, then no, long-distance is doomed. But that's probably not all he cares about. Maybe he's got a computer virus. Call him."

"Good point."

"And, yes…" Chip swallowed, "you're cute."

Ticia smiled and looked Chip up and down. "Not fat?"

"Hardly." He flipped his pen against his notebook. "What was in his last email? Was the content weird?"

"Andrew's content's always weird. That's what I love about him."

Love. Ticia loved this guy Andrew, and Chip's heart clenched and twisted. The biology textbook pictures were right. The thing was definitely a muscle, and suddenly Chip's heart muscle was too big for its space. It was butting up against his lungs, battling his ribs.

"Maybe he's having mom-stress again. She's unstable."

"Sounds familiar," Chip said. Had he said that out loud?

The word stared at him on his paper. *Yes.*

"Andrew's mom was in denial," Ticia said. "When they had to move on instead of move back, her plans got all fucked up, and she kind-of lost it."

"Huh?" Chip said.

"She had it all planned. Send the shipment mid-June and cruise Europe for a few weeks and then go back to New Jersey and meet up with their stuff. Classic exit strategy, you know?"

"Hmmm." Chip nodded. "A Kansas shipment takes six weeks to get here, I guess."

"Midwest is about the longest from the U.S. I mean, continental U.S. Your stuff went truck, train, ship, right?"

"I think so. It's due here in a week, when it clears customs."

"*If*, my friend. Never *when*," Ticia said. "Andrew's Mom wanted to take the QE2 back to New York. She didn't want to move to Austria. Neither did he, of course." She curtsied. "We thought his dad could commute from London, but the companies never allow that. Coke. Kraft. Procter & Gamble. The big HR guys come to Career Day every spring and they all say Keep Families Together." She clapped her hands with each word. "Fucking HR mantra ruined my possible future with the love of my life."

"What are you, seventeen? Kind of young to be thinking about *future*." Plus, these HR guys might have done Chip a favor.

"You've obviously never been in love." Ticia shook her head.

Chip put his headphones back on and stared at his notebook. The one word he'd written now seemed foreign. *Yes, yes, yes.*

Ticia pulled his headphones off again. "Look, I'm just… frustrated." She put her foot on the wall next to Chip's leg and stretched her calf muscle. Converse high tops. She'd drawn a checkerboard pattern over the white toe-cap. "Your shipment will probably show up in one week, just like they say."

"My mom hates the rental sofa." Chip nodded. "So I hope so."

Ticia switched feet and stretched the other leg. "You know, sometimes the mom has the expat deal and the dad trails, like my dad did before he became faculty here. STUDS. Spouses Trailing Under Duress. You'll learn the lingo."

Chip's pen tapped his knee, and he stared at her.

"Dude, this is my one area of expertise." She raised her voice. "I'm a lifer, ok? It's all I know. Here we still are, in a corporate rental for 14 years, which makes my dad nuts. We can't even talk about when we'll go home anymore. My aunt's a shrink, and that's her scientific definition of us. Crazy."

Chip opened his mouth, and Ticia touched his lips and shut it for him. His lips felt electric, a tiny flower blooming under her fingerprint. He wanted to lick the spot, to see if the electrical charge would transfer to his tongue.

"Expats who *move on* instead of *move back* talk about home-home, the place of their mother tongue. I don't even have that. Half the time my parents speak Spanish, like they're from East fucking L.A., and I don't understand them. *Comprende?*"

"I get it." Did every fight in this school start in a foreign language?

"I've said good-bye to more friends than you've had hot dinners. I've got no continuity, an incommunicado boyfriend. But I have this." She spread her arms wide. "I'm the queen of the fucking Global Village."

"Ok."

"Ask Jed Foster what nationality he is. He'll say 'American but I've never lived there.' Hansl Soderholm, same, but Finnish. The embassy has a great book on re-entry called *According to My Passport I'm Moving Home.* There's another good book – *Third Culture Kids.*"

"Maybe I should buy that re-entry book for my mom." Chip felt like Ticia was speaking level four French, but he was only level two. Her eyes were really blue.

"You don't buy it, shit head. It's free." She smiled. "U.S. Government issue."

"I think I prefer *dude*, you know – over *shit head*," Chip said.

She sat down and rested her hands on her legs. Black fingernail polish.

Chip looked at her thigh, nearly touching his, and his heart pounded. Muscle. Muscle. Muscle. He wanted to write the word down in a perfect phrase. But then of course, he'd never speak it. Where did his selective speech impediment come from?

"Why didn't you come hoist the Mexican flag with me?"

"Do I look Mexican?" Chip shrugged. His problem wasn't stage fright or performance anxiety, because it was only when he'd written the words. And he was not, by nature, a nervous boy. His parents saw to that.

"Fuck, homeboy. Everybody's welcome. I don't just mean you, homes, because you're from my home country, I mean everyone. You need to join the National Celebration Committee. Help plan the summer countries' events. Bastille Day."

"Bastille Day? My family's not big on the French."

"Swiss day is in August. You know their flag is square, for neutrality? It's the only one. Of course, Nepal's not a rectangle either. Theirs looks like an animal chewed it up. Still cool, though."

"No, thanks. I'm not a committee guy." Ticia's thigh was definitely touching Chip's. Their jeans were identical blues. He liked his firm response. Weak people wavered.

"We did it last year," she said after a minute. "Andrew and me."

Chip stared at her.

"That too." She threw her head back and laughed. "Five times." She held up a hand and counted off her fingers, thumb first. "Missionary, missionary, me-on-top, doggie style in the car, and uh… Kama Sutra page 42." She grabbed her pinky and wiggled it.

"I could do without the visuals." Chip smiled. Maybe, he thought, thank you just a little, for the visuals.

Ticia said, "He probably doesn't even fucking remember today's Mexico."

"Maybe he doesn't like your swearing," Chip said.

"Andrew?" Ticia burst out laughing. "He's from New York. I'm from LA."

"So you were born into this trash-mouth? Your vocabulary is in your architecture?" Chip shrugged.

"A bicoastal's different from a Kansas boy. My language is not the problem."

"Expat. Expat," Chip said suddenly. "I've enjoyed our little chat. I'll wear the logo on my hat."

"Don't do that," Ticia said.

"The chat? The hat? I sat on a mat with Yasser Arafat."

She stood, hand on hip. "How old are you?"

He wasn't a rapper. He was a loser. "I'm precocious," he said. "And tall for my age." She was so incredibly pretty in the sun. "Fourteen," he nearly whispered.

"Fuck me, Jesus." Ticia stepped back. "A fourteen-year-old Junior."

"I don't see what He has to do with it," Chip said.

"A word of advice." Ticia bent and looked Chip in the eye. "Good thing you're tall. Don't tell people you're fourteen."

Truth first. Chip could hear his father's words. *Truth matters above all.* "But I am fourteen," he said. He felt betrayed by Ticia Olague and his father, both. "And you asked."

"Wrong, sweet, naïve boy." She touched his cheek before she turned away. "All wrong. Eccentric is cool. Fucking freakshow is not."

Chapter 7

Carolann eyeballed the scribbles on a yellow sheet of legal paper. She'd been cross-referencing her sister's list all week, and it was hard to follow the arrows and footnotes. If they wanted to go to a different antiques store in England every day, it'd still take a hundred years.

"There are seven shops in that area around the Angel tube station. Maybe eight, or a dozen, on Maryann's list. She thinks we'll find the Beemasters thing within one or two places if we go there."

"I hope so," Lyn said. "Or this could get out of hand."

"We have to find it. Maryann says they're probably all over England. They're just not making it over to the U.S. Did you know they had little pitchers, they looked kind-of like gravy boats, and the women used them as toilets? Apparently their hoop skirts were very practical."

"Does Maryann know what they're for? If we find one, I'll personally buy it for her table." Lyn smiled.

"She probably knows. I read it in that English Porcelain book she gave me." Carolann tapped an open page of the London A-Z map. "A book I hope is on its way to our house, along with everything else. The weather's already turning, and we need our winter stuff. I don't like all this rental furniture. I don't like cooking with other people's pans. And the bed linens…"

"Our stuff is already in this country. It'll clear customs any day now. One thing at a time."

Carolann sighed. "I just want to get that debt behind us. Find that vase and go back a hero."

Lyn said, "When we go back, your sister will have some other axe to grind with you, even if you're lucky with the Beemasters."

Carolann looked at her husband carefully. What was he implying? The other axe her sister might have to grind had never been a fair topic of conversation, but thousands of miles away, maybe the rules had suddenly changed. Carolann was so anxious to see her elusive new neighbor Rowan again that she couldn't help but admit that for her, a small change was already happening.

"Carolann, I want to help your family as much as anyone, but what if we don't find that thing?"

"We'll find it. Maybe the next place we look."

"Of course, we could choose not to go back at all." Lyn looked at Carolann. "I just mean, today it's the Beemasters vase you girls broke, tomorrow, it's – I don't know – a whole new shipment of Pembroke tables or something for her shop. She'll run you ragged if you let her." He gently took the map book from his wife and closed it. He pushed the mail on the entryway table aside, and set the book down. "Not to mention whether we'll ever square the money."

Carolann stared at the book. "I have no choice." The beige carpet underfoot suddenly seemed frayed and patchy, trodden by millions of expats before her, they'd worn it out unevenly, with all their confident comings and goings through her entryway. She wondered if she'd lose her balance. She took a deep breath.

"You ok?" Lyn asked.

"Until I have some friends who might want to scour the antiques markets with me, I need you to do this." She'd never had close girlfriends by choice, so why did it feel like she now needed to blame her husband for this social deficit?

"I thought you were great friends with our new neighbor?"

Lyn's tone was sarcastic. "Aren't we going to her house for a party?"

"It was supposed to be last Saturday, now she says next Saturday. She's come over twice to reschedule, and otherwise, I've hardly seen her. So no, I wouldn't say we're great friends." Carolann felt like a child, desperate for the attention of a popular schoolgirl. Only now, the "popular girl" was a middle-aged English woman in bad sweaters, who had disappeared entirely, as opposed to just turning away from Carolann in favor of Maryann. "But that's beside the point, Lyn. I am not taking that train in to London without you. I don't understand how to read those train schedules. If I try to do this alone, I'm going to end up in... in... I don't even know. If I actually find a piece of priceless Beemasters, I'll be clubbed over the head or kidnapped and you'll never see me again." Carolann heard her voice become shrill.

"Don't misunderstand me. It's great for our family to go into the city. But I wish we could, just for once, not let your sister call the shots." Lyn took Carolann's hand in his.

Her heart pumped not blood, but poison and anguish. Was this a panic attack? She really didn't like the stuff, but she had to admit, a drink would calm her down. She'd drink it fast, and this time, it would have nothing to do with her husband.

"Lyn," she said, "of all people, I'd think you'd understand the thing about my sister."

"No." He slammed his hand on the A-Z book. "I said I would take you, and therefore, until we find that god-forsaken blue-and-white vase, wherever it is you want to go, I will take you."

The crack of his hand on the book echoed. Carolann nodded.

"Chip!" Lyn yelled up the stairs. "Right now. We're going antiquing. Your mother's ready to go."

Chapter 8

It was the blue-and-white vase that was causing all the hassle for Carolann in England, just like it caused the original trouble when the twins were seven years old. Of course, had the original trouble with the blue-and-white vase never happened, there would have been no rift between the little girls' family and their neighbor, Edith Heaney, and there would be no difficulty today. Carolann had no trouble linking cause and effect.

Mrs. Heaney had loved her English china. She had all different patterns, flowers and birds and Chinese people crossing little blue bridges. But the prized piece was the most rare pattern she had, a special gift from her mother, a Beemasters vase. It had a lovely little blue-and-white bee-keeper man collecting honey, an English fellow, Mrs. Heaney explained, as opposed to a French courting couple, or more common Chinese people. It was mint condition, which Carolann and Maryann understood to mean perfect. A "mint" so flawless no one would eat it.

The first time the twins gave Edith Heaney daffodils, she had put them in the blue-and-white vase, and immediately burst into tears. Rubbing her veiny hands at her eyes, she tried to explain. Something about England and her childhood, her mother, yellow flowers, fields of yellow flowers, and her father. It was hard to understand her through the sniffles and sobs. And the little girls were more intrigued by the grown woman's crying itself than any explanation of her reason for it. She mentioned American soldiers in Devon. Sedgewick Heaney working her father's farm. Making Sedgewick Heaney tea. Mr. Heaney was dead, and Carolann assumed Mrs. Heaney was crying because he was dead. If her father was dead, she thought her mother would probably cry a lot. The twins had never seen any grown-up cry, and Carolann trembled, half with fear, half with silenced laughter.

Mrs. Heaney stared at the yellow daffodils, like she was daring herself, like she enjoyed the pain of her memories. She used a sodden hankie instead of tissues. The twins watched the handkerchief carefully as the old lady rolled it in her hand and slowly stopped sniffling.

She mentioned plant derivatives in England, Europe, and the States. A future full of possibilities. Everything she gave up for the man she married. The twins understood almost none of it. Carolann understood more as it was described to her later, but in the moment, the twins understood the tears. They had caused the tears, and Maryann wanted more. But the next time they tried it, the flowers didn't make Mrs. Heaney cry.

Like all emotional moments, the experience itself and the expression of it may be triggered by one thing but softened (or indeed sharpened) by numerous other influences. Maryann was going to have to ramp up her game with the flowers.

The next time the girls brought her flowers, Maryann nodded at the blue-and-white vase, and Carolann knew what she meant. She nudged the vase toward her sister, and in an instant, Maryann stood, a big smile on her face, her *pretty-girl smile*, and she grabbed and dropped the vase on the hard floor, where it shattered.

Edith didn't cry – she screamed. Her face turned red, and lines bulged all the way down her neck and in her forehead like she was made of purple and gray and pink rubber, and she wasn't a human being at all. Maryann burst into a fit of frightened giggles. Carolann smelled metal and motor oil in the screaming. It was such a powerful smell, she thought surely her sister smelled this one too, but Maryann only stood there laughing. Carolann dropped to the floor to pick up the flowers and pieces of the vase. She laid her paper napkin on the spilled water, flattening its wrinkles into the dampness it absorbed. But Edith still screamed. And then she pulled Carolann from under the table and took the twins, one under each of her arms, like heavy rag dolls, and carried them downstairs to her basement. Her voice was raspy. Carolann would never forget that voice, nor the echo of the oil smell, when Mrs. Heaney set the twins down in the dark lab. "Stay."

Then Mrs. Heaney ran back up the stairs, sobbing and gasping, and she slammed the door. The girls heard the lock in the basement door and then silence. They heard Mrs. Heaney's front door creak open and slam shut. Carolann had wet her pants. She wondered if Maryann did too. The whole front of her dress was wet too, from the water and the flowers. The twins didn't move.

Murky light filtered through the dark, and the twins' eyes adjusted to take in the lab equipment in front of them. Charts and wires and glass tubes and shallow dishes and metal tongs with huge handles. Carolann had seen a Frankenstein book at school, and without moving any muscle other than her eyelids, she squinted in the dim light, looking for a slab and a monster with bolts in his neck.

"She's not a witch," Maryann whimpered. "She's a mad scientist."

"Is she coming back?" Carolann asked quietly. "She's going to kill us."

"Mama's going to kill us," Maryann said. "She's going to kill you."

"Me?" Carolann swallowed hard. "We broke it together." Mrs. Heaney was going to force-feed them like Hansl and

Gretl, and eat them. That would be better than their mother killing them. Or their father. He would kill them so it hurt. That vase was valuable.

"You grabbed it. You threw it across the table," Maryann insisted. "And then the loony bird tried to kill you. I saved you."

"I did not throw it."

"Everyone will hate the loony bird and not us," Maryann said. "We're just little girls. You dropped it."

"That's not what happened – will Mama believe that?"

"Mama believes whatever I tell her." Maryann's tone was firm.

"It was an accident," Carolann said. "Tell her that. Tell her you dropped it by accident."

"No, it was you." Maryann said, "You're clumsy. You drop things and see things and smell things. It was you."

Carolann stared into the dim blue light. The window near the ceiling was reinforced with chicken wire. "But it wasn't," she said.

"We're in this together," Maryann said. "This is how we get out of it."

Carolann nodded. Her twin sister was first, so she was older and smarter. Maryann knew everything.

But of course Maryann didn't know Barbara Ann's phone calls and accusations would lead to Edith Heaney's home being searched and desecrated, her privacy violated, and her lab all but destroyed. And her scientific journals confiscated and her judgment questioned. Maryann didn't know that for months, lowered voices in church would discuss why Edith Heaney ran off with an American soldier in the first place, instead of marrying one of her own. What was she trying to escape? What happened in England? What went on in those fields behind her father's farmhouse? Why couldn't she marry a man from her own town? Why didn't she have any children of her own? What was wrong with that woman?

The girls couldn't know that when their father heard of the broken vase and its value, the news would hit him like a shot, a bullet carrying the word *debt*. His daughters cost a woman something she said was irreplaceable. It was a balance he couldn't square. A debt he couldn't repay.

Cyrus was a man who lived firmly in the black. His reputation, his business, his whole sense of self were in the black. And now that his girls broke this stupid, ridiculously expensive old vase, he saw nothing but eat-him-alive, relentless and forever, red. Even as a little girl, Carolann knew plenty about living in the wrong color.

But as usual, Maryann seemed to know everything, Carolann agreed with the plan, and once their lie rolled out, it couldn't be rolled back. To reveal the various untruths later would each become a new betrayal of its own. It seemed easier, year by year, to glare at the neighbor's house across the way, look for a replacement of that vase in the antiques stores, to eventually right the balance if they ever could, and just leave the whole big thing at that.

It was a decision made when the twins were children, a wrong they were still, in turn, working to right. But the Beemasters pattern was proving itself nearly impossible to find, and even in England more than 20 years later, Carolann was discovering that Edith Heaney's special vase perhaps was irreplaceable after all.

Chapter 9

"I don't know what's gotten into him." Ticia spun the library chair backward and straddled it in front of Chip.

"Tell me about it," Chip slammed his book. "I don't understand Mr. Neame."

"Not Neame, bonehead. I'm talking about Andrew, my so-called boyfriend."

"Well, I'm talking about Neame. The man just pulled my headphones off my ears and said, 'I've got your number, mister. You don't fool me.'" Chip gave Neame the extra-deep voice of a puppet.

"It's a compliment," Ticia said. "You got another perfect score on a pop quiz, right?"

"Discovery quiz." Chip shook his head. "Starting point for a new unit."

"Whatever. It measures background knowledge instead of achievement, so what? It still counts on your grade and you got 20 out of 20, which is a little unusual. He just wants you to know he's watching you."

"Apartheid's been a dinner table topic in my house for years. I don't see the problem." Neame had looked Chip up and down, his long, curly ponytail bobbing with his head and said, *'I've been doing this a lot of years, young man. Be aware, I'm onto you.'*

"Just don't fuck up, sweetie. No problem." Ticia shrugged. "Now can we get back to my problem?"

"I thought you called Andrew and everything was fine,"

Chip said.

"Yeah, but it's been a week now, and still no emails."

Chip's toe dug into the tight-weave of industrial carpet. Was Neame implying that Chip cheated on a quiz measuring background knowledge? Wouldn't that be impossible? Chip had never been accused of anything in school or in church. He didn't know how to respond. And this wasn't even an accusation. It was a threat.

"My mom will kill me if I call Vienna every day," Ticia said. "Are you even listening to me?"

"Yes." Chip looked up. "You call *me* every day."

"You don't get it."

Chip shrugged. Maybe Neame would call his parents in for a conference. That would be a first. He had wanted to experience a few firsts. But God knows what his mother would do. Three one-way tickets to Kansas, first flight available.

Ticia said, "That fucker Henrik says Andrew's just too shy to break up with me, but that's what's coming."

"That's stupid."

"Yeah." Ticia stared at Chip. "But you're 14, and a virgin, and from Bumfuck Egypt. You write some awesome poetry, lyrics, whatever, and you're smart. But you could be wrong."

"You know nothing about me," Chip said. No one in England knew anything about him. Not Ticia Olague, and certainly not Stewart Neame. No one knew how his throat closed and his tongue tripped sometimes. He could answer questions and contribute to any class discussion off the cuff, but if he'd written the lines in advance, cared about them and nurtured them into meaning, he couldn't perform them. No one knew his parents. No one knew his problems.

"It's what you said." Ticia snapped her fingers. "I am damn cute. Andrew has to see me. I need to do Glamour Shot portraits like they have in San Pedro."

"Dress up in slutty K-Mart couture?" Chip imagined her in a low-cut nylon top and big hair. "That might work."

"I need a make-over," she said.

"No, you don't. Just take nice pictures. Don't look all fakey."

Ticia blinked her blue eyes. "Alannah self-published her photography book for her Personal Project. Maybe she'd do it. She's amazing. Portraiture."

"There you go. Look good, like the real you. That's got to be what he's in love with. Your confidence."

"Chip, I love *you!*" Ticia stood and spun the chair back into place. "You're wise beyond your years. Your big-secret 14 years."

Chip watched her leave. He couldn't control himself when Ticia left a room, especially in those jeans. Maybe that's what Neame figured out, that Chip was a pervert.

Ticia stopped at the library's big glass double doors and blew Chip a kiss. Of course her real kisses were for Andrew, the non-communicator in Austria, and the only ones for Chip were intangible.

His dad wouldn't say *pervert*, he'd use the word *normal*. Normal red-blooded American male, chuckle, chuckle. Neame couldn't fault Chip for that.

Perfectly acceptable big drama, Chip pretended to catch Ticia's kiss in his hand and stick it on his cheek, as he watched her jeans disappear. The door whispered shut, and rhyming words swilled, multisyllabic, through his head, through his hand, onto the blank page of his notebook in dark ink. Phrases to play with later.

Adorable, Deplorable.
Desperation. Above my station.
Elation.
Tragic agony.
Heartbreaking frustration.

Chapter 10

Lyn's career had reached an apex of sorts. He was earning good money. He knew he was envied back home for the overseas assignment so many other guys had wanted. Here and now, he knew he was doing an important job, helping the National Health Service live up to its original intentions from when it was formed after World War II. In its inception, it was a wonderful idea, and in its heyday, it was a shining beacon in world health. Now though, they needed help. Lyn Cooper's help.

In one year, he would make a good start. Already, only six weeks into the job, he knew he could begin to make a real difference – all the more so if they'd see the benefit of his assistance and offer him a contract extension. Soon enough, Carolann would have her own clothes and books and furniture and kitchen utensils, and she'd begin to feel at home. At least she'd get settled into the year of the contract. Even so, convincing her to stay in England longer than one year might be a bigger challenge.

Of course, new advancements in medicine were gained faster and faster during the second half of the last century. Lyn had to be careful to point out the research successes didn't just come from America, but throughout Europe and the UK as well. The United Kingdom, in fact, had always been a front-runner. Still was. In his speeches, Lyn was careful to pause long enough after saying so to really drive that point home. He was learning already how to read the silent signs of British disapproval, and likewise, the even more subtle clues when people agreed with him. To watch British Parliament in session on TV, one could be easily misled to believing the English were rather loud grumblers.

In actual fact, Lyn had learned quickly how much of what was "spoken" was silent. And if someone ever, God forbid, offered his opponent a compliment in argument or lively discussion, that was a cutting blow. *With all due respect to the right honorable gentleman...* Who would have figured that for an insult? Lyn Cooper, that's who. Day by day, Lyn was figuring out how to discuss the most sensitive health care matters with his British audiences.

Specialized machines for diagnosis and treatments were increasingly costly. The new drugs available, (offering prevention, or halting of progression, or even cure), were expensive. Even the elective treatments people could pursue all put terrible burdens on a suffering health care system. Expense was a universal hurdle, even if the two countries' approaches to jumping such hurdles differed.

Moreover, the layperson's access to knowledge (and resultant medical demand) was outpacing the NHS's ability to deliver medical care by miles. No wonder British people were frustrated. Lyn's first tour of six hospitals showed the same thing in all cases: down-trodden patients sitting in filthy "Accident-and-Emergency" waiting rooms. Even the nation's better hospitals resembled some of the worst he'd seen in the U.S. The reports he reviewed on paper also showed similar problems, most notably lengthy delays even for life-saving operations. People died, many patients died, for no reason other than the timing. In the U.S. this sort of death would be inexcusable. An outrage. (Though admittedly, every major American city suffered its outrages every single day). In the UK though, Lyn had found, there was a bit of British reserve injected into the outraged response, and although the loss might be outrageous, the overall comment was sometimes, *well, these things happen.*

It was as if there had been so many more past generations in this country, so many people whose lives had been lived and then briefly remembered, and then forgotten, the English were simply more resigned to the inevitability of death. Americans, in that regard, were like children, trailing behind the attitudes of their Mother Country. To an American, Lyn realized, every new injury or insult or outrage was raw, and its healthcare system battled fiercely to prevent any future affronts.

Lyn also discovered that the battle between straight-NHS patients and those who wanted to "top up" their health care by taking out private insurance, or by paying out of pocket for certain doctors or procedures was seriously muddying the English medical waters. From the outset, Lyn couldn't do a thing about the dangerous delays, or about the private versus public tangle, but he could help improve waiting room morale. He could help institute programs so that people better knew how to take care of themselves. He could encourage General Practitioners to use a simple database to keep their patient records up to date, accessible, and legible. It seemed incredible that the majority of doctors were still keeping patient records in their notoriously scratchy handwriting. No wonder the country was so sick and tired. Add more processed foods and American-style obesity to the mix, and things would only get worse.

From the minute Lyn had been brought over from Kansas to England, even though he was "on loan" from big pharma, he felt like Superman. He would fly backwards around the world seven times, turn back time to when the full package of technology and medicines and highly-trained personnel were more on a par with demand, and the NHS was at its best. He'd help them revive what they could, improve what they could, and scrap what they needed to, to start over.

Lyn understood triage, and he recognized the importance of morale. He felt more than qualified to get into the scrum and make decisions, and ultimately, he could see the troubled system into recovery. He'd need to start planting seeds soon, if he would be granted the contract extension to make a real difference where it was needed. For the first time in years, professionally and personally, he felt he was in exactly the right place at the right time.

Chapter 11

Carolann had to admit that it had been years since she'd seen Lyn confident, energized and striving for something important like he was now. It reminded her of when they first met. Whether her memories were changed over time or were accurate, he had seemed more alive then. Lit from within – a celestial golden-yellow. It was such a pure color, there wasn't even a smell. (Carolann rarely had one without the other). When his career was still challenging, his enthusiasm was intense and contagious. And although Carolann was ridiculously naïve and young and fragile at the time, she knew even then that she represented a good sort of challenge for him too.

In the early days, when they were first together, they were a beautiful couple. Silver-sheened royal blue and that divine yellow. Even if no one else saw her colors, they surely could sense it.

Being in England had destabilized both of them. Carolann knew she'd quickly grown into maturity after high school, she knew every smell and color of the events that shaped her at the time, but she couldn't remember, for certain, how she actually ensured her own growth. Surely it couldn't have just been marriage and motherhood that brought maturity and understanding upon her. She must have actively had something to do with it. If only she knew how she'd done it. If only she could do it again.

She had to trace it back. Lyn wouldn't approve – he wanted certain doors to stay shut. But if she didn't look back now, how would they handle Chip's imminent coming of age?

Lyn insisted he had the entire conversation planned. Soon enough, Chip would be sixteen, and Lyn would want to tell Chip the truth. Carolann understood why her husband was comfortable with the facts, but not with the details. No man wanted to picture his wife with someone other than himself, regardless of the ultimate benefits from that other union. But now, far from Kansas, Carolann realized the time was arriving faster than they'd planned. And in truth, she'd never fully agreed with or understood the conversation Lyn intended to have with their son. She'd better come to terms with it all. One step, one event, at a time. And then, she hoped, she'd help her husband do the same.

Carolann was seventeen when she woke up heavy with a booze flu and a throbbing awareness. She was new to drinking, but she knew enough. Acid filled her bloated stomach with opaque-egg-yolk yellow. Her head throbbed, russet and aubergine. Pain pounded through her skull, hard, brittle white bone, in the searing, bright blue morning light. She knew stress and fatigue brought on increased cross-wiring. After the night she'd just had, of course her senses were exploding. She wanted to call in sick to her summer job.

If Buck was already awake at his house, he'd be thinking about how to call her, and the best way he could do that would be through the switchboard at Memorial Hospital. Maryann's boyfriend Buck. Old boyfriend. Carolann's new boyfriend, Buck. Buck Roberts.

She tried to sit up and winced. Her sister's empty bed stared at her. She felt like she'd sat on a garden claw.

But at least Buck finally could know Carolann loved him more than Maryann did. She loved him more than she loved her parents, who would kill her if they knew what she did. She loved Buck more than God, who knew everything she did and everything she thought about doing. She loved Buck more than herself, headed for Hell. Eight hours passed at Memorial, but Buck didn't call.

A year earlier, Pastor Hugh had one day boldly asked the Girls Bible Study group: What do you get fornicating with a teenage boy? Answer: Nothing. (*If you're lucky*, Maryann had whispered).

Carolann finished her shift and couldn't face her parents at home, nor her sister's absence. She pulled her father's Oldsmobile into a parking spot at the closest bar. She had no fake ID, but she felt old. Why did people say drinking wasn't the answer? Obviously, people didn't know the question.

What did she really expect from Buck? At least he could have called her by the right name when they were in his car, maybe kissed her once more, before his tires kicked gravel at her, and he sped away, his red taillights searing zigs of shame into her street, denial screaming in his wake. *We did not do this. I did not do this.* The image returned to her often and loudly, those red lines of light, with acid rock.

The dim bar buzzed with a neon red glow. That same harsh-reminder red. A window air-conditioning unit spat moldy-smelling air into the room – three empty vinyl booths and a line of bar stools, one of them occupied. Carolann marched in, and she planted her elbows on the bar. The man on the stool seemed to be staring at her. Could he tell she was not of age? Not a nurse. Not a virgin.

Her arm stuck in a patch of brown residue. She scanned the lit bottles and took a deep, sickening breath. Cyrus would like the old air-conditioner. *If it aint broke, don't fix it.* Her father's favorite phrase that saved clients money.

The man on the barstool cleared his throat. Carolann concentrated on the bottles and rubbed her bare shoulders. Maryann wasn't just her sister, she was her twin. What if somehow, she already knew? Where was the stupid bartender?

If someone's sorry, do they have to say it out loud? Does confession downgrade a Catholic's sin to just a little mistake? An error in judgment, like their loony bird neighbor tried to say. And so what if God forgives your sin? He's not the one coming home from cheerleading camp to sleep in the next bed. Carolann's eventual entrance into heaven (or rejection there) had nothing to do with living every day in the same bedroom with Maryann.

A big, bearded man came from the bar's storeroom and stacked cardstock coasters. Big Foot in jeans and a t-shirt.

"Old Granddad and Tab, please," Carolann said. "Double."

"No ID – no double, no single, no nothing." He stared at her.

"Come on, you must know I'm of age." If she could slide a hundred dollar bill on the bar like they did in the movies, she'd get served. But she only had a twenty, and spending even one penny extra went so against the grain of her upbringing, she'd sooner suck whiskey from a stone.

The bartender turned his back.

"Right?" The man next to her asked.

Carolann turned, startled to recognize the man's face. He looked like Buck.

"You were in my lecture today."

She nodded. It was the eyes and the hair and the mouth. He had asked her directions during her lunch break, while she ambled through the hospital corridors, unable to sit. She had pointed out his lecture hall and then stood in the back while he spoke to nurses about asthma. He had probably registered the spark of recognition flare in her and then blaze out, when she realized, of course, he wasn't Buck. Now she'd be cursed to see her sister's boyfriend's face in every man.

"Health care marketing," the man said to the bartender. "Surely a hard-working nurse deserves a drink, and I owe her one, Jack."

"Name's not Jack. You buy yourself one, and what happens to it is your business."

The man who was not Buck turned to Carolann. "Bourbon's your poison?"

"Anything." She'd have to be the one to tell Maryann. Buck wouldn't do it.

"Let's line up some shots." The man patted the bar. "And a Tab."

Carolann shifted on her barstool. This guy was even older than Enrique, the hospital orderly she had kissed in the elevator weeks ago, at the start of summer, her first kiss, and one time later in the mop closet, green and turquoise, smelling of chemical pine. The man's hand rested on the rolled cushion edge of the bar. His fingers were short, and his nails looked stuck on with glue. (She later had to admit, she had noticed his hands right away).

"Knock yourself out, doc." The bartender set the glasses down. "Or her."

Carolann had come in for one drink, but now, she wanted several. There were no words to tell Maryann. Buck could hardly pass a spelling test, how could he know the right words?

The man laughed. "You might as well learn a thing or two about good whiskey. Tell me you're twenty-one."

Carolann smiled a tiny, tight smile. Not a loose, toothy teenager's grin, but a grown-up's. The boozy burden of memory was an adult's day-after ache. Excusing herself from her duties to attend this man's lecture was an adult coping mechanism. Of course she was twenty-one. She was forty.

"Smell the peat." The man picked up the first whiskey, his stubby fingers like those of a dwarf on the glass. "Nice deep breath."

It smelled like moss. Like navy blue. Soil, mud, mold, and sex. Like the ground where she and Buck fell down together next to his car, knocked to their knees, sloppy with desire, while Magic Maryann shouted into a megaphone two states away. Someone might have seen them before they left the party. In one long, fluid motion, Carolann sucked down the shot.

"Chaser." He handed her the Tab.

The whiskey burned her throat and made her shoulders shake. The aftertaste sizzled in her gut.

She had to tell Maryann what kind of guy her boyfriend really was, his pounding and pushing. She didn't even know if she'd liked it. She hardly remembered what it felt like, him on top of her in the car, other than *invasive* and *giddy*. And *gold*. If she did it again, it would probably feel good. Maybe the third or fifth time. People liked it. If the Church said to avoid it, surely that meant people even craved it. She thought of Buck's white t-shirt, his football-lemon smell, the steamy moonlight in his car. The pushing. She did crave it.

She gulped the soda. She wanted more soda, only chasers for the rest of her life. How much of the awful stuff did you have to suck down before you got the chaser?

"Next?" The man held up another shot.

She sipped the second shot and shut her eyes. *A man will try to bring his pet frog, to visit your lily pads*, their mother told them one time. *It is not a hotel, open to visitors. Only your husbands' frogs should ever visit your lily pads*. Carolann downed the shot. Buck's frog was enormous, and in the end, he had grunted like a toad.

"Different taste, right?" the man asked. "What are you thinking?"

He was handsome. Carolann smiled at him, aware of her eyelashes, the heated pink flush of whiskey in her cheeks. "Well..." She looked at the lit row of bottles glimmering behind the bar. Light pinging in the dark glass like rubies and sapphires. She knew gemstone sparkles reflected in her eyes, and everything was darkest amethyst, like when it started with Buck. And Enrique before he got fired. "I'd like to..."

She licked her lower lip and watched the man's Adam's apple bob in his throat. He would finish her sentence like they did, Buck and Enrique, and he'd move her beyond yesterday. He would lean in and kiss her.

But the doctor-guy sat silently waiting. Maybe he didn't have a frog.

She swallowed hard. "Maybe, if you have time, just to talk, I could use some advice."

He nodded toward a booth.

Carolann slid off her barstool. Her knees wobbled and she held the bar till she felt stable.

"Come on." Lyn took her arm and he smiled. "I'm safe."

Chapter 12

From the window, Chip saw the white Mercedes school bus pass his house to pick up the little kids at the end of the road. The street was wet and shiny, like it often was in the English morning, but the sun was climbing higher in the sky, sharpening all the contrasts outside like a glossy calendar photograph of October. Damp yellow leaves, green and orange, black branches, still heavy with the early morning drizzle. Sparkles of reflected light. He knew the minute he'd open the front door, the chilly air would smell like a thousand layers of fall, the same every year, century after century.

He returned to the kitchen and glanced at the clock. Seven minutes before the driver would double back to get him. Just enough time to finish breakfast, while his mother stood in the kitchen in her bathrobe, hands on hips.

Chip ate a spoonful of Cheerios. The English Cheerios had more sugar than the American ones. Carolann must not have discovered the difference yet. She rarely ate breakfast cereals.

Henrik always sat in the back of the bus, and by the time Chip got on, little kids from the end of the road had always filled in all the seats. Chip couldn't think how to ask Henrik to save him a seat, so he had to ride near the driver. In Kansas it wouldn't have mattered. If you sat on the bus with little kids, it just made church more fun when you saw them on Sunday. But the bus ride every morning in England was agony, sitting 12 seats away from the school's biggest rugby player, an incredible social opportunity wasted every day. Chip might as well arrive at school in a hot air balloon and a clown suit, the good it did him.

He sunk his spoon into the sweet milk in his cereal bowl and slurped it. The fact was, Ticia was really the only friend he'd made. And whatever his late-night fantasies might be, he wondered if she was just following school guidelines, rolling out the welcome wagon.

"Finished?" Carolann asked. "Bowl in the sink."

Chip stood. She was like a military commander on autopilot, dangerous in her rigidity, at least until she was dressed. Very briefly, she had seemed to relax since the move, but now Chip realized it had gotten worse, like she was scrambling to control minutiae – maybe because bigger things, like not understanding the shopkeepers' English accents, or her trouble setting up a bank account, or the driving on the left, were all beyond her. Her bowl-in-the-sink instructions had become unchangeable daily routine. Chip couldn't clear his plate until she reminded him, or it would upset the delicate balance. She said it when the bus was two minutes away. Chip grabbed his backpack, kissed his mother's cheek, and opened the front door.

"He's already here," he called. He glanced at the large clock in the entryway. Set exactly the same as the clock in the kitchen. Greenwich Mean Time. His mother had a thing about clocks.

"Fourth grade field trip today. I read it in the newsletter." She adjusted Chip's collar, same as always. "None of those kids are on the bus, so his route's faster this morning. But he can wait. You're to be picked up at 7:40."

"That's ridiculous. He's there." Chip looked at the bus. Henrik was in the back as usual, and no one sat near him. "It's two minutes."

"Two minutes today, ten minutes tomorrow. Schedules exist for a reason." Her jaw was tight.

Chip grabbed his thighs and squeezed. Every seat near Henrik looked empty, but if he didn't hurry, little kids might spring to life in that bus, like balloon people, they'd inflate in place and ruin his chance. "Mom, I'm going."

"Go." She nodded.

Chip ran to the bus, greeted his driver, and sat across the aisle from Henrik, in the back. Chip jerked his head up, and Henrik jerked his upward in turn.

The bus pulled away, gaining distance from Chip's house. He could see his mother's shape, as always, behind the white lace curtain, watching him leave. He watched her hand wave at him, but he sat on his fingers and did not wave back. Not today.

"So," Henrik said. "How do you like being the mop?"

"The what?"

"Tease-ya's new mop." Henrik's smile seemed crooked.

"Ticia?"

"You don't think she's teasing you?" Henrik shook his head. "Clueless."

"Screw off." Chip spoke faster than he'd intended. Great budding friendship.

"I'm just saying…" Henrik shrugged.

"Look, she's my friend." Apparently my only one, he thought. Why did he always have to be so assertive? They said that about him in Kansas too.

"No offense, but she's a tease," Henrik said. "Ask Maarten or Axel or Jonas or a hundred guys what kind of a girl Tease-ya Olague is. Did she go fishing with you yet? Caught the trouser trout? Ask Carlo."

"I don't need their opinions," Chip said. Carlo seemed like a decent guy, and Maarten. But what Ticia did behind closed doors was her business.

"It's just a friendly warning, since you're new. You should come over on Sunday and play basketball."

"Sunday's not good," Chip swallowed. "Any other day."

Why did his mother insist on the whole family "antiquing" together every weekend?

"Too bad. We always play Sundays. You watch our rugby games? Maarten's the best scrum half, like, in the history of the school. The guy's big."

"I know who he is." Maarten looked like he wore American football pads under his clothes. Big jaw and a crazy cowlick. He'd be scary, but he had kind eyes.

"He wants to meet you," Henrik said.

"Me?" Maybe subtleties of language were playing tricks. Even if Henrik had lived in England for years, English was still his second language, and prone to error. No rugby player even knew who Chip was. "Maarten said he wants to meet me?"

"That essay Neame wants next week, well, English isn't Maarten's best language. And it's obvious that neo-conservative hippie loves you, man."

"I don't think so." Neame definitely did not love Chip. "You want me to proofread Maarten's essay?"

"Something like that," Henrik said.

"Which topic did he choose?"

"Talk to him. He'll pay you."

"For grammar help? I'd do it for free. Like human spell check." Chip would be investing in his multicultural community – Neame would love it. If he helped Maarten with his English grammar, International Baccalaureate flags would wave in Chip's name.

"Talk to him," Henrik said. "And while you're at it, ask him about your new girlfriend Tease-ya Olague."

"She's not my girlfriend."

"Oh, right. You're just the mop." Henrik said. "The guy who holds her hair and cleans up her barf."

"Oh." Chip imagined holding a handful of Ticia's black hair.

"My point is, you might get a whole lot more than you

bargain for with her."

"If I do, I'll let you say you told me so." Chip reached out to shake hands with Henrik, confirming the deal.

"Yup." Henrik quickly shook hands with Chip.

A flaccid, limp-fish! How could that be? Henrik's clammy handshake didn't match his face or his voice, or his signature one-syllable responses. It didn't match his lips, or his chiseled Swedish cheekbones.

The bus pulled into the school driveway, converged with 40 identical white Mercedes school busses, and in a long, slow queue, it passed Security. Suddenly, Henrik was on his feet, backpack over his broad shoulder, not even a glance back at Chip.

Chip hopped down from the bus behind his new friend and called, "See ya, Henrik!"

The big Swedish boy turned around, like he was surprised Chip knew how to speak. He nodded at him and disappeared with a mass of athletes.

"Tell me you're not hanging out with that guy." Ticia fell in step with Chip. "Just 'cause he's on your bus."

"He's ok." Chip watched the group of guys veer off toward the gym, carrying his hopes in their wake. Anyone could help Maarten with his grammar. Chip would never hear of it again.

"He reeks like dog farts. I fucking hate him. I can't express it without profanity."

"I don't think he likes you a whole lot either." Chip smiled. "The English language is big enough, you shouldn't have to resort to that."

"They were on rugby together, and he told Andrew not to go out with me, that I'd be trouble because my dad's faculty. Like I don't have a brain of my own or something. Nor my dad. Like he can't make an independent decision himself. For fuck's sake."

Two minutes together, and already she'd used the f-word

repeatedly and brought up the boyfriend. "Your dad seems like a good guy," Chip said.

"He is. Everyone loves my dad. But that shit head told Andrew to choose him or me, an ultimatum like we're in fucking junior high. Of course, Andrew chose me." She curtsied.

"Of course he did." At least Ticia's handshake matched her appearance and her conduct. Still, a guy did need guy friends, and Henrik could be taught to shake hands better.

"Because I give a better blow-job." She laughed like a banshee and whacked Chip's back, perhaps harder than she intended.

"Hey –" Chip coughed. Why would a girl ever want to do that? "I was, I was…" He tried once again to change the subject. "I was thinking about a Friday study date – you and me."

"Can't." Ticia blew kisses to some girlfriends by the Nations United Fountain. "Friday I'm babysitting."

She might as well have slugged him in the gut. He was a total loser without any friends in any country, and no girl would be interested, not even one who gives blow-jobs and broadcasts it, and he didn't even have any friends back home, unless you counted the kids he taught Sunday School, and a girl like Ticia Olague was way out of his league. Even so… babysitting? "You could just say you're not interested."

"Huh?" Ticia stared at him. "Ok, homes, I'm not interested. I've never suggested otherwise, have I? But you just asked me on a study date, and I am aware that your GPA is going to be like the top in the school, and if I had the night free, of fucking course I'd come study with you, but I really am babysitting. Every Tuesday and alternating Fridays and Saturdays for my neighbor with the crazy-busy career in PR that I already told you about. Mrs. Jamison."

"Oh." Chip said. "Her."

"Anyway –" she grabbed his arm, yanked it downward

till he hunched, and she kissed his cheek. "Not in *that* way, cause I don't want to confuse you, but have I mentioned lately you're gonna fall madly in love with me?"

"Yeah." Chip laughed and looked at his watch. "I believe you said it ten hours ago."

"Well, then." Ticia's hand slid down Chip's arm. She intertwined her fingers with his and her hand felt small but electric. She pulled her hand away, burped from deep in her gut, and banged her chest. "Ugh. Streaky bacon for brekkie."

Chip shook his head. He wanted her to put her hand back, like its absence left him naked. Was falling in love a choice someone made, or the total absence of choice? Maybe love required absence first, like a black hole, or a vacuum. Chip's move to England had created a gaping new void, allowing him, (forcing him?) to fall in love.

He'd have to ask his dad about this new scientific theory. At least he'd get a considered response. And the man seemed to know a lot about love, how to make it work despite difficulties – fourteen-plus years of marriage to Carolann Field Cooper. Chip grabbed Ticia's hand and held it tight.

"You'd do anything for me, wouldn't you?" Ticia laughed. Again, she belched a long, loud staccato. A bit horrified, Chip realized she'd burped words: "You already love me."

Chapter 13

What Carolann didn't realize was that looking back at all was like opening Pandora's box. Once it was opened, it stayed open, and there was a lot more inside it to come out. She had no 9-5 to keep her head occupied, she had no Heart of America Church of God people needing urgent things from her. No Sunday spinach casserole conversations. *Parmesan on top? That's right, and bread crumbs.*

Instead, she now had all of her earthly belongings scattered all over her new home, after a group of moving men kept bringing boxes in and unpacking them, clearly not in the right places. Trouble was, Carolann had no right places. Kitchen utensils belonged in the kitchen, but beyond that, nothing seemed right. Her sofa was too big. Her dining chairs looked monstrous. Her four-poster American mahogany bed didn't even fit into the bedroom until they took off the posts. People said America and England were two countries divided by the same language – if that's what they said – but the size differences seemed more divisive than that. In the clothing stores, labels for an American Small was a Medium in Europe. The changes weren't exciting like everyone promised, they were annoying.

Of course, she missed home. And now, arranging all of her things while Chip was at school and Lyn was at work, she couldn't help but review what she'd truly left behind. Despite herself, she reviewed everything, even the colorful stories she'd once sealed away, telling herself they'd faded to black-and-white.

That Sunday when she was 17, Carolann had never felt more unwelcome in church. She sat gingerly on the pinewood pew, shifting her weight, tailbone to tailbone, in turn flaring the burn between her legs and then dousing the livid flames. Her head flared too, with the double humiliation of the thing with Buck and then the next night – spilling her guts to the doctor-guy in the bar. Of course, God could read her mind all the time, but in the church, it felt like she was thinking through a megaphone.

Buck's mother, Kim Roberts, had come alone. She wore a buttercup yellow sweetheart-neck suit that must have been new, and the site of her smelled like juniper. All the subtle variations in the yellows smelled different. Strangely, Mrs. Roberts sat three rows back, instead of up front with the Fields. If Buck came late, Carolann might sense his arrival behind her. She turned to check. No Buck.

The most embarrassing part of her body was crying pungent, sticky tears. She shifted left and leaned closer to Cyrus, breathed in his stale tobacco smell, and then right, closer to Barbara Ann, talcum powder and lilac. Her parents' thigh muscles tensed in turn, and seemed to scold her. Even Pastor Hugh fixed her in his gaze. Maybe he knew the chaos in Carolann's head, such noise that no one else could concentrate either.

Barbara Ann sighed loudly.

Carolann turned again. Mrs. Roberts stared straight ahead, her low-cut neckline nearly revealing a cleavage. If it weren't for her family money and generosity in the church, Carolann knew the ladies would talk about Kim Roberts' bosoms.

Pastor Hugh continued with the sermon. The Wisdom of Solomon. Carolann knew her mother was anxious to frost Maryann's Welcome Cake and do the windows. Cyrus needed to check the car's oil and call a Kansas City radio station for a traffic report. Carolann had already changed the beds, but she still had to vacuum. How much dirt from the past two weeks could the machine suck away?

The squirming itch between her legs shot through her, and, like a stone, she sat breathing – violently, aggressively still. She tried to focus on Solomon. Two would-be mothers, both claiming one baby was theirs. Solomon threatens to slice the baby in two so the women can share. Of course, the real mother renounces her "half," and begs the false mom to take the child, unharmed. Thus, King Solomon divines the truth. Carolann squirmed again in her seat. What if it's one mother with two children dividing her favor? Rather than tear the mother in two, one proper, loving daughter must sacrifice herself. That was it!

Barbara Ann Field might never recognize the rightful daughter, but that's what it was. That's what it always was, with Carolann. Righteous self-sacrifice. Though it didn't take the wisdom of Solomon to know people wouldn't get it. Carolann would have to keep the secret to herself, in her own head, where her sense of personal honor was sadly unreliable. Already, it vacillated toward shame.

Cyrus Field cleared his throat, an upheaval of phlegm and cigarette scum. He banged his fist on his chest, and finally, Pastor Hugh clapped his hands together.

"Before we finish today, a prayer for our families driving in to the airport. We look forward to a full house next Sunday and to the Panthers' first football game in two weeks." He winked at Buck's mother. "Let us remember our girls on that plane from Nashville. They entrust themselves to you, Lord, to deliver them safely home. They're in Your hands."

And the pilots' hands, Carolann thought. "Amen." She echoed the congregation.

Barbara Ann stood and smiled. Pink lipstick stuck to her front tooth.

Carolann tapped her own tooth.

Cyrus shook his head. "Make-up is foolish and costly."

"Come." Barbara Ann hooked her purse over her wrist and led her family to the vestibule.

"Not like Buck to miss church," Barbara Ann said to Kim Roberts. "I hope he's not ill."

"He'll be at the airport." Kim shook her head. "Carolann, you're such a good girl. Never miss a Sunday."

Carolann tried to smile. The summer smell of the room came at her powerfully. Clean and leaf-green, but there was more. Normally textures were trustworthy, but suddenly the floor felt like rubber, like it was melting, like it was mud. The smell played with her sense of time – it was no longer summer. It was anticipation. Chilly autumn rains and muddy feet that would stomp in and dampen the carpet that Kim Roberts bought. It was pinewood pews after rain. The old subtle release of last season's mildew. The place smelled like history and future and thousands of people who'd been there before her, like mold, and something inevitable, but never like Buck. The sting between Carolann's legs flared. When she next saw him, should she apologize?

"I bet you're anxious to get your sister home," Kim smoothed Carolann's red hair with her fingers.

"She's not as anxious as Buck probably is." Barbara Ann snapped her purse, and Mrs. Roberts let go of Carolann's hair.

"Oh, Bucky's anxious alright." Kim winked at Carolann.

The green and mud-brown blew away and left gold. The softened floor stabilized instantly underfoot. Carolann could almost feel Buck's heated body on top of her. His hipbones. His hair. The grind of his pelvis. Her stomach churned with a revolting, unmistakable yellow-gold joy. Even in the church, talking with his mother, Carolann couldn't help it.

"Lots to do," Barbara Ann said, leading Carolann out of the church. "Busy day. Busy day."

*

"I don't care if long-term parking is the cheapest," Barbara Ann panted as she hurried through the airport. "It's miles away." She ducked her forehead to wipe sweat on the shoulder of her blouse. "Curbside would have been free."

Cyrus huffed. "For shame. Curbside's illegal, and a parking ticket costs real money." He coughed and banged his chest as he walked. "We Fields set an example."

Barbara Ann fluffed her hair and put on a smile as she approached the crowd in the arrivals hall.

Buck was there holding a purple and silver balloon bouquet, wearing his football gear. His teammates and junior varsity cheerleaders buzzed around him like flies. He looked large. Carolann wanted to put her hand under his shirt, explore the mysteries of his contoured football pads and his skin. She had already run her fingers along the groove of his back, so couldn't she do it again, whenever she wanted? She wanted him to leave them all, like he left the party, and come talk to her.

"They're due in any minute," Kim Roberts gave Carolann's mother a quick hug.

Buck stayed where he was and Carolann smelled the people all around him. Perfume and body sprays. Flowers and black pepper, citrus and chemical testosterone. She also smelled the evil black-oil reek of kerosene, the fuel bringing the varsity cheerleaders home, and she felt sick.

Precedence establishes expectation, wasn't that the phrase? The hem of his shirt gapped at his lower back. Her hand would fit right in there, if he'd let it. Of course, he would not let it.

Cyrus went to read the monitor's flight information. Carolann watched him tap his cigarette pack into his palm. He'd been behind the wheel for an hour, heat and road dust blasting through the Oldsmobile's crossbreeze. Of course, her father needed a cigarette.

The crowd noise fell into a background hum, and Carolann watched Buck. He'd started it. He had leaned in Friday night and kissed her lips, and she'd just responded. A drunken but momentous decision to respond. But the rest of it played on fast-forward in her mind, the car and the clothes and crush of their bodies. She cringed. She had been the one to control most of that. And now, what happened next, with her sister, would have to be even more carefully controlled.

"I loved being a cheerleader," Kim Roberts sighed. "When the guys rush on the field and burst through the banner. Great memories."

Perhaps Buck heard his mother's voice. He turned and looked at Carolann and held her eye contact for an instant. It was the first time he'd even looked at her since he left her in the driveway. He turned back to his friends.

The flight landed, and Carolann saw her sister deplane, flipping her dark hair and then interlocking her arms with her two girlfriends, Bonnie and Kitty. The three girls hurried toward the crowd of Panther fans. Maryann's legs were tan and shiny. Only fast girls took a razor above the knee, but Maryann had shaved her thighs.

Suddenly, Buck rushed forward with his balloons, grabbed Maryann away from her friends, and twirled her. Carolann's stomach lurched.

Did her sister already know? Did everyone? What she did with Buck was her fault. No matter what, Carolann would say nothing – no apologies, no explanations, not a word – but she would shoulder the blame. But often, Carolann felt Maryann's emotions stronger than her own. Buck wasn't the boyfriend he pretended to be. Carolann suffered his infidelity for her twin sister. She wouldn't just shoulder the blame, she'd wear the regret for them all.

Cyrus stepped between his daughter and Buck. "Good you're home safe. Your mother and sister missed you."

"I'm dying for the ladies room," Maryann hooked her arms around her friends again, and the group skipped away.

Carolann turned to follow. No matter how much water she drank, she couldn't flush the infection.

"I need a pad," Maryann's voice called from inside a stall.

Carolann found a Kotex in her purse and handed it under her sister's door. Kim Roberts had followed the girls in, and she eyeballed Carolann.

"I wouldn't have guessed you two would be in sync." She stood at the mirror, applying purple "Panther" lipstick. "Cheerleading is all about sisterhood. So these girls – of course. But I sometimes forget you two are twins. Actual sisters."

"Gross." Kitty and Bonnie stood by the sink and exchanged a quick glance.

Carolann said, "We're not identical."

Maryann came out of her stall. "We're nothing alike. She's not a cheerleader. Not student council. Afraid to take chances."

"I take chances." Carolann said, "I have a job."

"You're not afraid." Kim Roberts nodded. "You just don't like to join in."

"I would if I –"

"Oh, honey…" The woman interrupted. "You're just different." The sound of her voice was thick and cloying. Carolann tasted it – hot glue in her throat. A big waxy lump that wouldn't budge. Shaped like an eight. Two big blobs, swelling. She couldn't breathe. The girls were staring at her. If she went in the stall and threw up, they would hear it. She tried not to gag.

Mrs. Roberts put her hand lightly on Carolann's shoulder. "It's not your calling, the silly high school stuff." She raised her other hand, showing the vulgar purple lipstick, extended from its tube. "Not for you."

Carolann smelled turkey, the smell of the purple

overwhelmed her and she choked. She was going to throw up in front of all of them. She was going to faint. And she still had to use the toilet. They were all staring. Her hands over her mouth, she ran from the room.

Chapter 14

Chip saw Maarten standing alone, near the busses. The whole weekend had rolled past without a single phone call. Not Ticia, not Maarten for help with his essay, not even a wrong number. And now a full day of school had passed, without any further social success. Mr. Neame didn't even call Chip's name in History.

Other than the moody song he started writing Sunday morning about Ticia, Chip hadn't found a single rhyme in days. His only friend, it seemed, was the enormous pimple taking on a life of its own on his chin.

His family's shipment had finally arrived from Kansas, and all of his belongings seemed foreign to him and unwanted. Even his mother, who'd been desperate to have her own things, seemed distraught and betrayed by each little throw-rug and bed-pillow and knick-knack that brought her no comfort.

Chip walked toward Maarten, hoping the tutoring thing Henrik had mentioned was not a joke. In any case, now that Ticia had disappeared off the face of the earth, he needed to meet other people.

Maarten turned to Chip and smiled. "Henrik says you might be able to help me." He quickly turned his attention to the soccer team, running the track.

His English sounded fluent enough. "Maybe. I'm Chip." He stuck his hand out and Maarten stared at it, unmoving. Of course, the zit on his chin was one thing… was his hand also sprouting something revolting? Quickly then, Maarten gave

Chip a firm handshake like he'd expected.

"You pretty fast?" Maarten asked.

"I don't know." Did Chip have to race this big Dutch kid too?

"It's due Monday," Maarten said.

"My class is due the same day. One week should be ok, depending on when you can show me what you've got."

Maarten nodded. Put his hand to his eyes as if there was blinding sun and he was desperate to find some other friends approaching across the blazing desert sands. Or he was searching for an oasis.

Strangely, the concrete paths toward the bus lot were still deserted. "Maybe you could take my bus and bring your work to my house tomorrow."

"Bring my work?"

"You know, whatever you've written, so I can help polish up your English. That's what Henrik said you need." Chip looked at the chilly gray sky. The clouds muted all the colors of the afternoon, and made him want to tuck his head into the collar of his jacket and speak quietly.

"What topic are we doing?"

"We?"

"Five pages, double-spaced is 20 quid. If you're any good. Henrik says you're good." Maarten stuck his hands deep in his pockets.

"He does?" Groups of students began to head toward the busses, and Chip knew certain details were becoming urgent. Which details, however, eluded him. Like fall leaves he had to catch in the air, undamaged, sorted by color and size, before they scattered in the wind.

Ticia hadn't been in school all morning. He'd only seen her from a distance after lunch, and she hadn't even noticed him. And he was probably leaking brain cells into the enormous pustule on his chin. No wonder he couldn't think straight. "Henrik said I'm good?"

"I don't care which topic, but it seems like women's rights is kind-of…"

Chip smiled. "For pansies."

Maarten laughed. At least the guy had a sense of humor.

"So you want to come home with me tomorrow?" Chip swallowed hard. Right after the comment about pansies, he sounded like he was asking Maarten on a date.

"I'd rather you just bring me the essay tomorrow, or whenever, all perfect. Or not perfect. Just keep me playing rugby."

Chip looked at Maarten carefully. "No, you're writing it, dude," he said, "I'm helping with your spelling. Tomorrow." Who was Chip impersonating? *Dude* was Ticia's word. She'd gotten into his head and taken it over and then abandoned him. Maybe Henrik was right about her.

Maarten shrugged and turned away. He walked off, toward the track. In an instant, Ticia bounded up to Chip holding a large envelope.

"Where've you been?" Chip asked.

"Wouldn't you like to know!" She laughed. "Remember my babysitting job? Mrs. Jamison's done some work for Dido."

"I guess."

"Mrs. Crazy-busy PR Mrs. Jamison?" Ticia looked at him like everything was normal. "Your homeboy practically launched her, you know. They're still friends."

"Are we?" Chip stared at the envelope and back at Ticia's face. Her eyes looked as blue as ever, clear and eager, like she hadn't been through any traumatic car crashes, ravaged by skinheads, joined the National Front, fallen in the bathtub and broken her neck. But the whole weekend?

"This was quicker than we expected," she said. "It came while I was in Amsterdam. That's where I was, ok? All forgiven?"

"Sue me. I was worried about you." Chip took the envelope.

"Did I mention you were going to fall in love with me?"

"Once or twice." Chip brought his hand up over his chin. "But you should have called and told me about Amsterdam."

"I haven't opened it, but it'll be the real thing. Jamison's the real thing." The shipping label on the envelope had Chip's name, care of Ticia Olague's address. He stared at the label.

"Dude, if I'd said I'm going to the International Schools' football tournament, you would have worried about that. And I have certain interests we don't share, right?"

"Football? I'm interested in football. They play soccer in Kansas, you know. And I too happen to have a passport."

"Look, I saw Andrew. It was strategic. Your parents wouldn't have let you go anyway. Brand new expats letting their 14-year-old son go to Amsterdam unaccompanied? I don't think so."

"Maybe your parents shouldn't have let you go."

"Open the fucking envelope. Or do you want me to take it back?"

"No." He still didn't open it.

"Look, my mom had depositions in Barcelona. My dad was at a conference in Stockholm. Technically, I was right between them. Anyway, it was one weekend, a few minor purchases. No big deal. And frankly, not perfect with Andrew. You've got to help me plan my next move."

"Jesus, Ticia, why don't I just date the guy for you?" Chip stuck his finger under the glued flap.

"The Lord's name in vain?" Ticia squealed. "Fuck, homes, your mother's right. England's changing you."

A glossy photo fell to the ground.

His heart flipped. Even upside down, the portrait facing Ticia, Chip knew who he was looking at. Ticia scooped the picture up, and danced it side to side in front of Chip. Eminem. Autographed!

There he was – big, bold, black-and-white. Tattoos, the headband, the chains, the stare. The biceps with his arms across his chest. His knuckles! Perfect, strong fingers. Chip thought he might cry. He could picture Eminem's hand holding the blue Sharpie marker, signing his name. *To Chip.*

Beaming, Ticia peeked over the top of the photo.

Chip fell to his knees. "I do love you." He hugged her around the hips, laughing. "I love you, I do love you. You're right! I am truly, madly, deeply in love with you."

Ticia laughed. "On your feet, cowboy. I love you too, and I'd throw you down and do you right here, if it weren't for that carbuncle." She tapped her own chin.

Chip squirmed to his feet. "And a small problem named Andrew."

"Yeah," she was still beaming. "Glad to know I'm forgiven. Next time I'll call."

"No way." He clutched the envelope, and his voice was firm. "No next time."

Chapter 15

"I'm glad you could come over today," Carolann said to Rowan, stepping aside to let her in the front door. "Of course I understand you've been busy."

"Not busy. I just wasn't ready. I…" Rowan's voice trailed off. She wore the same sleeveless sweater vest as the first time, and she ran the back of her hands down the soft front of it.

An American woman would be careful not to repeat an outfit like that with a new friend. Carolann watched her neighbor caress her own stomach. Rowan probably did not represent all English culture.

"Tea?"

"Please."

Carolann led Rowan into the kitchen. She took two mugs from the cabinet.

"Americans would drink tea, if more American homes had electric kettles," Rowan said.

"Probably right."

"I missed that, living in Texas."

Carolann nodded. Thirty-two years old, and it was the first time she was eager to talk about the synesthesia. Yet apparently, Rowan's seeming comfort with the topic had been a false promise. "I agree. The electric kettle is a wonderful thing." Her voice sounded hollow.

Rowan sighed. "So we agree on that. And we both see colors in our food. And…" she took a deep breath.

Carolann handed her a cup of tea. "And we're both twins."

Rowan's lips tightened into a pained smile. "Morwenna." Her head popped up and then lowered. "My sister's name." She leaned over the tea as if it had become imperative to smell it. She breathed slowly into the mug. Carolann lifted her own tea cup to sniff it. It smelled like tea.

Rowan's experience of tea – of everything – could be different. Did she smell soap or curry or sewage? Had Rowan been sent to her bedroom as a little girl because of the smells? Did Rowan's parents throw out her dinner when the chicken tasted blue? Carolann looked carefully at her neighbor, breathing quietly over her tea. As far as Carolann knew, Rowan had no children, but she had been married. Was Rowan's memory plagued with scenes in immovable color? Carolann wondered if she could ever ask Rowan what her colors were for sex.

"I'm ok." Rowan took another deep breath. "Shall we sit?"

The two women went to the living room – Rowan perhaps more familiar with the lay-out of the house even than Carolann was.

"Your furniture suits the lounge," Rowan said.

Carolann looked around. Her furniture did not seem to suit the lounge. She shrugged. It was not what she wanted to discuss.

Suddenly Rowan said, "Ovarian cancer two years ago. I can't talk about it. I prayed for it to be me. God doesn't do deals and trades." She squeezed her eyes and opened them slowly. "Still not ready....No..." Her eyes were glossy. She tipped her head back again, and tears rolled down her cheeks. "...Still can't talk about her."

"Oh." Carolann gently cleared her throat. "I'm so sorry."

Rowan lowered her face into one hand, and held up her other hand, a silent gesture asking for a minute.

"We don't have to talk about Morwenna," Carolann said. It was an unusual name. She hoped she'd said it right.

Rowan sobbed loudly, sniffled loudly, and then cleared her throat loudly. "You would have liked her though. That much I can say."

"My sister and I have never been close," Carolann said.

"What a shame." Rowan looked at Carolann. "Did something happen between you?"

Carolann stared into her own tea cup for a second. She hadn't even realized she'd drunk most of it already. It would certainly take Rowan's mind off her own loss if she could tell her what happened – the smell of it all, every sound, and all the colors. But Carolann was in no shape to speak it aloud. Nonetheless, in her mind, Carolann found herself at age seventeen, in the back of Buck's car.

Carolann. She didn't dare correct him.

"Maryann," Buck murmured again. His bourbon voice and her breathing, blended. Odiferous. Stirred murmurs and groans.

Carolann, Carolann. Hatred bloomed roiling and red, and she pulled him close. His hand moved around her backside, grabbed her rear like an animal's, a horse's rump or a pig's. He yanked her toward him, and the colors flared and sizzled into the burned scabby black heat of hatred. They'd had so much to drink, gulps from so many bottles, everything was blending together. Buck pushed his knee between Carolann's legs and pressed against her. Fully saturated blue and burgundy. *I love you,* she said in her head.

"It's not wrong." He whispered and stroked her face, his thumb tenderly tracing her cheekbone. Like he still wasn't sure she would do it.

"I'm not my sister," she said into his ear.

"Forget her." He kissed her mouth.

Hard words. *Forget her.* Almost profane. Carolann yanked open the button fly of her jeans. The colors shifted, the black-edged burgundy giving way to a pulsing royal purple, all-consuming. She was right in the beginning. Not hatred. Love.

His hands took her pants down, hip then thigh, they stuck to her sweaty summer legs. She fought them off. And then his. And their shirts. Easier. *Forget her.* His legs were muscled and hard. Smooth and soft with fine hairs. Boy's legs. Buck's legs! Her sister's boyfriend, Buck Roberts.

The wet skin of his stomach felt hot against her.

She kicked at their muddy jeans around their ankles and he bunched his cotton t-shirt under her head, like a pillow. It was warm. She always knew what his t-shirt would smell like – wood and grass and citrus and football. How many times had her sister come home wearing his smell? He slid his arm under her back, lifted her closer, lowered his head, and kissed her tan lines. His hair smelled sweet too, lemons and leather. She'd never been to either coast, but now she smelled ocean. The sun sparkling on the sea – she swam in it, the big, beautiful ocean. Buck's mother used expensive laundry soap that came in a bottle. It was blue.

He lightly brushed his lips along her collarbone, one side, slowly across to the other. He kissed her jaw and the quivering muscles in her neck and then pressed himself against her sternum. She could feel her blood pump through her veins. She'd wanted this for 17 years.

The two of them, together, became slippery. His tongue pushed at her, hard – the wet, rough animal muscle of tongue. She tasted bourbon in his mouth, salt on his neck. His car was riding waves, and with each dizzy pitch and roll, she felt her childhood get tossed away, irretrievably with Buck's. She kissed his earlobe. She kissed his eyes. The car smelled like sweat and steam and the sweet tang of brown sloshing slow-fermented sour mash. Her stomach lurched.

She breathed him in, deep. Buck tasted enormous and wonderful. And she thought: *he loves me, I will do this. Maryann's wrong... she's always been wrong.* She pushed her hips up to him.

"You can trust me." He slipped his hand down between the two of them, between her legs, and she squirmed against his hand until his fingers locked inside her, she gasped, and he held her tight. It was supposed to hurt, but this didn't hurt. He knew how to make it not hurt. It shimmered and flared and burst color – brilliant and warm – into every part of her body. Purple and turquoise and gold. It didn't hurt.

Here, finally, was the truth. Buck loved Carolann. Forget her.

"There's nothing to be afraid of," he whispered. "You can't get pregnant the first time."

"I'm not afraid." She looked him deep in the eyes, made sure he knew whose freckled face he was kissing. "I love –" He looked away, and she had to drop the last word. You.

"Maryann." He bucked and pushed himself into Carolann.

It was deepest starlit blue, pings of color, then immediately heavy and saturated, aubergine and reflective slate gray. Summer thunderstorm purple.

He pushed his pelvis into Carolann, his hot breath coming harder. He fogged the windows of the station wagon, parked only a quarter mile from the party, (beautiful, he'd called her beautiful when they got in his car), Jack Daniels steam diffusing blue moonlight as he moved.

He grabbed hold of her hand, Carolann's hand, not Maryann's, of course he knew the difference, Carolann had freckles, her sister had tears. Fake tears. Buck held Carolann's hand against the wool fibers of the stadium blanket in the back of the station wagon, and he moved. His soft hair was streaked with silver as he held himself above her chest.

In the pale glow, her nipples looked like big raisins. Like he could pluck one into his mouth, infused and fermented with Jim Beam, dark and plump raisins, now wrinkled with the sweet, concentrated juice of young fruit. She arched her back. "Carolann," she said out loud.

He slammed into her, his hipbones, again and again, and Carolann could almost feel herself bruise, big maroon bruises between her white thighs. She grabbed his lower back and writhed, violent. Is this what she was supposed to do? How did anyone know what to do?

She hooked her legs around him, and it hurt. All the bright colors vibrating chartreuse, vivid red, neon green. She was going to split open under Buck and explode. Lemon yellow. The pain eased away and left something raw and eager in its place. Lime, emerald, olive green, jade.

She gripped the soft flesh of his rear. It did not hurt. Indigo and again, the turquoise and gold. Their bodies rocked each other in his car. How would they tell Maryann? Cornflower blue, sunset pink. Burnished silver sparks. How long would the real purple marks of his hipbones show on her flesh?

His body went rigid. "Jesus God."

Carolann swelled and tensed, *Jesus God!* But she would not take the Lord's name in vain. *Holy fucking mother of Jesus Christ… God.*

Buck groaned something that wasn't a word, and flopped on her – done. He panted in her ear, his heartbeat throbbing between her legs. Carolann wiggled under him, elated and completed, and anxious, and desperately eager for more.

He rolled off her. She put her hand on his forearm, and he smiled. He looked right at her. Of course he knew which twin she was. She and Maryann looked nothing alike. He yanked his t-shirt from under Carolann's head and ducked into it. Between her legs, she was shimmering. An electric white light. She wanted it to build and catch fire. She wanted it to stop, reverse, to not have happened at all.

Too much bourbon. Too much bravery? They were starting to curdle in her gut. But it wasn't wrong! This was the truth. For better or for worse, she would have this thing with Buck, now, forever.

He clamored toward the front of the station wagon, fully dressed. Carolann wiggled her panties back into place and the shimmering dissipated. She was swollen and sloppy, and the elastic battled her. She jabbed her feet into her jeans. The denim stuck to her damp thighs. It had seemed a first glimpse of fall, the late August night, cooler than summer, a night for jeans, but it was a false glimpse, it was too soon. Now the car was all steam and heat. She should have worn shorts. She crouched on her knees and reached back to hook her bra. "We probably can't go back to the party," she said. "Everyone would…"

"No." He fiddled with his radio dial.

"Unless…" she stopped.

"No. I'll drive you home."

"Ok." She pulled her shirt on and watched the back of Buck's silken head, like she always did in school or church, only now he was waiting for her in the driver's seat of his car. The two of them, alone!

He turned up the radio's volume, and Carolann was jubilant. She climbed over the back seat. Pure joy. No disgust. No loathing, nothing loathsome. Horns and drums and strings and singing. She sat down next to him. She felt worked up, gold and red, thrilled by what they'd started. She tried to kiss his cheek, missed, got his ear, and laughed. He laughed. There would be details, days to come. But Oh! Right now… just the joy.

Chapter 16

"Was that your doorbell?" Rowan was staring at Carolann.

"No, I don't think so."

Rowan stood. "It was. That was your doorbell." She set her tea cup on the table without a coaster, and went to Carolann's door. "Anyway, I should go." Rowan opened Carolann's door to a young man in a black jacket. A large young man. "Mrs. Cooper?" he said to Rowan.

"Right there." Rowan pointed Carolann out behind her and pushed past the young man. "Toodles," she called behind her. "Thanks again for the tea."

Carolann stepped forward. A large black bicycle was chained to her front gate. The first time her doorbell rang, a man in a white apron wanted to sharpen her knives. At the time she had a drink in her, an actual drink, and was bold enough to slam the door. Next, someone rang the bell to pave her driveway. He'd seemed to have several drinks in him. At least with this guy, Rowan had seen his face, and could probably point him out in a line-up. Carolann set her jaw and looked up at the young man. "I'm Mrs. Cooper."

"I'm here for Chip." His voice was not deep. "I guess he's not home yet."

"Any minute." Carolann looked at her watch. "If you're a friend of Chip's, come on in."

*

When Chip arrived home, he saw a black bicycle chained to the gate.

"Look who's here," Carolann kissed her son on the cheek as he came in the house, lugging his bag of books. "Your friend Maarten. His family is from the Netherlands, where all the men are tall." She giggled. "But I guess you knew that."

Chip's stomach contracted like he'd been punched.

Maarten stood slump-shouldered behind Chip's mother with his hands clasped in front of him. "I thought maybe I could pick up those notes you were going to lend me. You said maybe today?"

"Don't you live outside the M25?" Chip could picture the antiques store map his mother had marked. "Like a hundred miles away?"

"I came from school," Maarten said. "Anyway, you got those notes?"

Chip stuck his hands in his pockets and shook his head. What did this guy expect? He was going to pull a completed essay out of the air and just hand it over? How could Maarten think Chip already wrote it? He'd only just met him, and they'd agreed to nothing.

"I made Rice Krispee Treats," Carolann said. "They're American. Stay for a snack."

Chip took a deep breath, like he was aiming an overtime free throw shot. He had homework of his own to do too. And a new autographed photo of Eminem to stare at. But Maarten actually seemed to want his help. "You'd better stay for a snack, dinner, and probably breakfast," he said. "We've got a lot of work to do."

Carolann coughed. "Maarten, I'm sure your mother expects you home."

"Nah." Maarten pulled at his hands as if they wouldn't release each other. "My parents are in Rotterdam."

"They've left you here alone?" Chip's mother shook her head. She'd have a heart attack if she knew about

Ticia's parents.

"My brother's here," Maarten said. "He's twenty-two."

"Well, I'm doing pork roast for dinner – Chip's father's favorite, since he'll be gone tomorrow night. Dinner at 8pm. And then we'll take you home. We'll put your bike in the car."

"Mom," Chip said, "I'm helping Maarten with his grammar and syntax. This essay we have –"

"History," she interrupted, nodding. "Women's rights."

"Uh, ok, women's rights…" He stared at Maarten. "Anyway, he's writing the whole thing, here, with my help, and it might take a long time. Maybe even all night."

Carolann said. "Wouldn't it be better to do over several days?"

"Nope. Just get it done." Chip turned to Maarten.

"Shit," Maarten looked sick, and Carolann gave a loud ahem.

Chip stared hard at Maarten. He could just say no and get back on his bike. He didn't have to use that language in front of his mother.

"You think I can get a C?" Maarten squared his shoulders. "I'm kind of interested in the plight of the poor."

Chip shrugged. "I don't know how Neame plans to grade. Maybe."

Maarten turned to Chip's mother. "If you have eggs in the fridge, I could make breakfast. I do a pretty good omelette."

Chapter 17

The boys were up late, and try as she might, Carolann couldn't join Lyn in falling asleep. She put on her robe and tip-toed across the hall to listen to the boys working. Chip was incredibly patient with his friend's shortcomings. And she had to give the other boy credit too. He was more committed to the project than she'd expected.

Lyn was right… Chip really was growing up. The future – Chip's future – was coming at Carolann faster and faster. Leaving Kansas behind had messed up the momentum and pacing in her life, both moving forward and looking back. Of course Chip wouldn't stay a little boy forever, and she knew someday she'd have to face his adulthood with Lyn. But "someday" seemed to be hovering around now, uninvited. She'd always deferred to Lyn with important decisions, like she'd been taught wives were supposed to, (or were supposed to *seem* to) but she would soon be entering uncharted territory. No parenting psychology books could offer advice. Of course, it was not something she'd ever discuss at work or at church, and Lyn was insistent. But what if he was wrong?

Without the obligations and protection of home now, the more Carolann realized she must discover her own priorities and strengths. Interestingly, the farther she was from her church, the more liberated she felt to let God, as she knew Him, guide her efforts. Often, Carolann felt like her real life had begun when she met Lyn and became his wife. But now suddenly, she thought the real person she'd always been was right there, within.

Carolann had met Lyn in the Topeka Bar and confided in him, and almost immediately, she had a bigger problem than simply sorting out her own elusive divisions between indignity and giddiness. She needed Lyn's help to solve it.

Her hand shook as she had flattened the napkin against her thigh to read his phone number. Of course, a sexually active girl needed a doctor outside her family community, and like it or not, even at age 17, that's what she was.

Her father never trusted phone lines that could be tapped – little ears sprouting like leaves on a vine. Cyrus only discussed financial matters face-to-face. Carolann's issue was certainly more personal than someone's taxes. She'd have to see Lyn in person. The best thing would just be to go straight to his office, after hours, and have him write her a prescription. Surely, he could do that.

The phone at his house rang. Carolann's mother rarely talked on the phone either. Private things required chairs, iced tea in summer, or hot cider in winter. Carolann's issue needed iced tea of the Long Island variety – in a gallon jug. She had no idea what she needed. Maybe he would have to examine her. No word travels faster than *slut*.

Straight off, Lyn asked, "So when can I take you out to dinner?"

"On a date?" Carolann smelled cinnamon. She had called him, so was she supposed to do the asking? Feminism messed up everything. Her mother's old Home Economics textbook – gospel, second to the Bible in their house – didn't cover it. "Soon."

"Easy, tiger." He laughed. "Italian and a movie Friday night?"

Cyrus always said fancy foreign food's the fastest way to the poorhouse. "Or hamburgers, sooner?" she asked.

"Day shifts end at 6pm, right?" Lyn asked. "I can pick you

up at the hospital."

"I could come to Kansas City." Carolann would borrow the car, refill the gas tank, and mark Cyrus' odometer book like Maryann always did. At Lyn's office, he'd have all the equipment, the prescription pad, the stuff they described in the book: stirrups and speculums. "I'll come to your office and then, you know, just have a quick drink."

"I know your quick drinks." Lyn laughed, a rolling blue baritone outburst. "I'll come to you Friday."

The itch flared fuchsia. "Ok." She didn't know how she could wait.

By the time she pulled her father's car into the hospital parking lot, she was on edge – mint green. What if the nice doctor-guy would tell her parents? She scanned the visitors' lot for Lyn's car.

Would she even recognize him? Her heart beat in her chest like she'd gulped down root beer with a live chicken. In the rear-view mirror, her face looked ridiculously young. Her freckles flashed, a roadmap sum of her experience. She was a connect-the-dots picture of a pattern too complicated to follow. Like astronomy.

She reached for the mascara she kept in her purse. Maryann was right – Carolann's eyes were pretty, but the rest was horrible. Her nose was too wide. Her lips were shaped funny. Her cheekbones weren't well-defined. That red hair did her no favors.

She added too much mascara. She couldn't get it right. Twelve-year-old, or trash. No in-between. If the doctor-guy couldn't write her a prescription without examining her, he'd have to do it in the car or the baseball dug-out or behind the Dairy Queen or the alley by the Five and Dime. They'd probably get caught. People went to all those places.

Lyn's car pulled into the lot, and Carolann's stomach lurched. She didn't even know this guy! Years later, when anyone asked her to explain her faith, she remembered that moment. As if God took the wheel and steered her decision. Not that she'd ever go into details when asked. But she knew.

She slid into Lyn's car. His dash looked greasy with cleaning product, and she didn't touch it.

"Your chariot, m'lady." Lyn beamed.

"Look, you don't have to take me to dinner. I sort of just need to ask you a favor."

He started the engine, checked the rearview mirror, and he pulled his car out of the parking lot. His small hands gripped the steering wheel. "Nonsense," he barked. "There will be time for favors later. But first, spaghetti. Scintillating conversation optional."

Carolann watched familiar houses speed by. She could end up with a much bigger problem than the infection she got from Buck. What kind of favors did he mean?

But true to his word, Lyn took her to an Italian restaurant, the same one Carolann's parents chose for the family dinner every year on their anniversary.

Lyn ate every bite of his dinner. Carolann split her meal in half, as if she might save some for later, but then she still only pushed the food around with her fork, distracted.

"Alright, let's hear it," Lyn said. "What's the favor?"

Carolann squirmed in her seat. Her thoughts scattered like gnats in a gust of wind and then corralled into focus. She stared at him. Everything went an overwhelming beige ochre and smelled like wet paint and sweat. She couldn't speak.

Finally, Lyn said, "When I met you in that bar, there was a lot going through your head."

"Kind of." The sweat smell hung heavy, but she could see through the beige. She squeezed tight. Fire ants. "But the problem's not exactly in my head."

"What then?"

She laid her hands flat on the Formica tabletop. Silver flecks in white and a sticky spludge of Bolognaise. She had done her nails, opalescent, especially for the party, which now seemed hundreds of years earlier. Her nails were chipped, flecked like the table, and bitten almost to bleeding.

"Listen, I meant what I said. If there's anything I can do…" Lyn looked into Carolann's eyes and didn't blink. "I will do it."

Carolann wanted to leap across the table and snuggle into his arms. "I've been drinking cranberry juice and eating yogurt, but it's not working. It must be bathing-suit bottom. My sister got it once. I think I need antibiotics or something. What kind of a doctor did you say you were?"

"Bathing-suit what?"

"Not bottom, exactly." She swallowed hard.

"Ok, well, I'm not exactly a doctor. I'm in Marketing. Go on."

"My mom calls it that. You're not a doctor?"

Lyn looked at her. "You told your mom?"

"God, no. I need a plumbing doctor, ladies plumbing. Not someone who knows my parents. I thought you were a doctor."

"Bathing-suit bottom." He smiled.

Carolann clenched her jaw. Anyone could walk into the restaurant and see them.

"Vaginitis," Lyn said quietly. "You're worried about a sexually transmitted disease."

"Yes." *Vaginitis* was the term she found in the hospital library.

"Chlamydia or Herpes. Syphilis. VD."

Carolann cringed. "Maybe I'm allergic to something."

"To someone." Lyn smiled. "Your sister's boyfriend."

Carolann felt sick.

"Look, it's probably a minor infection. These things get around."

Shared bodily fluids, the book said. Carolann felt even worse.

Lyn said, "We can get you a female doc in Kansas City for

a pap smear. You might like Dr. Wall. She's a good OB. Or Dr. Govender. Tough to get in, but excellent."

"Pap." Carolann whispered. The book at Memorial described the *insertion of a metal implement*. The burn flared. "Will it hurt?"

"You can't mess around with this infection. It could be serious, it could cause infertility." He cleared his throat.

"Good. Children are expensive."

He leveled his gaze at her and seemed to let an unasked question die in the air.

She smelled the gunk between her legs. Actually, the insertion of a cold metal implement might be heaven.

Lyn motioned to the waitress across the room, writing an imaginary bill on his palm. "They say it can be uncomfortable, but in your case, maybe not."

"Really?" Carolann pictured Maryann's curling iron, on ice. Bliss. A Popsicle. A bomb-pop! She'd cure it herself. A tampon in the freezer. "What do you mean, in my case?"

The waitress bustled over, pot of coffee in one hand, and the bill in the other. She tipped her head at the cash register near the pie counter. "Whenever you kids are ready."

Lyn nodded, watching the waitress disappear before he turned back to Carolann. "It'd be uncomfortable if you're tight or dry."

She flinched.

He put his stubby fingers on the table, like a card player revealing the trump. "Not to get overly graphic, but face facts, sweetheart." He patted her hand. "Right now this is a good thing… You're not exactly a virgin."

Chapter 18

The night after Chip and Maarten worked on the essay until all hours, Carolann assumed Chip might go to bed early. But it was almost his normal bedtime, and he was still awake. Carolann went to stand outside his closed door for a minute. When he was a little boy, she would fold laundry outside his room and eavesdrop on his conversations with his action figures. He had always revealed himself to be a well-adjusted, happy little boy.

At the time, Carolann needed regular confirmation of that. After what happened with Maryann, not everyone agreed that Carolann was attentive or smart enough or suitable as a mother. But if God decided she'd be a mother, who were they to disagree? From the beginning, Carolann worked tirelessly to be good at it. And what she'd always heard through Chip's closed door sounded fine. Though with kids' conversations happening through computers, how was a parent to know?

The rapid rhythm of his keyboarding worried Carolann. He'd never had girl friends. Carolann hadn't even met Ticia, the girl who called on the phone, and she was already panicked. Would the sound of Chip's typing somehow signal an imminent need for birth control?

During dinner that night, just the two of them, Carolann had been so focused on talking politics and History homework in Lyn's absence, that when Chip said he wanted to bring the girl to Rowan's clambake, Carolann was stunned. He retracted the request immediately. Hopefully, Rowan's clambake would be postponed once again, or canceled altogether. Carolann's family had no business mingling with new neighbors.

Carolann turned Chip's doorknob. It squeaked, and she paused. Of course he deserved a millisecond warning that she was there.

"I saw the time." Chip shut his laptop.

Carolann kissed the top of her son's head. He wore his pajama pants with a white t-shirt. Navy flannel, same as his father would be wearing in his hotel room in Bristol. Carolann wondered if Lyn was already in bed, or if a pharmaceutical rep had persuaded him into a pub.

She sighed. Public house. She'd been to every one of them on the High Street now, at least once, and some of the bartenders already knew her "usual." Diet Coke with lemon.

Chip moved past her in the doorway to go brush his teeth. Carolann looked out his window, into the darkness. The few times Lyn had to be away, she'd watch the moon and think of him looking at it too – even if she knew he was in late dinner meetings or nowhere near any view of the sky. She trusted Lyn's faithfulness entirely – and she knew few women who felt the same about their husbands. It seemed unfair that in turn, Lyn had to know she'd been with someone before him. And she knew, on occasion, it upset him.

At her sister's wedding, Carolann had been standing near the bride and groom for photos and she caught Lyn across the room, watching the three of them. She wished he could know that she felt nothing but sky-blue emptiness around Buck. There was nothing between them. Not then – not ever. She had motioned Lyn forward to join them, but he stayed where he was with the baby. Pings of alternating color returned to her then, heavy and saturated, aubergine and reflective slate gray. The substance of the tones had nothing to do with light blue, empty Buck. These deeper colors were complicated by her sister's wedding, by Buck becoming a permanent member of the family, and by Lyn. Her one night in Buck's car featured the same blend of color – summer thunderstorm purple, but now that color was Lyn.

Chip came back from the bathroom, and she turned.

She touched the blue top of a bright yellow bottle on Chip's desk. "Bubbles?"

"Yeah, the dorm council used them for an ice-breaker game."

"Remember how I never let you play with them in the house?"

"Play with them? You never even let me keep the bottle in the house." Chip laughed. "Why do you think I pulled it out of my backpack? I thought you'd want to put it in the garage with my finger paints."

Carolann smiled. "So what was the game?"

"The new people blow bubbles onto a circle of continuing students and whoever you hit with your bubbles has to reveal some personal information to the other guy."

"Like what?"

"My dad's the Defense Minister of Timbuktu. Bubbles everywhere. It was chaos."

Chip's mother frowned. "So what did you reveal?"

"Nothing." He shuffled his notebooks into his backpack and zipped it. "I never got hit."

"Good." Carolann unscrewed the lid and pulled the wand out, surprising herself, as the liquid dripped onto Chip's desk. It was only liquid soap.

"Anyway, I have no dark secrets." Chip looked puzzled at Carolann holding the bubble wand suspended. "Other than the espionage."

Carolann blew a bubble. "Counter-intelligence."

Chip grabbed the bubble from the air. "And Dad's a diamond thief and his car can fly."

Carolann said, "Being serious for a minute, I'm thinking about being a nurse again. Part time."

"Does Dad know?" Chip asked.

"No, we have to discuss it. The school needs help with the meningitis vaccines... it's nothing stressful." She blew another bubble and it burst on Chip's suspended ceiling lamp.

Chip glanced at his Eminem picture. "I could have said I'm a rapper, just signed with Def Jam Records."

"Never lie."

"I know." Chip sighed. "*Fix one problem, but create a bigger one.*"

She nodded. "Def Jam would be lucky to sign you." She said it as if *Def Jam* often featured in her conversation.

Chip shrugged.

"You're not limited, you know, being from a small town. You can be a rapper – you just prove the doubters wrong. Really do it. No need to lie about it."

"I guess."

When Carolann had handed in her notice at the hospital, her nurse friends offered the same platitudes her church friends had. The move will be a grand adventure. Embrace change. Don't fear the unknown.

But no one mentioned the joy of being unknown. The beautiful freedom of walking into the Waitrose where the checkout girl wouldn't comment when Carolann switched breakfast cereals or bought a bottle of Jack Daniels. The wonderful liberation of not knowing the checkout girl's aunt and her mother and her boss, and her first boyfriend's family farm house's linoleum pattern, and where they hide the key to the rifle cabinet. Of course, Carolann missed home – fitting in there, or understanding the ways in which she didn't – but she had to admit, the new freedom of being an expat was bliss.

"Mom?" Chip was watching the liquid drip from Carolann's wand.

"It's a rental." She laughed and blew again. The bubble grew on the purple plastic ring of the wand and took on all the colors of the room, spinning in its iridescent surface – the blues and purples and white light overhead, the golden moon outside, the pale peach streetlamp in front of Rowan's house. The bubble landed on Chip's shoulder, rested a moment on his white t-shirt, and then burst.

He touched the damp spot on his shoulder. "Ok, my big secret –"

Carolann looked at Chip carefully. The boy did have a big secret, but he didn't know it yet. If Carolann had her way, he never would.

"Zilch." Chip laughed. "I'm so boring."

"No, you're perfect and wonderful."

Chip took the bubble wand and blew.

She watched Chip's bubble land on her wrist and sit there. She smeared the liquid into her arm, and it felt slippery. "Oh my." She'd had one cocktail after dinner, only one, and she felt like time had unraveled itself. Her lifeline suddenly looked like a curling fuschia ribbon in Maryann's giftshop, crazy spirals, instead of linear. That was the trouble with Jack Daniels. Sometimes, one drink could spring a straight ribbon into a curley-que. Carolann really didn't like anything unpredictable. She pressed her wet fingertip into her warmed cheeks.

"You want to tell me about the diamond heist now?" Chip asked.

"No. I'll reveal something else." She glanced at his new Eminem picture. "This worries me."

"Eminem's innocent."

"The girl who gave it to you." Carolann frowned.

"Ticia's alright, Mom. She's nice and smart… and pretty, but you can't hold that against her. It's just – you know – friendship."

Carolann nodded. She needed connections. Information on the girl. She's a hooker. A cheater. A druggie. She'll break your heart, my sweet boy. Carolann needed that nurse job at the school.

"Give me some credit." Chip closed the bubbles. "I can take care of myself. I'm not stupid."

Chapter 19

Carolann flipped through the Antiques Guide Maryann had sent her. She and Lyn had already been out "antiquing" half a dozen times, covering Portobello Road on a Saturday, the Camden Market on a Wednesday morning (which left Lyn anxious to get in to the office) and numerous multi-vendor fairs. They'd found nothing. The lists of places selling English antiques seemed endless, and mapping out a successful plan appeared futile, but Carolann knew her sister would call any minute to discuss the ongoing search.

Right on time, 2pm, the phone rang and Carolann jumped for it.

"I don't think you're even looking," Maryann accused. "Did you go to the places I told you? Just find the goddamn thing."

"You find it," Carolann said. "You broke it."

"We broke it together," Maryann barked. "It got broken and our father's body is eating him up over it. You're having a great old time over there in England, and I don't think you realize how sick Daddy is."

"Is there something new?" Carolann asked, concerned.

"I don't know. Mama makes it sound like he's on death's door. She probably hopes he is."

"Did she update his life insurance again?"

"All he needs is to square the damn debt, Carolann. I don't have your 'medical background' but I know–"

"I'm looking for it." Carolann pictured her sister making

air-quotes around the phrase 'medical background.'

"Have you gone to Petworth yet? Chelsea? The Antiquarium? That's where you'll find it. You have to go often. Things come in to these vendors all the time. I should be the one over there doing it."

"If it's here to be found, I'll find it." Carolann sighed. "I leave my phone number everywhere. They'll call me." Lyn couldn't take time off for the quest. Luckily, Rowan had agreed to drive to Ardingly, the next big antiques fair.

"Do I have to remind you, Carolann? That god-forsaken Beemasters is English, like our parents' loony bird neighbor, and you're the one in England. If you haven't been to Chelsea yet –"

"I went to Chelsea."

"Lies will not find the thing. Gallivanting around Europe will not find the thing."

Before Carolann could reply, her sister had hung up. Carolann looked at the clock. Two-minute phone call. Maryann probably clocked it with an egg-timer. She could call her sister back – pay for the call – spare nothing, and answer the accusation. Or she could go to the pub. She knew where her energies would be better spent. Carolann put on her coat.

Lies and false accusations and withheld apologies. Edith Heaney was surely owed an apology, but Carolann couldn't go against her parents. And there were other apologies to make, but there too, she didn't dare. She was too weak. There was her own original sin – not being weak, but not being weak enough. The doctors said she really should have perished and reabsorbed into the womb.

In the fresh air, with the crunch of leaves and gravel underfoot, at least she could start to think clearly.

Of course, what she did with Buck was a sin. Or what she did to Buck. Or was it weakness? She'd given in to temptation, allowed herself to be led into temptation, against her expressed prayers. Was weakness a full-blown sin? Did God keep a sliding scale?

All those rat-a-tat t's: *lead us not into temptation.* Into temptation. She repeated the Lord's Prayer in her head as she walked. The rhythm of the words always smoothed distances.

It wasn't just the t's, into temptation – first it was the s's. The Sunday sound of them slithering, smoothly, one letter "s" sliding into the next, twisted snakes in their inseparable spirals. As a child, Carolann had memorized The Lord's Prayer without understanding its vocabulary, so all she experienced was the incessant s's. *…forgive us our trespasses, as we forgive those who trespass against us. Against us. Against us.* She could hear her footfall with the words. *Trespass against us. And lead us not into temptation, but deliver us from evil.*

She'd given in to temptation, despite all those whispered prayers… and at the first opportunity, she'd been too weak not to submit. And new weaknesses guided her journey ever since. Weakness and sin.

She wound her way through the narrow streets, taking in the smells of brown leaves and the sharp sting of the air on her face, and the white English sky and black branches above.

With a clear head and fresh resolve, she made her way home. If there was a Beemasters vase somewhere in England, she would find it and deliver it to her sister. Impossible as it seemed now, she knew that would be the easiest part.

Chapter 20

"You know if you find the god-forsaken thing, your sister will have some other bone to pick with you." Lyn sat down to dinner.

"We'll see." Carolann had to admit, her sister, older by three minutes, had always been domineering.

"She'll make you buy stuff for her store."

"The vase is why she got into antiques in the first place." Carolann gestured a reminder to Chip to put his napkin in his lap. Why the boy never remembered to put his napkin in his lap was a riddle for the ages.

"And why she resents your being a nurse," Lyn said. "As if her job could help your father's health more than yours ever could. She's off her rocker."

"What if it's here, in the very next place we look? And what if finding it really can help my dad?"

Chip coughed into his hand, and it sounded like he said "bullshit."

Lyn smiled – which Carolann found as shocking as Chip's cough. Did one put money in the profanity jar if the profane word was not quite intelligible?

"The old lady will probably die before you'd get it to her. She's probably already dead," Lyn said.

"She's still there. And we only have one year here. I have to try."

Lyn sighed. "So, the thing was valuable. Pay her for it. If your father's so sick, why didn't he pay her years ago? I'll pay her, for goodness' sake. How much?" He patted his pockets under the table, and coins jingled.

Was there ever a more belittling gesture a man could make during a discussion of value? Her big concerns were mere pocket change to him.

Carolann glared at him. She nearly stood and went to the kitchen to retrieve an imaginary necessity, but instead she forced herself to sit still.

Chip said, "Can I go to my friend Henrik's house to play basketball instead of antiquing? He has some guys over every Sunday. He lives close."

Carolann quickly said, "If this boy's mother calls our house to invite you, I will think about it. This is the Swedish boy from your bus?"

Chip's shoulders sank. "His mom's not going to call you, ok? I'm fourteen."

"Chip," Lyn spoke firmly, "Your mother said no."

"Actually, my mother didn't say no."

"Excuse me?" Lyn turned to his son.

"Why do I always have to go with you?" Chip said. "I have no role in this thing. With Grandpa's high blood pressure or this Beemasters thing. Why do I have to go?"

"Fine, you don't have to," Carolann said.

"You should be ashamed of yourself." Lyn stared at Chip. "He's your grandfather."

"No, Chip's right," Carolann said. "He doesn't have to come." She looked at her dinner, nearly untouched on her plate. She wasn't hungry. She actually felt a little relieved, a pale apricot-rose creeping in, it was more than relief, it was joy, that at least one member of her family didn't have to go antiquing.

"What about Henrik?"

"No," Lyn said. "You come with us. We are a family. Carolann, tell him what it's about. He can have a role in the thing, if that's what he wants."

The soft pink scattered and replaced itself with a see-through icy gray. The see-throughs were the hardest to read. Like jellyfish. Maybe that's what that color signified… she was under water, swimming among lazy-floating spineless beings that could be lethal if she got too close. She said, "It has nothing to do with Chip – even if I explain it."

Lyn set his water glass down hard and Carolann took a quick breath.

"Ok." She placed her hands on the table, either side of her plate, like cutlery, perfectly symmetrical. "Edith Heaney was a war-bride from England."

"Loony bird," Chip said.

Carolann bristled. "That old lady's been through enough."

"Sorry."

"She married Sedgewick Heaney when he was an American soldier stationed in England in World War Two."

"I know that much," Chip interrupted again.

"His company was training near Mrs. Heaney's father's farm in Devon. Some of the soldiers were there helping the local farms as well as their D-Day training exercises on the beaches. All the able-bodied English men were fighting the war on the continent. You can read the history. Look up Torcross. Look up Trebah Garden in Cornwall. You know the Omaha Landing in World War Two?"

"He knows it." Lyn interrupted. "*Saving Private Ryan*. It's where they left from, here in England. In fact, that's a place I wouldn't mind seeing. That's not on your sister's list is it?"

Carolann shook her head. "Anyway, Sedgewick Heaney was one of the guys helping Edith's father, he ended up marrying Edith, and they moved back to Kansas together after the war."

"They eloped," Chip said.

"I don't know the details."

"A sin."

Carolann shrugged. "She never quite fit in – her accent,

her English phrases. And she worked Mr. Heaney's farm like a son should have."

"They had no children because she's a witch. She has no uterus."

"That's ridiculous. Where did you hear that? Plenty of good women have no uterus. Or they have no children." Carolann stared pointedly at her husband and son. "She lost her husband before they had a family, but the point is, people found her odd. Didn't trust her. My mother was a girl at the time. I guess Mrs. Heaney wasn't much older than my mother. Ten years, maybe."

"Tell him about her basement lab," Lyn said.

Carolann raised her eyebrows. There were certain topics Lyn didn't discuss, and certain topics Carolann didn't discuss.

"I already know. She tried to kill you and Aunt Maryann when you were girls. You broke in to her science lab and she tried to poison you because she's a loony bird."

"No." Carolann shook her head.

Chip shrugged. "That's what I heard."

"Where?"

"Like 20 people told me. I've never *not* known it."

Carolann took a deep breath. "Mrs. Heaney distilled plant derivatives. She had tables and Bunsen burners down there. After Sedgewick Heaney died, people thought she would return to England, but she stayed and ran the lab. She published articles in agricultural science journals, including a booklet for the Future Farmers. They rejected that – they didn't want her anywhere near *impressionable youth*. They talked about something *untoward* in her past."

"Maybe she shouldn't have told people she'd eloped," Chip said.

Carolann shook her head. "My mother used to claim to be her only friend. Maryann and I went to her house every week while my mother got her hair done. It was a different era, really. We called Mrs. Heaney a loony bird, like everyone did, but she was a sweet old lady. Made us cookies… little tea parties." Carolann stopped for a minute.

"Like an aunt or a grandma." Chip nodded.

Chip's Aunt Maryann or Grandma Barbara Ann couldn't be what he had in mind. And Lyn's mother, even less so. Luckily, Chip never had to meet her.

Carolann continued, "When we were seven, Maryann and I broke her most precious thing, the vase. It was considered irreplaceable, so it created a debt that literally made my father sick. Even now. As you know, he considers money-management paramount." Carolann had a funny feeling about Edith Heaney even before she heard the stories in court, as a little girl. It seemed strange to try to explain it to Chip. She stood and returned to the kitchen.

"So does that help?" She heard Lyn ask.

Carolann returned to the dining room with a bowl of fruit salad. "She was so upset when we broke her vase, she needed to take a walk to calm down, so she locked us in her basement, thinking no harm could come to us there."

"And no harm did," Lyn added.

Carolann served the fruit. It sounded ridiculous. She wanted to say the whole family should go play basketball with the Swedish kid. "But my parents believed it was a grave error to lock us in that lab and leave us there."

Chip shrugged. "It's a 20-year feud or whatever, and if Mom finds that irreplaceable vase, everyone will suddenly turn out happy. I don't think so. Especially considering your parents got Mrs. Innocent Heaney locked up for child endangerment."

"Her record has been expunged."

The table fell silent. Evidently, Lyn would not insist that Carolann go into more details. Evidently too, Chip already knew more than he should. She could hear her own breathing.

Chip finally said, "I guess ours is not to reason why."

"Exactly." Lyn chuckled. "I do love a little Alfred Lord Tennyson with my fruit salad." He reached for the serving spoon. "So, we're all going antiquing together. If your mother's right and we get lucky in the next place we try, how about then I'll take you to shoot hoops in the park?"

Chapter 21

The next day, Carolann was going to walk to the post office when she saw Rowan out front, gardening. Carolann had never been neighborly, in any of the few places she and Lyn lived, but this was different. She changed direction. Feeling only a little awkward, she folded her coat under her seat, and sat down with Rowan. "So we're on for our clambake next weekend?"

"Right," Rowan said. "You think you'll only live here one year, but what if it's two or three or a decade? There are people on this road you should meet."

Carolann smiled. Strangely, she was almost looking forward to the party.

"I hope it's not too late for these," Rowan pointed at her bucket of bulbs. "I bought 10 different colors, stubby tulips, and I mixed them all together, so if we're lucky come spring, it should be a riot. Give it a stir."

"I wouldn't dare." She stared into Rowan's bucket of bulbs. "Mixing the bulbs! How stressful!"

Rowan laughed. "But I assume you like tulips same as I do, because they have no scent of their own."

"Very true."

"And you don't like the TV and radio on at the same time either?"

"Nobody likes that, do they?" Carolann reached in the bucket and pulled out a bulb. Its tiny white waxy shoot was just protruding from the brown papery casing. "How many years did you say you were married?" She nudged the shoot gently with her thumb.

"Too long," Rowan said. She took the bulb from Carolann and planted it. "Why?"

"I read that if a marriage makes it past 15 years, the odds more than double it will last. But the highest percentage of divorce is between 12 and 14 years. If only people put off the decision for a couple of years… who knows?"

"If I had stayed with that wankjerk bastard one minute longer, it would have killed me." Rowan jabbed her pointed spade into the ground and twisted it.

"No, sorry. Of course, I didn't mean you."

"Bastard," Rowan said again.

"Lyn and I are right at fifteen."

Rowan stared at her, and Carolann stood. "Need stamps from the post office or anything?"

"Fifteen's no magic number, honey. If you're married to a shit, you get out – first chance you have."

Carolann straightened her coat. "Luckily, I'm not."

Chapter 22

The post office was a small counter with two glass windows in the back of a general convenience shop on the High Street. Carolann saw a long queue, so she stopped to browse the greeting cards in the front of the store. Her wedding anniversary was one week away. In her family, greeting cards had always been hand-made… store-bought cards were indulgent and wasteful. Lyn didn't care what format she chose, as long as she remembered their anniversary and how fortunate they were to be married.

The infection between Carolann's legs disappeared almost immediately after Lyn brought her to his doctor friend, but a week later, she had a new problem. She found herself, once again, in the Italian restaurant with the nice-doctor-guy-who-was-not-a-doctor.

"I like the look of that banana crème pie over there," Lyn said. "We could skip dinner and go straight to dessert."

"No." Carolann smiled. "I'd better do things in the right order for a change." She would tell him the bigger issue in his car, where the darkness and distant neon lights would give her courage. She wondered if at that point, he'd finally try to kiss her.

"Them are Kansas apples," the waitress set a plate down for Lyn and winked. A generous scoop of warm applesauce nestled against the meat, glistening gold and cinnamon in the pork fat. She turned to Carolann. "Be right back with your *pa-sgetti*, darlin.'"

Lyn picked up his knife and fork and set them down again to wait.

Carolann looked at his hands. "Does it bug you?" she asked. "Your fingers?"

"I don't know what you're talking about."

"Were kids mean to you?" She could imagine the names: *Nubs, Mr. Thumbs. Kangaroo Mitts. Stubsy Malone. Midget McStocky Paws.*

He hesitated. "No."

"Sorry." Carolann looked at her lap. Her spaghetti arrived in a large shallow bowl. Making rapid work of it, she dug her knife and fork across the pasta, bisecting the plate.

"Do you always divide your food to share with your sister?" Lyn smiled.

"Habit." Carolann stirred her fork into the bowl, messing up the even division. "It's cheaper than two kids' meals. When you said you weren't a doctor, I thought maybe you were a shrink."

Lyn laughed. "A shrink is very much a doctor."

"I guess so." Carolann shook cheese into the pasta. "Well, the thing about my sister, my twin, she weighed seven pounds at birth, and I weighed four. They didn't know I was in there."

"Glad you were." He raised his water glass in a sort of toast.

"They went to tell Daddy that Maryann was born, and then I came out. All slimy. A runt. The doctor thought I was dead."

Lyn set his fork down.

"I was grayish-purple." Carolann stared into her pasta.

Lyn pushed his plate away, his pork chop also looking a bit purple.

"And then I moved and the doctor said, 'where did you come from?'"

"Who told you this story?"

"My sister."

"Maybe she made it up." He ran his fingers up his water glass and pressed condensation fingerprints into his napkin.

"No, Mama told her. They didn't think I'd live, which would have saved them a lot of money, over the years."

"I've never seen your sister." Lyn cleared his throat. "She could be Miss America. About to cure cancer and win the Nobel Prize. I don't care. But I do care about you."

Carolann looked up.

"You're the one who took my breath away in that hospital."

 Spaghetti noodles wobbled from her fork, mid-air.

"Look, I've never had a girlfriend. No one's ever walked into my life like that. I'm very focused, but when I saw you... your smile... your green eyes. What are you, seventeen? I'm twenty-four. That's not supposed to happen to a man in my position."

Carolann ate the bite of spaghetti. She heard drums. Pasta normally didn't give her drums. But Watusi Warrior drums banged in her head.

"And when you told me what happened with Buck, when you opened up to me, and let me help you, I thought: this is what makes a man feel alive."

"Ok," she said. Now she really needed his help, not just some antibiotics, but real help, so he'd feel like Superman. Or the opposite.

"Anyway, you shouldn't give that silly story another thought," he said.

"My father's an accountant, though, so I was a liability, a second girl. He's told me that himself. And they'd agreed to have as many boys as they wanted – they're cheaper – but they'd stop if they ever got two daughters. And there I was, so Mama couldn't have any boys. No more children. I ruined it. Only one daughter in the family budget. One big wedding, all that stuff. Maryann will get that because she was first."

"So what?" Lyn said. "None of that nonsense has anything to do with the kind of adult you choose to be. That's your responsibility, to govern your choices."

He was looking her right in the eyes. Did he mean Buck? That choice? She shouldn't have even said hello to Buck at the party. Could Lyn read her thoughts? She shouldn't have kissed him, gotten into his car. Taken off her jeans... she had undone her own jeans! It wasn't just a choice she made – it was more than just taking a chance. It was taking advantage.

"I think you're more mature than you realize," Lyn said.

She took advantage of the drinking, of her sister's absence. Didn't drinking make people forget things? Why did she have to remember every vivid layer, all the smells, all the colors, all the time?

Lyn said, "Anyway, a pretty girl like you deserves a beautiful wedding."

Carolann looked up, wide-eyed. "Maybe I should tell him?"

"Tell who what?"

"Tell him I'm... What if I'm...? He hasn't said a single word to me, but..."

"Your sister's boyfriend?" Lyn said. "Of course he's not talking to you. He's... Carolann, are you pregnant?"

She shook her head. She could only say it in the dark, if she was going to say it at all. They should leave. She couldn't eat. His plate was nearly empty. "Can we go?"

"Carolann," Lyn spoke clearly, "If you're pregnant with Buck's child, you tell him. You have no right not to tell him."

She nodded. "Or I could go back to Doctor Wall, and, you know... Do all doctors... you know?"

"First you tell Buck. It's his child. It's the biggest news a man will ever get."

Chapter 23

On Sunday, Carolann sat through church rehearsing what she would say and counting the seconds till the sermon would end. Right after services, Buck would go to the men's room, and she could catch him there. Not that she should have to chase him.

Pastor Hugh concluded his sermon. Carolann's heart pounded and she excused herself to hurry after Buck, the noise of her heels like a Doppler. Her wooden stack-heels on carpet-padded concrete. She knew he heard her approach. She would get no better opportunity.

She felt like she was moving through syrup. "Buck." She grabbed the arm of his shirt. She was ashamed to feel a twinge of excitement over needing his attention, touching his shirt. She was flooded with lavender. "Wait."

He turned. "Yeah." He looked up and down the empty corridor. "What?"

"I'm…I'm," she stuttered. "Listen, I'm late."

"So?"

Carolann also looked down the length of the hall. "I might be… I think I'm…"

Buck stepped back, away from the pressboard men's room door, but he stared at it with urgent intensity. The flat plastic man-figure affixed to the door was more important than Carolann and the baby inside her.

"My period's late." Saying the word *period* to Buck Roberts was about the last thing she ever thought she'd do.

"Christ, Carolann, couldn't you pick a better place to talk?"

"No." Was this the first time he'd said her name? It felt like a gift. Carolann stammered. "You're… Buck, it's your…" Why couldn't he finish her sentence the way Lyn could? *It's your baby.*

"No way. I never – what about the hospital guys you meet in the closets?"

"One guy. One kiss." How could he know about that? The only person she'd told was Maryann. "One time."

"Two times," Buck said. "At least."

He was jealous! "That was nothing. This is, with you, this is…" she still couldn't say it. *This is your baby.*

"Too busy to support your team." Buck shook his head. "You're nothing like your sister, you know."

"True. The way she feels about you and the way I do – they're not the same. I think I've proved that." She put her hand on her hip. "Anyway, this has nothing to do with her.

"Damn right," Buck said. "You have to go to a free clinic." His voice softened.

Carolann looked down the hall. Still empty. Apparently anyone who needed the restroom was using the one near the acolytes' closet. "That's not what I'm asking." There was a trout in her gut, flip-flopping for escape. "I thought maybe we could –"

"No." He slammed his hand on the men's room door, and the plywood shook in its frame. "You don't know what you're saying."

He pushed the door open. He was going into the men's room! But Lyn said Buck would do the right thing. Jars of baby food in cupboards, teddy bear birthday portraits at Wal-Mart.

Buck jabbed Carolann's shoulder hard, and before he went in the men's room, he growled, "Never."

Later on the phone, Lyn counseled Carolann to give Buck a week. Lyn's voice sounded calm, but Carolann couldn't shake the panic. She had a wedding to plan, an abortion to arrange, and a train ticket to buy, straight to Hell.

"It's just time," he said.

"I can't wait," she whispered. She could hear Lyn's light blue breathing in the phone. Felt like she could hear his heart beating, as if he were holding the receiver to his chest, drawing her anguish out of her, and gently discarding it. Like what would have to happen to the baby. If she didn't calm down, her body would expel the baby on its own. She couldn't explain her desperate anxiety over that.

Chapter 24

The waiting was agony, and Carolann didn't sleep. Friday evening, her mother called her downstairs.

"Your sister says you're emotional, tossing and turning, and keeping her up at night." Barbara Ann took Carolann's hand in hers. "Is there something you want to talk about?"

"No." Carolann pulled her hand away. One more day. Lyn would pick her up at 11am and fix the problem.

"Carolann, I already know."

She froze.

"*Senioritis*, I saw it on a talk show. You need cheering up." She pointed into the dining room, at the sewing machine she'd set up on the table. "Curtain skirt."

The curtains hanging over the kitchen sink window had been white with a red and yellow strawberry-teapot motif. Not a fabric Carolann wanted for a skirt, much less in a maternity size.

"Up on the chair, missy, for measurements. Get those jeans off."

Reluctantly, Carolann undressed and stood on the dining chair.

Barbara Ann sang, "*Cut but once, but be precise. Measure once, then measure twice.*" She stretched her tape measure around Carolann's waist. Barbara Ann looked up and smiled.

Carolann saw her mother's double chin stretch taut and disappear. From this angle, she looked young and pretty, like in old photos. Maybe the baby in Carolann's womb would be a girl with sweet little fingers that would grab Carolann's thumb and hold tight. Carolann tried not to think about the tiny presence inside her.

"Hips, seven inches below waist." Barbara Ann talked to herself and marked a chart by the sewing machine. "Those long legs of yours." She grabbed Carolann's hip and turned her. "I need more fabric or you'll soon have trouble with boys. Even uglies get in trouble with short skirts. Fat-and-uglies have it the worst. Nasty boys sense gratitude and vulnerability, and they take advantage. At least you're slim." Barbara Ann pressed the tape measure into the small of Carolann's back and bent forward. "Oh!" She stood up. "Mystery solved."

Carolann looked down, puzzled.

Barbara Ann tossed the tape measure on the table. "You're not sad with *senioritis*, young lady. It's just monthly girl-business. Go change your underpants. It's your curse."

Chapter 25

The next morning, Lyn turned his engine off in the hospital parking lot. "Do you want to give Buck more time?"

Carolann couldn't think how to respond. "No." Time. Two days ago, just a short time, she had a huge problem. Today, she didn't. "Buck doesn't need more time."

"Sure?"

"He hates me. He calls my freckles carrot puke."

Lyn shook his head.

"Though he didn't seem to mind my freckles that night." She closed her eyes. Talking to Lyn about Buck was like drinking the whiskey. It burned going down, but then it made her feel warm and grown-up. A plum-colored red.

Lyn said, "Buck's a jerk."

She nodded. She couldn't help how she still felt about Buck. She and Maryann had known him all their lives. The girls stayed in neonatal for a couple weeks, and then Buck was born, and the three babies were released from the hospital the same afternoon. She'd known him forever. She couldn't help thinking about the bright yellow-gold of the back of his car. Until she pictured the men's room door in the church. But it was irresistible, like picking a scab, each time she revisited the injury and risked a permanent scar.

"You deserve so much better," Lyn said.

"Yeah…"

"You already know what I think."

"What do you think?" She asked anyway.

"When I met you, I thought, I could fall in love with a girl like that."

Carolann didn't dare look at Lyn. She stared at his dashboard. She wanted to dig her fingers into it, white knuckling the maroon vinyl. She wanted to push her foot on an imaginary brake. Slow him down so she could pick up each little gemstone word he was saying, string them together and wear them on a necklace. She held her hand to her abdomen. What had Buck ever given her? Not even encouragement. Not even that night. Nothing.

Lyn's thumb pressed the button on the tip of his parking brake, and then he took one of Carolann's hands and touched each freckled finger in turn. "You have a problem, and I might have an answer."

"It's not a problem." His hand felt warm and strong. Deep evening starlit purple.

"Of course it's not a problem. It's a baby. You can keep the baby."

"No. Lyn, I…"

"So, the truth," Lyn said. "No secrets. Cards on the table."

Carolann looked at her spotted hand in Lyn's, her well-traveled roadmap.

"I already know all your secrets," he said. "Right?"

She nodded. How many secrets did he think a 17-year-old girl could have?

Lyn said, "Ok, mine. We'll do this one time. I… well, you're the first, understand? This is too much to talk about, too fast, but I don't see as we have any choice. So, you're my first."

First? He was a virgin at twenty-four? She hoped she hadn't cringed.

"You've noticed my hands."

"No," she lied.

"Truth!" Lyn shouted. "One time here. My fingers are malformed." He let go of her hand and held his up. "You need to know this. It's called brachydactyly. There are seven basic types, but mine's not among the seven. All my fingers are short, not just certain digits. I have no webbing, no curvature, no associated anomalies. But I can't palm a basketball. Couldn't play football. And I would never have been a guy like Buck, even if I could. Understand?"

"Brachydactyly," she repeated. It was dried-blood black and smelled like animal slaughter.

Lyn lowered his hands to his thighs. "I don't fit the medical journals, so the stats are meaningless, but it's fifty/fifty I'd pass it on. My mother tried to have me sterilized. But I'm a grown man now, and I'd like to have a family."

"Your mother… what?" Carolann glanced at Lyn's car door.

"A son or daughter I'd raise as my own."

"Daughters are expensive," Carolann said. The phrase rolled out as one long word, she'd heard it so many times. *Daughtersareexpensive.*

"An investment." He smiled.

"How old were you when your mother…?"

"Chemical castration. Young. Maybe ten. The doctors refused, genetic counselors and shrinks, but I wasn't standard abuse or neglect, so I didn't fit in their system. Wealthy family. No one knew what to do with me. My father certainly didn't know what to do with me, or with my mother. She couldn't get over it, and he couldn't get over that. It ended badly." He took a deep breath.

"But…" Carolann struggled. No mother could do that to her son.

"Anyway, I will get a vasectomy."

Carolann frowned. No 24-year-old guy could want scissors near his private parts.

"So I was thinking… Carolann, maybe the natural father doesn't, but I do… I want this child."

Carolann knew sometimes pregnant women came to the hospital with "break-through bleeding," and their babies were perfectly fine.

"I know you understand this," he said. "They hated me. They feared me." Lyn held up his stubby hands. "Never had more children because of this. They fought all the time because of it, and then my father killed himself. I was 16, and now my mother's dead, and none of it matters. They left me money. But you know what? My hands are what saved me."

"How?"

"I don't touch their money." He jiggled his gearshift, loose, in neutral. "Unless..." He looked into her eyes. "It's really important."

Hell of a date, instead of a drive to an abortion. Not even out of the parking lot, and it felt like they were headed full speed to a marriage proposal. "I'm not afraid of your hands," she said suddenly. "I think a child would be lucky to turn out like you."

"No." He shook his head. "That's not the deal."

So she was a deal, not a date. She turned to look out the window. Everything seemed fake, like a movie set, the trees, other cars, an old woman in a pink nightie, hunched in a wheelchair, all her years and regrets and choices behind her. A movie critic would say *very convenient, very symbolic.*

"I know what you're thinking," Lyn said. "Maryann's supposed to get married, the big wedding and Mr. Wonderful. And you're supposed to have a career. But you don't have time." Lyn gently took the end of her hair, a flame, between his thumb and fingers. "You don't have parents who will pay for your wedding, and you don't have Buck."

She nodded slowly.

"We'll use my mother's money. A thousand flowers. Bridesmaids. You name it."

The twins had looked at the all the wedding magazines in the church library, always making faraway plans for Maryann. Carolann looked out the window at the gray Kansas sky, a hint of sunlight struggling to shine through.

"The wedding is a gift I could give you and my father's memory at the same time." Lyn set a little black chunk on the dashboard between them, front and center, where people put Jesus or a hula skirt girl. A soft, velvet box screaming to be opened. But she wasn't even pregnant, was she? He'd call it off. The velvet block sat heavy on the dash, like a living thing, mocking her.

"I don't know." She could hardly breathe.

"Look, two years ago, Dytrepzone was a brand new drug, and I was a brand new guy, straight out of college. No one expected much of Dytrepzone, and no one expected much of me. They didn't realize its application for asthma at that point."

"Your lecture at Memorial."

He nodded. "When they discovered its potential, they tried to yank it from me, but I knew it was big." He held up his hands. "They thought I couldn't deliver it to market. Couldn't handle the presentations. But I showed them. My sales are excellent. Carolann, I will make a good husband. I'll show *you* that."

"But –"

"It's now." He looked at her tummy. "I'm here now. I want your baby. I want you."

"What if I'm not…" She held her breath. She had to be pregnant.

"You are." He pried the box open, his hands shaking. "You have to be ready, even if you don't feel like you are." The hinge creaked, and a brilliant diamond ring winked at her. "You could have my mother's, if you like it more. But I bought this for you, Carolann. Your ring."

She couldn't think. What if her father refused? What if she wasn't pregnant? What if she miscarried? Where did this guy stand on divorce? A father's suicide, shrinks and sterilization. This would be her child's legacy?

He pried the ring loose from the box, and slid the diamond

onto her finger. Fireworks! Her heart spun. How did any girl, ever, say no to a diamond ring?

"You said I look a little like Buck."

She nodded. Her finger felt hot, the ember of a shooting star landed there. The diamond seemed to gather and reflect light, even without sunshine. She closed her eyes. Would it burn out, fade away? Burn her? She opened one eye and squinted at it. The ring sparkled.

"Please…?" Lyn voice quaked. Like a skilled actor who'd stepped into unscripted territory. "You have a problem." The confident actor had found his lines. "And I have a solution. I could go to your father tomorrow if you'll let me. Trust me, Carolann. I'm your answer."

Carolann looked Lyn in the eyes like it was a dare. Could she sustain a marriage, sustain a whole life, on a dare? She smiled, and for the first time, Lyn kissed her. She melted into gold and turquoise and teal. She didn't want him to stop. "I have an idea."

"Name it."

Every part of her body felt both spring-loaded and released. "Don't you think we should, you know…" Carolann struggled for words. "Make it at least, a possibility that this baby could be yours?"

"Since you're already pregnant…" Beaming, Lyn started his engine. He quickly turned to her. "So that's a yes?"

Carolann nodded. "I guess that's a yes."

He drove straight to the Shoshoni Motel in Topeka, and ran like lightening into the reception, scrambled back out, and dropped their room key twice before he finally got it in the lock. But then he was more careful, slower and precise, and very gentle with the rest of his insertions. Nothing like Buck.

They'd taken a long soak in the bathtub, and talked about using her savings for baby things. Lyn made them both beards out of bubbles and they stood up, giggling at themselves in the steamy mirror, listing the items her two thousand dollars might buy. *Crib. Stroller. Diapers.* They both looked like wet naked Santa Claus announcing gifts, dipping to refresh their beards as the foam dripped away. *Jolly Jumper. Changing table.* Carolann was relieved the sink counter hid their lower halves. It was one thing to be naked, wearing nothing but a beard in a bathtub next to a man, but another thing to look right at it in the mirror. And really, she wasn't that kind of girl.

Chapter 26

The next day Lyn went to Cyrus for permission, and Carolann eavesdropped from upstairs through the bathroom vent. Her father's answer was not what she expected. All he said was that Carolann couldn't fry a chicken or turn a shirt collar. She wanted to race downstairs and shake her father. She'd known how to fry a chicken since she was twelve. But then Lyn described the house he was buying and the fact that he wanted his wife's name on the deed with his, and Cyrus grew quiet. Carolann could imagine her father downstairs giving Lyn the cold glassy-eyed stare he reserved for over spenders.

Carolann touched the wall behind the toilet. Its chalky eggshell paint was strangely clean and dry, despite the Kansas humidity. It felt like the skin of her fingertips might lift off and leave invisible fingerprints on the wall. If her dad said yes, she'd move out of this house, and become somebody's wife. She wanted her fingerprints to stay behind.

Cyrus spoke again, "Her sister will marry well, but Carolann... Anyway, why now? There better as Hell not be trouble."

"Absolutely not, Sir." For a guy so intent on truth-telling, Lyn seemed perfectly comfortable lying to her father. Carolann held her breath.

"Then why?" Cyrus asked.

"I love her."

Carolann gasped. She heard the thump of her father's fist banging his chest. The stiff salt and pepper stubble on her dad's jaw would look like tiny barbs, glinting shards of glass. He'd be working his mouth hard, chewing gristle. "Let me ask you something else, boy," he said, "Who does your taxes?"

"I do," Lyn answered.

"What percent did you fork over to Uncle Sam?"

Carolann listened.

"Twenty-eight last year," Lyn said. "For Federal and State. Next year I'll have a mortgage, to save a point or two."

"Smart," Cyrus said. "You let her make your curtains and bed linens from your wedding table cloths, if you insist on this fancy wedding. And never buy new furniture. Estate sales, hotel liquidators. People throw away perfectly good furniture."

"I know where to go," Lyn said. "I'll pay Carolann's tuition. I know she wants to be a nurse."

Upstairs, Carolann was in tears, struggling to stay silent. She pictured Cyrus chewing his bristled lip, calculating the cost of her meals, her school clothes, her new shoes. The transaction downstairs sounded crass, like bartering over a mule.

"I will be a good husband to your daughter, Sir."

"Well, then…" Her father's voice stopped, and Carolann caught her breath. "One word of advice. Make your vows in the church, and you keep them," Cyrus said. "When it's time to tell God and everybody you love Carolann, you step up and say it."

"Of course."

"And then for Pete's sake, shut up about it. The most valuable things in life are rare, understand? Possessions, people. Even, especially, words."

One month to the day from her engagement, Carolann married Raines Charles Lynwood Cooper, in the Heart of America Church of God. The maid of honor and mother of the bride wore lilac satin, matching the tablecloths. Carolann carried purple tulips to match Maryann's eyes. Barbara Ann Field planned everything except the cake, which Lyn insisted he would handle. He had a special *dreamcake* made by his good friend and childhood psychiatric nurse, creating more than a little animosity in the church, where the same woman had made every wedding, funeral, and baptism cake for 20 years.

In the early days of the catering business, Lyn helped deliver her *dreamcakes,* and he knew what he wanted. Three tiered rectangles of moist white cake with pink frosting and lavender frosting roses. The bottom layer said *for your future together* in script. On top was a violet sugar lake with a clear plastic bridge that glittered. An iridescent horse and carriage that looked like blown glass carried a tiny bride and groom over the magical bridge into their future. The cake reflected all the colors of the wedding, pinks and purples, fuchsia and pale green.

Maryann swished up in a swirl of amethyst satin, and she joined her sister near the cake. Barbara Ann had sewn matching sequin hearts on the twins' bodices. Smiling, Carolann looked around for someone with a camera. They would make a nice picture together. She wondered if Maryann had noticed that Carolann was finally pretty.

"Think Lyn's nurse-friend will make my cake, someday?" Maryann stuck her finger in the *dreamcake,* grinned, and pulled off a purple flower.

Carolann barked. "Don't."

"Two years." Maryann stuck the flower in her mouth and sucked it. "Buck and the guys bet less than a year."

"What?" Carolann turned sharply.

"But I know you better…" Maryann worked the finger in her mouth, "and my money's on two." Maryann plucked her finger free. "I mean, who would have guessed. You hit the jackpot with that guy." She tipped her head at Lyn, across the room, and she didn't look away.

Carolann snarled, "Don't." She put her hand to her tummy, sick with panic. She was now a married woman, to a beautiful man who thought she was having a baby, and her twin sister was doing eyelashes at her new husband. Carolann elbowed Maryann hard.

"Jesus, it's a compliment," Maryann sputtered. "Anyway, I don't know how you trapped him, but it's going to be a Hell of a job keeping him."

Buck separated from his buddies and joined the twins. "You, uh... make a lovely bride," he said to Carolann. He put his free hand into Maryann's hair and let it fall to her shoulder.

For one second, Carolann saw the pinky-beige of Buck's hand on the shiny purple of her sister's shoulder and her black hair, and she was jealous. But as soon as it had come, it passed. She smiled. Buck's parents probably told him to offer the greeting-card phrase, but he seemed genuine.

Lyn crossed the room to cut the cake with his bride. Flashbulbs lit the room. Carolann tried to smile. After the cake, after the wedding, after her mother would quilt the lilac tablecloth into bed linens, what then? And the biggest question of all... what of her empty womb?

Lyn wrapped his hands over hers on the knife handle, and they cut the cake. Suddenly resolute with clarity, Carolann knew what was required. She had a job to do, a marriage to build, and a new life to create, fast.

Chapter 27

Carolann watched Chip rummage through his backpack while his bowl of Cheerios sat in front of him untouched. She knew he liked his cereal a little soft, despite her insistence that letting it soften probably bumped it up on the glycemic index a point or two.

He pulled out a form letter. "I know this is kind-of sudden," he said. "They asked me to be an alternate for the Forensics team. This is the permission slip for the International Schools Debate Tournament."

Carolann took the paper. "When is it?"

"Friday," Chip said, dunking his spoon in his cereal. "I really want to do it. All day Friday."

"One week from today, Friday?" Carolann shook her head and read the form. "Your father won't like this late notice. And it's not at your school. Where is this thing?"

"They already have a team, since last spring, and they're all prepared. It's on nuclear proliferation and whether all countries have a right to it. They want me there because I can speak on it unprepared, they said."

Carolann sighed. "Who are these families that don't discuss current affairs and history with their children? So much of a child's education depends on their peer group. I trusted the families back home."

"So can I go?" Chip asked. "They leave Thursday night and come back Friday, late."

"Overnight?" Carolann shook her head. "Chip, this is

ridiculous. We hardly know anyone here, much less the people supervising this thing. Why didn't they have their team all planned in advance? I'm sure you'd be a great asset to them, but your father won't like this at all, and our anniversary is next Thursday night, and I... no." She stared at the paper. "And then Saturday is Rowan's party."

"If she actually has it." Chip shrugged. "Mom, they have a shot at winning this thing. They really want me."

Lyn walked into the kitchen. "Forensics team is an honor. Your school back home didn't have a team. You should go."

Carolann held the form up for Lyn to see. "It's in Switzerland."

"Then you'd better pack your skis." Lyn smiled at Chip.

"Lyn, don't be silly."

"We'll stay with expat families in Lausanne," Chip said. "I can request Americans."

Lyn nodded. "You're back when? Saturday? Maybe we ought to bow out of the thing at Rowan's."

"We can't do that." Carolann paused. "What American family? We don't know that their values match ours. Maybe they're from California."

"It's one night," Lyn said. "He can take that Eurostar train or whatever, I'm sure they're all going together."

"That train goes to Paris." Carolann shook her head.

"No, we're flying from Gatwick. It's all worked out," Chip said. "I just need your signature and my passport. I'll have a roommate from here." Chip tipped his cereal bowl and drank the remaining milk.

"What about customs in Switzerland? They're not EU, but would you have to go through a different line from the European kids? Who's going on this trip? Is the debate team mostly American?"

Carolann pictured Chip being shuttled off to another line, his passport gripped tight in his hand, while the other kids would funnel straight through to the baggage claim. He might get lost. She felt brown and slippery and sharp. Thumbtacks in slurry. She knew the textured color well, the nervous color of parenting, and she didn't like it.

"Carolann, we cannot control everything," Lyn said. "He'll be well supervised. It will be good for him."

"He's 14 years old."

"I spent eight weeks at summer camp at his age." Lyn took the paper from Carolann and signed it.

"Your parents weren't exactly role models," she said quietly.

Lyn glared at her. "He's going."

She said to Chip, "Are we talking limited nuclear reactors for energy with full UN compliance or... or... anything goes, here? People have rights, nations have rights, but be careful with that debate." She paused. "Rights aside, someone intelligent and trustworthy needs to keep a lid on things."

Chip stared at his mother, but she said nothing further. For the first time since they'd arrived in England, Carolann retreated back upstairs to get dressed, disappearing before Chip's school bus arrived. She did not say good-bye.

Chapter 28

Rowan rang Carolann's doorbell, holding a plate of biscuits. "Got a few minutes?"

Carolann opened the door wide. The cookies were loaded with seeds and looked like they might break a tooth. "A new sugar free recipe?"

Rowan nodded. "I'm still perfecting it… but they'll keep you regular." She laughed and followed Carolann into the house. "I won't stay long."

Carolann put two of Rowan's biscuits on napkins to go with their tea. If necessary, she could claim an allergy. "No antiquing today," she said. "My sister's got a new list coming, but I don't have it yet."

"I was going to ask if you wanted my chauffeuring services next week. Anywhere you want to go, I'm available." Rowan grabbed another cookie from the plate and ate it. "Any word on the nurse job?"

Carolann shook her head. "I don't think it helps that I'm so new here."

Rowan shrugged. "If it's meant to be, they'll see you're the right candidate, and you'll get it. If not, not."

Carolann sipped her tea. Rowan had a refreshing way of assuming a divine structure was at work supporting all the events predestined to happen. "I wanted to be more involved in Chip's school, but maybe he really doesn't need me there every day." Carolann hardly recognized herself, with her new flexibility and open-mindedness.

Rowan said, "You know, if I can't do our clambake next

weekend, it's going to be November, and I'll throw you a Thanksgiving party."

"You might postpone again? You know this thing really isn't necessary."

"No, it's happening Saturday. I do love Thanksgiving though."

Carolann thought Rowan looked expectant, perhaps hinting that she'd like to be invited to the Coopers' Thanksgiving dinner. "I'm afraid we don't do Thanksgiving."

"What kind of Americans are you, not doing Thanksgiving?"

"We ruined it. It would take too long to tell you the story."

"Nope, I'm staying." Rowan laughed and settled into her chair. "I assume this is a crazy tale you have never told a soul."

Carolann smiled. "Everyone already knows this one. But you're right. We certainly don't talk about it."

Rowan slapped the watch on her wrist. "I've got time."

"My sister had just had her baby." Carolann took a sip of tea. She hated to talk about him. That was a separate story, one she wasn't ever telling, but he did play a role in this one.

"Ryan," Rowan said.

"Yes. He was early. But Maryann still wanted to host Thanksgiving. He was barely out of the hospital. I'd hardly even met him. But that's beside the point."

"Go on." Rowan helped herself to another biscuit. It crumbled down her chest as she bit it.

"I'd been assigned the pie."

"Pumpkin," Rowan interrupted. "I love it."

"Yes, and pecan. We always did both."

"Did?" Rowan held her biscuit up mid-air. "You're serious about this. Thanksgiving in your family is past-tense?"

Carolann nodded. "Buck's mom was doing green bean casserole."

"With the cream of mushroom soup and the little fried onion things?" Rowan hugged herself.

"That's the one. You want me to just tell you the food?"

"Yes! No."

Carolann continued, "Chip was three. He was in his best little sweater, Lyn had one just like it from JC Penney. I don't know why, but that year I was really looking forward to it. Lyn drove us there, and I had one warm pie on the floor, between my feet, and one warm pie on my lap. Even through my coat, I felt that pie." Carolann shook her head. "Everything felt good."

"But then..." Rowan looked at Carolann carefully. "It wasn't all good."

Carolann shook her head. She had stared out the car window with the warm pies, looking forward to seeing her sister's baby. It brought her right back to her son's first days, when he was so tiny and tender, and she was equally fragile. She'd almost closed herself off from the split-second memories of Chip's earliest days, when Lyn revealed things she didn't want to hear, things about his childhood and his father's suicide, that he revealed to her in exchange for the flawless son she'd given him. But now those memories were left in Carolann's mind, not full words, not visual images, just tiny smudges, like shadows of white chalk on a blackboard. When Lyn told her about his parents, about finding his father's body, he transferred the burden of carrying the memories to her. And now that baby Ryan was born, another birth, another baby, she was forced to realize the chalky shadow words of Lyn's memories would not wipe away.

The beige and taupe ranch houses zipped by one by one, in Southern Kansas City. She only lived 20 minutes north of her sister, on the Missouri side, another end of the same city, but the geography was divided by a lot more than State Line Road. Way out south was a different world, where people picked out their perfect houses from a catalog, and had all new furniture that matched.

"Anyway," she said to Rowan. "My sister's house was in a planned community. White plantation shutters in the downstairs windows. Every house had hedges and two skinny trees out front, you know, with wire supports and rubber collars. And Maryann had a pearl blue Ford Probe at the time. And it was there, next to Buck's black Bronco. He was running a pretty successful car dealership – his father's business, and their cars were pristine. And my dad's Oldsmobile was already there, slotted into place, leaving the one spot for us."

Rowan nodded, apparently picturing the scene. Carolann liked the structure of those cars, the American-made solidity of the four cars seemed trustworthy and right. She went on, "And the warm engine of my parents' car was ticking and settling quietly, and I carried those pies, thinking my parent's car would still hold the smell of the dish my mother had brought. Yams, I think. And then Buck opened the door wide, and shook hands with Lyn, everybody pretending there had never been anything awkward."

"Why would it be awkward?" Rowan asked.

"Oh," Carolann shook her head quickly. "Uh, we've just never related to one another, somehow." Carolann shrugged. "As couples." It was what she sometimes said, when pressed, to her nurse friends back home.

Maryann took our coats and shooed me back downstairs when I said I wanted to come up to see the baby. Of course, Chip wanted to see his little cousin too, but she sent him back downstairs with me. Chip was adorable back then. He kept wanting to help Buck pour the cocktails. 'Help Uncle Buckle?' I think they'd been practicing pouring at pre-school."

"Uncle Buckle." Rowan smiled.

"So everyone was drinking, you know, like we do. Kim Roberts was a couple years into widowhood at that point, so we kept her glass filled, and we were all careful what we said.

But she was fine. My dad was cranky, as usual. He can't stand that we thank the Indians, 'the gol darn Injins' for the lessons on survival. Every meal in his book is thanks to God. Which is ironic, since I'm pretty sure at heart he's an atheist."

"Well, that's what I loved about Thanksgiving when I lived in Texas," Rowan interrupted. "It's a beautiful sentiment, being thankful, but it's not religious, so no one's excluded. I love Americans." She sighed, and folded her chubby hands together and rested them on her tummy.

"Actually, that was the night we told them we'd put in for foreign assignment." Carolann looked at the ceiling. "I'd forgotten that. We thought it might be Australia. And Maryann said to Lyn, 'She'll never go. You barely got Carolann to Europe for your honeymoon.'"

"Well, you showed her," Rowan laughed.

"They accused me of ducking out of future babysitting assignments." Carolann stared into the dregs of her tea. It really was not an amusing story to tell. And why were all the details pouring out of her mouth, unstoppable?

"And my mother said Lyn and I were the ones with medical connections, and we couldn't leave. Of course my dad was more practical. You go where a job takes you. Money's money.

But there we were eating our turkey and mashed potatoes, the baby upstairs, Chip in his little sweater, using a knife and fork and a plastic cup, and there was a sudden commotion out front.

Buck said to ignore it. Grunting noises. I thought it was an animal. And my dad was going on about gluttony and Buck's mom yelling at him to pipe down, and –"

Rowan interrupted. "Your husband married into crazy people. He really is a saint."

Carolann nodded. "Anyway, it was a girl, yelling to the whole perfect taupe and tan neighborhood: 'Buck Roberts is a TURKEY!'"

"So your sister ran outside and slugged her? I do love this image I have in my mind of your twin sister."

"No, she sent Buck, and she flipped her shutters open, so we saw the whole thing. The girl had a teeny tiny mini skirt and cowboy boots – no tights or anything, and she was heaving toilet paper rolls into the two skinny trees with the wire stays. And Kim Roberts said, 'Not another one,' like this was something that happened all the time. Girls who worked for Buck."

"Buck the newly married new daddy," Rowan said.

"Then the front door burst open, all this cold air, and the girl marched past the dining room like she knew where she was going, and went straight to the powder room. Buck followed her and she burst out of there, straight past him to us. She stopped and her jacket bulged open, and you could see everything through the white fabric of her shirt. Lyn's seat was right in front of her. He probably saw her internal organs."

Rowan laughed.

Carolann continued. "She introduced herself, like this was perfectly normal during a family Thanksgiving. 'I'm Judy. Receptionist. I'm sure you heard of me.' And my sister was yelling at her for tracking in mud and then she was there, barefoot, holding her cowboy boots in her hand, and her pale feet were mottled with blue. And to look at them made me hear the electric turkey carver, even though I knew no one else did. (Now that, I've never told anyone). But she had metallic burgundy nail polish on her naked toes, and it made me think she looked young and cold and unmothered."

"Had Maryann heard of her?" Rowan looked confused.

"No. But I'm sure she won't forget her. Or her announcement that Buck had given her an STD, which he then claimed was a 'salary till diem,' or money he owed her."

"Uncle Buckle was in big trouble." Rowan shook her head. "But quick with his Latin."

"Fake Latin." Carolann agreed. "But he promised to pay this girl, this Judy, her back-pay, and Maryann bought it, or pretended to, even though it was pretty clear what we were all witnessing."

"No one pushed him?" Rowan sat wide-eyed. "That's disappointing. Still, your life is better than the telly."

Carolann shook her head. "Once someone makes a stand, and it's his or her thing to deal with, we all follow along, like a pact. He said back-pay, and Maryann said, ok, so we all said ok."

Rowan took another biscuit and broke it in half. "I think this needs butter." She ate it. "So why did Thanksgiving take the hit?"

"Well, then Buck made the mistake of calling the girl Jody. And she screamed, 'Judy! Judy! Judy!' and finally stormed off. For some reason, Maryann turned on me, calling me Mrs. Perfect."

Rowan swallowed her hard biscuit.

"And then she turned on Buck, with a 'Jody, Judy, Trudie' sing-song. At which point Chip joined in with a song he knew. 'Bare naked nudie!'"

He was singing and banging his plastic cup on the table. That was our bath-time song. His naked butt on show, he'd go running down the hall singing 'bare naked nudie.' He'd probably hate my telling this story now."

Rowan smiled.

"It went on, 'bare naked nudie Judy!' Buck's mom was laughing like a goon. She was in her cups at that point. 'Nudie Judy,' Buck was at it too. And they were mocking her clothes and her boots, and then Lyn tried to tell everyone I had the same boots when I was slutty, which Maryann thought was a bad joke, because I was always a puritan and afraid to take any kind of chance."

"Your husband Lyn? When you were what?"

"It's an old tease he finds humorous."

"Oh my."

"But then my father, who never finds anything funny, threw his napkin on the table and stood up. He pronounced Thanksgiving an appalling waste of food, and we weren't doing it anymore. None of us. And we haven't."

The two women sat quietly for just a moment.

"My sister travels to a beach every year to avoid it. Usually Florida."

"With their son. That's nice for a family."

Carolann stared at Rowan. She said nothing.

"Well, let's hope I get this clambake organized. I wouldn't want to tempt fate, trying to force Thanksgiving on you." Rowan picked up Carolann's teacup with her own and brought them both to the sink. "For a family with no divorce or abuse issues, you all are still wildly dysfunctional."

"I'm afraid so." Carolann saw pearl. White, blue-gray, palest pink swirls. As she watched Rowan leave, she felt drained and also, strangely renewed.

Chapter 29

By Thursday morning, Lyn had spent a week encouraging his wife to accept his thinking about the debate tournament, and eventually, she did. Her slippery thumbtack brown had given way to blue. As they waiting for the bus, she handed Chip his overnight bag, its contents carefully checked, and when the bus arrived, she hugged him tight.

"Wish me luck." Chip pulled away from his mother.

"Knock 'em dead," Lyn called after him.

Carolann watched the bus pull away. "It feels like the first day, the first time he went to school on a bus."

"He's been away before." Lyn folded the newspaper and slotted it into his shoulder bag.

"Not where he had to bring a passport," she said. "But you're right. It's good for him. And good for us." She smiled.

"And you know what else is good for us on our 15th anniversary?" Lyn asked. "Dinner at the Good Earth. We haven't had a night out, just the two of us."

Carolann nodded. She hadn't been in to that place, even though it had a bar in the front. But she had reviewed the menu from the street. Pan Asian cuisine, and they served sake. She'd always wanted to try it. "Perfect."

Lyn added, "Then after dinner I thought we might have a couple friends over to celebrate."

Carolann knew his old joke, his code words for something else entirely, but somehow it seemed fresh… perhaps not his tease after all. Maybe he wanted to invite Rowan. In either case, her required response would be the same. "Oh? Which friends?"

Lyn smiled. It was the tease. Of course it was. In England, same as back home, they really didn't socialize with other people. "Jack and Coke." He laughed.

Her heart ached for Lyn, but she laughed, as usual. "Of course."

Lyn slid his hand inside his wife's bathrobe to hold her tight for a moment. Then just as quickly, he released her, kissed her cheek, and left for work.

Chapter 30

Thursday afternoon, Chip would have to leave his last class of the day early for the debate team trip, but his World Biology teacher, Mrs. Harding, had to leave even earlier. The Japanese translator was only available then for an essential parent-teacher conference. Mrs. Harding apologized and released the class soon after she'd taken roll. Did she really believe her students were disappointed and deserved an apology? Maybe teachers made a pact to uphold the pretence.

Anyway, Chip didn't mind the extra time to get ready. He was excited to go to Switzerland, but his confidence on the debate topic was wavering – and he was still in shock that his parents had agreed to let him go.

He had to bring all his weekend homework with him, along with his overnight bag. The cargo on his back, he marched toward the busses. The blue airport bus was parked near the administration building, past the regular white busses already awaiting their passengers, including the white bus that would drive past his house without him. His mother would probably watch it pass.

He was excited about his trip and sad about his empty white bus, and not sure whether India already had uranium. Normal classes had not let out yet, and Chip was grateful for the momentary solitude.

Out of nowhere, Ticia bounced up and pulled her backpack from her shoulder. "You are a lucky dog, you know that?"

"Why aren't you in class?"

"Admin Thursday afternoons. I run errands for my dad's office, among other things. Sometimes I get to study if it's not busy. And today it's not busy. Homes, you knew this. Keep up."

Chip nodded. "Hey, if a relatively stable country has access to another country's enriched uranium, do you think they would be more or less responsible with it than if they manufactured it themselves?"

"Don't know, don't care." She laughed. She leaned next to Chip and spoke into his shoulder. "I was thinking about you last night."

"Oh?" Of course, he'd been thinking about her too. Maybe if he'd invite her to meet his parents, some of the inappropriate stuff he'd been thinking would get out of his head.

"So my question is, how can you rag on my language, when you love rap?"

"That's what you were thinking last night?" He rolled his eyes. "Rap is satire, but your language is a reflection of you."

"It's youth culture," she said. "Everybody swears."

He shook his head. "You devalue yourself."

"Andrew says it's a language minority thing," she said. "Ask any American who's lived in Europe. Everyone turns trash-mouth. You'll figure this out in Switzerland."

Chip shrugged. "Your boyfriend lives in Austria where English is a minority." He pronounced *boyfriend* like a new strain of the Ebola virus. "In Switzerland, they have four national languages, and English isn't one of them. Whereas last I checked, people speak English here in England. If they need to swear over there to create some sort of false community, so be it. We don't need that here." He looked down his nose at her.

"Still," she swatted his shoulder. "Eminem is all *motherfucking, suck my dick without a condom on.*"

Chip smiled. Of course he should invite her to Rowan's party. And Maarten and Henrik and his parents. They'd talk politics and God, and everyone would get along.

"He really does drugs, too. It's not satire." Ticia looked at him, her eyes clear and blue in the chilly afternoon. "What if people like that message? Drugs are fun."

"They'll overdose, and the world will have fewer idiots," Chip said.

"Mr. Black-and-white," she said. "I can't wait for the first time you fuck up."

"Who says I will?"

"Neame." She laughed and tucked her hair behind her ear. "Remember?"

Chip nodded. Teachers filed out of the Early Childhood Center, children trailing behind like ducklings, bags and umbrellas hanging from them. Their biggest challenge would be remembering their clip-on mittens. Now teachers made veiled threats and back-handed compliments, and people asked for what they didn't want and apologized when they weren't sorry. And people lied in the name of truth and they cheated to honor something decent. Chip sighed like an old man. Probably no new country should have any nuclear energy.

"Shit, I almost forgot." Ticia pulled a large envelope from her backpack. It looked like the Eminem envelope. "Tough call here, but I want to give this to you now. Take it with you. I trust you."

Chip's heart skipped at beat. "Another autograph?"

"Yeah, I'm lining them all up. Will Smith, Kurtis Blow, Doug E. Fresh. The Sugarhill Gang…" She grabbed his shoulder. "I'm kidding." She pulled him downward, unzipped his bag, and wedged the envelope between his books. "I need your opinion. Just don't open it in public. I don't want this out in the digital world. Safer to send it with you to Switzerland in an envelope. You have to tell me what you think, asap." She stood and gave his arm a squeeze. "Rated R."

Her fingertips felt electric – small but powerful, they

zapped him through his sweatshirt. Little Chicana stun gun.

"Hey, our neighbor's having a thing Saturday. Day after tomorrow. You want to come?" Chip asked suddenly. His timing was terrible, but as his father always said, opportunities come when they come.

"Yes. I can get this back then, I guess. I can't wait to meet your mom."

"My parents will love you." Chip's swallowed.

"Dude, sometimes they don't. Too many earrings." She lifted the black hair above her ear. "Not to mention the tattoo on my ass."

A driver opened the blue debate team bus in the distance.

"I have to go." Chip imagined a snake wound around one side of Ticia's naked bottom.

"You want to know what it is, don't you?" She teased.

"No, I want to know that you'll behave yourself with my parents. I really have to go."

"Go on, use your imagination, sweetie-pie," She laughed. "Unless you're worried about invading my privacy."

"The thing might not happen anyway," Chip said. "It's already been rescheduled a hundred times."

Debate team members started putting luggage into the under-bus storage compartments.

"Now, don't fucking lose this thing." She patted Chip's backpack. "Rated R, and you don't even blink. I love that about you. Your lines don't blur. It's why I need your opinion – call me the minute you open it. Can you call me from Switzerland?"

"Ticia." Chip shook his head. "I'm thinking about enriched uranium."

She grabbed his hand. "No one's got backbone like you, homes. You're going to blow that debate out of the water. And I actually believe you… You're going to pioneer a whole new genre in music. No swearing, Happy Rap."

Chip jogged toward the bus and called back to her. "Crap."

Chapter 31

Carolann had already cleaned the kitchen after dinner, and she'd re-organized the coffee mugs. She couldn't help watching the quiet street for Chip's return. "We should have gone to the airport to meet the flight. In America, that's what we would have done."

"Would you come away from that window," Lyn said. "If the flight was delayed, we'd have had a call."

The sky-blue echo of Lyn's voice filled the room, and Carolann was grateful.

She saw headlights swing their beams down her street, and a bus finally delivered their son.

"Did you kick butt over there?" Lyn took Chip's bags from him.

"Tell me everything." Carolann hugged Chip, not yet fully in the house. "The debate, the people you stayed with, what did they feed you? Did you have fondue?"

Chip shook his head. "I didn't even get to debate." He ran his words together, a tired, moody mumble teenagers employed when they wanted to be left alone.

"They didn't need their alternate?" Lyn said. "That's too bad."

"Yeah, it was still a good experience, I guess. They asked me to write the newsletter article about it, so that's cool, at least."

"What was the family like? Where were they from?"

"I don't know, East Coast somewhere. Pennsylvania? They

were alright."

Eager for more details, Carolann led Chip into the sitting room. "Do you want something to eat? Are you thirsty?"

"I ate on the plane. Maybe I'll have some water and head upstairs." Chip yawned.

Carolann watched him carefully. His yawn seemed dramatized. Was he anxious to get upstairs because he didn't want to talk about something that happened?

Lyn went to the kitchen and poured Chip a glass of water.

"Did they have kids your age, this family?"

"No, they had a little adopted Chinese girl. She was pretty cute. And an older son who's already in college, so I had his room."

"And what about the other boy from here? Did you both sleep in the same room?"

"No, he had the guest room. Their house was pretty big. They had a bomb shelter. All the Swiss houses have them." Chip punctuated each of his sentences with sips of water in between. "If you don't mind, I'm going up to bed." He stood.

"Can I read the article you wrote?" Carolann asked.

"Yeah, when it's done."

"We'll hear all about it tomorrow," Lyn said. "I've got to hit the road early for the West Country hospitals thing, and then I'll need to stop in the office."

Chip nodded. "Is Rowan's thing tomorrow night? I kind-of invited my friend Ticia. Mom, you said it was ok, right?"

"Well, I... uh..."

"Go on up," Lyn said. "We'll need you sharp and sociable for that clambake. It will be great to meet your friend."

Chip stepped over his bags in the entryway and went straight upstairs. Carolann listened for noises from his bedroom, the squeak of his desk chair or footsteps, but she heard nothing. He must have truly been tired. Soon after, Lyn stood to follow Chip upstairs.

"You think he's ok?" Carolann asked.

"He's fine. If he's not, we'll find out soon enough."

Soon enough? If something was wrong, right-this-second wouldn't be soon enough. "I'll be up in a few minutes," she said. "I'll get his laundry sorted out." She grabbed Chip's overnight bag.

"Listen, I don't know how long I'll be tomorrow, but I promise I won't be late for the clambake party." Lyn disappeared upstairs.

Among the clothing in Chip's bag, Carolann found a large envelope. It probably held his notes from the weekend. Maybe there had been hand-outs or paperwork about the host family. He could have been anywhere. Lyn was foolish to sign that permission slip so fast, even if his reasons, carefully outlined after he'd signed it, had made sense. Now Carolann might learn more from Chip's notes even than from the finished article he planned to write. She pulled the envelope out of his bag.

Chip had been so quiet, so unlike himself, coming home from this overnight trip, Carolann felt obliged to invade his privacy. As his mother, she didn't have a choice *not* to read his notes. Having a teenage boy upset every balance. He was no longer a child, with no rights to privacy, and nothing private to protect. But he was not yet mature. He still required certain standards of parenting, now more than ever, if he was beginning to encounter bigger questions. And where the balance lay had to be determined by Lyn and Carolann, not by Chip. She knew she should look through his things, but she couldn't help feeling on edge, and ashamed of her eagerness to do so.

The night before, at their anniversary dinner, she'd drunk three tiny cups of warm sake and felt oozy and a wonderful color of metallic gold-flecked-teal before Lyn took her home and made love to her after dinner. The color smelled like the richest of coffee beans, oily and fresh, and it excluded all others. She hardly had to exaggerate her tipsiness. He was right when he'd said it had been too long.

Lyn was right about most things – but what if his decision to let Chip go to Switzerland had been wrong? Now it would be two nights in a row, with a real drink. She just couldn't open Chip's things without it. Carolann poured lemonade into a glass of Jack, and sat down with his envelope.

Of course, it wasn't lemonade. It was carbonated and clear, not lemonade at all, despite the English label claiming it was. Why couldn't even the simplest things from her life back home and her new life abroad just match up? She didn't know what she expected to read about Chip's overnight, or what she hoped not to read. Had there been alcohol? Had there been another sister in that family? A girl his own age, who snuck into his bedroom at midnight? Were kids doing things after the debate that Chip didn't want to do? If so, of course, she wouldn't find notes describing that. She needed to call the school on Monday to see where her job application stood.

Maybe the school had called her references. Anyway, her record was clean. They wanted someone to organize substance abuse workshops and administer the meningitis shot. Carolann was good at giving shots. She told children the truth – it would hurt, but only for a second. She told a little joke so the child relaxed, and then she just got the job done. She always said "ouch" when she pushed in the needle, and sometimes that took the "ouch" away from the patient. Sometimes, the child even laughed.

She sipped her drink. Now too, she needed to just get this job done.

She unwound a loop of string from a paper closure tab on the yellow envelope, her nimble fingers and burgundy nails making quick work of it. Her diamond flashed at her, and she could see the veins in her hands, like her mother's, like her grandmother's. She felt glossy paper inside, more like photographs than loose paper. It probably wasn't Chip's notes. Carolann hesitated and then slid the papers back into the envelope, and wound the string back. She took another sip of her drink. A small piece of paper fluttered to the floor between her feet, and she retrieved it.

"*Which one wins?*" the paper asked. The writing was tiny, but its loops looked like a girl's, flirtatious. It went on, each word getting smaller and smaller. "*Which one grabs you by the nuts, makes you hard, makes you love me forever?*"

Carolann felt a cold sheet of slate gray define the space around her. She would need a magnifying glass to read to the end. She desperately didn't want to read to the end, but now she had to. It was completely quiet upstairs. *Which one makes you think aisle, altar, have my baby? Which one makes you think about me, miss me, call me every night?*" Carolann grabbed her cocktail. "*You know what I want here, Chip. It was your idea in the first place, so which one?*" It was signed with a tiny "T" and a microscopic heart. Oh my.

Carolann downed her drink. His idea? But she'd been vigilant. And Lyn thought Chip wouldn't be "of age," and ready for his special gift, till his 16th birthday. For half a second, Carolann pictured Lyn as a boy about Chip's age, hearing the sound of a shotgun, finding his father behind the garden shed. She couldn't step into that memory, vivid as the story was. She couldn't question Lyn's need to tell Chip what he wanted to tell him.

But she could find out what was going on with this girl. She had to. She opened Chip's envelope again and slid the photos out of the package.

Chapter 32

Carolann rolled over in bed and winced. Light filled the room, and her senses sharpened one by one. Lyn must have opened the blinds before he left, when it was still dark. She checked the clock. If she didn't hear Chip get up on his own, she'd put on her robe and wake him in 12 minutes. Nine o'clock was late enough to sleep on a Saturday.

Her stomach felt stable and her head did not throb like it would have if she'd gone back to the bottle after she looked at those pictures. But still, she was sick. That girl would be coming to Rowan's party. If Carolann had drowned herself in bourbon the night before, who could have blamed her?

But guilty-parent drinking never solved anything, and Carolann knew Lyn was already asleep when she'd been downstairs with the pictures, so she had replaced the photos in Chip's envelope and put the bottle away, deciding she'd just keep the discovery to herself. It wasn't the first time she'd had to keep something to herself.

A surprising English sun pierced the morning air at a penetrating angle. It entered her skull through her eyes. It was a rare morning in England that she awakened to bright sunshine. She forced her eyelids open to take in the harsh, too happy, light.

If her eyes hurt, then maybe her head wouldn't. The blue sky did not hurt. The yellow-green and orange leaves and the ripening conkers in the tall tree outside her window did not hurt. There was still no noise coming from Chip's room. She had made her decision, but it could still be reversed. Maybe she should say something to Chip? Or was this a father-son topic, and once she'd tell Lyn, she'd get a free pass. But what if Lyn didn't like it that she'd snooped? No, the original decision had to stand. Somehow, she'd deal with the girl on her own.

She heard Chip get in the shower. When Maryann was training to be a teacher, before she'd quit school and had her baby, she told Carolann to time a boy's showers to know when he'd become interested in girls. When they suddenly take a long time, there's a girl. Half an hour alone, under running water. *Wink, wink.* At the time, Chip had been a little boy, and Carolann didn't want her sister *wink-winking* about him. Now, with those photos in her head, she glanced at the clock. Chip's showers normally lasted eight minutes.

She slid out of bed and pulled on her bathrobe. It was such a pretty day, all that unexpected English sunshine. She would mix raisins in Chip's oatmeal. Later, she'd put on a brave face and her favorite Carolann suit, so she'd really look like herself, even if she didn't quite feel it, and she'd walk to the garden shop. Or she'd take Chip to the Waitrose and they'd get flowers for Rowan's party. She brushed her teeth and looked again at her watch. Chip should turn off the shower water in three minutes.

Maybe the sunshine's volume and brightness were turned up too high, after all. Because it was so rare, the October morning sun seemed to be trying too hard – overacting for its bit part in a play. Carolann listened to the water rush through the pipes of her rented house. She too was on stage, playing oatmeal-and-raisins Super-mom.

What she truly felt like wearing was an old sweatshirt of Lyn's so she could blend in to the day. And she wished Lyn would come home, and she could put dinner on the table like normal, fresh lipstick on her mouth, and she'd pretend she knew nothing of the girl. Going to Rowan's party with her was going to be awful. One of the photos was topless!

With a lurching stop in the pipes, Chip's shower ended. Eight minutes, exactly. Carolann could handle Ticia.

"Oatmeal sound good for breakfast?" she called.

"Great." His hair still damp, Chip followed his mother downstairs.

Carolann neared the bottom step and gasped. The envelope was on the table with the mail, and Chip was mere steps behind her. She had to slip it into his backpack somehow. She quickly put a magazine on top of the envelope, turned around with a smile on her face and gave Chip a hug.

"You know, even if you didn't get to debate, I'm proud of you for going. Like Dad said, it's an honor you were asked."

He was still on the stairs, one above her, so she hugged her face into his chest, like a little girl with her grandpa. For just a second, she melted into him, drawing comfort from his young teenage boy innocent strength. He smelled like shampoo.

"You're in a good mood today." Chip laughed.

"I found raisins in the baking section."

"Excellent. Next you'll find American peanut butter and Macaroni and Cheese, and you'll never want to move back."

"Velveeta. Colby-Jack. Sugar Free Jello. And Graham Crackers, Nilla Wafers and Advil, and Rolaids and Triaminic and Wheat Thins." Carolann smiled. "Find me all those, and maybe we'll talk."

"Learn to drive more on the wrong side like Dad can, and then decide," Chip said. "Americans are supposed to be adaptable. You found raisins."

Carolann put the milk on the stove, and Chip turned on the morning news. Maybe while he was eating his breakfast, she could dash upstairs with his envelope and get it into his backpack. She hated having to be so deceptive. It was England's fault that she was forced to behave this way. Moving back had to be better than England. Although, that girl in the photos, that awful Ticia, was American. A girl like that could

be anywhere. A girl like Ticia could be in Kansas. She could
be in the Heart of America Church of God. (Of course, if you
listened to Lyn, and to the dark thoughts in Carolann's head,
Carolann herself might have once been that kind of girl). In
any case, she would never feel at home in England, but now
she wasn't sure she trusted her old home either. After she
served Chip his breakfast, Carolann excused herself. She had
things to do, and more than anything, she needed to get back
in bed.

Chapter 33

After the Westcountry Hospitals morning meeting in Bristol, Lyn drove the two hours straight back to Surrey. He had just enough time to stop by the house for a clean shirt. If he was going to speak to hospital administrators about cleaning up their acts, he should at least wear a pressed shirt, even on a Saturday. *Perception of truth becomes true in its consequences.* If he went in sloppy, he could show all the data, speak articulately, and deliver a compelling lecture, but the old school Brits would still never trust Lyn's expertise on his subject, the visual experience of the hospital as a crucial factor in the patient's healing. The patient's confidence in the hospital was paramount. Lyn would deliver this line clearly and carefully, but the administrators' confidence in his speech was also paramount, and a clean, pressed shirt was essential.

On the other hand, he couldn't look slick or too coiffed or tailored or rich or too American. He already had the too straight teeth of a prep school boy, and a certain unavoidable swagger. His accent only confirmed what these guys thought they already knew. No meeting went smoothly. No day was easy.

He knew better than many guys what he was up against. He had been in hospitals since he was a child, personally and professionally, and he knew how important his message was, especially in a country with a wonderful health care system that was nonetheless missing the mark of its potential by a mile. That's what the British government and his large multinational pharmaceutical company were paying him for, to help the NHS clean up its act. Lyn pulled into his driveway, fully intending, yet again, to deliver.

The house was quiet. Chip's coat was gone, so he must have gone to the shops. Carolann's car was in the driveway, as usual, and Lyn found that she had gone back to bed. He tiptoed into their bedroom for his shirt. He kissed his wife's forehead to see if she felt feverish, and she stirred but did not wake up. She felt warm, but not hot. Chip seemed to be doing well, but so far, the move to England had not been easy for Carolann.

Lyn quietly washed his face, changed his shirt and made his way back downstairs. Before his second meeting of the day, he would grab a bite to eat near his office, and read through the morning paper, or a new magazine. He quickly sorted the bills from the other mail in the entryway, grabbed the magazines, and stuffed them into his briefcase. As soon as he could enjoy a cup of coffee and a brief respite from the business of healthcare, he would put his feet up on his desk and really get down to business.

Chapter 34

"I can't find it." Chip stood over his open backpack, the phone to his ear. The last thing he'd wanted, after seeing Ticia's photos, was to keep them any longer than he had to. "Maybe they got confiscated at customs or something."

"You better find them, homes." Ticia's voice was cold.

"I didn't even look at them till the last debate was happening, right before we were leaving." He thought back to the few minutes he'd spent in the Swiss school's boys' room, looking at her pictures, and then the five more minutes he gave himself in the school's hallway before returning to the debate room. He would tell her to use the one with the hat.

A strangely-bright afternoon sun angled through the window at the end of the Swiss school's corridor, warmer somehow than the sun in England, illuminating languidly-moving dust motes. Even in stillness, even in silence, Chip thought, there was chaos and commotion in the very foundation of a school. He would have liked to write some lyrics about this rarely-visible movement, an inaudible racket. Somehow, he would filter seeing Ticia's pictures through those dust-motes, as a metaphor. A group of students walked by the lockers, and he quickly returned to the debate.

"Did you hate them?"

"No. God, no. Maybe you could have been a little more subtle, but no." Chip couldn't help but smile. Maybe the envelope was in his overnight bag, still downstairs. "I'll find it."

"You could have made photocopies, if you wanted them yourself. Those glossy prints are for Andrew. And I wanted to send the package to him asap."

Chip said, "If your relationship with marvelous Andrew is that fragile, you can't wait one extra day, maybe you ought to just call it quits and save yourself the postage." He wanted to say she should also save her dignity and not send the topless shot, but he had to admit, that might serve her purpose best. For any teenage boy, it was hard not to react to topless.

"Why? So I could go out with you?"

"No, thank you," Chip said. Right now, he did not want to go out with her.

"Do you still want me to come to your thing tonight?"

"Yeah."

"I don't know." Ticia was quiet for a second. "I feel like I don't know anything. He said he loved me. And love is forever, right? Across time, across distance. Always. What am I doing wrong?"

"Nothing." Chip would have hugged her, if she'd been standing there. "Maybe it's not you. But you're like…" he stopped to compose his thoughts, but they were complicated. "You're like, you're like…"

"Dude." Ticia banged her receiver onto a surface. "Broken record." She was back to her usual self. "You're skipping."

"Ok. It's like you're fictional," Chip said. "Like I made you up. You can only be defined in my head. I predict what you'll say about something, and then it turns out I'm totally wrong. Your opinions, stuff you'll say and do, it's like, not what I'd expect. Totally out of character. And it can even change mid-stream. It's like –"

"A let-down." Ticia said. "Big fat disappointment. Homes, I get that. It's probably what Andrew's thinking, if he's thinking about me at all, the fucker. You want me to be what you want me to be. But then I'm not. I'm –"

"Not a let-down, it's the opposite. You're the coolest girl I ever met," Chip interrupted. It was out. He'd given her an *est*. A superlative. "Despite your foul mouth."

"Seriously?"

"Yes."

"Fuck, yeah," she laughed. "Find those pictures, homeboy. I'll be there tonight."

Chapter 35

Chip's father held Ticia's envelope against his chest as he walked into his son's bedroom.

Chip took a deep breath. "It's not what you think."

Without turning, Lyn kicked his heel against the door and slammed it shut. Chip's heart leapt toward his throat. They had one hour before Rowan's party. She would be heading out the door any minute. He had to call and tell her not to come.

"You presume to know what I think?" Lyn slammed the envelope onto Chip's desk.

"No, sir."

"Ok, then. Number one, I think this is Patricia. Tricia. Correct?"

"Ticia. Yes, sir."

"Ok, check mark for Dad on point number one." His voice seethed with sarcasm. "Shall we continue?"

"But nothing's happening with her," Chip said. "I didn't take those pictures. They weren't even meant for me."

"They were here in our house, Chip, so they were meant for you. In fact, they were with our mail, which I took to the office. Fortunately."

"Oh." Chip's voice squeaked. "So Mom didn't see them?"

"I don't believe so. She would be devastated to think you're involved with a girl like this." Lyn stared at his son. "Do you want to hurt your mother?"

"No, we're not involved. Not like that. I'd never...I

couldn't… I wasn't thinking." Chip clasped his hands together in his lap. His desk chair suddenly felt huge. He had shrunk, like Alice in Wonderland. Ticia had feared he'd dropped the envelope at that Swiss school. This was worse. Chip's eyes welled up with the frustration.

"Look, she seems fine, and you know your mother. She hides nothing. If she'd seen these pictures, we'd know."

"But why were they in the mail?" Chip's voice caught. "You're not going to tell Mom?"

"No. It's as much her business as it is mine, but in this particular case, no. Now level with me. What's the story with this girl?"

"No story. She's my friend." Chip pointed at the envelope "And this isn't even how she is."

Lyn put his hand flat on the envelope and pumped his knuckles up and down on it, like he was debating opening it. "You hang out with a girl like that, you better be prepared to assume the consequences. You like this girl that much?"

"That's not how it is. She's a good friend."

"It can go from fun to serious, like that." Lyn snapped his fingers. He lifted the envelope off the desk and unwound the string closure. He slid the photos out. He glanced at her note, at its sloppiness, crumpled, smudged, and flattened. He pushed it aside. "Which one?" he said out loud.

Chip felt sick, like he had to protect Ticia, and protect his mother, and his father and himself, all from each other. He should never have tried to help Ticia with her Andrew problem. Look what he'd gotten himself into. His best advice would have been to quit Andrew in the first place. The guy lived in Vienna, what was she thinking?

Lyn examined the photo of Ticia in the hat, turned it to Chip, and then shifted it to the back of the stack to focus on the next photo. The topless one on the bed. Thank God you couldn't see everything, exactly, the way she was lying on her stomach, her back arched hard, so she could look up at the photographer who must have been straddling her to take the picture. It didn't show everything, but it showed curves. "Hmmm…" Lyn made a noise that Chip didn't dare decipher. "Quite an effective angle."

Chip cringed. How could he get his father to stop looking? A real man would stand up to his father, if necessary. Apparently, Chip wasn't a real man.

"She seems to have an artistic bent." Lyn snickered. "Emphasis on bent."

"Dad, could we not do this?" The third picture was the worst. Nothing showed, but the finger-and-tongue was horrible.

"Do what?" Lyn stared at his son. "You tell me. Can you control what you're doing? What you're interested in doing with this, this young lady?"

Chip had to call immediately and uninvite Ticia. She couldn't come because they'd all caught colds. Flu. Meningitis. Mad Cow, foot-and-mouth, SARS, malaria. Cholera, tetnus, typhoid. Infectious obsession with pornography featuring the uninvited guest. Bubonic plague.

"Son, it's like playing soccer with a…" Lyn stopped. Maybe the right metaphor had just escaped him. "…a defused land mine. Remember my hospital tour in Africa? The poor children I saw? Inevitably, those things blow your leg off."

Chip nodded. It wasn't a standard pick from Lyn's repertoire of aphorisms and what-ifs. Is stealing a piece of bread to feed your family still stealing? What's more important… the perception of truth or truth itself? *A tree falls in the forest and nobody's there to hear it…so who hears it first, the chicken or the egg?* Maybe, Chip thought, his dad didn't know all the answers, after all. Maybe sometimes, he didn't even know the right questions.

"She just needed some advice. This isn't really her."

"Judging from these pictures, maybe she doesn't even know the real 'her.' The prostitute-style earrings, that cute hat.

Her intentions are all over the place." Lyn continued, "Look, you choose a girl like that today, you better be prepared to spend your whole life with her. I'm not saying you wouldn't want to." He raised his eyebrows at the picture. "But girls like this are high risk, for-the-moment. Can you make that choice now, at age 14, to spend your life with this one girl, with only this one girl? What you do today impacts your tomorrow. I see these pictures and I have to question your understanding of consequences." Lyn raised his two stubby hands, palms up in alternating rhythm. "Cause. Effect. Cause. Effect."

"Ticia took the pictures for her boyfriend. I'm not... I've never even kissed a girl, Dad." Chip spluttered, "She's not interested in... They're not for me."

"Why not you?" Lyn stiffened. "Any girl would be lucky to be with you. Especially, a girl like this Patricia."

"Ticia, Tee-see-ya."

"See ya." Lyn saluted. "You ought to say that to her, while you still can. Before you get too involved."

"She's my friend." Chip shook his head. "And she's... I'm trying to help her get back on the right path. She's really a good person at heart."

Lyn squinted at his son. "I'm glad you know her heart, that you're not distracted by the outside image here. I'll look forward to meeting her tonight."

"Oh, no, I don't think she's coming after all." Chip searched papers on his desk for a good reason. "She might, uh, I think she has a thing."

Lyn nodded. He slid the photos back in the envelope and rubbed it in gentle circles. "Tough call, but my vote's the one with the hat."

Chapter 36

In Rowan's back garden, a dozen neighbors hovered around a wobbly buffet table of party appetizers. Chip didn't want to be there. He handed his father a Twiglet.

"Those smell fecal," Carolann whispered.

Chip shrugged.

"And be suspicious of pink packaging." She pointed to a bowl of prawn cocktail crisps. "The ingredients are all alpha-numeric chemicals. I read the label in the Waitrose. Now, where is your friend, Ticia? Is she often late?"

"She's not coming." Chip ate a pink crisp, and it dissolved on impact.

"Too bad." Lyn winked. "I would have liked to meet her."

Chip took a deep breath. He had told Ticia both his parents were sick, which wasn't entirely false. Since seeing those photos, his dad seemed a little sick in the head.

"The British diet." Lyn lowered his voice and held up a suet-colored ring of a highly-processed grain product. He wedged the ring onto the tip of his little finger and shook it – a child's pinky-swear. "Heart attack waiting to happen. "

"They boil or fry everything." Carolann made a face. "Watch the BBC. Bangers and mash, beans on toast. And what exactly is toad-in-a-hole?"

"Sausages in mashed potato. We have it in school. It's not bad." Chip said, "And bubble-and-squeak."

"People blame America's fast food for everything," Carolann said. "But I don't think Americans have a lock on obesity." She nodded toward Rowan and some other neighbors.

Lyn added, "That fish-and-chips shop down the road serves the food in greasy newspaper." He shook his head.

Between Lyn's concerns about hygiene and Carolann's obsession with fat, their conversation could go in an endless loop. Chip hoped the neighbors couldn't hear his family. Everyone but the Germans at school seemed to think Americans spoke too loudly.

"You know, if nutrition is a new focus in your lectures, I can help," Carolann said. "It *is* my area of expertise."

Chip raised his eyebrows at his father. His mother thought they needed a reminder of her expertise? Had accompanying Lyn on his foreign assignment made her nothing but luggage? Hadn't Carolann heard what Chip learned at school? She was now a *trailing spouse*. She had a definition in their expat community – which should help her feel settled, if not exactly "at home."

"I can't pick that battle here." Lyn shook his head.

"Why not here? Trans fats clog all arteries," she said. "British, Mexican, Vietnamese…"

Rowan stepped away from the canapés to join their conversation. "Chinese, Japanese, dirty knees, look at these!" She lifted her apron to reveal her trouser-legs and burst into laughter.

Chip and his parents stared at her, stupid smiles on their faces.

"Come." Rowan took Chip's arm. "Help me check the clam pit."

Lyn said, "I'll excuse myself for a moment." He crossed the garden toward Rowan's gate, presumably heading around the dividing hedge to the Coopers' home.

Chip watched him go, scanning Rowan's gate in case Ticia came to the party after all. His desperation split and followed two separate streams. He desperately did and desperately did not want Ticia to walk through that gate. Conflicting double desperation, he found, felt wildly more frantic than the desperation of single-mindeness. He had to focus. "Mom, you coming?" he asked abruptly.

Rowan led them through the neighbors to the far end of her garden. She lifted a corner of hot wet tarpaulin from the ground, releasing seaweed steam.

"Cool," Chip said. "A sandpit without a beach."

"Sunken bathtub." Rowan inhaled deeply. "Grab that stick."

Chip handed it to her, and she poked at the stones and lobsters nestled under the rockweed. Ticia had to see this bathtub thing – Chip wanted her there, after all. He could trust his father not to be weird.

"Nearly ready." Rowan dropped the tarp. Her fleshy arms and face went splotchy shades of pink. "You can show them how it's done back in Kansas. You have to get clams and seaweed flown in, of course."

If someone suggested "flying in" fancy foreign food to Chip's family in Kansas, there would be several heart attacks even before dinner was served. His Grandpa Cyrus would go first. With his dying breath, he'd insist on a trash bag in a cardboard box for his coffin, to counteract that foolish food expense.

Chip turned away from the clam pit and saw his dad jog through Rowan's back gate, with the reason he'd apparently gone home, a bottle of Jack Daniels, in his hand. Chip froze.

Rowan introduced some neighbors, Mr. and Mrs. Simon Fitzsimmons. Carolann conspicuously held up a crisp, poised her hand in the air and became fascinated with the couple's conversation. Chip knew his mother's strategy. She'd drop the crisp to the ground when no one was looking. His father had been stopped, bottle in hand, by another neighbor. Chip reached for a nearby hors d'oeuvres table and plucked up two beanie weenie sausages on toothpicks, with one hand, and ate them both at once.

"Lyn's a special consultant to the National Health Service," Carolann said to the Fitzsimmonses. "Health Care Marketing Management. He was brought in to right a few wrongs in the system."

The neighbors bristled, but Carolann didn't seem to notice. This wasn't how people reacted in Kansas. Lyn needed to walk across Rowan's back yard and take over the explanation of his job. Hopefully he'd somehow leave the bottle behind.

"He's an expert in the American profitability model."

Mrs. Fitzsimmons smiled politely and scuttled away. *Naked ambition* was the term Ticia had used in her Multicultural Studies paper. If an American lady bragged about her husband, had she stripped her husband down to nakedness?

"Perhaps you didn't realize I'm a doctor," Mr. Fitzsimmons said. "A surgeon. We like to use 'mister' instead of 'doctor.' Sort of a reverse snobbery." He chuckled.

"Then you know all about the system." Carolann ate the pink crisp and frowned. "So discouraging."

"I'm in private practice," the man nodded. "For my sins."

"I'm sure you appreciate how the NHS lacks some key features of the profitability model. It's understandable, really, after all the training a doctor goes through, med school, internship, residency, fellowships… and then some business person tells him *the customer's always right.* But the customer might be a feeble-minded high-school drop-out, with let's say, fibromyalgia. Plus, the British system of customer service is… well, I'm not sure the customer is ever right here." She smiled.

"More a necessary evil, the salesgirls might say." Mr. Fitzsimmons nodded. "I did some training in Los Angeles."

Carolann continued, "Lyn's teaching the doctors to recognize patients as customers. To invest in their practices, one patient, one prescription, at a time."

Chip scanned the crowd for his father. Lyn would say *GP*

instead of *doctor*. He'd say *surgery* instead of *practice*. And he surely wouldn't refer to patients as customers, even if that was the crucial point of his lectures.

"The American way does save lives," Carolann added. "Lyn started with asthma drugs, and now he runs Europe."

"I see."

Chip caught the man smile into his hand as he ate a handful of peanuts. He felt strangely conspiratorial.

"I think a blend of our cultures makes the most sense," Mr. Fitzsimmons said. "The NHS does offer something that's lacking in the U.S. Universal access."

Carolann stared at him. Two more neighbors stepped forward and were introduced. The conversation turned to their houses. Red bricks, pebbledash, stained glass, three-gable roof.

Chip saw Lyn near the gate, no longer chatting with neighbors. Now he was on his own, gripping the bottleneck of Carolann's favorite Tennessee whiskey, and two cocktail tumblers perched in his other palm. He opened the bottle.

Chip breathed in deeply, and despite the distance, he sensed the profound smell of the liquor. With a well-practiced arcing flourish, Lyn poured the amber fluid into two glasses he'd brought from home. He trapped the autumn afternoon sunlight in the crystal, loading the cup with golden history and significance, intense and reflective as a church window. As if his mother could smell the whiskey too and was lured by it, she turned.

She took a deep breath, over capacity, it seemed like her lungs needed to overfill before they'd register *enough*. She smiled at the neighbors. "Won't you please excuse us?"

Chip wondered if it was a respiratory equivalent of fat people eating till they were so full it hurt. His mother said many of her clients had that problem. Why did people's senses give them such messed up signals?

Carolann quickened her footsteps.

"I'm afraid you were right, Chip," Lyn said. "Message from Ticia said she can't make it." He held up the golden glass and turned to Carolann. "Your friend, Jack, my love, can."

If his mother was going to drink that stuff, Chip didn't want Ticia to come anyway.

Carolann took the drink. "Shouldn't we save this for after Rowan's party?"

Lyn shook his head and clinked his glass against his wife's. "Cheers."

Chip swallowed hard. It was too complicated, his father having seen those photos of Ticia, his mother in the dark. Chip felt like a human wedge, dividing his parents.

Suddenly, Lyn said, "Actually, maybe Ticia is coming. It was something about a ride, I think. Her cell phone cut off."

Carolann glugged a sip down, and she smiled like she was posing for a camera. "Maybe she didn't want to come."

Chip shriveled. One sip, and his mother had already begun to say things.

"She's lived here forever and must have many friends. What could you offer her? She's older than you." Carolann shrugged.

"Chip has a way with women, right, kiddo? With people." His father squeezed his shoulder.

Rowan joined them once again. "Look who I found. A princess in search of her knight in armor."

"Ticia!" Chip's voice cracked. His mother wasn't wrong about their age difference.

She smiled and curtsied. "A little trouble, but I made it. Long story."

"We'll enjoy hearing it." Carolann raised her eyebrows.

"Great to meet you, Mrs. Cooper." Ticia stuck out her hand. "I'm glad you're feeling better."

Carolann stuck her bottle of Jack Daniels under her arm and shook Ticia's hand. "Shame your parents couldn't get you here earlier. I would have liked to meet them."

"My dad's interviewing candidates in Brussels, and my mom got called to a strategy meeting in Rome."

"She's a lawyer," Chip added. Carolann generally respected women with careers.

"Hmm." Carolann crossed her arms over her chest. "That explains a few things."

Chip looked at Ticia and felt like he could read her mind. *What the fuck?*

"You're just in time for lobster. Let's get you some food." Rowan held out her hand. "There's enough to feed an army."

Ticia glanced at Carolann's bottle of Jack Daniels. "What I'd really love is a drink."

Rowan stared at the bottle. "Yes, you must be parched."

"There's water over here." Chip took Ticia's hand and immediately dropped it. The involuntary movement of his body alarmed him – right in front of his parents. "Follow me."

Ticia and Chip filled their plates. They glanced back at Chip's parents, and Lyn waved a stubby hand.

"Jesus, homes. You should have told me about your mom." Ticia plucked a cube from her potato salad and popped it in her mouth. "She could be like twenty-five."

"She's thirty-two."

"Holy shit. Guess that explains the straight up Jack. The last vestige of her youth. She was preggers prenup, I presume."

"Huh?"

"You're 14 and she's thirty-two. Therefore, teen pregnancy."

"We like to say *child bride*." Chip gnawed off a bite of crusty bread and stared at his plate in his hand.

"Weird." Ticia watched him chewing and sipped her water. "Anyway, I got nothing against teenage pregnancy. I'm Chicana, remember? My people would still number in the dozens if it wasn't for the faulty rhythm method."

Chip saw a rickety TV tray table. Two folding chairs

perched either side of it. "Should we sit?"

Ticia led the way to the table. "Hey –" she jabbed her fork in the air. "Don't keep secrets from me."

"What secret?"

"I heard what you did for Maarten."

"He told you?" Chip sat and scooted his chair back and forth to dig the legs into Rowan's grass to stabilize himself.

"Very cool, but why didn't you tell me?"

"I thought it could be misinterpreted."

"By me?" Ticia's chair rocked sideways and she righted herself, her feet planted squarely in front of her. "Don't insult my intelligence. Or discredit the value of our friendship. Shit. Did he pay you?"

"No." Money would have been worthless compared to what Chip actually gained helping Maarten. Several rugby players knew Chip now, by name.

Ticia said, "Jesus, it must be a burden for you, being so smart. Convinced the world around you can't keep pace. But you're going to be a sad, lonely man if you don't learn to lay out the truth and trust people to deal with it."

"Ok," Chip set his plate on the table and grabbed his own knees. "You want to know something true? That guy Andrew doesn't deserve you."

"Is that the truth?" She set her plate down next to Chip's. "Tell me more."

"I'm not saying I deserve you, or I'm right for you, or whatever – but maybe I am. I'd sure treat you better than that, that…" He wanted to say *asshole*.

"Guy?" she finished his sentence for him, saving him a dollar in his mother's profanity jar.

"I would treat you better than that guy." Chip nodded. "That's the truth."

Ticia touched Chip's cheek and he flinched. He looked around Rowan's neighbors, but no one seemed to be watching them.

"Baby, 14 doesn't do it for 17," Ticia said. "Honestly, that's the deal-breaker. Someday, it wouldn't matter. I'd be 24 and you'd be 21, like no difference."

Chip said, "There would always be a difference."

Ticia shrugged. "Dude, your mom's 32, but she could be our age, if it weren't for her hair and her clothes and stuff. And her attitude. And how old's your dad?"

"Thirty-nine. That's different though. I'm not talking about way off in the future, I'm talking about now. That shit head doesn't deserve you *now*." Andrew was a shit head. It was worth Chip's profanity dollar.

"Did you kids remember to invite Jesus to your table?" Carolann appeared, hand on hip, the other clutching her cocktail. "Let's not forget Him."

Chip swallowed. At home they only invited Jesus to Sunday lunch.

"Holy shhh... sugar," Ticia said. "Where's He gonna sit?"

Caroloann gasped. Chip examined his plate, the white insides of the steam-opened clamshells, the buttered yellow pebble-rows of corn on the cob. His mother once said all deep family conflicts hinged on that color yellow. Did the corn's irregular brick-pattern spell out the end of his friendship with Ticia? He could read it in the kernels plain as day. He bit into the corn, and butter oozed down his chin. He felt like a child, with butter already clogging his teenage pores.

"We need another chair." Ticia giggled.

Carolann stood in front of them, the beige pants, chain link belt swinging to her knee, her sky blue loafers with the brown rubber knobbles over the toes and up the heels. Chip could hardly bear to look at her, higher than her thigh, but he raised his head, dabbed his face with a napkin. Carolann was smiling at Ticia. She pointed to her heart and left a fingertip indentation in her sweater. "No, He sits right here." Carolann winked at Ticia and walked away, her chain belt clinking.

"She's trying to figure me out," Ticia said. "I get it. And me her. Right now, we're the two most important women in your life. No big."

"But the God stuff…" He couldn't finish his sentence.

"Normal. Look, they speak English here, but it aint home. You grab onto what makes you feel safe."

"Like my rhyming, I guess." Chip thrust his chin forward and back, like a pigeon. "This aint a test. My rhyme's the best. Listen up and I'll –"

"Shut up." Ticia kicked him under the TV table. "Next she'll want to reconcile with estranged family. The process is well documented. You do have some estranged family, I assume? Psychology. She'll pull out photo albums and display some heirlooms, if they're not all in storage."

Chip thought of the blue-and-white dishes his aunt collected. What did someone do with heirlooms if they didn't have an heir?

"Speaking of photos…" Ticia raised her eyebrows at Chip.

"We'll go get your envelope at my house after the party."

Ticia nodded. "If you hadn't found it, I seriously would have killed you."

"The hat, by the way." Chip smiled. "By unanimous decision."

"Who? You and your five knuckles?" She laughed.

"Nope. Survey on the internet." Chip saw his dad talking to a group of men. The pleats on his khakis bulged as he rocked on his heels. He was the same height as the English men, yet he looked bigger. He looked like a man you could trust.

Lyn turned and grabbed a garden stool to join Chip and Ticia. "Look at this cake! Any takers?" He held up two plastic forks.

"Just a bite," Ticia said. "Then don't let me have any more."

Chip watched her eat some of his dad's cake.

"So have you been to Ireland?" Lyn asked. "We're thinking

about the Ring of Dingle for the holiday coming up, or February if we're too late now. You kids have more vacation than school."

"I love Ireland," Ticia said. "Go kiss the Blarney stone."

"I think our rapper boy's already got enough Blarney." Lyn chuckled.

Chip saw Carolann's empty bottle of Jack Daniels on the buffet table. He hoped she'd been sharing it or spilling it out.

"Have you gone and traced your genealogy?" Lyn asked Ticia. "Olague?"

"Not in Ireland," she laughed. "No apostrophe in Olague. My family tree's south of the border."

"I'll be darned, you're a blue-eyed Mexican." Lyn laughed. "For once, Chip, your mother got something right."

Carolann came over, empty bottle in hand. "Jack's gone." She pouted. Her lipstick looked fresh. She batted her eyelashes at Lyn.

"Well," Lyn stood, "I was just going to suggest we make our exit. Chip, why don't you take the bus with Ticia and see that she gets home safe?"

"I'll be fine, Mr. Cooper," Ticia said. "Thanks, though."

"I don't mind," Chip said. He saw his mother's grip on the bottleneck. "I'll at least walk you back to the bus stop. Did you want to come to our house first?"

"Another time," she said quietly.

"Where's our hostess?" Lyn took Carolann's elbow. "We need to say thank you."

"You know best." Carolann's words came one at a time, strangely robotic. "Come on Chip. You can invite your little friend to our house another day. Your father thinks it's time to leave. All three of us."

Rowan came forward. "You're going already?"

"Lovely party." Carolann's eyes glazed. "Best go before things get ugly."

"Don't be silly," Rowan said, eyeballing the empty bottle.

Chip stood, hands in his pockets. "Maybe I'll just run back to our house with my parents, and then I'll be right back."

Ticia said, "I'll just, you know, see you at school." She stared at Chip, as if delivering a secret code.

"Ugly," Carolann repeated herself in a sort of trance. "Could get ugly."

"Nonsense," Rowan said. "I'll drive Ticia home after folks leave. You can help me clean up, dear."

"Sure." Ticia nodded. "I'd be happy to help."

"Perfect," Carolann grinned. "I'm sure she's used to that. It's in her genes."

"We're off." Lyn nudged his wife and turned her toward their house.

"Cleaning! My sister always has Mexican maids." Carolann cackled.

Lyn commandeered his wife away from the party, mouthing the word *sorry* to his hostess and to Ticia.

Chip stuck his hands deeper into his pockets and ambled hang-dog behind them without even looking back. Carolann was now singing, as Lyn frogmarched her home. Chip kicked gravel in the driveway and hung back while Lyn fumbled with his key in the lock and his wife on his arm.

"She hates me." Chip could hear Ticia through the hedge, and he stayed rooted in place.

"That was the drink," Rowan said. "I know a problem with drink when I see it. And she has a problem. But she's a lovely woman, in her core."

"Lovely if you think racism's lovely. That's fucked up."

"Out of character," Rowan said. "I know her sober. She needs to get a handle on the drink."

Chip wanted to shout through the bushes, but he didn't know what to shout.

Rowan said, "Her extended family's not here to do it right, so she needs us. Carolann Cooper's problem needs fixing while there's still a lovely woman in there to save."

Ticia said, "Poor Chip."

Rowan added, "He's lucky to have you."

"Not that he'd say so," Ticia scoffed.

"Carolann needs my help, and honey, especially now, I think Chip needs you."

Quietly, Chip went in to his house. He'd heard enough.

Chapter 37

Carolann watched Chip grab his headphones and head up to his bedroom. His door slammed. She probably had taken it too far at Rowan's party. Her intentions were solid, but tonight's performance didn't exactly win her Mother of the Year.

Anyway, a next-day apology was often part of the show. She opened her eyes wide, blinked them several times, and said to Lyn, "You realize what he's getting into with that girl, don't you? That... that..." Carolann couldn't find a better word.

"Let's get you upstairs." Lyn reached for her hand. "Get you some water to drink."

"In a minute." She sat on the stairs and sighed a long, slurring sigh. It was the best opportunity she would get. She was 100 % clear-headed, he believed she was 100% muddled, and she could therefore tell him whatever she needed to say. She had clearly heard Chip's door slam, and she knew noise didn't travel up the winding staircase of the house. She needed to talk to Lyn now. The urgency, the burden of it, overwhelmed her, and without warning, her eyes welled up.

When Carolann drank, even when it was pretend, it was always one or the other, in an instant, and sometimes both. Straight to the bedroom with her happy husband, or tears. And when it was tears, sloppy drunk tears, even fake-drunk tears, everything came back to the baby. Both babies. Her voice caught in her throat, and she heard herself sob.

"Not this again." Lyn groaned.

"I'm not… what I did was not…"

"You didn't take their son, Carolann." He glanced up toward Chip's room, sat down next to her on the staircase, and rubbed her back. "I wish we could just get that straight. Maybe we need to get you back to good works in the church. Feeling valued as a nurse. But you shouldn't need that cosmic balance. You're stronger than that."

"I just…"

"It's high time." He repeated, "it's time."

Time for what? Did he know about Ticia? Had he seen those pictures? Was Lyn saying he wanted to talk about Chip's paternity now? Or… which baby, exactly, did Lyn mean?

Yes, in effect, she could say, *I did take their son.* She sniffed.

"Let it go, Carolann," he urged. "You did nothing wrong. You never did anything wrong. We finally live so far from all of them. Look at it clearly now, from this distance, and just let it go."

She sobbed. She didn't need a single drink to watch her emotions cave in on her. How could he know what she had truly done or not done? She let her words run together, like a blubbering drunk, mixing scenes, mixing memories. "*I-didn't-know-what-I-was-doing, How-could-I-know? The-drinking, he-knew. He-did-it-he-was-almost-like-sick.*" The sound of her words flowed out fast on a satin ribbon of yellow, unspooling. "*It's-a-sickness. Like-alcoholism-like-abuse-mental-physical-like-rape. I-raped-him-you-know-that-right? And even after that I took their baby boy, I did it. I did do that. It was me.*"

Lyn didn't even try to understand her string of words, even as they slowed and separated. "You're destroying yourself," he said. "That was hard, seeing Chip there with his date, I know. Did you see him take her hand? Our son is… comfortable… with a young woman. And that's not so comfortable for us, well, not for me, as his dad, anyway. Seeing him growing up."

"We have to deal with it." Carolann hung her face in her hands. She'd had one, hardly more than a sip. But she was nervous and scattered and out of breath.

"He is growing up," Lyn said. "He is a remarkable young man. You are raising an extraordinary young man. And you can't drink his developing adulthood away. He deserves to know who he is, and who he's not, when the time is right. And it looks like that time may be on our horizon."

So Chip was indeed the son Lyn meant. Chip. He was right… there was every possibility that she didn't take that son from them. She was going to have to speak clearly and stop the charade. She took a deep breath. It was all yellow.

"It's a gift for Chip." Lyn held up his small hand and then set it on his wife's knee. "Soon. He'll understand and be grateful."

Carolann shook her head, her willful red hair no longer tame, she let it flop in front of her face. "He'll have questions. How did Mom get pregnant then? He'll want to know about this *alternate parenting.*"

Lyn interrupted and shushed her.

Carolann lowered her voice. "He'll want details. A petrie dish or a test tube or an adoption agency with a case file and a man out there somewhere in the world with a right to know his own son, maybe. What about this guy's mannerisms, or his biceps, his interests, special talents, high cholesterol, diseases? Chip will have questions. He'd have every right." Carolann looked at her husband carefully. "And what if we're wrong?"

"We're not wrong."

"He might not want that kind of gift," she said. "You're his father." She took a quick breath. "You're the gift. The only father he knows. He reveres you."

"This is repellent." Lyn again held up his hand and spoke firmly. "Vile."

"No." Carolann grabbed Lyn's hand and kissed his

fingertips. "Absolutely not." She knew her pronunciation of *absolutely* was probably too sharp, for a drunk.

Lyn pulled his hand away and slid his fingers under his thighs. "You didn't know my family."

"No." Carolann agreed.

"I don't expect you to understand. My father was … He looked so handsome… his cream dinner jacket. Not weak or troubled. His formal shoes. Except for the knees. What happened to his knees. He was so handsome. But he… You'll never know the crooked way his body fell on the ground. His hands. The smell of his blood, because of me. What he did because of me."

"No." Carolann could never fully grasp her husband's unfathomable childhood.

"But I know my son," he said. "Chip will understand the gift. He will not think any less of you. You are a strong and moral woman, and he will have no doubt about that. I will ensure that he has no doubt about that."

She nodded. The pronouncement of her being a strong and moral woman always sounded fragile. At risk of being proved untrue in a heartbeat. Her years of successful parenting and partnering dashed to oblivion.

He put an arm around her shoulder. "You did not take their son from them. You offered life to a baby who wouldn't have had it, you offered marriage and family to a man who wouldn't have had it. Chip will understand the strength of character you showed in that decision."

Of course she knew the timing. Chip could be Lyn's son a little early, or he could be Buck's, a little late. He had been a perfectly average sized baby. And what if she didn't take Chip from anyone, what if he was really Lyn's son? If so, she built a marriage on a lie – the false belief that she had taken the baby from his rightful father.

And still, the truth was she did take Buck and Maryann's baby from them. It was Carolann. The other boy. Her parents' other grandson. Ryan. It was unintentional, but she did it. And then she lied about it.

She laid her head against her husband's shoulder, and he ran his fingers through her hair. His believing she was drunk was so familiar and comfortable. But the lies were building on themselves, one by one, like slippery layers, unwilling to stay stacked, and she couldn't keep the foundation in place. Terrible brown and rust and dark green, and sharp edges and crispy burned-rubber black. But she felt the touch of his hand in her hair and the tremendous yellow. Vibrant daylight daffodil yellow, fresh road markings in sunshine. It was her color of poignancy and turning points. She knew it well.

She was going to have to replace the flimsy falsehoods with something stable. Each untruth, when pulled out and examined, could topple the whole thing, but it was time. She would not just stop the conversation, run to the bathroom and vomit – this time, she was not so drunk, so sloppy-silly rotten drunk, that she'd pass out, let him carry her upstairs and take care of her and love her. This time, she'd tell him the truth. "In effect," she said into Lyn's shoulder at last, "I did take their son. Took his life."

Lyn lifted her face and looked at her.

"Maryann wasn't wrong to call Paul Mayer."

"Paul Mayer's a jerk."

"He's not."

"If he wasn't Buck's football buddy, they never would have called the police." Lyn scoffed. "Grief can make people stupid, justify stupid behavior, but your sister had no right."

"Paul's the one who told her to drop the charges."

"You should never have even been questioned," Lyn said.

"The baby would have died anyway. You and I both know that," Carolann said. "But I bathed him." Her voice was void of emotion, she was somewhere else, her other self, revealing what she'd done. There were no more tears.

"You said you didn't."

"But the truth is I did. I bathed Buck and Maryann's child, and I swaddled him. How could I know? We had that Thanksgiving dinner and Ryan was upstairs sleeping, like any normal newborn. They never told me. I could say it was Maryann's fault for pretending everything was normal, but…"

"There was nothing normal that Thanksgiving," Lyn said.

"It wasn't her fault, though." Carolann pressed on. "It was wrong to lie to me, pretend he was fine. I am a nurse. And your field is asthma. Between the two of us, we knew more than most. But it was… his death, in the end… it may have been my fault."

"Asthma? Their baby didn't have asthma. His lungs weren't right. You've had too much to drink, my love. You don't know what you're saying." Lyn brushed the hair on her forehead with his fingertips. "We should get you upstairs."

But Carolann would not be shushed. "I didn't know how sick he was, how fragile. That's why they never let me look after him, they didn't want me to know. Why didn't they trust me to know?"

"Shhh." Lyn tried again to quiet his wife. "Did you use strong floral soap? Talcum? Toxins? Of course not."

"And then that shipment came in from England, and they wanted me to babysit, so they should have told me. They were gone six-and-a-half hours. Those stupid blue-and-white plates. That god-forsaken vase. As if Edith Heaney even wanted it anymore for her yellow flowers." The daffodils, searing yellow. Carolann felt bold. "It's tragic."

"Chip might hear you."

Carolann glanced up the staircase. What did it matter? It was the truth, didn't he want Chip to know the truth? "Lyn, I didn't know Baby Ryan was ill. I swaddled him in the goose-down crib blanket."

"Goose-down. What were they thinking?" Lyn's voice was firm. "It doesn't take a pulmonologist to know the problem there."

"He looked so sweet in it. He smelled so sweet, baby clean. His soft wispy hair and his little ears. I held his soft little delicate ear. I wanted it to know my thumbprint. So he'd know me, Auntie Carolann, another woman besides his mother who would love him forever. I held him to me, gurgling and happy. In that moment, I loved him like my own son."

She saw Lyn's eyes flash black. It was one thing to raise Buck's son as his own, but maybe hearing that she loved Buck's other child like her own was too much. But she continued. "In that moment, he was so peaceful, his little noises, perfectly happy, and then he had no noises, and I unwrapped him and tapped his back and that's when Mama and Maryann came in and grabbed him away from me, and I didn't even know he had a nebulizer and all that apparatus in the closet. They were only supposed to be gone for a couple hours to go through that antiques shipment, but they were gone all day and they didn't even call me from the shop, to check on Ryan. Six hours. I should have been told."

"They came home covered in dust." Lyn whispered into his wife's hair. "That's the worst. Dust, hay, cat dander. You did nothing wrong."

"They came back and Mama yelled, '*You bathed him!*' She was yelling and Maryann was squirting liquids into the nebulizer chamber and she held that green silicone mask over Ryan's tiny purple-gray face while the machine hummed and pumped, and his color came back. And I thought he was ok, we all thought he was going to be ok. His wrinkled forehead over the mask, it was pink again, normal, his cheeks and those sweet baby ears holding my thumbprint, and the thrum of the mist and his tiny hand gripping the clear tubing, those tiny baby fingernails, like everything was normal, and the thrum and my sister registered what Mama was yelling, I guess, and she sounded deep and throaty like an animal growl when she was yelling, '*You bathed him?*'"

Lyn looked stricken. But she'd never sworn it. As many times as they asked her before the funeral and after the funeral. Every month that Maryann and Buck tried for another baby that just never came, they asked and she said no, I did not bathe him. It was such a stupid lie, one that sprang from the moment she faced accusation, and then she kept it going, though it never served any purpose. How was she ever going to reveal any other true thing to Lyn? What would happen if someday Chip's future child would have misshapen hands?

"You lied." Lyn looked sick.

Carolann nodded and ran her tongue along her teeth. Her mouth was almost too dry to speak. "Yes."

"You're drunk," he said. "This isn't you. You do foolish things, say foolish things, when you're drunk, and this isn't you."

"He was a beautiful little angel about to go home to heaven. This world was not right for that sweet baby Ryan, but yes, I did bathe him. My mother and my sister searched through dusty shipping crates for that goddamned antique vase, and I bathed that sweet angel, and I swaddled him in goose down. How can I not blame myself? I killed him. I took their son from them. That son. I did that."

Chapter 38

Carolann held her breath. Without a word, Lyn stood and climbed the stairs. She had just admitted she'd killed a baby boy, so what did she expect? He still thought she'd drunk the Jack Daniels, and when Carolann had a drink, they never ended the night at an impasse. But of course, she'd never before mentioned that she'd killed someone. She checked the locks, turned off the lights, and went upstairs.

"I'm not a murderer," she finally said into their cold, dark room.

Lyn's breathing was stone silent, not a comfortable, forgiving rhythm of sleep.

Carolann's feet were cold. She couldn't reach Lyn's warmth.

"You didn't kill the baby," he said at last. "You carry an incredible unearned burden about that question. Stop. Go to bed tonight understanding that, once and for all. Let that burden go."

She reached for his shoulder. He was right, but she couldn't just let it go. When a person carries a heavy weight for a long time, it becomes part of them. The release itself would be painful. Lyn pulled farther from her and made a wall of his back.

"You didn't kill that baby," he repeated. "But you didn't trust me, the one person who shares every secret, everything. We had a pact, more important than our marriage vows,

Carolann. You didn't kill that baby. But you broke our pact."

This dangerous pact. What arrogance of Lyn's allowed him to put forth a vow more important than the one they'd made to God? And what power did he assume in enforcing it? What would happen if she could never address this hubris of his?

Lyn's breathing sounded hostile.

"I never meant to lie, but every month it got worse. Maryann blames herself, female troubles, *hormonal imbalance.* But it was Buck. How could I tell her? We knew Buck's history. Even before that Thanksgiving with Ryan."

"Enough, Carolann."

She stared into the dark, desperate to fix the height of her ceiling in her mind's eye. Ten feet above her? One hundred? No wonder people prayed to God in Heaven, above them. Were all religions' Gods in the sky? Burning candles to send worldly concerns upward, until the power up there took the smoke of worry and sent comfort, right into the believer's very core. But tonight, Carolann had no sense even of the ceiling in her bedroom. Only darkness. A hollow, hopeless void.

"Lyn?" Her whisper met silence. Her sister was childless, her barren womb too busy fighting infection to support new life, month after infertile month. Buck's history had everything to do with it. And Carolann was part of that history.

"Go to sleep," Lyn said.

Though childless, her sister's marriage seemed strong now. There were lies and half-truths told in every house. Lyn believed the son they were raising was Buck's child. How could she not feel accountable for her sister's loss? Carolann searched the darkness. She had no focus, no grounding, nothing to hold on to, to center herself. All was black. She needed a grid or a framework to grasp, but she was just floating.

"Bath or no bath," Lyn said, "you did not kill that baby. But you may have killed our trust, and without that, we are nothing, you and me. We have nothing."

Chapter 39

Something terrible and unspoken was happening, and Chip knew he couldn't stop it. Throughout the weekend, he shamefully replayed his departure from Rowan's clambake in his mind, leaving Ticia messages, while his parents navigated the house in opposition to one another. Mom went upstairs, Dad moved down. For the most part, Chip stayed in his room. Conversation was nearly nonexistent, and the whole house seemed that all its edges had become sharp. Plates and cups were carefully placed on surfaces, and doors were shut tight. His father's footfall was heavy, and he took the stairs at a stomp. By contrast, his mother walked on tip-toe.

Chip couldn't wait to get out of the house and go to school, but all day Monday, when he'd hoped to get Ticia's attention, she'd turned away. How could he apologize, if she wouldn't even talk to him?

At the end of the day, Chip dragged himself toward the busses. He saw Ticia jogging through the carpark toward an old white convertible Pontiac with its top down and a pony-tailed girl in the driver's seat, chewing gum. Did she not understand cold, damp October in England? The car was huge. Impossible to cruise English streets without taking off wing mirrors. It might as well have been a rhinoceros, brought in from the zoo. Nothing made sense. Ticia didn't look his way, and Chip didn't shout. Somehow, he knew she was aware of him watching her.

Ticia threw her backpack into the car's passenger seat,

turned, and walked to Chip. "I got your messages," she said.

"I'm really sorry, T." He didn't want to talk about it in the wide-open parking lot. But at least she was listening. He pulled out her envelope and handed it to her.

"You warned me about your mom." Ticia shrugged. "That's her problem. Her thing. But homes, you just disappeared after she said that stuff. You've got to realize your wacko family dynamic doesn't define you. You're 14, so you've got about four more years, and then you're your own man. And here's why I was pissed. I know the man you are already. The guy inside." She put the palm of her hand on Chip's heart. "So your mom got weird. Where'd the man go?"

Chip nodded. "I don't know…" There were a lot of people around, but no one nearby. Still, what could he say? No empty promises. Next time his mom would get weird, he couldn't trust the man inside him to step forward. Chip knew he could betray himself as easily as he betrayed his best friend. He owed some kind of loyalty to his mom too, didn't he?

Ticia glanced across the lot at the big car and the ponytail girl threw her arms in the air, impatient. "Anyway, Rowan thinks she needs help."

"In case you didn't notice, Rowan's a little weird herself."

"For real, sweetie. Your mom's got issues. I mean, she was my age, for fuck's sake, when she had you. How could she not have issues?"

Chip shook his head. "You think she drinks too much."

"I think she's weird about you, homes. Psycho over-protective, like you're fragile. Like you're the Queen's kid, and she's the nanny on probation."

"I'm pretty sure I'm my mother's kid. Forget it."

"Fine. Are you your dad's kid?"

"We had the same mailman all my life. The man is black."

"Then something else. There's serious tension chez Cooper." She shook her head. "Maybe you can't resolve it, but at least try to find out where it comes from. For your sake."

"I think you're barking up the wrong tree." Chip smiled.

Ticia unzipped her jacket pocket and pulled out a jewel-encrusted black calculator designed like a skull. "I'm not saying she forced your dad to get married or anything. That'd be totally vintage. But you are from Kansas. Maybe your people feel different about things?"

"No premarital nothing is how my people feel. Ticia, don't make my family your pet project. I know I was a jerk on Saturday. I –"

"We need clues." She glanced at the girl in the rhino. "What's with your dad's hands?"

Chip stared at her.

"It's like his nails are glued on. Like God was walking through his factory and sees a guy headed for the discard bin – weird hands – but then He takes another look and says, wait one hot minute. This is a good one. Go get me some fingernails."

"Jesus, Ticia. Shut up. This is not your thing to delve into. Not to mention, you've got God all wrong."

"Sweetie," she grabbed Chip's face with both hands and kissed his mouth.

Chip pulled away, stunned.

"Your mom's weird and your dad's got weird hands. I'm looking for connections."

The rhinoceros honked, and Ticia held up a hand over her head.

Chip sighed. "When I was about five, I asked my mom about his hands." He stopped talking, made way for the intense tactile memory, smooth and warm, mother and son ironing leaves in wax paper. "She said he was born that way, it's called brachydactyly. It's not disabling. I guarantee you that is not any source of family tension."

Ticia said, "At least you're admitting the tension. I love you too much to stay mad. You're just an innocent bystander. Not your fault. We have to figure it out. "

"Love?"

"Do the math. Your birthday's June 14, and your parents got married October what?" Ticia handed him her calculator, its crystal numbers glinting. It held her heat. "Start there, homeboy. What's your mom trying to drink away?" Ticia glanced at the Pontiac.

"Nothing. That's not even how alcoholism works."

"Name the biggest river in Egypt."

"De Nile. I get it." Chip handed her calculator back.

"Sweetie, your problem's not going away on its own. It's just going to get worse. Trust me."

Chapter 40

Carolann did her best thinking in the pubs. Thank goodness the High Street had plenty, because she had a serious problem. Monday morning, Lyn left for work with hardly a word. She got Chip on the school bus and walked to the end of the road to start her day in Jonathan Place, which opened at 9am. She stirred chocolate powder into her cappuccino.

Normally if Lyn was mad, he'd shout, she'd apologize, (if appropriate), and that was the end of it. The weekend's obstinate silence was entirely new, and Carolann felt out of her depths. She'd never confessed a lie to him before, but she hadn't realized their so-called pact was more than just the basis of their marriage, it was their marriage itself. She'd always given it more credit than that. A genuine relationship between man and wife, raising a healthy child, with a solid foundation. How could she make Lyn realize its true value? And what if his view of things was correct? Maybe it was only ever a charade, and she'd had it all wrong. Carolann sucked a last sip of cappuccino foam.

The Wheatsheaf didn't serve till 11am, so she waited on a park bench, breathing warm coffee-breath into her jacket. Today would be an all-day session, a solo pub crawl, with no guarantee of clarity. At least Lyn was talking to Chip, she thought. Ultimately, from the beginning, their son was her biggest concern.

Chip was only three months old the first time she tried to tell Lyn. The memory, the moment, was vinegar-sour and red.

The college day-care permitted Carolann to attend classes and return to the baby to breastfeed him, a book resting on his tummy, as he nestled into her. She studied while she memorized the whorls of fine hair on her baby's head. The contours of his delicate ears. His smooth, pale skin. His little fingers gripping her hand, gently holding the spine of her book. His clean baby fingernails, fragile as tiny tabs of wax-paper. From the beginning, Chip's hands looked perfect.

She wanted Lyn to know this child with perfect hands might be his son. She stood at the stove, stirring pasta sauce. Already, she knew how much garlic Lyn liked. A little salt. No oregano. Lyn was sitting on the sofa with the baby. Carolann watched him kiss the baby's tiny fingers, one at a time. In a moment, she set down her spoon, aware of the red tomato sauce on her white tile, and it seemed important, it seemed easy, and it seemed true. She said to Lyn, "He's your son, you realize. He's perfect, and he's yours."

Lyn's face clouded with an undisclosed pain, and Carolann saw the muscles in his forearms tense. His fingers tightened on Chip's ribcage under his little arms. The baby seemed to sense his father's reaction, and his body went still, his gurgling ceased immediately. The water on the stove was boiling, and the noise of it filled the house. Carolann blindly took the pot off the heat, and held it mid-air. She didn't dare look away from her baby. Lyn held the baby away from him, as if little Chip was suddenly a doll, something plastic, a trick of a new parent's nightmare. Something to throw out with the trash.

Carolann's arms were shaking. She looked into the scalding hot water searching for guidance, but there was nothing. Lyn's expression scared Carolann, and she held her breath. Little did she know at the time, that first time, it was the smartest thing to do. To say nothing.

And just as suddenly, as if a gust of wind had driven the bad memory away, Lyn's face brightened, he laughed, and the baby threw his little head back and laughed also. "A gift, my boy. Your brave mommy gave me a blessed gift. Someday we'll tell you about it because it's a gift for you too. Mostly for you. And your children. And your children's children." He poked the baby gently in the tummy and under the arms, and new peals of laughter erupted with each of Lyn's *children*. Carolann returned the heavy pot to the stove, cracked the bundled spaghetti sticks in half, and plunged them into the water. She took a deep breath, and silently, she continued making their dinner.

The Wheatsheaf was a dark, cozy pub, and she hated to leave, but she made her way to the Bear. Lyn was angry after her confession, but it was such a stupid lie, and she knew she was doing the right thing, an honest thing, maybe for the first time in her life. Was this the definition of irreconcilable differences? She'd never understood how two people in a marriage became irreconcilably different.

Carolann went from the Rebel Henry to The Black Sheep for marinated olives. If she sat Lyn down and told him another big truth, that she suspected his genes and those of their beautiful son were shared, what would he do then? Their charade would be over. She popped the last olive into her mouth. High fat, but very healthy. Sometimes, she knew, a thing should be looked at from two angles. She loved all of him, all the time, including his hands. Drunk or sober, in sickness and in health. If Carolann accepted it, why couldn't he?

He'd refused to see a marriage counselor. If the thing was over, and he knew it to be so, he'd said, it was over. But he still wanted a few days to decide. Meanwhile, was Carolann supposed to sit back and wait? If telling him the truth was the right thing, how could it kill her marriage? She was a child when he married her. Now, she realized, so was he. Suddenly, Carolann had matured. If she were to leave him, she'd leave him a child. If she'd stay, they'd grow old together, exactly as they'd vowed to do. Of course, their marriage wasn't over. Its very existence, their finding each other at just the right time for both of them, was as much proof of God as she'd ever need, God in the sky, God in her heart. She had to make that clear to Lyn. A human being couldn't just tear apart something honoured by, something created by, God.

She had spring rolls in Pan Asia Gallery, and in Aphrodite Taverna, tomato soup. She could travel the world through the pubs and restaurants or through genuine geography, but her same thoughts and judgments would be with her, unshakeable. What was that no-escape phrase Chip wrote in his Multicultural Studies paper? *Wherever you go, you're there too.* That was her problem. She'd have to get out of herself, step out and look in, like expats supposedly did all the time, to gain fresh perspective.

The waiter took her soup bowl away and nodded his head at the dessert counter. He had a mustache. "Can I tempt you?"

Carolann nodded. "Baklava, please."

He smiled. "In for a penny, in for a pound."

She knew she was doing the right thing. When Lyn shouted and slammed things, she might back-peddle and apologize. But she'd started this fight on purpose and it needed to play out to the finish. In for a penny, in for the whole savings account.

She paid her bill and walked to Oxfam. The charity shop received donations and refreshed their window display throughout the day. Maybe she'd get lucky and the elusive blue-and-white Beemasters vase would show up for a fiver. Lyn might stay angry, but at least she could try to make her sister and her mother happy.

She'd already called or seen every antiques dealer Maryann

mentioned. Everyone was on the look-out for the piece. The old loony bird had said it was irreplaceable, and maybe it was. But it could still turn up in Oxfam, and Carolann would be a hero. All of Maryann's tears and Barbara Ann's yelling would be washed away in a river of gratitude. Today, though, as usual, there was nothing blue-and-white in Oxfam. Not in the window, not in the musty-smelling shop. Carolann moved on.

Even if she found the thing, the burden of debt might be too heavy to lift. Mrs. Heaney seemed a hundred years old when the twins were girls, so by now she might be senile and not even recognize the prize. And after 20 years, the whole town had woven the story into its framework. Everyone knew its details, the debt, the endless search for the god-awful vase. If Carolann actually found it, the tight-knit community around her family might unravel.

In the distance, Carolann saw Rowan turn from their road onto the High Street. Head down, her chin was tucked into a fluffy turquoise scarf, but Carolann knew she'd see her in a second. An awkward apology was due, of course, but Carolann wasn't ready. She pushed on the next pub door available. The White Horse was kind of a rough one. The stained carpet smelled like old beer and stale men.

"The usual?" the barman asked her, pulling a pint glass from his shelf.

Carolann nodded, leaning on the bar. Her purse dangled from her forearm. Just as well she didn't have an expensive piece of china to lug around.

The barman poured two small bottles of Diet Coke into a pint glass, and Carolann paid him.

A scruffy man in painter's clothing came into the pub and clapped some pound coins on the bar. "Well, lookee here," he eyed Carolann up and down. No "h" in the word "here." He must have been from somewhere other than Surrey, and his strong accent was perhaps filtered through something stronger than Diet Coke.

She smiled a cold, tight-lipped smile at him and turned away.

In the barman's mirror, she saw the filthy man staring at her hair. He said something that sounded like "gingham" or "singer."

Carolann didn't understand the words, but she knew the tone. It would probably be smart to make a quick exit, but Rowan would be on the street, probably very close to the bar – not to mention she'd just paid for her drink.

Did the barman raise his eyebrows at her? He seemed, almost imperceptibly, to shrug his shoulders. If he was going to be so British and subtle not to even offer her a grunt of dismay, then she could damn well be American and defiant and stand there in his pub next to a grungy man with a disquieting tone. In the mirror behind the barman, she watched her own reflection next to the man, and through the window behind her, she saw Rowan's cotton-candy hair bobbing its way up the street. Carolann would just stay long enough to let her pass.

The pub door opened to a gust of chilly street air, raising a mildew smell from the carpet. The scruffy man whispered into Carolann's hair. Something-something-Hampton-something.

Carolann moved a step away.

He stepped closer and repeated himself, louder. "Rub my Hampton up your ass-crack."

"Cute." Carolann turned and saw Rowan behind the man, wide-eyed. Carolann set her drink down on the bar. Its dark liquid could be Guinness. She couldn't blame him – or Rowan – for that mistake. "I assume Hampton's a pet name? Like the wee little bedsit apartments in Hampton Court... very, very tiny?" She held up a finger and thumb. The women's club report about their Hampton Court tour turned out to be a useful thing to have studied.

"Hampton Wick, dick." he said. "You want it up –"

"Up? You can't get it up? Poor man. How humiliating." She raised her voice. "Teeny tiny, and you can't even get it up. You should see a specialist."

The bartender stepped forward. "We don't serve your kind." He pushed the coins back at the man, who surprisingly pocketed them and left. The bartender moved to the other end of the bar without looking at Carolann. Perhaps he'd prefer not to serve her kind as well. Though by now she was a "regular" and felt a certain amount of acceptance.

Rowan said. "I saw you come in here, and wasn't sure if you knew what kind of place…"

"Listen," Carolann's heart was pounding. "I owe you an apology. Rowan, your party was lovely, and my behavior was inexcusable."

"It was the drink." Rowan tipped her head at Carolann's glass. "My ex was a drinker. It took my sister ten years to convince me. Don't wait ten years, Carolann. Do it now. This spring, when I go to Glastonbury to thank my sister, you can come. We talk on our birthday, through the Tor. The feminine sacred."

Carolann nodded slowly. If she spoke, she would laugh out loud at Rowan's bizarre mysticism.

"Honestly. It's a vessel. It vibrates with ancient feminine powers of healing. Maybe you can reconcile with your twin sister. I know that would do you good."

"I'm not sure." Carolann's conflict with Maryann was insidious and too firmly founded to be healed by a magic tower in England.

"Well, the point is, you can beat this." Rowan tapped Carolann's glass.

"That's not —"

"No excuses," Rowan interrupted. "It takes strength. H.A.L.T. Hungry, angry, lonely, tired. First, know the reason you reach for it."

"I'm a nurse. I know the acronym," Carolann said. "And that's Diet Coke. I pick the letter T for thirst."

"Well, I'm glad you're familiar with H.A.L.T." Rowan raised her eyebrows. "It wasn't Diet Coke at my house."

"No, it wasn't."

"There are resources available. You've got an alternate T, and maybe there's also a different H?" Rowan said. "*Husband*?"

"Lyn's not a big drinker."

"I noticed he's the one who went for that bottle."

Carolann took a deep breath. "Lyn does like me to have a drink."

"Co-dependency breeds more dependency. You can beat it. I'm going to tell you something... that bastard I married was an angry man, and his anger was reducing me, but it also was revealing me, making me better."

Carolann listened.

Rowan mimicked her ex-husband's angry voice. "What the fuck is this dinner supposed to be? What the fuck does that mean? How can you be so fucking stupid?"

Carolann cringed. The barman would think she'd gotten herself into another conflict.

"He'd fucking this and that, and I'd just shrink. My shoulders, then my biceps would lose millimeters, smaller and smaller, I began to take up less space around him. I used to be tall, and suddenly I was shopping petites." She laughed at her own joke. "But inside, I was not disappearing, I was just fitting myself into tighter spaces." She made a fist and squinted her eyes. "Getting hard. With his insults and his drinking, it's like I was chipped away and distilled to a sort of purity, hardened to my essence. Light-reflecting, or holding light, I honestly believe this. I became myself, eventually. A substance so hard it cuts glass."

"A diamond." Carolann nodded.

"But the trick is to quit cutting when the facets are perfect, and you still have the biggest rock possible. That's when you get out. That's what my sister helped me see, just in time. Two and a half years, she's been gone."

"I wish I could have met Morwenna. Maybe I will join you at that tower."

"End of April." Rowan smiled. "She'd like that."

"Meantime, I asked Chip to invite his friend Ticia to a pre-Thanksgiving dinner Friday after next. An apology dinner, really. Nothing to do with Thanksgiving. You know our story. But I'll make turkey tacos and tamales. I hope you'll come too."

"Mexican food?" Rowan raised her eyebrows. "For Ticia?"

"Beans and rice are a complete protein." Carolann smiled.

"Remember I lived in Texas. I love Mexican food. You sure that lovely girl will take your gesture the right way?"

"I hope so." Carolann drew in a deep breath. "All in the presentation, I'm sure." How could she add, *I'm really not a drunk or a bigot*. And Chip's friendship with her seemed absolutely genuine.

"I'll bring the pudding." Rowan nodded at the bottles behind the bar. "And when you're ready for help, I'll help."

Chapter 41

C hip was watching his mother shred lettuce in the kitchen when the front doorbell rang. He opened it to find Ticia standing there with a bouquet of flowers.

"For your mom," she raised the flowers, stepped in, and hugged Chip. "And I got the other stuff too." She patted the side of her bag.

"No DNA thing." Chip glanced back toward the kitchen. His father would walk out, rubbing his hands on a dish towel any second. "We're not doing it."

"I'm doing it," she said. "My gift to you, sweetie."

"My family's not your project. I thought you'd have moved on to another one by now."

"Good to see you again, Mr. Cooper." Ticia stepped forward as Chip's dad came out of the kitchen. "Happy weekend-before Thanksgiving." She lightly kissed Chip's father's cheek as if she and Lyn were the same age and shared the same social circles. Chip couldn't help but stare.

"Lyn," his dad said. "First name basis – please."

Carolann came through carrying large bowls of diced tomatoes and shredded lettuce in each hand. No greeting kisses were possible therefore, and Chip was relieved. He didn't think his mother would appreciate Ticia's comfortable "adulthood."

"Hi, Mrs. Cooper." Ticia clasped her hands in front of her, looking awkward and more her age. Maybe grown men bring a teenage girl up to adulthood whereas grown women keep them in line as children.

Carolann said, "I'm glad you could come. First things first
– I want to apologize. What I said at Rowan's house was out
of order."

Ticia shrugged. "Forget it."

"I assure you I haven't forgotten it, nor will I, but you're
very gracious. Please make yourself at home." She hoisted the
two bowls in red and iceberg-green gestures of welcome.

Chip's jaw dropped. He had told Ticia it would be an
apology dinner, as instructed, but he assumed the apology
would be implied, or at best, mumbled. He had so much to
learn about how adults made mistakes and then made up
for them. He was still trying to interpret the moody silence
still lingering between his parents since Rowan's party. It
had followed them throughout their holiday, meandering
the streets of Dublin, the Ring of Kerry and the Ring of
Dingle. If it weren't for the Murphy's Irish Stout and a better-
than-Bob-Dylan guitar player in O'Leary's Pub in Kilkenny,
they might have spent the whole week together dead quiet.
But once they'd both had a drink, the tensions between his
parents seemed to ease out, as usual. Even so, Chip certainly
had more to learn about navigating the confounding waters
of adulthood.

"Can I help with anything?" Ticia asked. "I could put the
flowers in a vase."

At that moment, Rowan stepped into the house behind
Chip, an enormous bowl of puffy pink blancmange in her
arms. "I wanted to do a Mexican pudding, but the only recipe
I found was cinnamon fried ice cream. Horrible! I don't even
think the Scots would fry ice cream."

Ticia laughed. "I do love a deep fried Mars Bars now and
then."

"Yes! And deep fried pizza. I'm really a foodie, not a fattie,
despite appearances." Rowan laughed. "If I am re-incarnated,
I'll come back Scottish. But tonight, I've got the good English

pink stuff for our multicultural celebration." She handed the bowl of inflated pink peaks to Lyn. "This was always Morwenna's – " she stopped herself and took a deep breath. "My sister's favorite."

"It is indeed pink!" Carolann laughed.

"Yes, but the taste is… " Rowan looked into the bowl Lyn was now holding. "Opalescent blue."

No one spoke.

"And saxophone." Rowan winked at Carolann.

"Whoa, what do you put in there?" Ticia shrugged off her jacket. "I can't wait to try it."

Chip saw she'd worn a long-sleeve t-shirt that said *Carpe Diem*. When did Ticia not seize the day? He hung her jacket in the coat closet and helped her find a vase for her flowers. She used Carolann's kitchen scissors to snip the stems off at the base and then put the flowers in cold water. Chip had seen his mother do this with flowers. Maybe all women knew how to handle cut flowers. Now that he'd observed the process, had he diluted his masculinity? Henrik and Maarten definitely wouldn't know shit about flowers. More information he'd gained only to keep to himself.

"Let's go wash our hands." Ticia led Chip from the kitchen into the entryway loo, where they stood side by side, soaping their hands. Chip had to remind himself she'd had two different friends who'd lived in his house, and she knew the lay-out long before he did. "Do you want to save your parents' marriage or not?" she asked. "I'm doing you a big favor here, kiddo."

"No. Not tonight."

"You're only here for one year. You can enter into adulthood, fully functional and balanced. Take home a happy family as a souvenir from England."

Chip dried his hands. "Or a disaster."

The phone rang just as they were sitting down. "Leave it," Carolann said. "They can call back."

Lyn said, "It's probably your sister with more antiques vendors for you."

It rang again.

"That's why I said to leave it." Carolann smiled a quick, tight grin. "The machine gets it and she'll be thrilled I have to call her back. She'll save a dollar."

Lyn added, "And she'll be thrilled if she misses your call back, because then you'll be saved by her answering machine."

"Yes." Carolann stared at Lyn.

Chip explained, "My Aunt Maryann's greeting is a Bible verse and then it says *praise the lord, leave a message.* Sometimes, she emails to tell us to call her machine, if it's one of her favorite verses she thinks we ought to hear."

Rowan giggled.

The phone rang again. Whoever was calling was more persistent than Maryann normally would be.

Ticia waited half a beat to see if anyone would run to answer the phone. No one did. "My mom has a crazy sister too," she said. "Well, not crazy. Far from crazy, in fact. She's a psychiatrist. They love each other, and they compete with each other. I guess it's a classic love-hate sister thing."

"I thought your aunt had a llama farm," Chip said. The phone rang one last time and stopped. The silence seemed to echo. "In central California far from civilization."

"She does," Ticia said. "Llamas spit, but apparently, interacting with animals is stabilizing for unbalanced people. She's incensed that my family doesn't have a dog or iguanas or anything. She doesn't even have kids, but she still tells my mom all about how to be a parent."

"Sounds familiar…" Carolann looked up. "Sisters."

Chip watched Rowan, unusually silent. Had everyone forgotten she had a beloved dead twin sister?

Ticia continued, "Standing joke in my family – if I really mess up, they'll send me to that llama farm. No Internet. No

Cable. They don't even have TV."

"No internet?" Chip shuddered. "That's not a joke, that's a nightmare."

Rowan flipped her knife over, once. "Carolann, everything smells wonderful. Would it be presumptuous of me to offer to say grace? You do say grace before meals?"

"We sure do." Lyn winked at Chip. "If we don't forget."

Ticia clasped her hands, closed her eyes, and bowed her head. Rowan raised her glass, and the three Coopers lowered their chins but watched Rowan.

"To family. Old and new." She set her glass down. "Thanks, God."

Ticia picked up a taco, tipped her head and took a bite. She kissed her fingertips. "*Muy rico.*"

"*Muchas gracias.*" Carolann giggled.

Rowan nodded, chewed. Nodded and chewed. Chip realized his mother was either very brave or very foolish to fix tacos for his Mexican friend and the British expat from Texas. Finally, Rowan leaned back in her chair and patted her ample stomach. "Lovely jubbly."

"How many for coffee?" Carolann stood, counted raised hands, and scuttled away toward the kitchen.

Ticia said suddenly, "Mr. Cooper, uh, Lyn, I'm doing dentistry for Career Day. Maybe Chip told you?"

"No," Chip barked.

"I'm supposed to graph some adult tooth patterns before my meeting with the dentist tomorrow. Especially the back teeth, and the gums and get buccal swabs. My mom's out of town. I need at least one more volunteer. I was hoping–"

Carolann stuck her head through the doorway. "Career Day's not till March."

Chip gasped. How did she know when Career Day was? "No, it's not," he said. "Not March."

Ticia looked at Chip. The world's most incompetent liar. She and Carolann simultaneously responded, "Yes, March."

Carolann continued, "It was in the newsletter last week. Lyn, I meant to tell you I signed you up for health care. I didn't realize there was dentistry."

"Cool," Ticia said. "The school's Admin thinks no one reads the newsletters."

Lyn flattened his hand on the table. "I have that NHS conference in March, Carolann. I wish you'd have asked me."

Chip watched his parents. He still had no idea what triggered the recent tension between them. The last thing they needed was a new conflict.

"If I asked, you might have said no." She came in and stood by the table. "Today's children need more parent involvement. Do it for Chip. Right before spring break. I'll help prepare your slides. Whatever you need. March 23rd."

The phone rang again. Of course it was the same ring tone, but somehow it sounded more insistent in the silence. No one moved.

"That's exactly one month before my birthday," Rowan said. "Don't forget about Glastonbury."

Carolann nodded, and the phone rang.

Ticia said, "Actually the school will assign a student liaison, which is what I'm doing for Dr. Sales. He's my dentist, and I'm doing this powerpoint thing, helping with his prep before his official student liaison is assigned. And we're meeting up tomorrow, so um, can I do my mock dental exam on one of you?"

Carolann turned back to the kitchen.

"Do me, dear." Rowan hefted herself out of her chair. "We salute your involvement in school. Should I lie on the floor?" In an instant she was flat on her back on the carpet.

Chip heard his mother finally answer the phone in the kitchen.

"Actually," Ticia said to Rowan, "It'd be better to have one of Chip's parents, so if I need more records later, I could just ask Chip. Plus, it's all within the school community. They think that's important." She looked at Lyn, and Chip saw her expression as identical to the one in her topless photo – the one his dad especially liked.

Rowan sat up, her stomach resting on her open legs. "Just as well." She laughed. "I've never liked the dentist."

Lyn ran his tongue around his teeth. "Can I just tip my head back?"

Ticia pulled a handful of cotton buds from a box in her purse. "Sure." She spread swabs and a small plastic spatula on the table. "I'm not exactly sure what they can see from these gum samples, but I guess I'll find out."

"Bacteria causes cavities." Rowan shrugged. She took an armful of plates into the kitchen.

"Chip, I hope this benefits your education. I'm not sure I can do the thing in March."

Ticia held Chip's father by the chin. "As they say…" she sounded just like the dental hygienist. "This won't hurt a bit."

The fact that Ticia had found a DNA testing lab and bought a home-sampling kit for Chip was shocking enough. Those things must be expensive. He couldn't believe he was now watching his friend scrape food debris from the inside of his father's mouth. The results might be skewed by blancmange… the report would name Chip the son of Jello.

Rowan tip-toed back into the dining room.

Carolann came from the kitchen, her face ashen. "I'm afraid I've had some bad news from home. My father's very ill. They're not sure what it is. They want me there for the… well, the *duration* is the word Maryann used."

"Go," Rowan said. "First flight tomorrow. I'll drive you to Gatwick or Heathrow."

"We'll all go," Lyn said.

Carolann shook her head.

Rowan said, "You don't mess around with a health issue. And you can make things right with your sister. Go."

"To be honest, it may be nothing. He's a hypochondriac. But they're very upset. My mother called first."

"Your mother has never called here, Carolann." Lyn said. "To pay for an international call, it must be serious. We will all go."

"Can I miss school?" Chip asked. "We have those projects in Theory of Knowledge."

"We never should have moved." Carolann rubbed her arms.

"That's Maryann's opinion," Lyn said. "Not necessarily shared."

"If grandpa's dying, I know I should –"

"He's not dying." Carolann turned to Chip. "You don't have to go."

"Chip can stay at my house," Rowan volunteered. "No change to the bus schedule since I'm right next door. He won't miss any school. Chip, you can stay in my yoga room. I'll show you the ropes I've installed on the wall. The floor mats make a lovely guest bed. It's great for deep relaxation when you're not studying."

"Oh," Chip said. "Uh…"

"I'm happy to have him," Rowan said. "You stay in Kansas as long as you need to. I hope you'll make it back for Glastonbury. That's where you'll get the divine influence you might need, if it doesn't work out with your sister in person. Anyway, that's weeks away. Maybe we should go sooner."

"I don't think I should miss school, but…" Chip didn't know what else to say. He definitely didn't want to stay in Rowan's yoga room.

"They want me to move back home immediately." Carolann shook her head.

"I bet they do," Lyn said.

"Anyway, they'll run some tests tomorrow, and he's got a scan or something next week, so we'll wait for results, I guess, and then I'll know better what to do. Maryann's probably got it all wrong."

"She's your only sister. Your twin. I need to get you to Glastonbury soon," Rowan said. "When is your birthday? Is there another significant date you and Maryann share? First Communion?"

"We're not Catholic," Carolann stared at Rowan.

"First Menses? Was it the same month? Same astrological season?"

Chip stared at Rowan. No way was he sleeping in her yoga room.

Ticia leaned into Chip. "Dude, stay at mine. My parents won't mind."

"First things first," Lyn said. "And first, we find out Cyrus Field's true bill of health."

Chapter 42

Eight weeks and many medical tests passed while Carolann waited for definitive news. Cyrus Field did not have cancer. It wasn't diabetes. Not epilepsy, obesity, cystic fibrosis, asthma, lupus, or pernicious anemia. One day he felt great, two days later, he couldn't breathe, eat, or get out of bed. There was mention of a rare bacteria from sub-Saharan Africa. Very unlikely – and testing would be expensive and inconclusive at best. Carolann began to know full well what the problem was – if she wasn't finding the vase, Barbara Ann just wanted her nurse-daughter home.

The first buds were beginning to show on the trees when Maryann called to tell Carolann to fly back. Their father was in the hospital for round-the-clock care.

In the meantime, the health crisis back home shifted focus away from the impasse in her marriage. Lyn and Carolann reached an unspoken accord to let things ease out. Carolann revealed no more big truths to her husband, and he settled in to an acceptance of what she'd already said.

"So it'll be just you men here at home." She folded a shirt into her suitcase.

"Chip's happy," Lyn said. "But I still wonder if we shouldn't all go."

"It was a lovely offer from Rowan, but not entirely practical. You can't really take the time off."

"What do you think your dad's got?"

Carolann shrugged. "A bad case of exaggeration."

"I hope that's all it is." Lyn watched her tuck rolled socks into the shoes she was packing.

"You should take Chip on that Beatles tour of Liverpool. Get his mind off his little friend." It had become clear, over the weeks, that Ticia truly had a boyfriend in Austria, though Carolann still didn't trust Chip's interest in her.

"I don't want you getting confused…" Lyn examined his fingernails. "You're going back there, and you might forget where home is."

"I won't." Carolann wondered if he would say the name Buck. Chip was almost due his "special gift," so the real father must have been on Lyn's mind.

"Don't let them push you around." Lyn handed her a pair of boots for the suitcase. "Take advantage. Try to make you stay."

Carolann nodded. "My return flight is in three weeks. I'll be on it."

Lyn stepped forward to hug her, squeezing the boots between them. The heels dug into her ribs. It was the first and only time in their marriage she was going somewhere without him. Carolann felt reassured by his hug. "You know when you told me about your vasectomy?"

Lyn pulled away. "You mean after I'd done it?"

"Yeah. After. Were you afraid to tell me?"

Lyn shrugged. "It was already done. What was there to be afraid of?"

"But I still wanted more kids."

"Impossible."

Carolann slotted the boots into her bag, and neither spoke.

Lyn finally said, "Carolann, are you plannng to tell Maryann about bathing Baby Ryan?"

"No."

"Good. This is no 12-step program where you have to come clean to everyone you've ever hurt. You owe them no ridiculous confession. You owe your sister nothing."

"Right." She zipped the suitcase. "She wants that vase, and I don't have it yet. So I'll go back, help my mother navigate the hospital with my dad. Check his blood pressure, try to get a diagnosis and an action plan, and then I'll come back here. Home."

Lyn sat on the bed and stared out the window. "They want me to re-up the contract."

"Another year?"

"Indefinitely. It's a good job. It's an excellent job."

"No."

"Or year by year. Though the pay structure's different. The contract requires your signature as well as mine. I couldn't even think about it if you'd refuse."

"Good." Carolann tucked her passport into her purse. "I refuse."

Lyn shook his foot at the ankle, his attention turned back to the gray sky outside.

"This shouldn't be a surprise," she said. "I never wanted to go abroad in the first place."

"You shouldn't be going back there without me."

Carolann scoffed.

"Something you said after Rowan's clambake..."

"What?" Carolann asked. He wanted to bring it up now, minutes before she'd leave the country?

"About that night – before you met me."

There was the yellow. The night itself, the experience of it was purple, dark summer thunderstorm purple. But the memory of it, discussing it with Lyn, brought the yellow.

"You used the word rape."

She stared at him. Slate gray. With a hard, bright, reflective glare.

"Carolann, if that's what happened, if this is a recovered memory, somehow, you'll have to deal with it. This trip is about your dad. But if Buck raped you –"

"He didn't."

"Maybe the distance has given you sudden clarity."

"That's not what I said."

"Do you even know what you said? Rape is demeaning and violent. Whether the rapist knows his victim or not, it's a crime. Black-and-white."

"And shades of gray sometimes. Other colors."

"No. No variations. It is evil and invasive and violent." Lyn shook his head. "If that's what happened, and this is the first time you've seen it for what it was, you'll experience the horror of it all over again when you see him. I assume you will see him."

"Not necessarily." Seeing Buck hardly mattered.

Lyn continued, "Emotionally, those scars don't just heal. Even if you suppressed the memory. Don't go today. We'll make other arrangements, and I'll go with you."

Carolann sat on the bed and rested her arm on the suitcase. She spoke without looking at Lyn. His arm rested on the suitcase between them as well, a reassuring bulk. "It wasn't him," she said. "It was me. That's what I tried to tell you about that. I took advantage."

"For Christ's sake," he said. "You were a teenage girl. That's not how it works."

"How's it work, then?"

"He was drunk," Lyn said. "You were drunk. You took advantage of each other. You have it all wrong."

"I'm guilty of –"

"Of nothing. How dare you equate yourself with, with… It's senseless. I can't stand to even talk about it."

A woman who'd seduce her sister's boyfriend and then raise the boyfriend's child without his knowledge would be a terrible person. But of course, that wasn't her true story. Even if her husband thought it was. Lyn didn't think she was an evil seductress – he thought she was a weak teenage girl. In fact, he demanded that of her.

She said, "I… I wanted to steal something from my sister. Something Maryann valued. I was obviously never in love with Buck." Carolann looked at Lyn. She knew he liked hearing that confirmation.

He nodded.

"The opportunity presented itself. But I didn't realize what I was taking. And that I couldn't give it back." Was today the day she would finally tell him? *Chip is your son. I have let you believe something untrue. His hands are fine, but I believe Chip is your son.* She couldn't say it unless she knew. Chip could indeed still be Buck's. He could be the son of either of the two men.

"What?" Lyn asked.

"Men can be raped," she said. "More than seduction – forced into having a sexual encounter they didn't intend. It isn't always so clear-cut. You weren't there."

Lyn slammed his hand on her suitcase and the bed reverberated. He stood.

"He sure wasn't innocent. But I did take advantage."

"Listen to yourself! Think about true victims. Think about their struggle to heal. Attacked, damaged by vile criminals. You have no right to redefine this. You blur the lines to suit your bizarre burden of guilt, and you victimize these women all over again." His face was red, and his neck bulged.

"Then it's a matter of vocabulary. We need a better word. It's not a sociological argument, though. This is between us. You and me."

Lyn stared at her hard. "Do not drink anything, Carolann, while you're home. You sometimes say silly things. The vocabulary you choose is important. And you're way off base. Can you promise me?"

"If you're not the one pouring my cocktails, sure." She took his hands in hers. "I promise."

Lyn nodded. "That night you did something immoral. You were promiscuous. I do understand your shame."

Carolann felt the familiar tension in her shoulders. Sometimes Lyn used the word *wanton. Loose. Easy.* She didn't like the story – how he'd saved her from her licentious nature – but she worked hard to make it true.

"But every day I'm grateful to you for the gift of our son. And for our marriage. I didn't want to bring up the contract renewal yet, but –"

"One year. We agreed to one year." Carolann shook her head.

"It's a good contract. They pay Chip's tuition, the house, utilities, the car –"

"I hate to drive here. Wrong-side steering wheel, wrong side of the road, and the roundabouts. You make one wrong turn, and it takes 40 minutes to correct it."

"But you've made such progress."

"I look in the rear-view mirror and it's not there. I reach for the hand-brake, and it's on the other side. Turn on the radio, and I can't understand what they're saying. No."

Lyn said, "It's good money."

"My father has lived every day with *the bottom line* in his sites. I'm not doing it. Life is not all about money."

"It's important work. I'm of value here."

"When do they need to know?" Carolann looked at Lyn carefully. When she came home, she'd have to tell him a few things, and she had no idea what he'd do, or in turn, what she'd do. She would not be married to a man's shoulder. She would not crawl into bed, night after night, with a wall. "Let me say good-bye to Chip so we can go to the airport," she said. "Right now I just want to get home."

Chapter 43

"So, how's it going with your dad?" Ticia asked.

"Weird." Chip slammed his locker shut. "We don't know when my mom's coming back."

"Is your grandfather dying or what?"

"Of exhaustion, maybe. My mom says he wore himself out, complaining, so they committed him."

"More like he wore them out. Wore out his welcome with your family."

"And my mom's there doing everyone's laundry."

"At least it's a big American washing machine." Ticia looked down the hall. "I need to tell you something."

Chip's heart skipped a beat. He had nearly forgotten the DNA thing, Ticia swabbing his dad's buccal regions. "Ok... what?"

"Something kind-of intense," she said. "Let's go somewhere private."

"I've got the hour free."

Ticia led him toward the lower school playground. There was no one outside in the chilly drizzle. A damp row of tricycles awaited riders if the weather cleared before afternoon recess. The little playhouse beckoned, dark, and dry inside. Chip knew it would smell like wet pine. Instead she headed for the chain-link fence at the school's perimeter, to a little-used recycling area just outside. Ticia pulled on the fence, and it gave way to a decent-sized gap. She shimmied through and pushed it wide for Chip.

"We're not allowed." He shook his head. Crushed beer

cans and plastic milk bottles littered the ground beyond the fence.

"Ten minutes." She pulled the fence open wider. "My dad's faculty, remember? I got to talk to you."

Chip squeezed through the gap. She grabbed his hand and led him between two giant metal bins – a blue one for clear glass and a green one for green. She sat on a rock wall behind the bins and patted the damp granite next to her. Chip sat. Small shards of glass crunched like sticky beach pebbles under his feet, and it smelled like old wine.

"He finally did it," she grabbed her knees. Ticia's eyes were red, and her face looked puffy. She'd been crying? And this was the first Chip had noticed?

"Who?"

"Andrew, the shit head, broke up with me. On the phone."

"Oh. Uh… that sucks. You ok?"

She took a deep breath. "Yup. Over it now." She smiled.

Chip jammed his hands under his thighs, and he watched her for a minute. He leaned away from Ticia to see around the big green bin toward the school. Maybe someone was already out there on the playground. A teacher, even. Neame! "Should we go back in?" His voice squeaked.

"Not unless we're done out here, sweetie." Ticia looked him in the eyes. "You've been very patient."

Chip swallowed hard.

"I think it's finally your turn, baby."

Cold wet rock wall, sharp edges under his hands, under his rear. Wet jeans. Decomposing, organic smell of beer and wine dregs and fermentation. She hopped off the wall and stood in front of him, between his knees. She reached forward and held his face in her hands. Chip was only shaving a year, and now Ticia's hands were on his jaws. Did she feel stubble? He was off campus and out of his league and unsure if his cheeks felt like a baby's face in her hands. Her black hair glistened with rain drizzle and Chip stared into it, controlling his breathing.

She stepped forward and climbed onto him, onto the wall, straddling him. "You ok?" she asked.

He knew his voice would squeak again, and he nodded. His mother always said girls might take advantage. People didn't think girls could do that to boys, but they did. If he looked down, he'd be staring right into Ticia's chest. If he looked up, it'd be her lips. She had him caught between a rock and a hard place – he finally knew what that phrase actually meant – and he kissed her. Found her open lips, gently pushed his tongue into her, and she kissed him back. Soft and hard and exploring and insistent. Jesus! Kissing Ticia Olague!

She was on his lap, wedged in close to him. He had his hands on her backside. He pushed a cold hand in under her shirt and felt the smooth contours of her back, and pushed the other hand deep into her hair, thick and soft.

"I thought you were ready." She pulled away, laughing. "But I didn't know quite how ready."

"Don't fuck with me, T. I'm not just rebound material. You know that."

She ducked her head and kissed his neck. His ear. His neck again.

Whatever she'd ask, he'd say yes. She could fuck with him to her heart's content. He'd be rebound... he'd be unbound, over-wound, he'd run aground, he was screaming, but he made no sound.

She stopped. "I shouldn't."

Oh yes. You absolutely should. Chip said nothing. Should.

She whispered in his ear, "On the other hand... what the fu—"

Chip pulled her hips in close to him and his mouth stopped her foul language. This was going awfully fast, for his first kiss. With his best friend. *Shouldn't? Should.* She wriggled into him. She was too old for him. Neame had his number. What was he doing? How did anyone ever say no to this girl? To any girl? Coitus interruptus? No way.

He was swollen and swelling more, and if the world suddenly exploded and Chip was smashed to smithereens, well, fine.

Ticia pulled back again, yanked her hips back from his groin and looked down between them. "Baby packing a fatty in there?"

"What?" Interruptus, all right. She was mocking him. He was taking a blow for all mankind.

"Baby poppa chubby?" She threw her head back, laughing.

He glared at her.

"You got it wrong, baby," she said. "I'm joking around. That's what I do. But I'm not teasing you." She looked down between their legs again. "I'm not going to rush it, but I do want this. And I think, I hope, you want me too."

Chip nodded. She fit so nicely into his coat, how could he help it?

Suddenly Ticia froze. She whispered, "stay still."

The fence squeaked open, and they could hear three or four solid footsteps. Men's footsteps.

A teacher Chip didn't know stepped right in front of them, stared at them, and without saying a word, dropped his Diet Coke bottle into the recycler. The glass banged inside the metal container and shattered. "Ms. Olague," he said. "Your father know you're out here?"

"Not unless you tell him, Mr. Head. It's more innocent than it looks."

Mr. Head looked Chip up and down. "There's a rule against leaving campus, and you're aware of that. Are you not?"

"Yes, sir," Chip said.

"He's new to the school. I needed to talk to him out here. You don't have to tell my dad."

"What your father decides about you is his prerogative. You're his daughter. This young man, I certainly hope, is no relation. And he admits he knew our closed campus rule."

"Neame already has something against him, and he's a straight-A student. Come on, you know Stewart Neame."

Mr. Head chuckled.

"My dad doesn't have to hear about this at all. You have no idea what you'd be starting."

Chip had never seen her plead.

"I'm afraid you don't know what you have *already* started," the teacher said. He turned his back and went ahead of them through the gap. "Let's go."

Ticia leaned into Chip's ear as she climbed off his lap. "I got an idea what I started." She scampered after the teacher.

He couldn't help it – he rolled along behind the teacher toward the office. Almost eager in his nonchalance, he finally had that tough-blasé, laid-back walk down. He shook out a leg inside his jeans, adjusting himself as they walked.

She squinted her blue eyes at him as they walked, a silent apology. A little walking firebomb, manganese Tinkerbell.

But now that the fire was lit, it was lit. He shrugged, like he'd seen worse, he'd handle it, he was a man here, he could take it, whatever it was. It could be suspension, expulsion, a permanent blot on his record. But whatever it would be, it was *worth it.*

Chapter 44

Carolann pulled a load of her father's wet shirts from the washing machine to hang them on plastic hangers. She wondered when he'd last analyzed the cost-saving differential between line drying versus an efficient clothes-dryer. In their family, Cyrus' pronouncements were rarely questioned. And he was probably right – a dryer was an energy hog.

No test results had yet revealed concrete news about his health, although each time they talked of releasing him, he suddenly ached or couldn't breathe. Mostly though, it seemed that Barbara Ann was the one with the problems, most of which centered on a desire not to look after her own house. Carolann had now been in Kansas for 12 days. She had filled both the regular freezer and the deep-freeze with home-cooked meals for her parents, she washed and re-hung curtains, cleared gutters, and bled radiators. She dutifully confirmed that her father's blood pressure matched the numbers recorded by hospital staff.

There was little else she could do to be helpful, and there was no question she'd be on the return flight as scheduled. If Lyn would have her after she revealed a few difficult truths, she realized she wanted to stay with him in England. It was an entirely unexpected realization. If.

Maryann came into their parents' laundry room, hands on hips, and watched her sister. "It's not like I wasn't doing it," she said. "But I'm not as fast as you."

"You called me back from a foreign country for this?"

"I thought you'd have some pieces for the store by now. Inventory's low since Christmas."

"I'm not looking for inventory for your store."

"I noticed."

"If you want me to buy for your store, you need to ask me."

"You'd never do it. What *do* you do all day?"

Carolann snapped the wrinkles from a shirt.

"Well, you're not working your ass off for little boy wonder. You have no background in education, so it can't come from you that he's Kid Perfect."

Carolann didn't want Maryann talking about Chip. "I've found a thousand blue-and-white things, if that's all you want."

"Mint condition? Would you even recognize mint condition?" Maryann grabbed one of the freshly-hung shirts and yanked creases into its sleeves. "As usual, Carolann, you miss the whole point."

"My mission is the Beemasters vase. And I thought I was called home because our father's condition was serious, and I'm a registered nurse."

"You want him on his death bed?" Maryann scoffed. "Melanoma and kidney failure? Aneurysm? Would that make you happy?"

"No."

"Cardiac arrest? Daddy in a box?"

"Don't be foolish."

"I swear Carolann, all they talk about is how goddamn wonderful you are. You had to come home. Forgive my sad, sorry, fat ass."

Carolann looked at her sister. Maryann had, in fact, put on weight. When had she started swearing like this?

"Carolann this, Carolann that." Maryann pressed her hand on the metal top of the washing machine till it buckled and twanged. "My shirt collars are never ironed like yours. I can't cook a lasagna that holds together like yours."

"Since when do they eat lasagna?"

"Since the fucking fourth of never. I'm sick of driving an hour from Kansas City for them to tell me I don't measure up to you."

"You've always been the privileged first-born. Better than me at everything."

Maryann shrugged. "I envied you. You had it easy. No expectations."

"But they paid for your college. Your summer activities. Cheerleading camp. Your wedding." Carolann heard her voice falter.

"Yeah, I've got Buck. You've got your own money. Independence." Her voice trailed off. "I can't stand being jealous of you."

"Buck's business is solid. You have a beautiful home. Your shop…"

"Buck is a fucking lot of work. Always was. Holding back, proving my fucking worthiness. Left him begging and turning to other girls in high school. Sluts."

"That was a long time ago. Life isn't high school."

"Life *is* fucking high school. Every time I refused him, Mama said I proved I was worthy of *us*. You're about the only one who didn't – he wasn't into you because of your hair, and your freckles, and you were always weird and skinny, and your nose —"

"Enough," Carolann said.

"Point is, even if you'd been the first-born, you know, Mama and Daddy promising you the wedding and school tuition and all, Buck wouldn't have gone for you. But I still envied you. You had choices."

Carolann took a deep breath. "Why did you let him do that stuff?"

"A man has needs."

Carolann shook her head.

"He told me every time." Maryann smiled. "Every slut was in love with him. Melissa Brown, HT with her hairy tits."

Carolann said, "I thought HT stood for Hoity Toity – snob from Chicago."

"Grace Edwards. Becky Preston. Birthmark on her ass."

"Grace Edwards?" Carolann repeated.

"They all thought they were his first, stupid cunts."

Carolann raised her eyebrows.

"But it was all practice for our marriage. And I held off, not because of God, or Mama or Daddy. It was Buck. Being worthy of Buck."

"Wow." The husband was more important than God in her sister's marriage too. It ran in the family.

"Everyone knew except you," Mayrann sneered. "The back of his car, Buck and a slut rocking the Buick. You thought Buck was the Golden Boy."

"No," Carolann said. "I knew."

Suddenly Maryann fell silent, watching her twin.

The way Carolann would answer her sister's question, or choose not to answer it, gave her power.

Maryann waited.

Carolann was silent.

"Anyway, Mama was right."

Carolann nodded. She couldn't wait to get back to England. Petty concerns were easily confused for larger issues in Kansas, and Carolann was eager to leave them all behind.

"But they're in need now, more than ever. Mama and Daddy both. You have to move back home."

"I'm honored they like how I starch a shirt, but –"

"Fine," Maryann spat. "I get it. If they treated you like I've had it lately, you must have been this close to slitting your wrists." She held up her pink acrylic nails, thumb and forefinger nearly touching.

"Suicide is a sin."

"Yeah, right." Maryann flipped her fingers into a gun

charade and shot herself in the temple. "Why are we doing their laundry anyway? They should hire help, except our father's too cheap. I don't know how she puts up with him."

"Vows," Carolann said. "Remember your faith? Call your own answering machine sometime."

"Fucking machine's broken. Vows! Let me ask you – don't you think we could have paid off Mrs. Loony Bird for the broken vase – big symbol of her wedding vows or whatever – a hundred times by now? People shouldn't form attachments to material things like that. We did her a favor, trashing that thing."

"Not sure she sees it that way."

"You kidding? She wrote that thing off ages ago."

"Does Dad believe that?"

"He should. Our mother and the loony bird discussed it right before your wedding. Were you too gaga to notice?"

"No, I knew Edith Heaney brought me a gift, and Mama pushed her out the door. I never even knew what the gift was."

"Who cares what the fucking gift was. Probably some ugly picture frame piece of crap. Mama slammed the door in her face, and we got our closure that we needed."

"You mean if I found the perfect Beemasters, we weren't even going to give it to Edith Heaney?"

"She must be 98 years old."

"But all your vendor lists and progress reports, to give our father some kind of comfort. Square the debt. Cotswolds, Petsworth, Stoke-on-Trent."

"Glad you're enjoying your exotic world travels. I'll hold down the fort in Bumfuck Egypt while you scamper around doing reiki massage with your hippie neighbor and having garden parties with the Queen."

"You have no idea." Carolann's heart pounded, thinking about Rowan's little car zipping through West Country hedgerows at high speeds. Or being in the tubes 100 feet under London with dirt and mice and muttering weirdos and incomprehensible announcements about bombs and evacuation.

Maryann said, "You have no business sense. I'd sell that fucker for three times the price you'd pay over there. At least. And I've got buyers. At least I have a built a solid network of buyers, thanks to that stupid thing."

Carolann turned her back and hung her father's last shirt. "We still owe Mrs. Heaney," she said. "We never even apologized."

"Apologized? Do you know what made her snap?"

"We broke something of value to her." The entire town, county and state of Kansas knew the story.

"That triggered her memory..." Maryann pressed her lips together, her slick of cinnamon apple lipstick looked sticky. English women wore more muted lipsticks, and Carolann realized she preferred the subtlety.

Maryann continued, "She was a lit fuse, ready to blow. Post-traumatic stress or something. You're the nurse, what's the psycho thing that makes soldiers jump off buildings or shoot up people in shopping malls? The loony bird told Mama about England, the war, those men."

"What men?"

"Men who gang-raped her or something. Or one guy." Maryann shook her head. "I don't know. It was the war. Atrocities."

"I never heard about this. There were American soldiers over there – decent guys – which is how she met Sedgewick Heaney, who she loved."

Maryann shook her head. "Maybe she loved him, but she was unbalanced. Damaged goods. Ask Mama sometime why the old loony bird ran off and eloped, which is a sin."

"Gossip is also a sin," Carolann said. "Not to mention, half the stories about Edith Heaney were invented by us. We should go apologize right now."

"You broke the thing."

"Both of us."

"I can't." Maryann shook her head. "Buck's coming home early for dinner. And Mama won't approve. Call the hospital and tell her. Daddy will have his aneurysm you want."

"Our neighbor deserves our apology."

"Don't stir things up, Carolann. She locked us up, Mama saved us, and the courts couldn't make anything stick, so just leave it alone now."

Carolann looked at her sister. *Nothing will stick.* When Baby Ryan died, Maryann called Paul Mayer, Buck's football friend-turned-policeman, and Paul came to Carolann's house to ask questions… not blasting his sirens, but flashing his lights, red and blue, red and blue… he left them rolling in the pewter twilight for 20 minutes while they talked in the front room, so everyone would wonder. Paul eventually told Buck and Maryann, *don't pursue it, nothing will stick.*

But people talked. They fell silent in the grocery store when Carolann walked through the produce aisle, they eyeballed her returns in the video library, they stood at a distance from the sandbox where she watched Chip play in the park. A girl in school told Chip his mother was a baby-killer. Fortunately, Chip already knew Carolann Cooper to be a strong and moral woman, which he told his classmates.

Maryann said, "Don't say I didn't warn you."

Carolann followed her sister out of their parents' house, into the chilly afternoon. She glanced toward the neighbor's house, not far away. It was still painted nicely.

Maryann got in her car, slammed the door, and rolled down her window while the car pumped gray exhaust from its tailpipe. "If you've got a checklist of betrayals and apologies in your pocket, I'm sorry I can't stick around to hear mine." Maryann cackled like a hyena, plucked her head back into her car, and drove away.

Chapter 45

Lyn dialed his wife's cell phone number for the third time in ten minutes. Even though he had not yet successfully rehearsed the bad news, he wanted to reach her voice-to-voice. Suspension from school, unblemished academic record now blemished, budding maturity confounded by unhealthy interest in girls. One girl. Carolann would never agree to extend their contract now. About Chip, she'd been exactly right.

Even worse, Chip seemed proud of it. He was hanging his head and apologizing, but then Lyn would catch him walking with a swagger. What was the boy thinking? Off-campus, kissing a girl. There had never been any indication that Chip would behave like this. Once again, Lyn called Carolann's cell and went straight to voice mail.

Carolann was probably in the hospital tending to her father's invented symptoms. Lyn's father-in-law may not have been genuinely sick before, but if he knew what Lyn was spending on international calls to a tri-band cell phone, he'd croak.

Music blasted in Chip's room, and then the speaker volume was quickly lowered. Rap, as usual. Maybe Lyn should ban that rap music. He'd never had a kid home on suspension before. He'd never been suspended himself. What to do? Carolann had never been in trouble in school either – she wasn't any more likely to know what to do than Lyn was. Though having her in another country didn't help. He stared at the keypad on his phone. It had been 20 seconds since he'd last called. Should he go into Chip's room, make a snide comment – put the boy in his place with sarcasm – or an overt reprimand? Or not? The boy was no longer a toddler testing an overheard swear word… Chip was fast-approaching manhood. He desperately needed the right guidance. Lyn needed to understand what was going through Chip's head.

It was Buck! That's where Chip got his misjudgment. Of course, Ticia was the first girl who'd caught his attention, and once she did, in an instant, Chip was Buck's son. His eager, risk-taking, hyperactive libido… that's what Chip was made of. It nearly cost Buck his marriage. Directly or indirectly, it cost him the terrible price of being childless. Was that Chip's possible future? Lyn massaged his scalp with his fingers. Carolann sometimes accused Lyn of being overwrought. Letting worries and jealousies and over-thinking get the better of him. Maybe in this one instance, she was right. Many successful men were once suspended in high school – expelled, even, or they dropped out, or they never went to college. Everybody finds their own paths to their successes and failures, despite the best laid plans of their parents. Chip wouldn't necessarily turn out like Buck. Though at least Buck had good hands. Buck, who was probably mere minutes from Carolann at this very moment with his marvelous hands. Perhaps they were in the same room. Lyn needed to speak with his wife. He needed to get her back home.

Chapter 46

Carolann walked up Edith Heaney's gravel driveway, same as the twins used to do every Thursday afternoon as little girls. It was smaller than she remembered. One brave purple crocus had dared to bloom – the stark purple color that made her smell licorice – and several others were testing the air with their leaves. Carolann rolled the thin fabric of her pocket lining in her fingers, and watched the steam of her breath in the cool air. It would be good to finally speak with Edith Heaney. There was plenty Carolann could say to her sister too, but those conversations would do no good. Truth, in its essence, had to be carefully weighed before delivery.

Not long ago, Carolann would have described the Heaney house as *imposing*. Now she saw just a small Kansas farmbox, with a roof and windows, and faded paint. Could Carolann truly have been gone only a few months? Evidently, distance, more than plain time, is what firmly shifts a person's perspective.

She pressed the doorbell, and after several minutes, the door creaked open a crack. An old lady squinted out. "Yes?"

"Mrs. Heaney? I'm Carolann Field, from next door. Carolann Cooper now." A worn, recycled smell escaped the home, like an old vacuum in need of a bag change. Dust and fatigue and floral air-freshener aerosol. The smell was probably genuine. "I'm one of the twins from next door."

"I know who you are."

"I, uh… I live in England now."

"I heard about that. Is everything ok? Your parents are ok?"

"My dad's in the hospital actually, which is why I've come back. Maybe you know I'm a nurse. It seems that he'll be fine."

"I see." Edith opened the door another half-inch.

The smell was both stale and sweet. Old wool, maybe, and mildew. "I think we live just a couple hours from where you grew up in Devon. That's where you're from?"

Edith stood staring at Carolann in the doorway. "That was a long time ago," she whispered. Finally she opened the door wider, stepped forward, and touched Carolann's cheek. "It agrees with you." She smiled. "An English rose."

Carolann didn't expect Edith's reaction. Her dry hand, like powdered bones, on her cheek. Edith dropped her hand to Carolann's and pulled her inside the front room. The smell was strong, but the house was immaculate. Carolann sat on Edith's flowered sofa. "It's only for a year, but I'm starting to settle in," she said. "Maybe we'll stay longer."

"That happens sometimes." Edith sighed. She ran her wrinkled hand along the threadbare antimacassar on the sofa arm. The veins in her hand stood proud but vulnerable, thin-skinned tubes of purple on the delicate mottled pinky-beige hand and wrist.

Carolann hoped no nurse would ever have to run an IV line into that fragile hand. "I guess you haven't been back often," she said.

"Twice," Edith said. "When my mother died, God rest her, and my father. Should have gone back when they were alive. People make such a fuss for funerals. Dead person's never going to appreciate it. Neighbors had to accommodate me like an after-thought. If you stay overseas, come back more often. That's my advice."

Carolann nodded.

"The English countryside is beautiful in spring. I suppose

that's my other advice. Make time to enjoy it. Near where I lived. Pure gold."

"Was it hard for you to move here?" Carolann asked. "Moving abroad must be easier today, with technology. You were courageous. Mr. Heaney must have been a wonderful man."

"He was a good catch." Edith smiled. "I live with the thought that I come from there and not here. My *otherness*, my *Englishness* defines me here, even though I almost don't know what being English means anymore. I would be as foreign there as I am here. In some respects, more so. I must have an American accent now. It's not the life I once imagined for myself. But you bet, he was worth it."

Carolann smiled. Mrs. Heaney did sound different from people in England, but she sure didn't sound American.

"But I accepted that *otherness* a long time ago. It's like a beloved old sweater I wear every day. Even when no one sees it, it's there, next to my skin." The old lady looked out the window, toward Carolann's girlhood home.

"I'm sorry about what happened with us," Carolann said. "With my family. That's what I wanted to come over here and say."

Edith looked at Carolann carefully.

"I'm sorry about the vase we broke, and the way we behaved, my sister and me. And my parents. And the police. All of it."

Edith nodded, her eyes sharp and clear.

"My mother said later it just got out of control."

"I loved you girls. Both of you, despite what —"

"It was fear," Carolann said. "We were afraid, then our parents were afraid. Fear got the better of everyone."

"You were a dear little girl, smart and resourceful. So different from your sister. Your mother was blind to it, and I —"

"They wanted boys." Carolann stared at Edith Heaney. "I

was the second girl, and girls are expensive."

"We get what the Lord gives," Edith said. "And we should appreciate it. That was my mistake, of course, telling your mother that."

"No, I think it was... I only just learned... it was something in your past that scared my parents, something in England. We broke your vase, and something —"

"Your sister broke it. Your mother wouldn't accept that."

Carolann looked at Mrs. Heaney. "But your background – you'd been through some difficult times in the war, right? No. Forget I asked that. Your personal story is none of my business. I came to apologize." Carolann didn't know what to say and what to hold back. The truth was so slippery. How would she ever deliver the right words to her husband when she got back home? "Also, I wanted to tell you I'm still looking for a replacement for your vase. I know there was no better Beemasters. But if there's one in England, I hope to find it."

"Oh, honey, it doesn't matter. Before I left the country with Sedgewick, after we married, you see, my mother gave me that vase. In springtime, she always put my father's yellow oilseed flowers in it. I loved those yellow fields. Those fields brought Sedge and me together. I was her only daughter, you see. It was a beautiful gesture. That was its value to me. I tried to explain that to your mother, why I reacted the way I did when your sister broke it, but she wouldn't hear it. What background?"

"I'm sorry about all of it – the way my family reacted."

Edith said, "Sedge had been working with my father – a number of American soldiers worked our farm. They believed the yield of cooking oil could bring a nice profit in Kansas. Sedgewick was smart. He was right about the climate. The University of Kansas has made good use of his research – his and my father's. That work continues today. Your mother knows all of this. Your father did our financial records. Of course, you know my husband's lab. Barbara Ann knew

RAPESEED

everything. You know, I valued my friendship with your mother as well. Such a shame."

Carolann shuddered. All the children knew about the old witch loony bird's lab. Most never even knew Edith's real name. "Do you hate my mother?" Carolann asked. To hate one's mother seemed the privilege or the burden of the mother's children, and no one else.

"Of course not." Edith shrugged. "Hate wastes your days. Who knows how many I'll even have left. And I think about your mother now – her only grandchild so far away. I'm sure it's hard on parents when their children grow up and move on."

Carolann nodded. Of course, Edith had once been that child who moved away. She probably also knew something about Barbara Ann's other grandson. Small town... Still so many untruths, layers of deception and misunderstanding woven into its fabric.

Edith said, "I sometimes wonder if the criticism of a woman's child, or the way she is raising her children, might not be the most hurtful thing a woman can hear. A very deep wound."

"I guess every mother does the best she can do." Carolann thought of the long and broad-ranging list of concerns Maryann had, over the years, about Chip and the way he was being raised – all of which sent Carolann delving into secret, exhaustive research. Autism, hyperactivity, allergies, attachment disorders, sociopathology, strep throat, faulty tooth-flossing methods. Too smart for his own good.

"I told your mother that favoring one twin over the other was a mistake. I was clear about who smashed the vase and who lied about it."

"We both lied," Carolann quietly admitted.

"Your parents favored your sister. Until that day, it was never my business to say so." Edith shrugged. "But I had no idea the cost."

Carolann nodded, overwhelmed. Grateful and vindicated, yet terribly weighed down by the fact that if Mrs. Heaney observed the imbalance in her upbringing, it must have been true.

What else did Mrs. Heaney observe? This old loony woman might be wiser than anyone knew – she might be the key to reality, backwards through time, and on into the future. If Carolann dared ask her advice, would Mrs. Heaney tell her to divulge everything to Lyn right away? Should she voice her concerns – even potentially unfounded ones? What kind of a marriage prohibited a wife from worrying out loud? What kind of husband demanded only the glossy falsehoods of coupledom?

Carolann needed some kind of sign, telling her how to proceed. If there was a God up there, couldn't He tell her what to do? Of course, God was there. Carolann knew He was there. She was ready to know His answers. Of course she wasn't confusing the old loony bird's wisdom for God's truth. But why wasn't He offering her the words?

Mrs. Heaney broke Carolann's train of thought. "My dear girl, you've done a lovely thing coming over here today. Somehow, I believed you would. I hoped you would. I tried to come see you on your wedding day, that morning, do you remember that?"

Carolann nodded.

"Goodness, that was a long time ago. You have a teenager at home now. I bet you're very proud of that boy. I suspected that deep down, you would want to come have a chat with me someday. Patience is the answer to most things we desire. A lot of years, but you're just as lovely as ever, Carolann. Thank you, sweet girl. It was just a matter of time."

Chapter 47

Chip sensed his father's presence in his bedroom doorway yet again, and he turned to find Lyn standing there, hand on hip. Kind-of a woman's stance, like he was trying to step into both roles at the same time, dad and mom. He really seemed to need his wife back home. Chip had never before felt sorry for his dad. Everything was getting very mixed up.

Lyn shifted his weight. "If you write a formal letter of apology to the school's administration, they might clear your record. It's probably stronger than a verbal plea."

"I could do that, but I don't want to seem fake. Like too American. False remorse. Maybe I should say it out loud. Go before the board?" It sounded very official and well-meaning, this *going before the board* idea.

"Your mother should be home in an hour, if she's not delayed. We'll see what she thinks." Lyn jammed his hands in his pockets, puffed out his khaki pleats, and disappeared into the house.

Chip had one more day of suspension. His father was beginning to repeat himself. At least when Carolann came home from Kansas, she'd have new concerns to voice, maybe tears and shouting… new guilt and compunction, and she'd call God in on it. But Chip didn't regret it. He lay down on his unmade bed and thought about Ticia's lips… and her tongue. He'd have to clean his room before his mother got home. He scanned the surfaces. It would take 10 minutes.

But what was the matter with Ticia? He'd had one email

warning him that she couldn't talk or text or smoke signal. Her mom was freaking out, calling her psychiatrist sister and inventing new rules for their family to live by. But if Ticia had been able to send one message, why not another? Just to tell Chip that she didn't regret it, or she did, or part of it, or none of it, except for the part about getting caught. Maybe she thought Chip was pathetic. Too young, after all.

He tried to shake off the paranoia. He and Ticia had a unique connection, beyond their thing behind the recycling bins. Still, one short message from her would help. He got up and stared in the mirror. He didn't look like a guy who'd kissed Ticia Olague, and yet, he *was* that guy. He had every right to look like it. And if they hadn't gotten caught, he would have been a guy who'd done more than that. Ticia would not have climbed onto his lap if she didn't mean for it to go farther. He pulled the black bandana from his drawer – an impulse purchase Ticia brought him from Kingston when she first learned what kind of music he liked. He tied it onto his head, re-tied it, and tied it again. Put on a hooded sweatshirt and a chain he'd pulled from the sale box at his Aunt Maryann's antiques shop. Thick gold-plated links – it originally had a big daisy pendant that Chip had removed with pliers.

He laughed at himself. Chip's grandfather would applaud his resourcefulness, with the daisy chain. So would the school's Environment Club. *Reduce, re-use, recycle!* But today Chip was not into after-school clubs. Ticia Olague! He slung his jeans low on his hips, so his boxers showed over the top, and thought of his hand inside the back of her shirt, her hips right up into him, and her tongue. For the one-thousandth time, he had to think down a mounting erection.

Even if she didn't send him a message, he'd know in an instant when he'd see her at school. Would she try to avoid him? She could not regret it.

The doorbell rang. Chip heard his father on the stairs. His mother had said people came to sell cleaning supplies or repave the driveway. Gypsies, according to Rowan, *Gippos*. Chip had never seen a real-life Gypsy. He wondered if a crystal ball might reveal what Ticia was thinking.

He heard Lyn fumble with the lock. For a second, Chip felt sorry that his father had taken time off work to stay home with him. The guy in the mirror didn't look like someone who cared about his father's career or felt sorry for anything. Chip scowled.

"Where is he?" It was a woman's voice, angry and loud. Obviously not a Gypsy with a bag full of kitchen sponges. "Is he out? He's under suspension and you let him go out?"

Chip froze. He was the only other "he" in the house. The only guy there "under suspension."

The woman raised her voice. "Meeting his drug dealer? Out vandalizing cars? How many girls is he screwing around with?"

"Who the Hell are you, in my house? Who the Hell *are* you?" Lyn's deep voice took control. "I think you're mistaken."

"Are you Lyn Cooper?"

Chip hurried downstairs. He stopped before he even reached the bottom. There was no mistaking who the woman was. She looked just like Ticia. Same blue eyes and black hair. Lara Olague.

"You!" She pointed at Chip, something rectangular in her hand. A video-cassette.

Chip quickly pulled the bandana from his head and yanked up his jeans. He wanted to step forward to shake her hand. An appropriate move, but now the bandana was in his hand.

Mrs. Olague waved the video. "This is your influence! You people never think about consequences. Ticia's gone, understand? Do you understand anything about consequences?"

"Gone?" Chip's voice faltered.

"Con-se-quenc-es!" She shouted each syllable.

"Would you like to come in?" Lyn swept his arm in grand gesture.

She slapped the tape in her hand. "No, I would not like to come in. It's too late for what I'd like. I'd like for my beautiful girl to have never met this boy. You knew what she was doing, you were helping her, the drugs, the videos, her experiments…"

"What?" Chip shook his head. "No." The only experiment he knew of involved his father's DNA – one of the top ten items of their unfinished business.

"You knew she was filming herself," Mrs. Olague talked right over Chip's thoughts. "Or did you do it for her?"

"What? She what?" Chip yelped, then lowered his voice. He stuffed the black bandana into his back pocket. "I don't understand what she did. Is she ok?" He thought of the photos he'd encouraged her to take for Andrew. Maybe she did more than take still photos of herself. His groin tightened with a rush of skidding thoughts. But how could that be Chip's fault? Why was Mrs. Olague bringing the video over to Chip's house? Was she going to leave it with Chip?

"And to think your mother applied to be the school nurse." Mrs. Olague sneered, "Outrageous."

"Did she?" Lyn cleared his throat. "Well, Carolann's an excellent nurse. Her record is impeccable."

"She applied to administer the new meningitis vaccine and develop a drug awareness program for the high school. The irony kills me."

"When did she interview?" Lyn seemed stuck on the wrong train of thought.

"A while ago, Dad."

"She didn't get the job?"

"Where is Ticia?" Chip asked. "What do you mean she's gone?"

"As if you didn't know she was doing drugs." Mrs. Olague

hung her head in her hands. "So many…"

Chip thought he'd be sick. "Where is she? She'll be at school tomorrow, same as me, right?"

"Hello?" Carolann, looking travel-weary, stepped into the entryway, behind Ticia's mother.

"The impeccable nurse arrives." Lara Olague glowered.

Carolann's attention went from her husband to the irate woman to her son. "What's going on here? What…?" She pointed at Chip's hoodie and his necklace.

"It's… It's…" Chip stuttered.

"I thought you wanted to be a stay-at-home mom, finally," Lyn said. "You applied for a job at the school?"

Carolann pulled her carry-on bag from her shoulder and dropped it. Her driver set her large suitcase just inside the door and tip-toed away.

"Ticia's not home where she belongs?" Carolann asked. "Is she alright?"

"No, she is not alright." Mrs. Olague sneered, "But thank God this tape specified who should do her eulogy, which, by the way, he is absolutely not welcome to do." She took Carolann's hand and slammed the tape into it. "Apparently, your son is quite the poet. This is enough to make a mother sick."

Chapter 48

The rewind hum of Lara Olague's videotape clicked to an abrupt stop, and no one spoke. Lyn turned the power off the machine.

Carolann turned to Chip. "Well?"

"I never knew! I had no idea she was doing this stuff."

"Alright. Go on up to your room, so your father and I can discuss this."

"I should stay. Her mom thinks – I should be involved in the discussion." Chip stood and thrust his hands in his jeans pockets. "Her mom thinks I'm... you know – implicated."

"Later." Carolann nodded at the doorway. It was clear Ticia had been doing some very foolish things, but there was nothing to suggest Chip had any part of it. Nonetheless, they needed to handle it right. She watched Chip retreat from the room and counted a few extra seconds till he'd be out of earshot. "A llama farm in California. As if that's what that girl needs," she scoffed.

"This is probably the last thing you need, straight off an international flight." Lyn rubbed his wife's back.

"At least they've got a lid on things back home, more or less. My dad's back home, back on his feet." She pointed at the blank TV. "This is terrible."

"The psychiatrist sister has probably been waiting for an opportunity like this for years. Dishing out *I told you so* with a heavy hand." Lyn added, "I'd think a lawyer-mom would be an excellent role model for a girl like Ticia."

"They were lucky Ticia wasn't hurt. That girl's been up

to no good for a long time." Carolann let her voice trail off. Chip might have known nothing about Ticia's drug use and videos, but there was no question she was trouble. Carolann also could relish a moment of *I told you so*, but she knew that wouldn't be fair to Lyn, nor would it be entirely accurate.

Apropos of nothing, Lyn suddenly asked, "Did you see Buck?"

"No." Carolann was grateful for a new topic – any new topic. "I would have told you on the phone. I told you what I was doing there." She knew Lyn would have certain questions, but now was not the time. Not when their son's best friend had nearly killed herself, right after making a recording that said she wanted Chip to do her eulogy.

"He didn't come with Maryann to pick you up at the airport?"

"Well, yes. I already told you that," she said. "He's heavy. My sister too." Even though she hadn't compared the two men in years, she knew Lyn still did. Lyn had never had any trouble with his weight.

"Lack of discipline," he said. "Food, drink, tobacco, women."

Carolann took a deep breath. Normally, Lyn's next phrase would be "*the man's his own downfall.*" And she would be expected to agree – normally out loud. But now there was a much bigger issue at hand. Watching the footage of Ticia smoking hash, and its aftermath, climbing out her bedroom window onto a tree branch, joking and confident for the camera, was now too big an image to push aside.

Lyn said, "I just wondered if your sister's answering machine message was supposed to be a profound message."

"Maryann said her machine was broken. You called her house?"

"Not broken," Lyn said. "It's just playing the same verse on repeat."

"When did you call her?"

"When Chip got in trouble and I was trying to find you."

Carolann nodded. "If Chip did drugs, hash, I mean, anything, we wouldn't do what Steve and Lara Olague have done." She needed to assert that she and Lyn were still aligned in their parenting. What if parenting Chip would soon become their only point of connection? The irony made Carolann nauseous. If Chip was truly Lyn's son, surely that was as much Lyn's fault as hers. But that was exactly her worry. Maybe he'd punish himself, just like his own father had done. The lie tied the three Coopers up in a much prettier package. Pandora's box with a bow on it. Carolann knew her father's mantras. *No undefined debt. Leave no unknowns.* But his advice was about adjustable rate mortgages. Not to mention, even about money, the man could be wrong.

"I don't even know what she smoked." Lyn shook his head. "Is hash worse than weed? Reefer? Spliff? I need a guide to the continuum. I do know today's marijuana's a heck of a lot stronger than our contemporaries might have smoked. Spend any time at all in an ER, and you know that." He stood and then sat back down. "But we're not the Olagues, thank the Lord. And your sister is not a psychiatrist with all that training, and a llama farm in Central California, and an offer on the table."

"That girl was trouble," Carolann said.

"And her mother thinks Chip is trouble. Are we being naïve?"

Chip walked back into the TV room. "No, Dad. You're not being naïve," he said. "I am not on drugs. I will not do drugs. And I did not get Ticia on drugs. If I'd known she was doing that stuff, I'd have tried to make her stop. Which is probably why she didn't tell me. The reason for my suspension was a stupid error in judgment, I snuck off campus during my free period, like three feet off campus, and that was not a sign of bigger problems. I'm not on drugs."

Lyn nodded. "We believe you."

"But her mom doesn't," Chip said quietly. His lip quivered. "Maybe her dad does." One minute he towered above his parents and spoke like a man. The next he was fourteen. Chip sat on the coffee table, facing them, awaiting answers. Always, Lyn and Carolann Cooper had answers.

"Give them time." Lyn touched his son's hand. "Maybe they'll decide the llama farm thing is an over-reaction."

Carolann watched them. Lyn was a good father to Chip, whoever's DNA the boy shared. Lara Olague sent Ticia to her sister because she (perhaps unfairly) doubted her abilities as a mother. Carolann remembered that she was once unsure how best to be Chip's mother or Lyn's wife. She had prayed. Eventually, somehow, she understood that God gave her Chip, God gave her Lyn. He would give her instructions. Carolann learned that when she asked the right questions, answers came. Even if she forgot to ask questions, somehow she'd figured things out.

"They didn't even let her say good-bye," Chip said. "For a school that makes such a big deal of welcoming and *farewelling*, you'd think they'd give a long-term student her due farewell. Ticia's been at that school her whole life."

"All bets are off when kids are on drugs," Carolann said. "And I'm not entirely sure her parents are over-reacting. This could have been very, very serious. It may be very serious."

"You're probably happy she's gone."

Carolann shook her head. "Happy? No."

"You probably prayed for God to get her out of my life."

"Not like this. No."

Lyn said, "Thank God she wasn't injured. This was her third video experiment. Who knows what she planned next. Falling out of that tree was probably the best thing that could have happened to her. A successful cry for help," Lyn said.

"A cry for help is a botched suicide." Chip quickly glanced at his father. "That's not Ticia."

"But your friend did need help. Now maybe she'll get it."

"The tree thing was dumb," Chip said. "But she's not a druggie shooting up heroin in the street. She filmed herself getting high and she scientifically recorded the results, timed the decline of her fine-motor skills. How many people can even remember the preamble to the Constitution, much less write it in calligraphy? I mean, sober? Her research might even help science! She's smart and I admire her. And she knows what she wants." Chip took a deep breath. "She specified what she wants. The school should do a memorial thing for her farewell, and I should do the reading, like she said."

Carolann said, "She's not dead. The eulogy idea was a joke in poor taste."

Lyn added, "I won't fault her scientific method, but those were illegal substances. And I think when she said if she fell to her death, have Chip do her eulogy, well, maybe that didn't sit well with her parents. They'd have to assume..."

"What?" Carolann interrupted. "What would they assume? Chip, is there something else you need to tell us?"

"Like what? Like she's pregnant? I knocked her up and like, six of her friends at the same time? And now we all have Herpes and Syphilis and A.I.D.s. Jesus, Mom, I'm fourteen." He fidgeted with the old-lady's chain around his neck. "And I've never done drugs and I never will."

Carolann smiled. *Knock her up*? Probably not a line from his rap music. Carolann was pregnant at 17, while Chip's young viewpoint seemed anachronistic and borrowed from outdated movies. "*Formal Send-off*," Carolann said. "The school should do a ceremony for Ticia's friends to have some closure. And it could be combined with the drug awareness event. Her father is a Vice Principal. He should do this."

"Will you tell him?" Chip asked.

"It's not my concern. No. Talk to the person who got the nurse job."

"That's a point," Lyn said. "I knew you were considering it, but I didn't know you'd applied."

"I should do that reading though," Chip insisted.

"I'm surprised you'd want to – something so personal, in front of the whole student body." Carolann registered Chip's startled reaction. She had seen the poem he'd written for Ticia when she was in Amsterdam. He'd left it open on his desk. Probably the same lines Ticia herself had seen. But facing his classmates with his private devotions was something he clearly hadn't thought out.

"It could be a good challenge for him," Lyn said. "Like that job might have been for you. Maybe everyone in our family needs some new risks and challenges."

Carolann stared at Lyn. "That was a little part-time job, not a risk. Not that it matters now."

Chip said, "Everyone loves Ticia. Well, most everyone. If we have a ceremony about her and about drugs, I think they'd be respectful even if I get all nervous and screw up. It might be a good way for me to start."

Lyn turned back to Chip. "You're new there, maybe this will be your only year in that school. Maybe it's better to stay under the radar, kiddo. If Ticia's mother thinks you were involved, others might assume the same. Should you avoid that focus?"

"No one would think that about me." Chip shook his head.

"Maybe now you understand what we've said about reputation." Lyn looked from Chip to Carolann. It sounded so familiar, an accusation from a distant, irrelevant past.

Carolann stared back at him until Lyn stood, seemingly finished with the debate. She said to her son, "Ticia wanted you to do her eulogy. So if you want to do a memorial thing for her, you go to her dad. Lay out your case, and I, for one, will support you."

Chapter 49

Carolann recognized the BBC newscasters' faces on the TV, but she processed almost none of their words. They seemed to have jumped from the upcoming Chelsea Flower Show to something in government. Maybe it was jet-lag. She'd only been home a few hours, her whole body was probably still decompressing. She stared at the screen. Parliament, elections, the right honourable gentleman. *Labour, conservative, Green party, but those were the days of Maggie Thatcher and let's not forget Paddy Pantsdown.* Hearty laughter. An inside joke shared by the entire country, but somehow, specifically excluding her. Nothing pertained to Carolann.

She'd been gone for half a year, and already it was just as Edith Heaney said. She didn't belong back home, and she didn't fit in here. Did the English people revere Maggie Thatcher or revile her? Carolann would never share their history, their jokes, their ability to drive with ease down their narrow, narrow roads. And now, with Chip's problems at school, the possible disparity of her marriage was coming to the light as well. The TV screen returned to images of the flower show. Lilac rhododrendron, healthy and bold, sunlit dew on the petals. Carolann exhaled. Flowers, she could do.

She could hear Lyn moving upstairs, in their bedroom. The floor creaking under his weight, a closet door slammed. Anger? It was hard to tell. Carolann sighed. Her view of Kansas had seemed subtly but irreversibly changed, and now, even the English landscape had changed – she saw it when her plane neared Gatwick. The patchwork green-and-gray had shifted to a springtime green-and-blue, with promises of warmth. She and Lyn had enjoyed years of successful marriage. Why would she indulge in any assumption that it might not continue? She listened for another clue from upstairs.

Was he changing into pajamas? Would he still come down, double lock the doors, and take her upstairs by the hand? Black cotton-knit pajama pants from a first class long-haul flight. Carolann guessed there might be a hundred fathers of kids at Chip's school with airline pajamas, a subculture. So many of Chip's classmates were children of high-power corporate guys. Even here, Carolann and Lyn didn't quite fit.

She heard the stairs creak as Lyn came down, still dressed. He held up a bottle of Jack Daniels. "Thought maybe you could use a nightcap."

"I don't think so." Carolann crinkled her nose. "I've turned over a new leaf."

"This thing with Ticia really got to you?" Lyn smiled. "Never mind, we'll get you back in the saddle."

"Let me be clear," Carolann said. "I don't need it. If you need me to drink it, let's talk about that."

"What?" Lyn set the bottle down on the coffee table. "It's just a drink, Carolann. Something you have certainly never turned down in the past."

"My past..." she interrupted herself to think carefully about what to say.

"Your past...?" Lyn seemed to be taunting her. "Your past?"

"For a long time, I've felt ashamed. But I really don't have much of a past, so to speak."

"A few little mistakes." Lyn shrugged. "And you've made amends... You are a strong and moral woman."

Carolann focused on the brown liquid in the bottle, and the black label with stark white text. Even with the top on, she could smell its pungent aroma in her mind. It poured strength into her, just sitting there, closed. "A few little mistakes." She repeated the phrase. This needed correcting.

"You know we got lucky with Ticia," Lyn said suddenly. "She's gone, but there will be other girls on Chip's radar. Do you think an unnatural interest in girls is... might be... genetic? Do we need to worry about this? Do something preventive? Pre-emptive? You just saw Buck. You know better than I do."

"For God's sake, Lyn. Your son is not unnaturally interested in girls," Carolann said. Should she say it now? *Your son.* "No. Chip is a normal, healthy 14-year-old boy, of the red-blooded American variety."

"Buck took advantage of you. That's what's in *his* red-blooded American blood."

"I've tried to explain how I'm the one who took advantage there."

"Right, you raped him." Lyn's voice was laced with sarcasm.

Carolann was undaunted. "But who did you take advantage of, Lyn?"

"No one." The muscle in his jaw clenched. "I never overstepped a single bound with a woman, ever."

"Don't misunderstand me." Carolann softened her voice. "You stepped forward to rescue a young girl from an unhappy home, you stepped forward, willing to raise another man's child as your own, and you have been an exemplary father from the start."

"And husband." He turned his back, hands on his hips. Bold plaid shirt. His all-business bold plaid of success. Deserved success. American men's firm handshake, closing the deal outside of the office, as expected, as earned, wearing the khakis, the loafers, and that shirt.

"Excellent husband," Carolann said. "But in the beginning, my *past* presented quite a convenience. Would you have ever asked me to marry you if I wasn't in trouble?"

Lyn turned back. "You were a knock out."

"I was seventeen. You took advantage of a good opportunity." She looked at him to be sure he understood. "And I'm glad you did."

He pushed his hands into his pockets.

She continued, "And I wouldn't have been brave enough to say yes if circumstances were different. I was drinking then, Lyn, certainly that night with Buck. And in the early days with you. But I love you. It started as gratitude, but it became a real marriage almost immediately, a loving, respectful relationship. My so-called *past* is irrelevant. I'm not a girl in trouble anymore, and you don't have to be a white knight. What we have now isn't a fairy tale, it's real, and we don't need manipulation to hold it together. It's stronger than that. We are stronger than that. And even if you can't accept your hands, I can. I do. And I don't need a drink to prove it."

Lyn looked at his wife carefully, his face betraying nothing, his hands deeply hidden. She watched while he seemed to debate retreating upstairs, or staying. Slowly, he pulled one hand from his pocket but did not raise it.

She nodded.

He reached for the liquor bottle and held it up. "Sure?"

Carolann stood, took the bottle and set it back on the table. She kissed his hand. She kissed his mouth. The rest of what she had to say to him would wait.

Chapter 50

The kitchen was steamy with the aroma of cooking pasta. Carolann dipped a spoon and swirled the boiling water. She moved her hand over the sauté pan to check its heat from above. Warm. Chip reached over her shoulder for a glass. She said, "So have the Olagues made a decision whether you'll speak?"

"Not really. Mr. Olague says they're reluctant but willing. I'm not sure they're thrilled about the whole event. It's one thing to do the tribute-memorial thing – everyone wants that to happen – but making Ticia the substance abuse poster girl is something else. She's always been, you know, academically amazing, head of all the clubs, faculty kid. Drug use wasn't part of her transcript, so now it's kind-of complicated. Mrs. Olague's sister keeps talking about releasing the stigmas, whatever that's supposed to mean."

Carolann tipped a plastic chopping board over the trash and scraped brown onion paper and end-slices into the bin. "Tuesday doesn't give you much time. Will you be ready?"

"I guess I'll know when I'm on that stage." Chip took a deep breath, his hands tight on the counter edge. He filled his water glass from the tap and drank it half-empty.

"Tuesday is Rowan's birthday and the thing in Glastonbury. Are parents invited to this ceremony? I can stay here and skip Rowan's thing."

"I don't even know if I'm doing the speech. If they decide it's all happening, I guess I have no choice."

"You always have a choice. Ticia's doing well in California, and they believe you weren't involved in her misbehavior, so right – assume they'll want you to do it. Regardless, you still have a choice."

"I write a lot of stuff. It doesn't mean I should, you know, perform it." Chip swallowed hard.

"You've wanted to give it a shot."

"In front of the whole school?" He shook his head.

"You don't have to do it. Do you want me to come?"

"It could be awful. Whether or not you're there, I could really mess it up. I might not even do it. And Rowan is kind-of desperate to take you to Glastonbury."

"You are my priority by miles, Chip." Carolann considered Chip's response. Maybe he didn't want her there. "Rowan thinks I'll reconnect with your Aunt Maryann somehow, through this giant pagan tower. Spirit powers of the goddess." She fluttered her fingers in front of her eyes.

"Rowan had a good thing with her twin sister." Chip shrugged. "I think you should go with her."

She nodded. "Look, it's all about confidence when you get up on stage. You're at a tricky age. Is it your parent's presence or your parent's absence that's more empowering? I'm no expert. I went from catching fireflies at your age to... well, adulthood. Maybe we should ask your father. He's good with public speaking."

"He's no expert either. He's hiding in his office." Chip laughed. "Anyway, you should go with Rowan."

"If my sister and I can't connect through Christianity, with half the world's population believing, I'm not sure the pagan vibe is going to do it."

"Like Stonehenge? I thought Glastonbury was a Woodstock thing. Maybe Rowan just wants a friend for her road trip. Maybe Rowan's smoking a little marihoochie herself. You sure she's not a bad influence on you?"

"Pretty sure." She smiled. "Rowan is a good friend." Carolann dipped a tomato in the boiling water and deftly skinned it. She wanted Lyn to walk in and re-affirm Carolann's being a strong and moral woman, and in all likelihood, Rowan too. "Do you know, not a single friend came by my parent's house while I was there? They brought a hundred casseroles, women from the church, but no one stayed to visit."

"Yeah, because they all heard you'd become a pagan. You've probably been excommunicated and you don't even know it."

Carolann laughed. "Anyway, Maryann was thrilled I'm going to Glastonbury. She's got blue-and-white vendors near there."

Chip said, "Do you think I could just put a printed copy of my speech in the box they're sending to California? Like on vellum? They're video-taping the whole tribute, including the guy coming to talk about drugs. I could put in a teddy bear in the box, and you know, a scroll, like with a ribbon."

"That box will be loaded with teddy bears. Ticia is a good friend to you, and in some ways, I misjudged her. Maryann's machine got me thinking." Carolann smiled. *"Do not judge according to appearance, but judge with righteous judgment."*

"John 7: something. I think that one plays a lot. Dad mentioned it." Chip pulled a glossy onion from his mother's pan and watched her stir the penne noodles.

"If you think you can, you should do that memorial. Ticia deserves that." Carolann pushed her son's hand away from her sauce pan. "Go call your father down for dinner."

Chapter 51

Monday night, Carolann couldn't sleep. She didn't want to go to Glastonbury with Rowan. She wanted to be in the school's auditorium to watch Chip deliver his eulogy poem thing in the morning. Chip wanted her to go with Rowan, but he was only 14, and he was wrong. A boy starts with bravado, and then he grows into real bravery. Where was Chip on the continuum? Carolann was the adult… more qualified to figure that out than Chip would be. If he was going on-stage to recite his words, he should have his mother's support. Just thinking about it, Carolann's stomach was jumpy. Chip must have had a flock of geese in his gut. And she knew she'd encouraged him to do the thing. It could definitely go horribly wrong. Finishing out the school year could be a daily humiliation for him.

She could sneak into the back of the auditorium, and unseen, send him good vibes. Rowan could do a magic goddess spell for him. Carolann breathed deeply. People in her church back home frowned on magazine horoscopes and false gods, and now she wanted to ask her neighbor to do witchcraft for Chip. What did Carolann's God, who'd served her so well throughout her life, want her to do? She knew He'd tell her. He answered all questions, even those yet unasked. By morning, she'd know.

Calmed, Carolann pulled the covers back and got out of bed to call her sister. She needed to double check the name of the village in Somerset. Carolann dialed Maryann's number.

It was nearly midnight in England, so Maryann was probably home, fixing dinner for Buck.

Maryann's phone rang, and Carolann had a vision of her sister, licking butter from a finger, tea towel in hand, shutting the refrigerator door to run for the phone. Unless of course Buck was working late, and Maryann was eating three boxes of Lean Cuisine in front of the TV. Carolann shook her head, thankful that as far as she was concerned, Chip's father was Lyn – and not Buck. The phone rang again. Somehow, while her sister's telephone rang, even the split-second memory of Carolann's thing with Buck seemed wrong. It should not be in her head and not in conversation with her husband. Maybe never.

Maryann's phone rang and rang, rhythmic and constant, unlike the higher pitched double-ring Carolann had come to know in England. The American ring tone was soothing… and she hated to admit it, but so was the fact that her sister wasn't answering.

Suddenly, the phone clicked, but no one spoke. Only clicking-clacking, electronic noises. She stared at the paper in her lap. Rowan would probably recognize the village name anyway. But between the clicking, there was a whir of foreign phone line connection. "Maryann?" Carolann prepared her mini speech, repeating in her head the details about customs and excise taxes, import-export mumbo jumbo. As if the antiques vendor wouldn't know how to do the paperwork.

A suave male voice burst into life on the phone line, a soap opera doctor or ranch owner, somewhere in the middle of its script. "… *shall make you free. John 8:32.*" Carolann stared at the receiver. The scripture played again. "*Ye shall know the truth and the truth shall make you free. John 8:32*" Carolann felt like she was on Christian Candid Camera. The machine was running on repeat, delivering its divinity. It left no option for her to leave any message.

She hung up the phone. *The truth.* Carolann sat back on

the sofa. *Ye shall know the truth.* Should Lyn know the truth? Carolann stared at the phone. The Lord works in mysterious ways.

Her sister's machine delivered canned scripture. Like sticky-note reminders for people who didn't trust themselves to keep in mind their own important relationship with God. That had never been Carolann. With a message as blatant as that, there was a paradox. It wasn't overt, it was ironic. At last, Carolann knew exactly what God was telling her. She wasn't stupid. She'd gone to church all her life, she'd listened to sermons, and sat for ladies' Bible study Wednesday nights, and she was someone who'd never needed overt. The guidance she'd asked for was delivered.

The truth was the truth, and God already knew it. Likewise, Carolann was good with God, and she knew that. The only true connections in the universe, divine or human, are woven by subtlety. And now Carolann knew not to betray her sweet husband and break his heart with something, some "great truth" he certainly never needed to hear.

Chapter 52

The high school auditorium was packed with students and faculty and plenty of parents. Chip sat in the front row, reserved for the substance abuse guy and students presenting songs and tributes. His throat was dry. It was awfully personal stuff, he'd written. He could still back out. Maybe he'd only read part of it.

Girls wore costumes, hot-pink feathers, glitter, cowboy hats, and thigh-high boots. Ticia's Moonwalk Marathon friends sat near Chip in their tie-dyed bras over t-shirts, the same as they wore for the breast cancer marathon in London. (Good thing Chip's mother was heading to Glastonbury – she wouldn't like those outfits, no matter the cause).

Everyone had inside jokes with Ticia, stories they shared. Chip had had less than a full school year with her, that's all. They'd never raised funds together, trained for marathons, headed committees. He didn't belong. Ticia had already read his whole poem anyway. Why did she want him to do this thing? In his normal clothes, he felt worse than underdressed… he felt exposed. He crossed his leg over his knee and watched his foot shake up and down. The white leather tennis shoe looked too clean, even it was calling attention. His mother must have wiped it with bleach. He lowered his foot to the floor.

Carolann had watched his bus pull away from his house, like he was a child. Of course she wanted to come. But Chip was not a child. He did not need his mommy. He could read this poem for the audience, for the video camera, for

Ticia, like she'd asked. He'd tell himself it was someone else's writing, and his tongue would behave itself. His throat would not close. Anyway, his dad would be there, in the back.

A boy could not become a man with his mother watching, but his dad – that was different. Maybe Chip should try to rap it, like it was originally intended, instead of speaking it like a lovesick weirdo. He should have asked those glitter cowboy hat girls to dance while he performed it. But that wasn't what Ticia wanted. She wanted him to read his words, his poetry. As long as he didn't stumble up onto the stage, he could do this.

*

On Tuesday morning, Carolann didn't hide behind the dining room curtain, but stood right in the doorway and watched the white bus roll away with her son. She was physically unable to step into the shadows. It was no less an event than his first day of school at age five when the big yellow American school bus took him away, and she'd cried all morning, excited for him, impressed by him, and in equal measure, on his behalf, worried sick. Rowan was due in ten minutes, and Chip's classmates were probably already filling the auditorium. Carolann thought she might be ill.

"For a country that revels in their anti-French jokes, they sure love their French cuffs." Lyn held out his palm, holding a pair of blue enamel cufflinks. "A little help?"

Carolann took the cufflinks from him and fitted them into his cuffs. He had stayed home with her that morning when five-year-old Chip started school. And today, Carolann realized, Lyn must have stayed home to see how she was doing with Chip's morning departure, as he usually left before Chip's bus came.

"I hope you're impressed they gave me cufflinks.

Apparently, good looking American guys get cufflinks, and ugly old men get pens."

"They just want us to keep buying you these new shirts from Marks and Spencer. It's an evil ploy." She was trying to be light-hearted, but she knew her voice sounded shaky.

"You alright?" Lyn nodded his head toward the front door.

"He's growing up." She sighed. "Here comes Rowan." She took her purse, the antiques vendor information, and a bottle of water for the road.

Lyn kissed his wife and grabbed his briefcase to follow her out the door. She watched him drive off and then buckled herself into Rowan's car. Carolann stared straight ahead.

"Ready?" Rowan asked.

"Yes." Carolann nodded.

"Chip got off to school ok?" Rowan started the engine of her Citroen.

"Yes." She took a deep breath.

"He's going to do the speech?" Rowan headed the car out toward the High Street. At the end of their road, she would take a right toward the Motorway instead of a left toward Chip's school. She pushed the gearshift into second, and then third, gaining speed.

Carolann nodded. "Looks like he is," she said quietly. She was the boy's mother, and she felt more emotionally invested in the event than he now seemed to be, even. And now Lyn was on his way to the office, as usual, instead of heading for Chip's school, where he should also be to support their son. She should have asked Lyn to go. Chip hadn't specifically said he didn't want his dad there. She only heard him say she shouldn't go. Why hadn't she asked Lyn to go?

"And you're ok?" Rowan asked. She slowed to the stop sign, and flipped her turn signal upward, to turn right. Motorway.

"A-ok," Carolann said. As if a lighthearted reply could eradicate the rock in her gut. "Okey dokey," she added.

"Liar." Rowan flipped her turn-signal down. "We're going to that school. We'll stay in the back. If Chip sees you and gets mad, well, blame me."

The rock in Carolann's gut was no longer a rock. It suddenly became a kidney stone, silver-gray, and it shattered like starbursts into a million tiny fragments of sand. The powder passed right through her and evaporated into blue nothing. Rowan pulled the car out into traffic toward Chip's school, and Carolann felt the leak of her silent tears.

*

The event began with a video about peer pressure and self-esteem and avoidance of drugs and alcohol. Chip had seen similar videos at church lock-ins, and every one of them terrified him. Strangely though, this one seemed completely benign. Maybe he was immune to the film's scare tactics since he was already riddled with stage fright.

When the video ended, the school's headmaster, Herbert Cupp, welcomed Ticia's father to the stage. Chip expected a slide show, set to music, of Ticia and her friends, school events, parties and so on. Instead, Steven Olague read a letter his daughter had composed before she left for California, apologizing for her bad judgment. Chip thought it sounded like someone had dictated it to her, but it set an appropriate tone for the event. Mr. Olague finished to the sound of reluctant applause. It seemed like no one quite knew what to make of the letter, of Ticia's sudden departure, nor the strange blend of occasions in the auditorium. Steve Olague sat back down, and the stage lights were dimmed. The slide show and music would ease the awkwardness. Chip realized the sequence of events actually made sense.

"Lights, please." Mr. Cupp stood on stage with the microphone. He held his hand over his eyes, shielding them, and nodded at the stage crew in the light booth. "And now I'd like to introduce a student new to our school, and relatively new to Ticia's circle of friends, but a very important one at that. Chip Cooper."

Chip heard his name and a rush of its echo inundated him, flushed away all his confidence, and pinned him to his chair. People on either side of Chip turned and stared. The headmaster looked at him and nodded. Chip grabbed the arms of his chair, and his body stood.

"Perhaps some of you heard," Mr. Cupp continued, "that before Ticia climbed out her window, which ultimately is how she fell and was then found unconscious, she made a bit of a joke – not so funny, really – and said if things didn't work out, she'd like Chip to read her eulogy. Well, we are thankful that things did, more or less, work out, and welcome Chip to do this reading nonetheless."

People applauded again, slightly less awkwardly, and Chip found himself at the top of the stage steps, crossing to the podium. He unfolded his paper and flattened it in front of him, knowing the lines were all in his head anyway. He scanned the audience. His father was in the middle, smiling. He knew the room's capacity was only a couple hundred, but the stage lights were hot and bright, he couldn't even see to the back, and it felt like thousands of eyes were on him.

"I uhh…" he began. "I wrote this when Ticia was in Amsterdam for a long weekend, and she kinda forgot to tell me she was going." People laughed quietly, and he continued. "So for like four days, I was uh, pretty worried. Because she called me pretty often, and then suddenly that weekend, no calls. It was October, I guess. But later I showed this thing to her. Anyway, so this is what she wanted for her so-called eulogy."

A sea of faces stretched before him. Like sponges, everyone was eager to hear it. Of course, this was what she wanted… for people to see the depth of his feelings for her. They'd be impressed, maybe envious, and she'd love that. The inside of his mouth felt like sand. Everybody deserved to have someone love them like a fool. He could do this. His heart beat so hard it might hit the podium and knock him flat. He coughed into his hand and ran his tongue around his mouth. If he passed out, that might be more fool than she'd wanted.

"The minutes stack on minutes." His voice was strong.

"Hour after hour." The microphone helped.

"The silence of the telephone," he looked into the camera in the front row.

"Grows more profound with power." Chip halted. What was he thinking? The line was pathetic. Rhyming *hour* with *power*! His throat was parched. *Power*, he heard himself repeat. *P-p-power*. He was sputtering. His throat closed. He looked at the audience. Every face was blank. His mind also was blank. He looked at his paper. "The thing…" It was covered with unrecognizable words, like in a nightmare. "The thing I need…" A child's scribbles. His lips were glue and stuck to his gums. The roof of his mouth was parched. His tongue stuck to it.

"Take your time, man."

Chip looked toward the voice in the audience and saw Maarten. Chip thought he might cry. Henrik sat next to Maarten and nodded. Henrik, who had warned Chip he might be getting more than he bargained for with Ticia, and who could just as easily yell up to the stage: *I told you so, man*. He nodded again. Chip ran his dry tongue over his teeth and took a breath.

A few people clapped – a pretense of honoring Chip's completed speech so he could take himself off stage.

Chip raised his palms to the audience and then grabbed the microphone.

"The thing I need the most can never really be
You are you, always only you

Always separate from me.
But you're so still and silent. The phone that doesn't ring.
All the words are just pen and paper, song that doesn't sing.
But you are never silent, Ticia, and never only noise.
You're joyful reverberation
A dance of grace and poise.

Now minute after minute… hours turn to days
Play it like it lays, kid. Play it like it lays.
(Someone whooped in the audience, very well-timed).
Agony of silence, again she doesn't call.
Misery of mutiny. Each minute, my downfall.
Again she doesn't call my phone. Once more again, and now.
But I can't hate the girl, I am not allowed.

Each new silent second, another stark betrayal.
Maybe she lifts her fingers, but her phoning fingers fail.
But Ticia's never failed me. That can never be.
What did I do? What happened to her? What will become of
me?
Never feels like never. It can never be.
You are always only you, you see
Separate from me.

But this girl is never silent. That can never be.
My phone can't not ring another minute.
My head can't think without her in it.
She's replaced the person I was before
With someone better, something more.

Now it's never going to happen.
It's never going to be.
Never's always never.
Until the reverb rings again, and Ticia calls for me."

Chip swallowed hard and looked at his audience again. He looked into the camera and said into the microphone, "Ticia, get well and get on back here. We all miss you." He saluted, his papers knocking into his head and flapping by his ear. Probably very uncool. There were ten-thousand eyes, one-hundred-thousand ears. The whole world was silently listening. And suddenly, the whole world stood up, applauding, like in a movie. Horses galloped in, trailing clouds of sparkles, and flags waved. Or everyone stayed seated, but there was hearty applause, and Chip was happy. It wasn't the best, most profound thing he could ever write, but the words were for Ticia, the words were true, and the words were his. "Thanks," he said into the microphone, and then he smiled into the camera, directly (across the time, across the distance), at Ticia.

Chapter 53

Carolann's fear for her son had been almost palpable. And her realization that she was looking down at the back of Lyn's head made it worse. He hadn't lied, but he'd certainly let her believe he was headed to the office. But once Chip eased into his words, it was like another person, an adult version of Chip had taken over. This was not her 14-year-old boy, her would-be white-boy rapper from Kansas. This was a young man, a future president, a corporate leader, a genuine gentleman. She felt like a fool for thinking he'd need her. And if he hadn't continued after the shaky beginning, what would she have done, really? For that matter, what could his father do? As Chip finished to thunderous applause, she felt Rowan squeeze her shoulder.

"Do you want to stay till the end and let him know you were here, or talk to Lyn, or should we…"

"No." Carolann cut her off. "Your sister's waiting for you. Let's go."

The women quickly made their way out of the auditorium, as the morning's emcee announced the next presentation, a singer who would need two minutes to set up.

"Mrs. Cooper?" a man's voice called to her outside. "Do you have a minute?"

Carolann and Rowan stopped in front of the Peace for all People Sculpture. The springtime sun reflected off the bronze.

"I thought that was you." The man jogged toward them. "I remember meeting you and your husband at the welcome pic-nic. Steve Olague. And of course you applied for the nurse position."

"Yes," Carolann said.

"Uh, I'm sorry about that. You know, in the end, we took the person with NHS experience…"

"I understand," Carolann said. "And I'm sorry about…" She nodded toward the auditorium, but didn't know how to finish her sentence. She shouldn't be offering condolences. This wasn't a funeral.

"Chip did a great job." Steve interrupted her. "Ticia was right about him. And my wife and I appreciate some of your comments as we've discussed our situation by phone."

Carolann nodded.

"Listen, this came in the mail, and I opened it." He pulled an envelope from the front of a binder. "I don't know what they were up to. Something for career day. The mind boggles. They used the school's med-lab account, which I will take up with Ticia. It will need to be reimbursed. I'll invoice you. It's not for…" He shook his head. "Anyway, this was addressed to Chip, but care of Ticia, and in light of…" he gestured back toward the auditorium, "well, I opened it." He smiled and handed Carolann the envelope. "This thing aside, he did an excellent job up there."

"Thank you." Carolann read the envelope's logo. *Biogenics*, somewhere in Scotland. The tuition at that school was high enough already, even if Lyn's company was paying for it, but they certainly didn't want to be charged for Ticia's extra-curricular science projects. Carolann put the envelope in her purse and trotted next to Rowan toward her car.

Chapter 54

"Grab that map off the back seat, would you?" Rowan said, "Every year I take the wrong exit. I need you to navigate."

"Ok," Carolann reached over her shoulder for the large spiral-bound book. Rowan's car was warm and comfortable, and it didn't smell quite as mildewed as it normally did. Carolann had to think it was because her morning had some element of closure to it. She'd just been witness to a real accomplishment. A rite of passage for her son. She was glad she'd seen it, and glad Chip's father saw it too, in fact.

"M4 to the M5, and then it should be signposted," Rowan said.

Carolann flipped large map pages forward and back. Maybe she'd get to Glastonbury and hug the big tower and have an unexpected cosmic meeting of the minds with her sister. And then she'd find that blasted Beemasters, come home and tell Lyn she wanted him to extend his contract in England, and they'd all live happily ever after. The page in front of her showed Sheffield – nowhere near their starting point, nor their destination. Carolann flipped back to the book's beginning.

"You didn't want to talk to Lyn after Chip's grand success?" Rowan asked.

"No." Carolann said it too loudly, and then let silence wash over the car.

Rowan said, "You know, the bravest thing I ever did was

divorce that awful bastard." Her strawberry-blond hair looked like a halo. The car had flip-out windows instead of roll-downs, and Rowan nudged the glass for a bit of air. "People think it's weakness, but I'm telling you, it takes courage to go through a divorce. You have that kind of courage, Carolann."

"I'd hope so." She turned and looked out her side window, into the wing mirror. A Volkswagon bus was close behind them, probably heading for another pagan place. Carolann did not want to divorce Lyn. She did not want him to divorce her. "I hope never to need it."

"If he's not good for you, and you know it, you should summon that courage."

"You've got my situation wrong. Your ex was a drinker. And he was cruel. You won't even refer to him by name." Carolann watched the enormous concrete expanse of the M25, the crawling stop-and-go traffic of greater London.

"Yes," Rowan said. "His behavior made me compromise myself. Walking on eggshells. Pretending to be one thing, feeling like something else."

"Not all men are like that. With Lyn, it's not like that."

"I don't hate men. Don't misunderstand me. It was my sister's dying wish that I kick that bastard out of my life, and I wish I'd done it sooner. Morwenna could have had years with me whole. She died too soon." Rowan's eyes filled with tears and she wiped at her face with her forearm. The car swerved dangerously.

Carolann grabbed the wheel and straightened the car. "Should we pull over?" The car seemed like a child's toy. If they pulled over, Carolann would probably have to turn a crank in the front to restart it.

"No," Rowan sniffed. "Just saying her name still does it. Today's a rough day for us, till we can talk. I'll be fine."

The road noise was soothing as they continued.

Carolann said, "With Lyn, probably in all marriage, there's pretense. But the woman I pretend to be is generally the one

I want to be."

"A drunk?"

"Not anymore," Carolann said. "We've dealt with that."

"You know what that is, don't you?"

"It's not a problem any more. We're past that. Thanks partly to you."

"Well, that's not just Lyn. It's all men." Rowan glanced sideways at Carolann. "The great shame of men is that the things they want us to do to their bodies disgust them. The penis and the mouth – the unwashed penis should not unite with a person's mouth, and yet they desire this connection, they crave it, regularly and often." Rowan glanced at Carolann again. "They do not understand, cannot believe, that the mouth, that pretty mouth, desires it equally. Women are hungry!"

"Well, I'm not sure that's – "

"Oh, yes. And if that pretty mouth desires it, the woman is either a liar with her demure posture, or she is a whore. If she's a liar, he hates her; if she's a whore, he hates her. Yet he loves her, and his man's body craves what she may possibly – especially if she's had a shot of tequila – be willing, even eager, to do."

Carolann sat and watched the road. She said, "I'm not sure all men suffer that shame. Haven't you ever accidentally clicked one of those channels in a hotel?"

"Porn? Sure. That proves it. No shame in vicarious thrills – only on a screen. It's why that whole industry's so big. They want what they want, but they are disturbed by it, in the cold light of day. What they want is horrible."

"If you're right, and I have no idea if you are, but doesn't it work both ways? Don't women want that same... I mean, aren't men hungry?"

"Not the same. For men, it's a means to an end. Even a selfish lover will perform now and then because it's a nearly-guaranteed orgasm for his partner."

"Oh, I, uh…" Carolann was in medicine. She could discuss the human body and biology without hesitation. But the word *orgasm* seemed to cross a line.

"Luckily," Rowan added, "some men even define themselves by that success."

"Maybe it's Americans. We all come from Puritans."

"Nope. All people. All nations." Rowan checked her rear-view mirror and yanked the car across two lanes. "I've gone without for so long, I've got it pretty well figured out. I'm now a second-time virgin. The more distant you get from any hard truth, the easier it is to tell it. And I'll tell you now, all men need their women to drink."

"Well, not Lyn. Not anymore." Carolann smiled.

"Does he still like to describe your wild past?" Rowan asked.

"Our marriage started under unusual circumstances, and I don't think he trusts that it's developed into something real. I actually love him." This was truth at its core, but she felt overwhelmed with sadness that in trying to express it, she might sound insincere, and she was a bit ashamed of the need to speak it aloud.

"Crazy. Are you afraid he'll find out you love him?"

Carolann said, "He thinks I need him, and I owe him something, and need outweighs love. If I tell him I love him, and then for some crazy reason he thinks I don't *need* him, well, that's too fragile."

"I did love that bastard, once upon a time," Rowan said. "Yes, love is fragile." She gripped her steering wheel. "Bastard."

"When Lyn proposed," Carolann said, "he offered me a healthy, stable family. I needed that."

"Everyone needs that, but he treats you like a child," Rowan said. "You are an independent woman. Some women can't drive, can't even pump their own petrol."

"I hate driving here."

"Fine, but you're stronger than that. Don't exaggerate your weakness to please him."

"What we have is stable. False stability's got to be better than none."

"Truth is better than that, my dear," Rowan said. "You tell this to the Tor today, and see what answers you get."

Carolann sighed. "Magic."

Rowan shook her head. "Talk to your sister first. No love, no marriage can replace the love of a twin. I'm a twin, with or without Morwenna on this earth, and I think I understand your situation. And I'm here for you, when and if."

Carolann glanced sideways at Rowan but said nothing. Her jaw twinged.

"Morwenna!" Rowan threw her hands up and hit the ceiling. "Not the bloody crying again!"

Carolann grabbed the steering wheel to hold it steady.

Rowan wailed. "Morwenna! Let me say your name without crying. Three years... It's been three years... Morwenna, Morwenna."

"Should I drive?" Carolann watched the road, a long curve approaching. The last thing Carolann wanted was to drive Rowan's stick-shift Citroen on a five-lane highway with relay-race-style passing laws.

Rowan wiped her face, and took the wheel. "I'm fine."

"Could you quit saying her name?" Carolann dug around in her purse for a tissue.

"I'm fine now. Perfectly fine."

Carolann handed the tissue to Rowan.

Rowan took a deep breath. "Anyway, what about Chip?"

"Chip's doing great. You saw him."

"If you're not true to yourself, what example does that set? If you compromise his mother by staying in a destructive marriage?"

"That's not fair." Carolann slammed the map book against the dash. It did not make the loud noise she had desired. It felt like her blood flowed upward.

"Ok, stale marriage."

"Lyn is the best father a boy could have." Her veins had all reversed themselves. "You know nothing about it."

"Ok." Rowan sniffed again. "I'll back off. I'm obviously emotional today."

Carolann reached for another tissue. Instead of the Kleenex though, she grasped the envelope Steven Olague had given her. She pulled it out and opened it, unfolding the paper on her lap. It was indeed addressed to Chip care of Ticia, lab test results of some kind, his legal name on one column, *Raines Charles Lynwood Cooper, Junior*, she loved the important, dignified sound of his name, a future President – all those poor American kids born outside of the U.S. who could never be President. And another column, lengthy with numbers, DNA strand this-that-and-some-other thing. And another name, so similar to Chip's, *Raines Charles Lynwood Cooper – no junior*. Similar numbers, some arrows. *Buccal swab*. A paid-in-full annotation for nearly £200, the sample date back in November, the night of their turkey tacos. The night of Ticia's dental experiment, with Lyn's head tipped back in his chair while Carolann had been doing her best to play hostess.

Lyn was Chip's father.

And for some reason, Chip and his friend Ticia had wanted proof of that. Carolann couldn't breathe. "No."

"Bad news?" Rowan tried to see the paper.

Carolann hung her head. "Fuck." Hearing the awful word in her mouth felt better. A punishment and absolution rolled in one. "Fuck." She was 32 years old and she'd never known how good blasphemy felt.

"Whatever it is, you tell it to the Tor."

"I can't go home now. Never. Drive me to that suspension bridge. I want to jump."

"Suspension Bridge is in Bristol – it's out of our way. Plus, your big hoop skirt will just float you gently to the muddy banks. What's up?"

"This isn't the 1800's. Give me arsenic. Give me a noose. Give me –" She stopped herself saying the word *gun*. She would not touch on Lyn's history. Carolann took a deep breath. What could she possibly have said to trigger her son's curiosity? Maybe it was something Lyn said – hinting at future discussion. What had Chip overheard?

Rowan waited, driving several silent miles.

Carolann finally ran her hands through her hair and said, "I hope the goddesses at your magic tower have good advice."

"You want to start with me?" Rowan asked.

Quietly, Carolann spoke into her lap. "I slept with Buck." She waited for Rowan to gasp, to yank the wheel of the car, but Rowan did nothing. "My sister's husband."

"When?"

"High school. I seduced him. Took advantage." Carolann watched the clean countryside fly by. Green fields, neatly tended.

Rowan said, "You're too hard on yourself."

"It was only the one time…. the thing with Buck. Then I met Lyn and I slept with him, once, before we were married."

"A frenzy of premarital sex. Is that what you're upset about? Get thee to a nunnery."

Carolann looked down at the paper on her lap. She felt like a weight had been lifted only to reveal something even heavier and alive and unbearable in its place. "He thought I was already pregnant. We both thought."

Rowan slapped at the paper on Carolann's lap. Not a living thing. A dead thing. Ink and tree pulp. "Tell it to the Tor. You'll know what to do."

Chapter 55

In the back of the school auditorium, Lyn put his hand on Chip's shoulder and squeezed. "Well done, son, once you got going. I'm proud of you."

Chip said, "I'm glad you were here." Students passed by on their way out of the auditorium, and several gave Chip a pat on the back and congratulated him.

"Public speaking is the toughest thing in the world," Lyn said.

"Good genes, I guess."

"Nope." Lyn shook his head. "All you."

"Mom probably should have been here too."

"You're becoming your own man now. She understands."

Chip nodded, remembering the image of his mother in the doorway watching him leave.

"Your success means the world to her. To both of us."

Chip watched his classmates file toward the exits. Stewart Neame still stood near the side exit – even so Chip knew if he continued talking to his father, he might be late to History. His friends would make his excuses for him. In fact, if Stewart Neame was as attentive as he claimed to be, he'd already know exactly where Chip was.

Lyn said, "Soon enough, your upbringing will define you less than your core self will. You understand what I mean? Your actions and your intentions will mean more than anything your mother and I can influence. Whether or not we're watching will be of less and less importance."

"Nature trumps nurture around age fourteen?" Chip

raised his eyebrows. "You sound like New Age Rowan."

"No, I think nature and nurture both get trumped by the man you intend to be and the choices you make accordingly."

"Ok."

"You can aim to please your parents, society, God. Point is, it comes from within. Ultimately, you are in control of and accountable to yourself, – primarily, if not only – yourself. Apparently that does begin to happen, in your case, around age fourteen. You're becoming an impressive young man, Chip. Come walk me to my car."

"I have History," Chip said. "Mr. Neame's the one —"

"The teacher who's *on to you*. I'd like to meet him."

Chip nodded toward Stewart Neame, rocking on his heels near the side exit. "He'll be in a hurry, though."

"This won't take long." Lyn headed toward Neame. "Trust me."

Chip followed, wishing Neame would turn and leave, but the teacher stayed put.

"Mr. Cooper, I presume." Neame stepped forward and shook Lyn's hand. "Fine job up there, Chip."

Lyn smiled. "Quick question, if I may…"

Why did his dad have to stir things up? There was no way Mr. Neame with his curly hippie locks and Lyn Cooper were going to have an instant meeting of the minds.

"Toward the beginning of the school year, even when Chip was making excellent grades in your class – in all classes, – you expressed some concern about him. Do you want to let me know what it was about?"

Neame leveled his gaze carefully at Lyn. "This…" He waved at the stage. "More or less."

Neame was concerned that Chip's best friend would smoke hash, fall out of a tree and get a concussion, and Chip would have to get on stage to deliver her eulogy to be mailed to her aunt's llama farm?

"Look, sometimes expat kids from small town America, good kids, stand-outs in their communities back home… well, they get over here and find a good opportunity to redefine themselves a little. They may shed their positive attributes in the process as well. Maybe they get led down a path they didn't intend. Very dangerous."

"That's not Chip." Lyn put his hand on his son's head. He had to reach up to do it.

"Let me ask you this," Neame turned to Chip. "Did you wear those black t-shirts every day back home? Did you slouch in your seat and write lyrics in class?"

"I pay attention in class." Chip stood tall.

"I understand. Listen, maybe you weren't entering that expat spiral. But the first week you were in collared shirts and clean hair, and by week three, you had a new look. It doesn't do a kid any harm to know they're noticed. That an authority figure is watching. That's all."

"Where we're from," Lyn explained, "Everyone is not just noticed, they're carefully watched. People know if Chip's changed his style of t-shirts and how much the shirts cost and exactly when his size went from 14 to 16 to men's small. Not just Chip – everyone."

"Well, I'm glad you got the bad-ass swagger out of your system." Neame nodded at the stage. "Nice tribute. She'll appreciate it."

"Thanks, I guess." When did teachers start saying *bad-ass* in front of a dad?

"Can he walk me to my car?" Lyn asked.

Neame dipped his head in a reverent sort of nod one reserves for royalty. His long curls brushed his lapels. Chip followed his dad outside.

Lyn held the door. "Strange man, but he seems to have your best interests in mind." He stopped near his car. "Chip, there's no doubt you'll hold leadership positions over the years. Professionally… also personally. Remember this.

People make mistakes… sometimes enormous, seemingly unforgivable mistakes."

"Ok."

"This is important. I want you to remember this. Judge people first by their intentions. Unfortunately, your response may have to be directly proportional to the error, and it may seem quite harsh. That's leadership. But always bear in mind the intentions."

Chapter 56

"Ok, Sleeping Beauty, we're here."

Carolann felt a gentle pressure on her shoulder, someone pulling at her, and her body registered the slowing of the car, after the higher soporific speeds of the west country motorway whizzing beneath Rowan's little car. She recognized the subtle anxiety of being in a freshly parked car after a long drive, and the need to rise to action.

She rubbed her face and ran her fingers through her hair, massaging her scalp. She must have slept most of the ride. Her mouth tasted like glue.

"Lucky for us, I didn't get lost," Rowan said. "I didn't want to wake you."

"What time is it?" Carolann looked at her watch.

"The traffic wasn't bad." Rowan patted Carolann's knee. "Ready to see Avalon?"

Carolann opened the car door and stepped out. The air smelled like the countryside. Green grass and cows. Things they ate, things they'd digested. The sky was blue and wispy with clouds. She pressed her hand into the small of her back and stretched her shoulders.

"I know you're unsure," Rowan said. "But this is a pilgrimage. Separate from the thing with your sister. Decide to honor the sacred here, – it is a decision – and it will serve you well." She zipped her ample fleece jacket over her bosom. A human-sized blue teddy bear.

"So this was Merlin's home and Sacred Druids?" Carolann's

pulse quickened as they hiked the path.

"And King Arthur and Guinevere's graves are here… And Jesus was here." Rowan suddenly stopped walking and looked up. "Behold."

Atop a very big, grassy hill, sat a squatty looking tower, like the remaining top of a church sunk deep into the ground. The structure was square, but it looked phallic, too exposed somehow, and vulnerable, as it poked out of the ground, seeming to want to hunker down and hide. A strangely masculine image, for the physical manifestation of the goddess. Proof, perhaps that in everything masculine, there is feminine, and in all things feminine, there is masculine. The nub of "tor" reminded Carolann of her baby son's newly-healed circumcision.

"Is it what you expected?" Rowan asked. "Don't judge the experience till later. Soon after, and much later."

"You know my family may actually still be here next year," Carolann said.

"Good." Rowan grabbed Carolann's arm.

There were a few people dotting the hillside, making their way toward the top. Others were making their way back down, backpacks and cameras slung over their shoulders.

"Do you talk to your sister out loud?" Carolann panted.

Rowan shrugged. "Sometimes. You feel it already, don't you? The intersection of ley lines. The feminine power is speaking to you."

"I don't know about feminine power, but this hill is kicking my butt. You're not even out of breath."

"Yoga!" Rowan laughed.

Carolann laughed too, but she was wary. As she climbed the hill, she realized she did not want any mystical confirmation of the divine. She didn't want to abandon her healthy cynicism. Carolann liked her own personal belief in God and her understanding that this belief was a choice she made every day. Not blind faith, but an active decision. Her decision.

She breathed deeply and filled her lungs with the fresh April air. "When it speaks to you, when your sister speaks to you, is it scary?"

"Not at all," Rowan was now panting. "See the seven terraces?"

"Jesus climbed the terraces?" Carolann tried to pictured Jesus hiking the path she was on. "If this was already the site of the Sacred Feminine, or whatever you called it, was Jesus here to meet up with a bunch of other divinities? Like a party? Buddha cruising the hors d'oevres table while Mary and Joseph did the tango…" She stopped climbing to catch her breath.

Rowan laughed. "You Americans love to talk when you're nervous. Are you nervous?"

Carolann said, "We do?"

"Press on," Rowan said. "No one knows quite what the terraces are. Defensive ramparts, or grazing patterns, or a medieval labyrinth. Maybe a zodiac. You'll see concentric circles converging. When we get to the top, I'll show you a few things. Then you ask your questions in your head, and I bet you come away with answers to a whole different set of questions."

Carolann wanted to smooth the path for a true friendship with her sister, if possible, but she did not want the magic tower answering any other important questions. Some people believed that man invented God, and not the other way around. Human beings could not easily control their impulses, so they invented religion. Or if not that, exactly, then Man certainly discovered the fact of God's existence fortuitously, to serve his own need. The public debates would never be settled – the chicken or the egg – or religion or the people who needed it – and none of that mattered.

Carolann's worldview was solid. God did exist – He had always been present and always would be, and He would express Himself to His believers in His own way. Not necessarily the way a pastor in Central Kansas expressed things on His behalf. The collective mysteries of the universe were not to be solved by even the most philosophical members of humanity, and the perception of faith was a deeply personal thing. These beliefs were firmly held, developed over a long period of time, and Carolann didn't need any ethereal goddess voices messing with her truth.

When the women reached the top, they sat on a big stone circle, druid cash, Rowan said, and surveyed the green landscape. Farmland divided by muted burgundy hedgerows, a thousand shades of green rolling away, far and wide. Blue sky overhead, with gentle wisps of golden sunlit cloud. The way Carolann felt was an exact match for the colors she saw – a rarity.

"Breathtaking, right?" Rowan put her hand on Carolann's shoulder. "I'm going inside. See that bench under the arch?"

"Yes."

"Meet me there in half an hour."

Carolann walked the perimeter of the Tor alone. *Ok, Maryann,* she thought to herself, *if there's some divine message you think I ought to receive, now's your chance. I'm listening, sis. Bring it on.*

Nothing.

Nothing you want to tell me? Carolann formed the question, word by word, in her head.

Nothing.

You want me to reveal some things to you? Things you may have wondered about? What do you want confirmed, Maryann?

Nothing.

Carolann heard no voices. Even in the privacy of her own head, she heard no response at all.

You want me to move back to Kansas and look after our parents? Would that make everyone happy? What would that solve?

Nothing.

And if I find that perfect Beemasters vase, what exactly will change?

Absolutely nothing.

And if I do find it, and it's all done, the mission accomplished, what will we have to talk about then?

Nothing.

Carolann smiled. She watched the green grass ripple down across the hill and a breeze seemed to envelop her from all angles, wrapping her in emptiness. She felt a rush, a sort of hollow void, a chill in the air that somehow carried off all her emotions and her history, and it left her clean and blank and pure. She shivered. And then the moment passed.

No further questions.

Nothing.

No earth-shattering revelations, no subtle tremors, no vibe whatsoever. Carolann sat on a jutting corner of the Tor itself and shrugged. She reviewed the conversation she'd had in her head, aware of her role in both sides of the dialogue. It was one of the easiest conversations she'd ever had with her sister. She smiled and just sat, memorizing the landscape. She let her fingertips rest on the cold rock under her. There was no heat, no music in her fingertips, no vibration, no texture other than cold, muted gray-gold rock. She bent her fingers to feel the subtle variations in texture. If it was sacred, if it was something divinely feminine, it was not speaking to her. It felt solid and certain beneath her, as it probably had for hundreds on hundreds of years. Catching rain, absorbing sun as it sat there, season by season. Only rock.

Carolann leaned her head against the Tor to sun her face, and her thoughts returned to Surrey. Chip had done a fine job, in the end. And Lyn was there, doing a fine job, as always, as Chip's father. Stream of consciousness became flowing river of consciousness, not like the voice of a goddess with a message to deliver, just her own thoughts, questions and answers, one after another, or all at the same time, rushing.

She realized she'd had little opportunity for true self-reflection, living in a town where everyone is busy reflecting on each other. The new freedom felt like a drug. She opened her eyes to the sun and closed them again, leaving bright red in her eyelids. Drugs. That poor girl Ticia was no drug addict. Of course Carolann understood this, she was a nurse, but how could Ticia's parents be so mistaken? Now the poor girl was in Central California with a psychiatrist llama-farming aunt, going through rehab. God knows who she might be meeting in rehab, and what she might be learning in there. If Carolann hadn't been so busy trying to protect Chip, she might have helped steer Ticia's parents in the right direction, or a better direction, with their thinking. Was it too late? Carolann took a deep breath.

Steve Olague was asking where they'd gone wrong. Lara Olague seemed more focused on the future... what could they salvage and how to get Ticia back on track. Maybe that's why children need two parents... one to look at the child's past as it rolled out for the record books, and one to keep an eye on the future. But a person's time on this earth isn't linear, and it isn't one-directional. Sometimes, Carolann realized, two parents still aren't enough to cover the spectrum. Ticia's family needed her help.

"There you are." Rowan appeared in front of Carolann. "You want to stay a while longer?"

"Guess I lost track of time," Carolann said. "Everything ok?"

Rowan threw her arms wide. "Morwenna. See that? Morwenna. It's a birthday gift. And you...?"

"Well, n–"

"What did I tell you? You've got clarity now, right? And so much more will become clear. All your questions, worries, fuzzy edges. You've tapped the goddess within. Now let's go find that vase for your sister."

"Let's go get lunch – on me. Crepes Suzettes prepared by a unicorn in ballet slippers with a magical flute."

Rowan clapped her hands. "And sparkles! Happy birthday to me and Morwenna! I love a good old-fashioned flaming *flambee*. The ballet slippers are a bonus."

Chapter 57

Chip watched students streaming toward various buildings. Ten minutes earlier, he was elated. Now, his whole body felt heavy.

"You alright?" Lyn asked. "Can I take you to an early lunch?"

"Better not." Neame had said he did a good job. His father said he did a good job. He felt good when he finished, to enthusiastic applause, and got off the stage. But now it seemed no one would meet his eyes. Henrik and Maarten had both disappeared.

"Sense-of-self is an elusive thing. But you did great up there."

"Yeah." He could think of no other reply. Maybe his thoughts had oozed all the way down through his body. Gravity had pulled them away from the clarity and organization of his head, and dropped them like solidifying lead in his boots. Poison now leaching up through the soles of his feet. He glanced at his father. Maybe it was his fault. Something was definitely his fault.

"You're going to miss her," Lyn said. "And you're angry."

"I guess." Chip stuffed his hands deep into his pockets. Was there lead in there too? All his clothes were loaded with toxins.

"Ticia did a very foolish thing, and now she's gone, so of course you'd be disappointed."

Chip shrugged. "But if you miss someone, you'd think good things about them." Chip heard himself speaking rationally, his anger set aside so it wouldn't filter into his conversation with his dad. When had he learned to compartmentalize his emotions? "It's like she made me certain promises she just broke."

"Your friendship may weather the distance. Don't be surprised."

"I was stressed out about the presentation thing, and now that it's over, there's all this other stuff. Like before, my brain closed off a bunch of stuff I was thinking."

"Cognitive dissonance," Lyn said. "That clash of opinions will ease out."

"Maybe," Chip sighed. "But you're right. I'm pissed at her."

"Mad. Not pissed. Right?"

"Yeah."

"But it was a good opportunity for you to challenge yourself up on that stage. And Ticia not only gave you that opportunity, she pushed you into it. The irony is she's been such a good influence."

"Yeah." Chip smiled. "That's true."

"Let me ask you something. Were you jealous that she didn't include you in her experiments?"

"The drugs? No way."

"It wouldn't be inexcusable," Lyn said, "to want to experiment. Making the decision not to is a moral victory… but the interest, the initial desire, might be expected."

"Get real." Chip kicked at his father's tire. "No."

"I just needed to ask, point blank. Rather than miss something important we ought to talk about."

"I hardly even drink caffeine."

"You know," Lyn said, "nobody hands you a guide book when you bring your baby home from the hospital. Sometimes your mother and I ask questions we shouldn't or tell you things when you're too young to hear them, or teach you things we shouldn't. We sometimes get things wrong."

Lyn clicked his security key through his pant pocket. The car barked twice.

"No, you don't," Chip said. He remembered a conversation he'd had with Ticia a few weeks earlier, when he told her of his grandfather's suicide, and Lyn's upbringing. You can't undo his past, she'd said. All you can do is make up for it, a little bit at a time. You create his future with him, as he discovers what kind of a father he's turned out to be. Chip looked at Lyn. "You didn't have a great dad," he said, "but I do. You're a really great dad."

Lyn opened his car door.

"Seriously, when I have my own family someday, I hope it turns out exactly, 100%, like what you and Mom –"

"No. Not 100%." Lyn sat in his driver's seat, and he stared hard at his dash.

"Are you kidding me?" Chip leaned against the roof of his father's car, in the way of Lyn shutting the door. "Give me a little credit. I'd be proud to have my kid turn out just like you."

Lyn started his engine, and he did not look at his son. "Don't keep Neame waiting." Chip moved back a step, Lyn yanked his door shut, and drove away.

Chapter 58

"Are you terribly disappointed, or are you angry?" Rowan asked, poking a fat golden chip into her mouth. "It seems like you're angry."

The whole pub smelled like fries. Decades of transfats in the red-and-brown patterned pub carpet. Carolann sat on her hands, annoyed with her body's desire to eat one. "I don't know why Maryann thought he'd have one. That shop sold furniture. And the man was rude."

"It might have been your accent. Your almighty dollar."

"That guy supposedly sells to the U.S. market." Carolann sighed. "There must be one, somewhere."

Rowan ate another chip, blobbed with mayonnaise.

"It seems like it's never going to happen. I'm sick of it."

"It never is, until suddenly, *never* doesn't matter, it evaporates in an instant, and the thing happens. Unless you give up first."

"Edith Heaney said I should. But I want the thing for Maryann."

"You and Lyn have explored some good places, at least. Tetbury, Burford... And you and I have been having some adventures."

"I don't owe it to my sister." Carolann said, "I owe her nothing. Sisterhood is not about debt or guilt or evening scores. Maybe that's what I figured out at the Tor. But she doesn't think I'm even looking for it, so I want to prove her wrong."

"To our quest." Rowan lifted her pint.

"And Happy Birthday to you and your sister." Carolann clinked her glass of mineral water.

"Me and Morwenna." Rowan looked up at the pressed lead ceiling tiles, filmy with smoke, age, and wisdom of decades of overheard conversations. "Morwenna," she repeated.

If Maryann died, Carolann couldn't imagine crying three years later, just speaking her name. The apparent dichotomy between the two sets of twins struck her. If Carolann died first, Maryann wouldn't cry a whole lot either – not once the funeral was over, and people turned away. Maryann always had a talent for separating face and heart. With Maryann, everything always looked as it should, regardless of the underlying truth. But truly, there was no reason the Field girls couldn't have a sisterhood more like Rowan and Morwenna did. Carolann had to make the first move – she had to find that Beemasters vase. "Did you see that car boot sale poster?" she asked.

Rowan nodded. "They'll be pretty well packed up, by the time we'd get there."

"Perfect time for bargaining, if we find something." Carolann shrugged.

"You're in no hurry to get back?"

"No." Carolann pictured the lab report in her purse. "No hurry at all."

An hour later, Carolann was shifting antique plates from one stack to another on a fat man's rickety display shelf. His handwritten cardboard sign said £2. Even upside down, Carolann recognized the pattern. "Oh!" she heard herself yelp, as she turned the plate around. "Beemasters!"

"But it's a plate," Rowan said. "Your sister wants a vase, no?"

"I would think she might like a plate, for two quid," Carolann said. "No smudges in the transfer, no thumbprints, no chips, no cracks, no crazing. She'll want this."

The bored vendor finally stood up from his aluminum-frame lawn chair, suddenly more alert. He pulled the elasticized waist of his jacket down over his gut. It snugged right into place, atop his skinny legs in gray trousers. "That one's a rare pattern. It's more."

"Your sign says two quid." Rowan shook her head.

The man took the plate from Carolann, set it back on the stack, and shoved his hands deep in his pockets. "Twenty. That's the best I can do."

"Two quid." Rowan pointed at the man's little sign. "Anyway, it's not the thing she's been looking for."

Carolann didn't want to argue. Her sister would pay a hundred pounds. But she knew she'd already said all the wrong things if she wanted to negotiate, being eager and pointing out its selling points. Rowan would have the right things to say, plus the right accent.

"He's having a laugh. It's not the right thing. Don't waste your money."

"Hmmm." Carolann had lived in her father's home too many years not to at least pause over *waste of money*. But if Maryann only wanted to sell the thing in her shop, she'd be thrilled with a plate. Maryann might be so happy Carolann found the plate – anything in the Beemasters pattern – their new friendship would finally take hold. That possibility would never be a waste of money. "I'll take it."

The man wrapped the plate in a sheet of newsprint. And Carolann paid him.

"Smug bastard," Rowan said as they walked away. "He didn't even know what it was."

"But I know," Carolann hugged the plate to her chest as they walked. "It's not the vase, but this is exactly what I need to give Maryann. It will finally show her... well, it will prove to her... oh, you know what I mean. Anyway, I know."

Chapter 59

Lyn slid his train ticket through the electronic ticket-eater, as Carolann liked to call it, waited for the metal gates to flap open like strangely-English, modern saloon doors, and grabbed his ejected ticket as he pushed through the pass. He hurried down the stairs to the train platform, the soles of his shoes scuffling along each concrete step, as he kept pace with the other scurrying late-morning commuters. In the beginning, Lyn had real trouble with the train tickets. Sometimes he slid it in upside down. Sometimes it was folded and unreadable, or it was yesterday's ticket. Forgetting the infamous British reserve, people groaned and huffed behind him in line. Scoffing British Rail guards had to click him through the handicapped door with luggage and baby strollers while he apologized. Shame the simple word *sorry* always revealed his American accent.

Maybe if he'd get another year in England, he'd learn to say sorry like the Brits in the train station, if he had to say it at all. One year was hardly enough to get settled. He needed one more, at a minimum. And it would be nice for his son to finish high school here, now that he seemed to have hit his stride.

"Excuse me?" A woman in a beige trench coat stepped forward. "Does this one stop in Clapham?"

"No," Lyn said. "But it stops in Wimbledon."

"Thank you." She flipped a scarf over her shoulder and moved down along the platform.

Lyn watched her walk away. He was finally becoming

himself again, in England. He'd always been a guy people looked to for directions. Early in his career, other reps said Lyn "bordered-on-anal" he was so attentive to detail, and he was proud of that. In England though, his deep voice, used to commanding attention in the office and restaurants, now seemed too loud. Foolish and posturing. And until he learned to tighten his vowels and soften his R's and throw a few local slang words in for clarity, he'd had to repeat himself frequently. Now he had it down. He checked the schedule board for the next train. Two minutes. He saw the woman in the trench coat look at the electronic board and smile at him.

Chip had it down too. Where did that kid get the words he came up with? And his ideas? Even when he wasn't speaking, Chip seemed to understand and purify and distill meaning, and express the undiluted truth, just through his eyes. His hazel eyes, same color as Lyn's, same color as his uncle's. For a fraction of a second, Lyn lost himself in a wash of remorse. Why couldn't Chip be his own blood?

The train came and Lyn got a seat. He couldn't help but watch his misshapen hands on the newspaper he held up, pretending to read. Chip had done a superb job speaking that morning – the boy really was becoming a man – and as a result, Lyn and Carolann had to resolve their biggest issue. Lyn gripped the newspaper tight – shielding other passengers from his chaotic thoughts and hopefully, helping him corral and organize them within his small private space.

Chip would not have to confront a child with misshapen hands or any other horrors of brachydactyly, like Lyn's own father had been forced to face. Maybe Chip really could accept the problem, but what about Chip's future wife? She might be as incapable as Lyn's mother had been. No one knew until they actually confronted these things. But Lyn knew it well. As a little boy, he had watched his parents' marriage unravel, he watched their dinner table discussions become more forcibly controlled, furniture moved more aggressively in one another's presence, doors shutting louder and louder… until the day he found his father's bleeding body by the shed behind the garage. Lyn was extremely relieved he'd averted future heartbreak for Chip. Even if it meant he couldn't be the boy's honest father. And surely, Chip would recognize the gift when Lyn and Carolann would reveal what they'd done. They'd agreed to the plan even before Chip's birth, so why was Carolann suddenly balking?

The train trundled along, and Lyn folded the paper, closed his eyes, and tipped his head back on the cushioned headrest. His father had appeared asleep, but crooked somehow, or twisted, and in totally the wrong clothes. Why did he put on his white dinner jacket to kill himself?

Lyn had approached carefully, aware even before he was aware, of what he would find, (what led Lyn out there in the first place? He knew before he knew…) And he saw his father's lifeless hands, crossed one over the other, a smear of darkening blood across his wrist, across his crystal watch face, across the white sleeve of his suit. It was like he'd shot himself in the heart and then decided to check the time before it was too late. His father was dressed as James Bond, and he wore his best watch, and his manly fingers looked strong and long and normal. Lyn felt proud of him and jealous of him and his strong hands, and horrified and betrayed and sickened, and sad, terribly, tragically sad, and jealous and proud, even for his father's stillness, and the contortion of his pose on the ground, and the blood.

When he went to tell his mother, he walked quickly to the house, but he walked. He didn't know he had knelt by his father's body. In his mind, he had only stood above him, it was obvious the man was dead, he'd had no need to kneel, yet his jeans were damp and cold and pressed with dark mud at the knees and down the shins, as if someone else had been wearing his pants. He felt the cold on his legs as he walked.

He ached for his father and slowed his pace, desperate to give the man one more moment's peace, as he'd finally achieved it.

Twenty years later, Lyn knew the value of the gift he and Carolann had already given their son. Through the boy's mother's surprising indiscretion, and then her extraordinary decision to confide in a near-stranger – and to trust Lyn's reaction – the two of them were granted the very opportunity Lyn had prayed for when he prayed for a family. God did that for them. Prayers answered.

The train from Surbiton pushed on toward London, clacking as it crossed an old bridge, painted and chipped and repainted many, many times over. The velvet seat's fabric was worn away to a shiny gray canvas, with no nap left at all. Lyn ran his fingers along the bare patch of it by his leg. The time to present the gift of truth to their son was coming sooner than anyone expected.

Chapter 60

C hip got home from school and made himself a peanut butter sandwich. His mother wasn't there to greet him, and the house felt empty. He wondered if she'd found what she wanted in Glastonbury. Once both his parents were home, they'd talk about his poem-tribute together. Chip had surprised himself, once he started over and got going. About a dozen kids congratulated him about it during the school day, starting the minute he walked into Neame's classroom. He'd had no idea some of those people even knew his name. Probably before the presentation, they didn't.

The one he really wanted to talk to though, was Ticia. And she was probably hunkered down on a plastic chair in a church basement, talking about drug addiction with a bunch of people who actually knew it firsthand. And then she'd go feed llamas. Chip stared into the fridge, waiting for something to suddenly look appealing. Nothing did. He closed the fridge.

Why was Ticia's mother so sure her psychiatrist sister knew best? And how did Chip's mom deflect all of his Aunt Maryann's criticisms of her? He re-opened the fridge. There was cheese. There was broccoli. There were blueberries. He almost never had the house to himself, he realized. He was no latchkey kid. Maybe he couldn't blame Ticia's mother. She was probably a great lawyer, with all kinds of good feedback and bonuses and victories in court. So who could blame her, not knowing what kind of a mom she was? Nothing to measure maternal success, except maybe the kid's report cards. And now the kid had a drug problem. Of course she had to send her off to the shrink sister at the llama farm.

Chip poured out a bowl of blueberries. His mother would be pleased with the antioxidants. He popped a handful into his mouth. If Ticia got to come back from California for her senior year, Chip wanted to be in England. He knew his dad wanted to stay too. But his mom didn't, and with important domestic matters, matters of the home, and where in the world home ought to be, Chip knew his mother called the shots.

Chapter 61

Rowan's car juddered along the motorway. A nearly-audible silence settled between the two women, and the plate wrapped in newsprint sat heavily between Carolann's feet. Rowan still seemed unhappy that she'd bought the plate. Maryann would probably be unimpressed too. Or she'd be pleased with the one piece and insist that Carolann do regular buying for her store – something Carolann was not prepared to do. In any case, it certainly was not something Edith Heaney particularly wanted. Even a replacement vase didn't seem to matter to her. And whatever the unresolved history was of her time in England, her so-called background – she seemed perfectly content with her memories. Carolann sighed. She couldn't worry about the newsprint-wrapped item at her feet. She had a lab test paper in her purse to worry about first.

Rowan kept her hands on the steering wheel, approaching a large bend in the motorway. "Almost there…" They began to pull out straight. "You were asleep on the way down, but this is even better from this direction. And the light's really good now too. It's almost as good as visiting the Tor."

Carolann gasped. Huge bright yellow fields opened up before them, checkered shocking shades of intense yellow, divided by greens. She was speechless. Miles of fully-saturated color. A crescendo of yellow. She stared out the window. Pure unspeakable beauty.

Rowan smiled. "I'm glad I didn't wake you earlier."

Brilliant lemon yellow, apple green, vibrant gold,

pineapple-buttercup, more vivid yellow than Carolann had ever seen. "My goodness."

On either side of the narrow gray strip of motorway, stunning, impossibly bright fields opened below the blue horizon. Cloudless sky above, green grass below, just at the side of the road, and everywhere, everywhere, as far as Carolann could see, the rolling enormous fields of yellow. She expected music in her ears, but heard instead an incredible, pure silence. Tears streamed from her eyes.

"You know that artist, Christo?" Rowan asked. "That was in Kansas, wasn't it? Where he draped the sidewalks in this color?"

"Kansas City," Carolann wiped her eyes. "My school went to see it from Hoyt. We had a new teacher from Chicago who kept trying to introduce us to *culture*."

"Only this is better than culture," Rowan laughed. "This is nature."

"What is it? Mustard?" Carolann was mesmerized. "Forsythia? Daffodils? It's not mustard?"

"Nope."

"Safflower?"

"Oilseed. That, my dear, is the glorious, spectacular color of rape."

"Rape?" Carolann whispered. It wasn't a word she wanted to speak out loud. The word didn't match the divine color. As Lyn often insisted, that word was black-and-white.

"Rapeseed," Rowan whispered.

"Do you think everyone sees it like us?"

"I do." Rowan nodded without turning from the view. "It doesn't take a neurological condition to be flooded with music and emotion when a person sees the color of rape."

"Out here, maybe everyone's a synesthete. If they want to be, I mean." Carolann had never considered the possibility that someone might want to be synesthetic. The idea alone made her feel glittery.

"Everyone is a synesthete," Rowan glanced at Carolann. "At least on some level, I think. If they're willing to tap into their creative self. We're just lucky we have that tap open all the time."

Oilseed rape, Carolann's nutrition studies had covered this. Rapeseed oil, used for margarine or in cooking. Healthy Fats. Her favorite oxymoron. Not long ago, people didn't believe in such a thing. But of course, time and research can alter any belief, once the truth is brought out. "I think the Italians sauté the rapeseed flower with garlic."

Rowan said, "The French call it colza. They use the oil like the Brits and Americans do."

Carolann nodded. "We grow it in Kansas. I've never seen fields this big, not so big, not so bright. But I know someone who grows this in Kansas."

"Your neighbor. You told me. With the lab."

"Stop. Can you stop the car somewhere?"

Rowan checked her rearview mirror, threw her gearshift into neutral and flipped her turn-signal. "Side road by this bridge – I sometimes stop here, even though you're not supposed to, really. It's only this exact time of year. My birthday. And only when we're lucky, me and Morwenna. I thought you might like this view." Rowan pulled the car to a stop by a high bridge over a stream.

Carolann threw open her car door and stepped out to the edge of the road. "It must be the climate, the quality of light in the countryside – I've never seen anything like it."

"This isn't exactly legal, here." Rowan looked back at the motorway. "We'll only stay a minute."

Carolann said, "My mother thought Edith was raped in England, and that's why she eloped with a foreign man. Maryann said it was soldiers, and that turned her loony."

"The sweet old lady you just saw in Kansas?"

"The trauma... she's never been unstable, not really, but my mother thought... what a misunderstanding, all these years. What a waste." Carolann took a deep breath. The air was fresh and clean.

"No human being is capable of fully understanding their parents," Rowan said. "Half the time, we can't even understand ourselves."

Carolann smiled. The golden acres calmed her, focused her thoughts, and made her feel both centered and energized. She was all confidence and purpose. "It's unbelievable."

"We should go," Rowan said.

This was rape. This splendid golden view was rape. Sometimes, evidently, rape wasn't black and white, and it wasn't varying shades of gray. Sometimes, in very particular circumstances, it turned out, rape was an unbelievable sunshine yellow. Carolann suddenly knew how to handle the truth, what to do with that piece of paper lurking in her purse. The truth, she now knew, was multi-faceted, at odds with her very religion at times, the truth she'd always been taught. She now understood that the truth isn't necessarily a cure-all, it's not always the answer. It had to be examined, understood, carefully purified and distilled down not just to what's true, but to what's right. Reconciling a past thing was only so useful. At some point, it would not serve any possible future. She took in the wide expanse of magnificent sunlit yellow, and she knew. "I need just one more minute."

Rowan sat in the driver's seat. Carolann grabbed her package wrapped in newsprint. She tore off the paper and jogged to the edge of the bridge, looked quickly over the railing at the stream flowing clean and blue and bottle green over the glassy wet gunmetal gray and sapphire rocks, white bubbles, tiny peaks and troughs in the water, sunlight and diamonds, the stream itself seemed to sing. Carolann held the blue-and-white plate over the music of the flowing water. She nodded once, without even thinking, but still somehow confirming her intentions as she looked at the blue-and-white plate in her hand, and in a flash, she let go.

Chapter 62

Carolann turned the key in the lock and let herself in. If everything was still running like clockwork, Lyn would be home in an hour. Chip would already be home, half-way through the punnet of blueberries, if she knew her son. She hung her coat on a hanger and went to the small desk in the entryway. It would take her less than a minute, but it could define her whole life, this move she was making, this one moment.

She could have found the paper she sought in the dark. Three newspapers, two stacks of coupons, one bulky envelope from the IRS, one bulky envelope from the Inland Revenue, and then, stapled neatly together, 11 pages entitled: Renewal of Contract. She flipped to the last page, the family page. Suddenly, she was John Hancock. Though he'd wanted independence from England, while Carolann was signing up for just the opposite. She pulled a bright blue permanent marker from the desk and signed her name to Lyn's contract.

She went into the kitchen.

"So…?" she said, sitting next to Chip at the breakfast table. "Were you happy with your decision to do the speech?"

"It went alright," he nodded. "It was kind of rough at first, but then –"

"You started over and your voice was smooth and even, and you didn't stutter." Carolann finished his sentence.

"Pretty much." Chip stared at his mother.

She took a deep breath. "I was there."

"You were?"

"I understood why you didn't want me to go. Public speaking is the hardest thing in the world for people, on any topic, much less something personal. Honestly, I respected your viewpoint, but I… I confess, I…"

Chip interrupted her with a laugh and shook his head. "Dad was there too."

"I saw him." She nodded.

Chip shrugged. "I guess a parent has the right to second guess their kid's judgment and act accordingly."

"Interesting phrase. Very familiar." Carolann smiled. "I was so proud of you, Chip. We both are. And Rowan."

"Rowan was there too?" Chip shook his head again. He ate another blueberry. "How was Glastonbury?"

"Beautiful." Carolann picked out a small handful and fed herself one at a time. "Rowan had a nice conversation with her dead sister."

"Did you talk to Aunt Maryann?"

She shook her head. "I was a little distracted by something Steve Olague gave me this morning." Carolann placed the lab report on the table next to the bowl of blueberries and flattened it under her hand. "Something for you, actually." The metal tabletop felt cool beneath the paper. She smelled the blueberries' sweet tang. She turned the paper to face Chip. Aware of her fingertips, her hearing… she waited for her son to recognize the report.

"It was a…" Chip pushed the paper away. "It was a school project. Like a science experiment. Of course I already knew Dad was… it wasn't meant to…" He interrupted himself again, flipped the paper back around and read it quickly but carefully. "Does he know we did this?"

Carolann took a deep breath.

Before she could say a word, Chip spoke again. "I mean, of course I'm his son. I was conceived on your honeymoon. I know that. You two fell in love at first sight. I know all that.

I knew."

"You were not conceived on our honeymoon."

"Oh, God," Chip said. "Don't tell me."

"When your father and I were married, I was already pregnant."

"I have homework. I – too much information." He stared intently into the blueberries. "Your personal life is none of my –"

"You were conceived on our first date, more or less," she said.

He stood and put his hand up, blocking her. "I've got a humongous History assignment."

"Sit." Carolann pressed her hand, once again, against the paper. "You weren't totally off-track to ask this question."

"Neame assigned a ton of reading." Chip raised his head and looked at his mother. "How not *off track*?"

"Your father thought I was already pregnant when he met me."

"He thought…?" Chip's voice trailed off with the realization.

"He thinks. He still thinks it."

"Thinks what…?" Chip stared at his mother.

She nodded slowly.

"He thinks he came in like a hero and rescued you, poor pregnant teenager from BFE charity case. Is that it?"

"It's complicated," she said.

"So this is great news." Chip said. "We're not a charity case, we're a real family. We can wrap the lab paper up like a present."

"It's not so simple." Carolann winced. "He… because of his…"

"Hands." Chip finished her sentence. "I get it."

"I never knew for sure, but now I know. He may be devastated. But I need to tell him about your conception."

"Oh man, Mom. Could we quit with the… This is really

between you guys. Can I go upstairs?"

Carolann continued, "We always thought the day would come we'd someday tell you the reverse. That you were never genetically at risk for brachydactyly."

"So who's my dad?" Chip suddenly asked. "I mean, who was my dad?"

"Your dad's your dad." She shook her head.

"So that stuff Dad jokes about…" Chip pursed his lips. "Were you with a lot of different guys?"

"No," Carolann said. "It was one time. A mistake. I knew him from the hospital, and he was only there that summer. This is a lot for you to take in, Chip. You are a mature young man, but I recognize that this is a lot. Anyway, you never knew him. I barely knew him." This was a lie she knew made sense.

"It's not like I'm judging you." Chip shrugged. "It's none of my business. I mean, it's not like I'm perfect."

"Yes, you are." Carolann laughed. "But I did think I was pregnant. Your father fell in love with me and my unborn baby at the same time, you might say. But then it turned out, the unborn baby was actually his son. He's so proud of you."

"But now, I'm really not perfect, after all." Chip took a deep breath.

"He found his father's body." Carolann shook her head. "We can never understand what he went through. But you… you will still mean the world to him even when he finds out the beginning wasn't quite what he thought. I will tell him." She tapped the paper.

"Why?" Chip pulled the paper from her hand and held it tight. "You'd break his heart."

"What if that report said something different, and you two didn't match?" Carolann asked. "Would that news break *your* heart?"

"Maybe. Kind-of. But it says what it says." Chip shrugged. "So I can't answer that."

"But you questioned it, and you wanted the truth. I have to tell him the truth."

"I didn't question it. Ticia questioned it. I never wanted to know anything. I thought everything was all good. The thing's addressed to me so it's mine. So it's my decision. Dad's not questioning it. He's not asking for any truth. Let's burn it." He tore the paper in half, then in quarters. Carolann watched his long, normal fingers at work.

"Stop." Carolann rested her hand on top of Chip's. He was always such a brave boy. And naïve, just like she used to be. "Someday, you realize, the question may arise again."

"What about it? Someday's forever away," he said. "Maybe I'll slip in the bathtub and die tomorrow. Maybe I'm sterile, or I won't even want children. I could get sterilized, so we never have to think about it again. Will they do that to minors? Drugs or surgery or what do they do? You can sign something."

"Absolutely not," Carolann said.

"If Dad wanted it, I'd do it."

"No."

"Well, maybe my wife will be a package deal, like a widow with two kids. Maybe I won't even want to get married." He threw his hands up and looked his mother in the eyes. "Maybe I'm gay."

Carolann blinked. "Are you gay?"

"No... Pretty sure I'm not gay."

She pictured him behind the recycling bins on the rock wall. Too bad the kid got caught out there. That kind of memory ought to be private. Or at least not reported by school faculty to one's mother. "I'll keep this." Carolann slid the torn pieces of paper toward herself and puzzle-pieced them together. "I understand your wanting to protect me as well as your father."

"Yeah, and me too. Things are fine the way they are. It's just a stupid test. Ticia's gone and not talking about it. She doesn't even have Internet. No one knows a thing about it. Don't make Dad mad. Don't tell him."

"Protecting our family is not your job, kiddo. You're fourteen. You're going to have to let me be the parent here, the guardian. Trust my judgment even if you don't agree. I'll hold onto it and keep it safe."

Chapter 63

"Hold on to what?" Lyn walked into the kitchen and dropped his briefcase on the floor.

Carolann slid the paper scraps into her lap. "You're home." Her voice squeaked.

"Don't tell Dad what?" Lyn said, leveling his gaze at Chip.

"Nothing," Chip said quickly. "That's not what I said. I… nothing."

"Not exactly nothing…" Carolann said. "In fact, I'd say it's very much *something*."

Lyn turned his focus on his wife.

"I said *maybe* you'd get mad, not definitely," Chip said. "How long were you…?"

Eavesdropping is the word Carolann wanted to insert into her sweet, struggling son's (completely false) sentence, but she didn't dare. "I'm guessing Chip wants to know how long you were there, and what you think you overheard?" The unsaid word throbbed in her head. *Eavesdrop*. Should she accuse him?

"Fine," Chip suddenly shouted. "Fine, then. I said *definitely*. You'll definitely get mad. And I didn't want Mom to do that. There's no need to make you mad over something stupid. Something that's totally my fault in the first place. It's no big deal, it should not have been a big deal."

"Chip…" Carolann tried to slow him down.

"Take it easy, son," Lyn added.

"She was there, ok?" Chip glared at his father. "I told her

not to go, because I knew I'd be nervous, the whole public speaking thing, I wanted you there but not her, but she went with Rowan, and she saw the whole thing. It's probably why I screwed it up in the beginning, excuse my French, but my throat closed up just like I knew it would if she was there." He panted, then continued. "And she told you, she promised, just like she told me, she wasn't going. She would not be there, because she respected my viewpoint. But she went! So I said you'd be pissed when you found out."

"Well, hey now," Lyn began. "You think you've got me pegged, but it's possible that I…"

"Are you happy now?" Chip looked like he might cry. "That Mom lied? To both of us? And made me totally screw up the biggest thing I've ever tried to do on a stage?"

"When did you find out she was there?" Lyn asked.

"She just told me. I have homework. I need to be upstairs, but she told me to sit down so she could tell me she was there."

Carolann watched her son embroider his fabrication with more and more decoration. It was a potentially useful decoy, but she had to stop him.

Lyn put his hand on his wife's shoulder. "Then your shaky start really can't be your mother's fault. I'm not mad. To be honest, I don't think you're being fair. You were nervous in the beginning, that's all. And you recovered beautifully."

"No thanks to her." Her glared at his mother.

She wanted to save Chip from making a total fool of himself. But she knew he was trying to save her – not from making a fool of herself, but a self-sacrifice.

"Fair?" Chip said, "You've taught me all about fair. Feelings don't equal fair, remember? You have to separate the two." Now Chip stared hard at his father, almost daring him to absorb the phrase. Maybe be ready to apply it to some other situation. "Anyway, I have homework." He left the room.

Lyn poured himself a glass of water from the tap. "So you

saw it."

"Rowan and I went before we got on the road." Carolann ate the last blueberry.

"Think he's going to be the next great rapper?"

Carolann smiled. "I think he can be whatever he wants to be."

The floorboards creaked overhead as Chip settled into his desk chair up in his bedroom.

Lyn drained the water and swallowed. "But you did say you weren't going."

"And you said you weren't going," she replied. Her fingers gripped the rolled bits of lab report in her fist.

"Not to him," Lyn said. "I told him the truth, unlike you. He wasn't entirely wrong to be angry, was he?"

"Look, Chip and I are fine. He understands why I went."

"He didn't seem fine. He seemed…"

"Stressed out," Carolann said. "He's been under a lot of pressure lately. We all have. The contract, the question of moving back. Your wishes one way, mine the other, and then the thing with Ticia. That girl is effectively his first love, and now, immediately after he ignites a spark with her, she's whisked off to a psychiatrist's office in another country, and they're both suspended… it's no wonder he's stressed out."

"All true. I wish our thinking about that contract was more aligned," Lyn said. "I cannot figure out why you think you owe your whole life to your sister and your parents. Why you insist on moving back right away. That disagreement alone is tearing the kid up."

Carolann shook her head. This wasn't the way she wanted to tell him she wanted to stay in England. That news should be a celebration, not a weapon in her arsenal.

Lyn continued, "Stress aside, he knows how much we value the truth in this family. No wonder he was broken up when he thought you lied to him, Carolann."

"I didn't intend to go to the school, but Rowan saw I was

desperate, and she headed the car that direction, and yes, I let her. I was relieved. Did I lie to him about it? I suppose I did," she said. "But Lyn, I did not lie to him about this. And I didn't hide it from him." She slapped her hand onto the table and four even rolls of sweaty paper escaped her grasp. "And I never lied to you."

"What is this?" Lyn stared at the rolls. "Carolann?"

She nodded.

Lyn assembled the pieces of the puzzle and read the paper. "You did this? When?" His voice was shaking.

"No, Lyn. Read who ordered the test."

Lyn stared at the address line of the paper, holding the four pieces onto the table with his two hands. He stared and stared. He breathed through his nose and kept his fingers dead still on the papers' edges. His entire body seemed to seethe with restrained energy. He didn't move. He just stared.

"They were taking swabs, with that dentistry project," she said.

"At Thanksgiving?" Lyn's voice was no longer shaking. It was slow and metallic, inhuman. "How could you?"

Panicked, Carolann felt backed into a corner, like the seven-year-old girl who watched her sister smash their neighbor's prized vase, her defenses shattered on the floor and scrambled, skittering in sharp blue-and-white pieces away from her, she wanted to grab each and every one into her fingers, into her palms, even if the shards cut her, dropping her red blood, bright on the floor, on her clothes, she wanted to piece it all back together and grab at every one of her reasons she'd never said anything to Lyn about this before. She wanted to put them in order and methodically outline the whole thing, until logic spelled out the acceptable truth, shard by sharp shard. "I couldn't," she said finally.

"That poor boy." Lyn looked anguished, but his voice sounded angry. "That nonsense he cooked up just now… that poor boy."

"Your son," Carolann said.

"No." Lyn shook his head and stared at his own misshapen hands on the papers.

"He's your son."

"I was proud of him," Lyn said quietly. "Proud of the father I was to him."

"You are," Carolann said. "He's unchanged."

"Everything's changed." Lyn's head raised suddenly, anger in his eyes like an animal's, they flashed yellow, anger had replaced the anguish. "It's everything. It's nothing. This marriage is nothing. It never was a single thing."

"But that's absurd. He's your son."

"Never."

"No," she said quietly. "Just listen, Lyn."

"You lied to me from the very beginning. Classic soap opera story from a hick-town, you trapped me, saying you were pregnant and you weren't even pregnant."

"Don't be ridiculous. We both thought I was pregnant. I'm not going to tell you I didn't wonder later. But until today, until this paper, I did not know. And I have never, I mean this, never, had a problem with your hands. I never met your father, God rest his soul, but I cannot agree with him, with what he did, with what you live with."

Lyn growled. "This was never supposed to happen."

"Listen," she said again.

"Listen? I can't even look at you. You knew. You knew from the beginning. That poor boy. What's going to happen when Chip, when he…"

"We deal with that when and if," Carolann said. "He understands that."

"He understands what exactly?" Lyn's hands let go the papers, which sprang into rolls once again. His fists opened and closed, opened and closed.

"He understands the future's uncertain." She tried to rest her hand on her husband's, but he yanked it away.

"Great," Lyn said. "His future's uncertain. And our future's all planned out, all played out, all done. You go on back to Kansas and take that poor flawed boy with you as soon as this school year's done. There's no need for a spouse's agreement on that contract. I'll tell them I have no spouse. No child and no spouse. Carolann, we had everything. It looked like we had everything. But it was nothing. And you knew it."

"I already signed it," she said.

"No." Lyn grabbed his briefcase off the floor and turned.

"You're going?" Carolann yelped. "Where are you going?"

Lyn glared at her and pushed his arms into his trench coat. Saying nothing, he walked out of the kitchen.

"Hold on one minute," Carolann stood, full of fire. "I suspected it, but I never knew for sure. Lyn, life is unscripted, unsure. I never knew what I'd truly be getting with my decision to marry you, and you didn't have any idea what you'd be getting from me, but here we are."

Lyn pulled open the front door.

Carolann continued, "And it's all been a blessing. And what did we just find out? We thought it was false... built on sand. And now we learn it's built on solid rock.

"It's nothing," Lyn said firmly. "It's built on nothing."

"If you crush it now, because it's not what you thought, you're an idiot! You always call the shots, Lyn. Your vasectomy, the move to England, the purple wedding cake. I've always bowed to you, and now, I defer to you, once again. You call it. You look this thing up and down and see it's real, see it's rock solid, see what a wonderful son you've got, the real deal, what a wife you've got, what a life... and if it's not exactly what you've always wanted, fine. You say the word, once it's carefully thought out, and I'm out. I do love you, and I respect you that much."

Lyn shook his head no.

"I won't chase you. I won't push you," Carolann said. "I

will wait. But I won't run after you, and I won't beg."

Lyn walked through the door and slammed it shut.

The house was desperately silent. Chip must have heard the door slam. Carolann sat on the stairs, the gust of chilly evening air still fresh in the room. How stale and warm would her house be before she next spoke to her husband? She listened for the crunch of Lyn's footsteps on the gravel, for the start of his car. But all she heard was anger. She saw his renewal contract on the table, aware that her signature throbbed in blue, bold and proud, 11 pages down. Her eyes filled with tears, but she did not cry.

Thunderous footsteps ran the length of the upstairs hallway, and Chip took the stairs, leaping. He jumped past his mother at the bottom of the staircase, and yanked open the front door.

"Get back in here, asshole," he yelled after his father. "You owe me that much. This is not my fucking fault!"

In an instant, Lyn stood hands on hips in the doorway. Carolann was on her feet behind her son.

"Who the hell are you?" Chip seethed. "You're walking out of here and not even saying good-bye because of your fucked up hands and your fucked up father's fucked up suicide?"

In the shocked silence, Carolann cringed. *Fuck you* were the only words that might come next. And the truth was, she didn't want to stop him.

Lyn stepped in. "There's a right way to do this. We will call lawyers tomorrow." He took off his coat.

"How can you do that?" Carolann shook her head. "You can't quit your son. This isn't his fault."

"He has no idea what his faults are. He has no idea what's inside him. Fifty/fifty, Carolann. Maybe what's coming down the line next is worse than what I got. Feet too, other problems. I was lucky with just the hands."

"Blessed," she said. "Not lucky. We are blessed with a healthy son." She put her hands on Chip's shoulders, and he shook them off, hard.

"I believed you people. Trust in God, tell the truth, when were you going to tell me that you've always been full of shit? Big fat fabrication. Bible study, profanity jars. You people. God damn." He spat the last word.

Lyn shook his head. "We're still your parents. Your relationship with your mother remains unchanged. If you're angry at me, if your profanity's directed at me, so be it."

"Bullshit." Chip scoffed. "You know what? Fuck that paper. I'm not your son at all. You're all about truth and "face versus heart" and all that righteousness crap. People say I have your face, but I sure as hell don't have your heart. Turns out your heart's a big fat fucked-up lie."

Carolann glanced at Chip and then spoke quietly to her husband. "If you stand firm on it, I will move back to Kansas. I will raise Chip with hope that you'll come to accept him. And accept me. Accept the fact that everything you thought you had was not a farce after all, you had it, it was real. When I married you, I vowed to accept you and your judgment in place of my own, if I had to. I used the antiquated vow *to obey* for a reason, and I will do that, if it's your decision."

"It is," Lyn nodded, defeated but firm.

"This is bullshit," Chip repeated. "You think you're going to just find some other wife who will... who will... drink your Jack Daniels on command?"

Carolann nodded at Chip and mouthed the words, *go on up.* He scowled at her, and she nodded again. She let Chip ascend the stairs and then sat down on the lower steps. "But you're wrong about the odds, Lyn. Fifty/fifty only applies to the seven known types of brachydactyly, and yours presents outside the seven known types. No one knows anything definitive about your anomaly. And even those odds are outdated. Lyn, you are more in the medical community than I've ever been, so surely you've done the same research I have."

"I didn't have to," he sneered. "It was never going to be passed on." He marched toward the kitchen, stopped, walked into the dining room, and then back toward Carolann on the stairs. Like a human pin-ball, he bounced room to room, ringing bells, and lighting lights, but scoring no points.

"Today there are surgeries," she said.

"What do you know about it?" Lyn stopped in his tracks. "You know nothing."

"Two docs in LA, a guy in Denver. You've read about these things. I know you have. Some incredible things happening in India."

"Stop. We're not going to India. It's too late, Carolann, everything, all of it, it's too late. It's what the vasectomy was about. Stopping it. I should have let my mother find a guy who'd do it when I was a kid."

"You know the guys right here in England who separated the conjoined twins?"

"To hell with conjoined twins. This is my problem! It was supposed to stop with me."

"They can even alter genes now, in utero. Fix a problem before it happens."

"I did fix my problem! I fixed it! My mother should have tried harder."

Lyn sat on the stairs, where they'd been when Carolann confessed her culpability about Baby Ryan's death. That seemed a lifetime ago. Carolann wanted to reach for Lyn's hand, but she didn't dare.

"Chip asked about sterilization," Carolann said softly.

"I would have let her. Of course I would have let her. She just couldn't find anyone to do it," Lyn said.

"Not for you. Chip asked about himself," Carolann said. "Chip doesn't want it, he's healthy and sensible, that kid of yours. He would think it's sick what your mother did to you, the way she treated you, if he knew. But he said he'd be sterilized if you wanted that. He'd do that for you. I'd do that for you. We'd sacrifice everything for you."

"He said that?" Lyn held his head in a grip and squeezed his eyes tight.

"He reveres you, like I do. He'd make any sacrifice, I believe that. I understand it because I'm the same. That is our family."

Lyn looked at her.

"And look what he already accomplished." Carolann pointed at the kitchen door, at the room containing the quadrants of lab report paper. "Without our even realizing what he was up to. He'd probably get on the Internet, book himself a flight to a clinic in Poland or something within 24 hours, and he'd have it done, if he thought you'd want it. If he thought you'd only accept him if he did it."

"Do you think he should? Not today, but later, before he gets married?"

"No, I do not," Carolann answered. "And honestly, if I thought for one second, you would encourage it, I'd be on a flight with our son tomorrow. To get him far, far away from even the thought of it."

Lyn held his face in his hands. "I can't do this."

"I said he'd sacrifice anything for you. I said I'd sacrifice anything for you. But not our son. I'd draw the line there. I will not sacrifice his future. You're a grown man, and your decisions are your own. But I will always be my son's mother, his protector, even against you. But I know you love him. And you love me." She looked at her husband carefully. "He is your son."

Lyn lifted his head. "I can't think about raising him. About his future. You didn't find my father's body, Carolann. You didn't see his suffering, every day he was alive. I can't do this."

"It's not black and white," she said. "Some things seem 100% or fifty/fifty, or absolutely perfect or totally impossible. That's not life, Lyn. It's not odds, it's just... what it is."

He watched her speak but didn't move. He didn't touch her.

"But I can tell you this. I don't mind your hands. I love you. And I know you love that boy of ours, and you are a better man, a better father than your father was. You are not held back by any disability, and if Chip had inherited it, I fully believe he would also not be held back by it. And his child, if ever he has one, will also not be held back by it. Or maybe he or she will. But that's not our job to prevent or protect or preclude from ever happening. Our job, Lyn, same as it ever was, is to try to love each other and to raise that young man right. And whatever your hands look like, and whatever you think of my morals and honesty, you have to agree, we've been doing a fine job."

Lyn sat and stared. "You already signed that contract?" He looked at the stapled papers on the table. "You want to stay in England, you decided you wanted our family to stay?"

"It's what's right for all three of us." She nodded.

He put his hand gently on her knee, took a deep breath, and exhaled. "Already," he repeated.

"And it's what's real." She clasped his hand with hers. She squeezed him gently, and the muscles and tendons of his hand slowly relaxed as he finally let her. He turned his hand over and held hers. The moment went pure and it fluttered, palest pink. A clean, evening breeze and sundown and salt smells. The music was silence. Lyn's hand was warm in Carolann's. It felt good.

"Already."

Acknowledgements

For John, who may be the best writer's spouse in the history of writing. This novel is also for Jack and Edward Fraser and for Jane, Ron, Tim, and Heather Freund. Mary Albanese, Meg Gardiner, and Michelle Bailat Jones have lived through this novel's creation with me and made the ten years great fun. So too, Adrienne Dines, Suzanne Davidovac, Tammye Huf, Kelly Gerrard, Lauren Christopher, Margaret Fletcher Saine, Sophie LaRouge Knight, Iris Kuerten, Mary Wilhelm, Linda Ward O'Hara, Emma Ward Govender, Julie Borgelt Hardison, Paula Fentener Van Vlissingen, and Jackie Hayden Wilson. Paul and Gina Bertrand should note that as promised, there is a character named Paul. A good guy, in fact. Tim and Stacy Mayer might like him too.

Mary Knapp Parlange, Christine Geiger, Amanda Click, and Alannah Wilson generously shared their personal experiences of synesthesia. I'm grateful to UCLA's Creative Writing program — specifically to inimitable Carolyn See and to Irish novelist Brian Moore who promised no "industry help whatsoever" yet helped secure my first agent at Curtis Brown and my commitment to living a writer's life. Thanks also to Pascal and the Lavaux Literary Salon, the Geneva Writers Group, the American Women of Surrey Writers, the wonderful, generous instructors and participants at the Iowa Summer Writers Festival, to Necessary Fiction, and of course, to Gobreau Press.

Thirty years ago, high school Creative Writing teacher Greg Vogt said he'd see my books on library shelves. Took me a while, but turns out, he was right.

Readers' Group Discussion Guide

A prior English teacher, Nancy Freund strongly believes in the benefit of discussing books and of literature's value in a community. No two people read a novel the same way. Their personal experiences encourage new themes and ideas to emerge during discussion, enhancing each individual reader's understanding of the story. The following questions are intended to trigger a few interesting conversations about *Rapeseed* and its characters. Gobreau Press welcomes your further comments online, at Goodreads or other readers' social networks. Please let us know what inspired you and your discussion group.

1. Carolann discovers several things in common with her neighbor Rowan, and vice-versa. What commonalities draw each to the other? Are they the same? In examining friendship between women or sisters, do both women generally value the same experience and attributes in the other, or is friendship more enhanced by difference? Do you think male friendship works the same way?

2. Carolann seems obsessed with the minutiae of time-keeping. In what ways are issues of time and sequence vitally important to her? Why?

3. Carolann's neurological condition of synesthesia alters her memories and applies changeable color-schemes to her experiences. Despite the unusual brain phenomenon of cross-wired senses, Carolann's understanding of her past experiences is very perceptive. Do you think she is a reliable narrator, or do you find yourself questioning whether or not she

has a full grasp on the truth? In what ways does she seem unreliable?

4. The original title of *Rapeseed* was *The Color of Rape*, inspired by the striking visual image of an English rapeseed field and the play on words therein. Which title do you think fits the novel better and why?

5. In more than one scene featuring Chip and Carolann, the characters are seated on rocks or rock-walls, their fingers exploring the rock's texture. In what ways are these scenes pivotal in the characters' development? How does Carolann's experience at the Glastonbury Tor compare to Chip's experience by the recycling bins?

6. While Carolann Cooper is the novel's protagonist, her son Chip's character also follows a developmental story arc. In what way do his rap lyrics reveal his character? Which of the two characters do you feel arrives more firmly at a new understanding of his/her life and goals?

7. One of Chip's early rap lyrics asks the question, *what if what you want, you already had?* In what ways is this line important in the novel?

8. Some neuroscientists believe all babies are born with synesthesia that untangles itself as the child matures. Some believe everyone has subtle versions of synsethesia all their lives. Chip is not a true synesthete, but he experiences certain smells and colors profoundly. In what other ways has Chip inherited the traits of his parents?

9. In the school auditorium, Chips feels "more than underdressed... he feels exposed." In what way is

the theme of exposure important in all three Cooper family members' lives? How do they differ in their attitudes toward privacy?

10. Carolann feels isolated and different because she is a synesthete. What else separates her from her twin sister and makes her feel alone?

11. How does becoming an expat allow Carolann to view her position in her home community more clearly?

12. Stewart Neame expresses concern about Chip redefining himself in a dangerous way – something he calls an *expat spiral*. Is he right to be concerned?

13. Is Chip is a realistic 14-year-old boy or is he a caricature? Is Ticia more or less real? How does the author handle these two teenage characters' different styles of dialogue and their opinions on one another's dialogue?

14. "Worked hard to make it so." How does this line define Carolann's understanding of her marriage and family and how does it inform her decisions moving forward?

For more discussion, come visit! www.gobreaupress.com.

About the Author

Nancy Freund is the author of four novels to be published by Gobreau Press, specializing in "expat and elsewhere fiction." Born in New York, raised in Kansas City, and educated in Los Angeles, she is a citizen of the U.S. and the UK, and lives in French-speaking Switzerland. Writer-in-residence for webjournal Necessary Fiction in September 2012, she has also had shorter works published in *BloodLotus Journal*, *The Istanbul Review*, *Offshoots* in Geneva, and Zurich-based literary magazine *The Woolf*. She is the 2013 winner of the first Geneva Writers Fiction prize, for *Marcus*, chosen by American novelist Bret Lott.

Rapeseed is her debut novel.

Connect online:
www.nancyfreund.com
Twitter: @nancyfreund
Facebook: nancyfreundauthor
Pinterest: nancy freund
Goodreads: Nancy Freund

Lightning Source UK Ltd.
Milton Keynes UK
UKOW05f1010030717

304560UK00001B/48/P